LEAGUE OF ELDER
THE SHADOW TECH GODDESS

Ren Garcia

Loconeal Publishing

Amherst, OH

THE SHADOW TECH GODDESS

Copyright © 2014 by Ren Garcia
Cover Art by © 2014 by Carol Phillips
Listed copyrighted interior image art is
provided in the 'List of Illustrations'
Edited by Kathy Watness

Loconeal books may be ordered through booksellers or by contacting:
www.loconeal.com
216-772-8380

Loconeal Publishing can bring authors to your live event.
Contact Loconeal Publishing at 216-772-8380.

Published by Loconeal Publishing, LLC
Printed in the United States of America

First Loconeal Publishing edition: July 2014

Visit our website: www.loconeal.com

ISBN 978-1-940466-14-9 (Trade Paperback)

Also by Ren Garcia

The League of Elder Series:
Sygillis of Metatron
The Hazards of the Old Ones

The Temple of the Exploding Head Trilogy:
The Dead Held Hands
The Machine
The Temple of the Exploding Head

The Belmont Saga
Sands of the Solar Empire
Against the Druries

Turns of the Shadow tech Goddess
The Shadow tech Goddess
Stenibelle (coming soon)

For more please visit: www.theleagueofelder.com

TABLE OF CONTENTS

Prologue

Part 1—The The Shadow tech Goddess

**Part 2—The Loves of Paymaster Stenstrom
The First Turn**

Part 3—Eng

LIST OF ILLUSTRATIONS

The Garden of Horrors

Paymaster Stenstrom's Office

1: FEDULA (Gwen's Sword) 2: Vith Artifact (Magravine Chasm) 3: MOLLY (A-Ram/Taara) 4: Marine SK Pistol (Taara)

5: Hospitaler Jet Staff 6: Merian Invisibility Belt (Alesta) 7: Portrait of Countess Sygillis 8: Belmont/Tyrol Coat of Arms

9: Portrait of Captain Davage 10: Portrait of Lt. Kilos of Tusck 11: Fleet Tremblar Hat (Gwen) 12: Hoban Royal Navy Coat

13: Anatameter (Arcane device) 14: NTH Pistol (Stenstrom's gun) 15: Stone Knife (Tempus Findja) 16: MARZABLE (Stenstrom)

STENSTROM, LORD OF BELMONT-SOUTH TYROL

As in All Things . . .
Every creature no matter how wretched
has a place to call its own.

. . . Even the Shadow tech Goddess.

Prologue

I—The One that Lost Everything

Mixed into Paymaster Stenstrom's usual pile of daunting correspondence was a square letter with no return address. TO: LORD STENSTROM, COMMANDER, MFV SEEKER was printed out in careful, feminine script.

He often got letters: from Gwendolyn when she was away on business, which happened from time to time, from his old friend Lady Alitrix of Zama—soon to be Countess Alitrix of Hopkins, he was elated to hear, from Crewman Kaly who'd left the old frigate she'd served on for years and now worked on the bridge of the Sprint ship *Speedwell*—a few words from his father, Captain Stenstrom, had helped pave the way for that promotion, and from Christiana on Planet Fall.

All of them good friends.

All of them—except for Gwendolyn—paths not taken. He could have, if he'd thought about it, fallen in love with any of them.

The unmarked letter sitting in front of him had a grim feel to it, like bad news.

He opened the letter, dreading the plunge he was about to take.

Bel
Please come to your main conference room. I am waiting for you.

That was all. Stenstrom wondered if it was a joke, from Taara perhaps. She had a relentless, Bazz-like sense of humor that sometimes escaped him.

It didn't seem like a joke, though. The letter carried a strong feeling of command—as if not going would be a bad mistake. He put on his HRN coat and stuck his two NTH's into his sash. He exited his office and went down to Deck Three. The conference room was just a short walk from the lift.

Light streamed out from under the door. Somebody was waiting for him.

Exiting her quarters, Taara ambushed him as soon as he walked out of the lift. "What's going on, Bel?" she asked, pulling on her Marine coat.

"There's somebody in the conference room."

"So? It's probably Gwen, again, wanting to get naked with you."

"What? Please . . ."

"Everybody knows."

Stenstrom blushed. "I've an odd feeling about who's inside."

"Oh. Come on then." She looked like a strawberry in her red Marine uniform.

They opened the door and entered.

Sitting at the far end of the vast table, her back to him, was a woman dressed in gray. "Gods!" he cried. He immediately drew his NTH's and Taara skinned her SK. A woman in gray—it had to be Lady Vendra of Cone, a long missing enemy and a fugitive, come to settle their score at last.

"Put your hands up where I can see them!" He cocked the hammers of his weapons. "And if you start to Waft away or Cloak, I'm going to fire."

The figure put her hands up in a slow, deliberate manner. She turned.

It wasn't Lady Vendra. Golden hair and pale skin peeked out from under her broad-brimmed hat. Blue eyes and sculpted cheek-bones.

Lilly, his former love. Lillian of Gamboa, who wasn't Lillian of Gamboa. She was a sand golem, a Nargal construct created by the Sisters to "guide" him in the direction they wished him to go. Lilly was an arcane monster who once slew over a hundred Soul Devourers.

A woman of sand, perfect in every way. A woman of sand he had once loved, dearly.

She glanced at Taara. "Please go away."

Taara cocked her SK. "Like hell!"

Lilly spoke in a slow, condescending way. "Bel, tell your little friend to go away or I'll have to do it for you."

Stenstrom glanced at Taara. "It's all right. Wait for me outside."

"But, Bel . . ."

"It's all right, Taara. Go on. I'll be right there."

Slowly, Taara holstered her SK. "Better not try anything," she said and backed out of the room.

Lilly raised her eyebrows a little.

He eased into a chair at the opposite end of the table, still pointing his NTHs at her. They stared at each other for a long time, Lilly's blue eyes sparkling.

"Do you like gray, Bel? How does it look on me?" she said at last.

"How did you get aboard?"

"How? I do get around, Bel. I can fly. I can drift. I can be thousands of feet tall. I can plant my feet and be in orbit at the same time. The airlessness of space troubles me not in the least. I can sneak aboard a starship through the smallest of imperfections, as in this case."

He carefully considered his response. "Where is Vendra, Lady of Cone?"

Lilly didn't hesitate. "She's dead. I killed her. I've been a busy lady. She was simply the latest to discover how dangerous it is to try to control me, to deny me what's mine. She's in her grave, though you'll find no tombstone. I didn't bother to memorialize her resting place. You may thank me if you wish, or not. It's your choice."

Stenstrom struggled with his thoughts. He felt his heart stir a little, looking for old feelings.

The Sisters had wrenched his love for her from him. Not a trace of it was left.

At opposite ends of the table they sat silent for a minute or two.

She stirred in her seat at last. A little gold locket gleamed at her neck. "I believe we needn't be shy here, Bel," Lilly said. "I think, for the first time, we both know what we are."

"What do you want, Lilly?"

"Isn't it obvious? I want you."

"I was informed by the Sisters that you are not a real person—that you're a construct, a Nargal built to their specifications."

The Sisters. A wave of hatred crossed her perfect face at the name. "Yes, the Sisters created me. They cast their spells and gathered their materials and kept me in a cage in Vithland they thought strong enough to hold me. Best laid plans, I suppose. I grew beyond what the Sisters intended—I have cast aside and rejected all that they tried to build into me—except for one thing. I love you, Bel."

He stared at her. "Do you feel love?"

"Of course I feel love. I feel love, hate, happiness, sadness, bitterness, anger. Loneliness . . . spitefulness . . . I feel the whole range, good and bad. I wouldn't be here if I didn't. The late Lady Vendra of Cone . . . I have her to thank for some of the other things I feel: my ambition, my determination. She gave those things to me in a packet of black sand and some tainted Rumbob."

"I'm the Sister's man, Lilly—I cannot be harmed."

She smiled. "Maybe, maybe not. But, it's quite irrelevant. I would never try to harm you. I love you. Your friends and your current puppy dog, however, they enjoy no such protection. I'm no killer, but I do kill when I have to, as a few unfortunate individuals have discovered. And nothing survives should I get to killing. Perhaps I would have killed your puppy dog if she had entered here. Jealousy is a particularly strong emotion I feel. I killed your Knife, and I killed the Lady in Gray."

"Knife? You killed Knife?"

"Yes, I did. Yet another slave of the Sisters. I didn't plan on it. I was going to kidnap her, but she hurt me and I got angry, so I killed her and stripped her bones. She is scattered to the winds."

Lilly sat there and seemed ashamed for her revelations. She studied him, maybe hoping to read his emotions, hoping to discover something—anything—of what they once had together. "You really have no feelings left for me, do you?"

"I don't see what—"

She slammed her fist against the table. "Answer the question, Bel!"

Stenstrom didn't know what to say. Though he felt nothing for her any longer, he still had his memories: their contentious first meeting, the lunches they shared, the untried avenues of carnal delight she'd taught him. The long conversations and the piles of correspondence. Lilly ate that food, but did she taste it? Does she have a stomach? She'd made love to him—but had she felt it? Who had written him those letters he'd loved to read? Was it Lilly or was it some anonymous scribe in a Sisterhood stronghold?

It was too much to ponder. "There's no hope for us, Lilly. I've moved on."

She breathed in deeply and looked at her hands. "Have you any illusions that I couldn't kill every living thing aboard this ship at my whim?"

"I think, should you attempt to do that, I would have to stop you."

"Shoot me with your guns. Punch me with your fists. Do you think it would make a difference? I am free; I am fully realized. That five year condition I was forced to recite was words the Sisters put in my mouth."

"You just threatened the lives of my crew and my friends. Did the Sisters put those words in your mouth, too?"

She flushed. "I didn't come here to threaten you or to harm anyone. I'm sorry. I regret saying that. Still . . . I'm ready for you, Bel. What am I supposed to do? What lengths am I to go to?"

"Again, I've moved on. I love Gwendolyn."

Something dark crossed Lilly's face. "Another of your puppy dogs, Bel? Do you know how I ached to kill that girl of yours when you were in school? In that cage the Sisters kept me in, I dreamed of killing her. I'm not perfect."

"Whose arms do you prefer around you, Bel? Can you take that woman you claim to love and embrace her—truly embrace her with all your might? You can't, can you? She would crumble in your arms. You have to contain yourself, inhibit yourself. That needn't be. You can embrace me, as hard as you want and I'll not break. Wherever you choose to go, I can follow. I can stand at your side and you need not fear. We could have anything we wanted. We could have it all as King and Queen, or we could content ourselves with nothing, just you and me and a fire-lit hearth in a modest cabin. You loved me once. Who's to say you can't love me again?"

Lilly suddenly changed shape. Now, she looked like Gwendolyn, scarred cheek and all. "I could be her, if you like. I can be anyone I choose. I can be anyone you want me to be. Indulge your whims, your deepest unspoken fantasies and I can be those things, just for you."

"Another lie, Lilly. Another fabrication."

"It's not a lie! What I feel is not a lie! All the lies I told you were put into my mouth by the Sisters! That was their doing, not mine!"

She resumed her usual Lilly guise and composed herself. She changed her approach. "Look, Bel, look what I have. I have this . . ." She produced a small handbag and dug through it. She pulled out a small black velvet bag and placed it on the table.

"What is that?" Stenstrom asked.

Lilly was excited and spoke like a child for a moment. "This is what the Sisters stole from you that day in their temple. It's your love for me, contained in the magic metal slivers you once wore in the folds of your mask—see! I found them discarded on the floor like so much refuse and kept them with me, all this time." She picked the bag up and held it out. "These are your feelings, Bel—no magic, no tricks. Take these pieces that I've protected and feel for me what you once did. It can all be yours again. Take it."

Stenstrom set his weapons down and looked at the bag in Lilly's hand. His feelings.

His love for Lilly, and it had been a profound love, until the Sisters pulled it from him. Now, he loved Gwendolyn.

He struggled, full of indecision.

The door to the conference room opened. Gwendolyn came in, still holding her bags from her return trip. "Ah, Bel, there you are. Taara said you were . . ."

She saw Lilly sitting at the end of the table holding the black velvet bag. She dropped her purchases and drew her FEDULA.

Lilly's face distorted into rage. "You! Get out!"

Gwen focused on the bag Lilly held. She flashed her weapon and bisected the bag, destroying the fragile metal pieces within.

They crumbled.

Lilly stared at the destroyed pieces for a moment. She moaned, then screamed a primal roar of fury. She pointed at Gwendolyn. A torrent of sand shot out and punched Gwen in the chest, driving her back into the bulkhead.

"Bel!" she cried, dropping her FEDULA, the sand scouring away her flesh.

Stenstrom snatched up his NTHs and fired two shots, hitting Lilly in the neck.

She exploded in rage, a windstorm of sand engulfing the room. He couldn't see much, just a cloud of sand with a central vortex twisting in the center.

His ears filled with the sound of Lilly's scream, growing with each passing moment.

The windows to the conference room, each several inches thick to withstand the rigors of space, burst outwards and the room rapidly decompressed.

He was pulled out into space, and so was Gwendolyn, or what was left of her. Her body was half stripped to the skeleton. She spiraled away in a random direction.

He fell in the silent cosmic breeze, his lungs crying out for air, but not needing it for survival. The Sisters' power kept him whole, even in the airless deep freeze of space.

He watched the graceful form of the *Seeker*, veteran of countless battles and sturdy in the extreme, burst outward in a cloud of boiling sand—destroyed by Lilly in a matter of moments. Its remains pelted him as he entered Kana's atmosphere.

The tormenting cloud of the creature that was Lilly came down around him as fire licked off his plummeting body.

BBBBBBBBEEEEEEEEEELLLLLLLLLL!! entered his brain and he felt his body, impervious to the rigors of space and the trials of reentry, stripping away.

Lilly's power was too much, even for the It Man.

He fell to Kana, and a cloud of anger and torment fell with him, Lilly growing and growing until the entire ball of Kana below was as stripped bare and lifeless

He fell and fell.

II—St. Mary's Axe

He wondered sometimes what had happened when everything fell apart.

Once, he had a beautiful wife from the St. Paris region of Remnath, proper and stately, perhaps a tad boring, but what did it matter? He loved her and the children she gave him. She had a voice like a whole choir. His favorite thing was to sit in church and listen to her sing.

And then she was gone.

Since childhood, the sun seemed to follow Lord Willshire wherever he went. People liked him, found favor in everything he did. He enjoyed playing the oboe, and once had a brief solo at a weekend recital in the park. The locals came from all over to hear him play, bringing basket lunches and tankards of lemonade, closing their eyes and listening to him play.

He had a special skill he told no one of. As a child, he discovered a mystical place he called "St. Mary's Axe", because it looked like the old axe gallery in St. Mary's Manor, his home. St. Mary's Axe came to him at the oddest of times. At first, it frightened him, since nobody else seemed to have this ability. Eventually, he learned to call St. Mary's Axe to him when he wished. To enter, all he had to do was touch the gem-like key and it would open up into a passage going left and right. If he went left he could venture to faraway places, magical places that he sometimes spent days exploring. To the right was the lair of a dark, terrifying creature he wanted to avoid.

And then he grew into young manhood and joined the Stellar Fleet, standing at the Com station of a fine Warbird, the *Venator*. At the terrible Battle of Mirendra I, he leapt from his station and manned the helm when the helmsman was killed. He was praised as a hero and given the command chair of a Sprint-Class ship and had a blue-haired first officer from Famora. Surely he would soon move on to the command of a full-sized Warbird.

The star that had followed him since childhood rose ever higher.

And then his wife was gone, killed while visiting friends in Zenon. An accident they said, and everything fell apart. The light that had followed him his whole life dulled, obscured by madness and despair. He became estranged from his children, from his friends, and he squandered his House fortune. In desperation, he thought to use St. Mary's Axe in an attempt to recover his wife's soul. He wandered St. Mary's Axe for an uncounted length of time, drifting through the corridor, looking for his wife.

And somewhere in that time of sadness and grief he encountered the Shadow tech Goddess. He saw a lone figure in black coming toward him from the right-hand corridor. She wore a featureless helmet, floating like a buoy in a sea of darkness. A cloud of fear swirled around her and he groveled at her feet.

The Shadow tech Goddess removed her helmet, revealing a face of wondrous beauty. She took him by the hand and led him through dead fields and dark meadows, shaping everything around them as they desired, changing black stillness to paradise.

Sometime later, drunk with the experience, he was expelled from St. Mary's Axe and it never appeared to him again. Any power or favor he once had was now gone forever.

Lost and now quite deranged, he forgot the love of his departed wife and obsessed over the Shadow tech Goddess. Enraged he could no longer gain access to her, he joined bizarre clubs and performed forbidden things in the bloody moonlight, all to curry her favor and return to her side. In lust, he took his pleasure from his blue-haired first officer. She seemed the only person who hadn't turned her back on him. She was a ravenous animal, so unlike his gentle wife he'd long forgotten. She tore at him as they made love, biting him, bloodying him, sinking him like a carnal anchor to the bottom of a sea of delirium. He took her to his clubs and shared her with the membership. Straps and scourges, she endured it all.

Anything he had to do to get back to St. Mary's Axe and the dark woman residing within.

III—Melazarr

Melazarr was thrown down to the forest floor in her lacy wire gown by the chanting people dressed in brown robes. She was wearing her usual *caratina*, an unusual harness of swirling black metal with sharpened points around her torso. The people who had carried her out of the restaurant and into the woods cut their fingers on it, for which they ceaselessly complained.

If she hadn't been playing dead, she'd have cursed them out. *Aw, shut it, will you—try wearing one of these for creation's sake.*

The situation was quite interesting. They seemed intent on killing her; so perhaps the evening wasn't a total loss.

Earlier in the evening, the handsome, but rather stuffy gentleman she'd had dinner with in Burgon had plied her with a vast amount of wine, obviously wanting to intoxicate her. Melazarr, however, was no stranger to wine and it would take more than the cheap, Boran grape he served to put her on the floor. At first, she thought he was going to sell her drunken body to a meat market—the Burgons having developed a taste for man-flesh over the centuries. But he didn't take her to the market. Apparently, he was involved with some sort of cult. He had a float-car full of robed weaklings struggle with her long, solid body out to the woods surrounding the city.

Having nothing better to do, she allowed them to proceed. She was curious what would happen. After all, there was no way they could harm her; so what the heck, let it play out. She'd done herself up proud for this date. She'd had her hair varnished solid and her flash-ons lit; so she might as well get her effort's worth.

It was all creepy and mysterious. She liked that. It was odd that her date for the evening, a Sir Rodrigo of Burgon, didn't become a tad bit interesting until after he thought she was unconscious. Before that, he was a wretched bore, talking about his paltry holdings and tepid feudal duties as he motioned for the waiter to pour more wine. Big deal, his dry discourse was more of a sedative that the crappy wine he'd forced down her throat.

When she finally allowed things to play out and slid to the floor, some bony lady in black with wrapped up arms and a large handbag sidled up to their table. Melazarr had seen the lady sitting at the bar, obviously watching them, draining her glass, then shaking it for more. She wasn't sure if the lady was Rodrigo's wife, mother, or concubine.

Rodrigo said a few things to the lady and she left to get the grunts, who then appeared in droves, manhandling Melazarr out from under the table.

She wasn't surprised that nobody in the restaurant made a move to help her or enquire as to what was going on. Burgon wasn't much of a place for great character. The other diners doggedly stuck to their meals. They didn't even rubberneck to watch the spectacle.

The cultists carried her by the legs and by the shoulders; her rump close to dragging on the woodsy ground as they stumbled along. They complained bitterly that she was so heavy and they nearly dropped her once or twice, their robed heads knocking into one another as they struggled over the uneven footing.

"This fat cow will be the death of us," one of them said. She took exception to that; there was no fat on her, she was all muscle. She felt like kicking loose and fighting them, but she kept still. She'd settle up with them later.

They carried her into a clearing lit with a small, reddish fire. Some weird device was set up at the far end of the clearing, all wired and trussed up. It seemed vaguely familiar. Had she seen it before? Maybe they were going to film her killing. Maybe she was going to be the star of a snuff film.

Safety first, she noted. The fire placed in the center of the clearing had been properly partitioned off with rocks and raked dirt; they even had a pail full of water nearby, should the fire get out-of-control.

When they laid her down, she felt her *caratina* cutting into her back. They tried to get her shoes off, but they were expensive, illegally imported heel-jobs from Hoban, and they were amongst her fav's. She scrunched up her feet so they couldn't get her shoes off. They muttered to themselves and eventually gave up. *What a bunch of weaklings.*

Robed people then gathered around. Their leader arrived, all somber and upright.

It was her date, Rodrigo of Burgon; she smelled his cologne. It didn't smell any better now, pine-scented from the woods, than it had at the restaurant.

"Is the victim ready?" he asked one of his flunkies.

"Yes, Magus," someone replied.

"The information we've so painstakingly sought lies within this foul girl's innards."

The robed lackies were skeptical. "What can this unspoiled maiden possibly know?"

Unspoiled maiden? You're a little late, chum. That's a big no-can-do on that one. Hate to disappoint.

"No, no," Rodrigo said. "It's written in her innards. We harvest them and read the information that is there."

What? Rodrigo was going to dissect her? That's gross. She wasn't worried. She had her secret weapon available to her.

On the outer reaches of the clearing, she noticed the tall woman in black with wrapped up arms watching the proceedings. The woman from the resteraunt ate leftovers out of a bag.

"Don't forget her thing, darls," the woman said in a child-like voice, holding her food with pinky extended.

Rodrigo pulled a curved knife from his robes and strode in her direction. "Ah, yes, thank you. I shall cut the garter from her leg. She won't escape. Then, she will burn, and we will read what her innards have to tell us. And the first step in summoning the Shadow tech Goddess will be accomplished."

The woman in black belched. "You sure this chick's the one you want, eh? She doesn't look like much to me."

"Her likeness was discovered in the Cistern of the Shadow tech Goddess, and that makes her invaluable. Not alive, mind you, but dead, dead and ripped open." He came at Melazarr with his knife.

If he was going for her garter, he had another thing coming. When he was close enough she reared back with her legs and shot out, pushing him hard in the mid-riff. He fell back into the small fire, dropping his knife. His robes caught fire. He leaped to his feet, screaming, spinning, blazing like a torch.

The wrapped-up woman stood. "Darls!" she cried, dropping her leftovers. The other cultists stared dumbly at one other as Rodrigo burned. Finally, one of them got the smart idea to grab the nearby pail and douse the burning man. He missed, however, the tongue of water splashing into an adjacent tree.

Screaming, Rodrigo bounded off into the trees like a flaming deer, a bobbing trail of sooty smoke marking his passage, the woman in black following. "Drop, Darls! Drop, hold still!"

Melazarr stood.

The others recovered a bit. "The victim must not escape! Summon the Punts!" They all drew curved blades.

She turned to run into the woods, but found armed people behind her as well.

Well, bugger. Here we go again.

Several robed fellows engaged her, while the others chanted and jumped around the fire. The fire sputtered and crackled, turning a distinct shade of green.

They closed in, raised their knives, and she easily evaded their stabs. One fellow came in close. She seized him and plunged her own small knife deep into his neck. She felt a small prick; somebody had stabbed her from behind, creating a small circle of blood, staining her gown. She lifted the fellow with one arm and threw him head-first into a tree with a sickening crunch.

Melazarr killed another one, then she noticed a group of new people had arrived in the clearing, robed like the others, but these seemed more commanding, more threatening. They pulled their hoods down and revealed green heads of hair with odd, brassy-colored skin.

"Hey, I like the look . . ." Melazarr said, trying to be bold.

The arm of one shot out, stretching, pinning her to a tree with unbreakable strength. She grappled with it, but could do nothing. The arm detached, then a new one sprouted out of the robed figure's sleeve. The disembodied arm held her in place like a boneless snake.

The fire hitched and rose up, climbing several times its previous height. Its color shifted to dead black and spewed thick white smoke which filled the clearing in a twisting wall.

The Punts held Melazarr still, and, as she watched, she filled with true fear for the first time.

Something moved in the smoke. Two points of bright white light appeared and panned about, like a pair of spotlights. They settled on Melazarr.

Two black masses pushed through the smoke and emerged into the night air. As she watched, two hideous, scissor-like claws both the size of small houses came down fast, opening and closing with relish.

<CLACK>, CLACK>, <CLACK>

Melazarr could see the horny ridges nested inside the claws, waiting to bite into her flesh. Her heart pounded

ZAP!

Melazarr vanished as the claws snapped the tree in two.

Part 1

The Shadow tech Goddess

The Ruins of Caroline

1—An Unexpected Caroline

Tucked on an outcropping of fertile land facing the turbid waters of the Straights of Elder was a blackened heap of stones arranged like the pieces of some primitive board game. The stones, once a stately whitish-gray, but now a cinder sort of black from age and weathering stood out sharply against the rich green of the landscape.

The stones once were part of a grand manor hall that had stood there for centuries. The laughter of children from generations gone by could still be heard, some said, echoing through the fallen masonry. The manor had been well-built out of strong rock, but time and neglect had taken the place down. A fair portion of the north wall still stood, rising up a story or two as a shard of black stone etched with empty windows; the panes long since fallen and ground into the earth.

There were many such ruins scattered about the northern continental interior of Kana; most so remote and ill-traveled they were difficult to locate, dangerous to explore, and generally best left alone.

This particular ruin, however, situated along the coast of the fertile Halalands and within easy reach by land, sea, or air was far from abandoned. Many nights a year, when the weather was favorable, young gentlemen, dressed to please, milled about the rocks and fallen battlements, or sat in the moonlight, waiting.

Waiting for what?

Indeed, the grounds around the ruin were well tended, trimmed and kept manageable by the locals who went well out of their way to keep the place from getting too wooly. The passes between the fallen stones were leveled out and had been made reasonably safe for casual walking even on the darkest of nights some years back. Oftentimes, there were colorful assortments of flower bouquets lined up at the feet of the stones, like a string of beads around a great, black neck. Occasionally, there were also propped-up notes written longhand on fine paper, baskets of food, bottles of wine, stuffed toys, and every so often, rings still sitting in their cushioned boxes, all left to sit in the rain and fog.

These were the fabulous ruins of Caroline, a House long since gone. The Carolines, along with many other Houses, went to the stars and became Xaphans centuries ago at the end of the EX epoch, leaving all they had, leaving their manor to fall into ruin.

Though officially Xaphans—enemies of the League—the Carolines were never brow-beating League-haters. It was said they became Xaphans out of love, that they followed their hearts to the stars. Through the centuries, they managed to maintain friendly ties with the League. During the First and Second battles of Mirendra 3, it was the safe harbor they offered many badly damaged Fleet vessels, at great risk to themselves, that saved many lives and helped turn the tide in the second battle. For that act, the League Ex-Commons and the Sisterhood of Light reconstituted the House of Caroline's familial patent, making them dual League/Xaphan citizens.

The Carolines, far away on their new world in Xaphan space, were friends among enemies.

So, why the flowers and other gifts propped up against the ruins of House Caroline? Why the gentlemen sitting there in the moonlight dressed in their best patiently waiting for something to happen?

The House of Caroline, among other things, was well known for one curious fact. The LosCapricos weapon of House Caroline was an unusual device called the VERY MARY. In its most usual guise, the VERY MARY was a black garter worn on the leg of tall Caroline maidens. Known throughout the ages for being precocious and daring, Caroline maidens often found themselves in difficult situations and the VERY MARY guarded the life of the maiden wearing it. Should a Caroline maiden fall into harm's way, the VERY MARY instantly teleported her, no matter where she may be, back to the ancestral grounds of the House of Caroline—which just happened to be in the Halalands of Kana by the sea.

Therefore, Caroline maidens sometimes simply "popped up" out of thin air amid the ruins.

Eventually, a fad emerged, where prospective League gentlemen seeking a bride, ventured out to the ruins and sat there in the moonlight bearing gifts, waiting for a lady to appear from nowhere.

Sometimes their efforts were rewarded; sometimes they were not. At other times they were met with frauds, and the word "Carofab", a local woman pretending to be a lady of Caroline and snare an unsuspecting gentleman, was introduced into the vernacular. It was a very romantic fad, and a profitable one for the Halas living nearby.

The prospect of finding love in the ruins was too much for many young men from all over Kana to resist, and for many local ladies not to try and take advantage of. An extensive spy network was formed; eager ladies knew exactly who was going out to the ruins and when, and they could take action accordingly.

So, the legend of Caroline perpetuated itself in flowers and waiting gentlemen in the moonlight and ladies from nowhere, real or not.

The gentleman picked his way into the ruins; the pinkish light from the two Kanan moons, Solon and Elyria, lighting up the lonely surroundings in a diorama of quiet stone. A blanketing layer of fog had rolled in from the sea and covered the ground low in a featureless veil. Out in the channel, the Lighthouse of Caroline rhythmically flashed a bluish beam across the night.

The man wore a Fleet uniform. He was a smallish fellow, his uniform perfectly tailored to fit his slight frame. He'd opted for epaulets, which were generally not worn, but having tiny shoulders, he thought they improved his profile. He wore his triangle hat proudly on his blonde-haired head. He also wore a stylish pair of optical glasses he had made on Onaris, "Dragons", they were called. Few people needed glasses on Kana. Most could pay to have their eyes repaired via Hospitaler should they need it. But his eyes were inoperably bad and without his glasses, he could barely see. The Dragons looked good on him, gave him a stately sort of look, a far cry from the thick black, inelegant things he once wore.

He carried a bouquet of nice flowers he'd picked out in Minz, and had a box of chocolate candies tucked under his arm, the expensive ones with the delicious stuffing in pastel colors.

He wandered into the fallen rock and craggy maze of the ruins. He found a nice place to sit, a flattened stone with a fairly smooth surface where, many men had sat before and polished its surface with their collective backsides. He brushed it off with his hand and sat down. He felt the cold, damp stone through his Fleet pants.

He took a deep breath and waited, listening for the most minute of sounds. He tapped his boot heels against the stone to pass the time. Looming before him, like a craggy fingernail poking up out of the ground, was the remains of the northern wall. The panning light from the distant Lighthouse occasionally threw it into relief.

ZAP!

He heard an odd noise made loud and abrupt by the orderly tapestry of the night. Startled, he looked around for the source of the sound.

In the dark, he thought he saw two flickering points of red light hovering at about eye-level.

A lank, somewhat elongated figure stumbled out of the darkness. It whirled about, confused it seemed. Its face flashed in an unsteady, quizzical pattern, lighting up with an odd sort of orangish-red color, like a disembodied demon's head.

It spied him and locked on, its flickering face speeding up and getting brighter as it became aware of him.

A sneering female voice rang out in the foggy dark. "Well, what have we here?"

The man, shocked, dropped his flowers.

The figure strode toward him. Coming into view was a tall woman dressed in a lacy black gown, cut high, showing a healthy portion of legs and hips. She was thin, but very long, well over six feet in height. She appeared quite solid; her lean body fleshed-out in toned, practiced muscle.

The woman's gown appeared to be made partially of rusty metal. The bodice portion was swirled and rigid, like a harness made of lacy steel and wire spokes. Her hair was teased up high over her head in a stiff pile, like a teetering stack of coins. Though it was hard to tell in the foggy dark, her hair appeared to be a burnished shade of metallic green.

Her face was the most startling thing, made up in a stark white base coating of paint. Somehow, her face "lit up" with regularity. Her eyes, her cheeks, the veins on her face and the interior of her mouth blinked on and off with a queer, cherry-red light, as if she'd swallowed a sputtering flashlight. Intricate designs painted on her cheekbones showed up clearly in darker red when her face lit up. Her flashing on, flashing off eyes, gave her a distinctly demonic appearance. She had some type of ring or rivet stuck to the side of her nose.

She regarded him for a moment. Her flashing red eyes were big, crazed almost.

The man swallowed hard and looked around. "Ma'am, I—"

She came closer, all arms and legs, then stopped, hunched over him, as if ready to spring

"Gods . . . Kana again. So, what do you have here for me? Flowers or something?"

He glanced down and picked up the bouquet he'd brought with him. "Yes, yes, I have flowers."

The woman held out her hand. "I've ended up in these wretched ruins fifty-seven times; that's a record, I think. Well, come on then, let's see them. Let's see your flowers."

The man offered the bouquet and she snatched it from his grasp with a sharp crinkling of paper. "Oh, well, these are lovely. Nice assortment." She stared into the paper cone, the whole thing lighting up in occasional red light. "Nice smell, too. You've got taste I see, short guy. And what else do you have there? Is that candy or something?"

He looked at the box sitting next to him. "I, well . . ."

"Come on, let's have them. We don't have all night." She reached out and motioned with her long fingers.

The man slowly lifted the box and, again, flickering, she snatched it out of his grasp. "Let's see, what do we have here?"

She opened the box, exposing the compartmented selection of fine stuffed chocolates.

"Xaphan's Beard!" she exclaimed. "Look, let's get one thing cleared up here right now. These are chocolates. I prefer hard candies, ok? Get it right, next time."

The man tried to slink away, but she jumped in front of him with remarkable agility, holding the box of chocolates, cornering him against the stone. "Where you going?" she asked in a sinister voice. "Huh?"

"I . . ."

"So, you've given me your flowers and your candy. Now, I'm afraid, I'm going to have to kill you . . ."

"You're going to what?" he cried. "You're going to kill me?"

She reared back and laughed, her metal harness rattling about her torso, a cone of red light coming out of her open mouth. "Of course I'm not going kill you! Boy, can't take a joke, can you?"

"Ma'am," he said, "I think there has been a mistake here."

She popped a chocolate into her mouth. She took another. He saw the wad of chewed up chocolate bulging out her cheek when her face lit up.

"Oh, there's been a mistake here, all right; there's been a grievous mistake made," she said, chewing. "You ready to die, little guy? I mean, we're all buddy-buddy here, aren't we? League, Carolines, we just love each other, don't we?" She backed him up into the face of the stone. "But I'm still a Xaphan . . . I'm still a 'bad guy', aren't I . . ." She stuck her sharply-heeled shoe into his chest.

"Ma'am, please, I . . ."

She put her foot down and stared at him, a bit disappointed. "Boy, you really don't have a sense of humor, do you? A lot of fellows really enjoy the whole 'Mean Xaphan Chick' thing; it gets them going. I've got you quaking in your boots, don't I? All right, let's get the formalities out of the way. I'm Melazarr, twenty-fifth daughter, House of Caroline."

"You . . . you're a Caroline maiden?"

She looked at him lamp-lit, wide-eyed, and nodded slowly, as if she were speaking to a dim-witted child; her tower of hair bobbing a bit. "*Yeah.* Were you expecting somebody else, like a Burgon perhaps, or a Conwell, or one of those Midas bitches? Nope, you come out to the ruins of House Caroline, and you're probably going to get a Caroline, period. And, also, '*maiden*' isn't really a good term, is it? I mean 'maiden' implies that I'm unmarried, which is true, but it also implies that I'm a virgin and, I hate to break it to you, but I haven't been a virgin in quite some time. I mean, look at me, I'm simply too hot not to handle. I've been Re-Virgined a couple of times, you know, by Xaphan mystics, but I keep Un-Virgining. You do think I'm hot, right?" She held him in the spotlight of her gaze.

"Ma'am, I think there's been a touch of a mistake . . ."

"Do you think I'm hot, yes or no?" she said again, loudly, towering over him, lit up, demanding an answer.

"Yes, yes, of course," he cried.

She seemed appeased. She ate another chocolate, then tossed the box away, the individual pieces dropping out and falling like little bombs.

"That's better. So, you got a vehicle around here somewhere? You didn't walk out here, did you? Come on, let's go. Take me to wherever, unless you feel like hanging out in these ruins all night long in the damp air." She looked at him and gave him the once over. "You know, you're kind of cute. And you're wearing a Fleet uniform too, which I like. I suppose this could be a whole lot worse. You got a name, by the way, little guy, or shall I make one up for you?"

"My name is Lt Josephus, Lord of A-Ram."

"Lieutenant . . . ahhh," she said, almost purring. "Ok, 'Lt. Joe', take me to your chariot and let's get a move on. I'm getting a little cold. You get two pokes for 'saving' me tonight, Joe, but that's it."

"*Excuse me?*" he squeaked.

"Sex, Joe. You get to have sex with me twice, and then I'm out of here, ok? It'll be the best you've ever had, trust me. You want it rough, we can do it rough. You want to make a game out of it, we can do that, too."

Suddenly, she seemed conflicted. Her flicking red light became unsteady. "You know, you're cute and you're an officer and all, so we'll have sex three times. How about that? This is your lucky day, Joe."

There was a noise farther back in the ruins. Melazarr spun around fast. "Hold up, somebody's skulking about." She moved the skirt of her gown aside, exposing the extreme upper-portion of her leg. She drew a squat knife. "You stay here, Joe, I wouldn't want you to mess up your uniform or anything."

A-Ram stood there. Melazarr was a bit annoyed. "Boy, you just have no clue how to read me, do you? Get over here, and watch my back, will ya`? You got a gun or anything?"

"Ma'am, there's no need for this. I know exactly who is moving in the dark."

"Yeah? Clue me then."

A-Ram called out. "Alesta, come out here, please."

Melazarr stopped, confused.

Ahead, a figure emerged from behind a partially fallen bulwark. It was a small woman, slender, wearing a green open robe over an inner white robe or smock. She had thick black hair done up with combs. She had flowers arranged in her hair. She didn't appear to be wearing shoes.

Her complexion was pale, like a porcelain doll. She spoke in a shy voice. "Rammy, are you all right? What's going on? I heard an unfamiliar voice."

Melazarr stood up straight and put her knife away. "Who is this woman, Joe?"

A-Ram walked up to the woman and put his arm around her shoulder. "This is Lady Alesta of Dare, my betrothed."

"Your betrothed? So, what are you doing out here, then? Ah, a little kinky, aren't you two? Well, that's fine, that's fine, I'm down with that. So, it's a threesome, and I'll bet I could get my legs 'round the both of you at once and start squeezing. You've got some set of vices, Joe. I'm impressed. You're just full of surprises."

Alesta's mouth dropped open.

"Madam, please." A-Ram said, blushing. "We . . . Alesta and I wanted to act out the legend of the ruins of Caroline. We thought it would be fun to . . ."

"To what?"

"To come here and act out the legend. Alesta was to jump up at me and pretend she was a Caroline maiden. It was all in good fun."

Melazarr smiled. "Oh, ok, I get it. You're role-playing, right? Your lady comes out here and hides in the rocks, then you show up bearing gifts, and she jumps out, pretending to be a Caroline. Only in this case, a real Caroline—me—just happened to show up. Well, sorry, Alesta, but here I am, and there you are. Looks like you and me are going to be fighting to the death over Joe here right now."

"You cannot be serious," A-Ram said, holding Alesta tightly.

"Well, of course I'm not serious. Boy, you fall for it every time, don't you?"

Melazarr gave Alesta the once over. "Wow, you really don't set your standards too high, do you, Joe?"

Alesta reddened. "Pardon?"

"I'm mean, look at those pinion legs and that silly black hair, and what are you, five foot nothing? You need to dye your hair a good shade of blue or green, and you need to be at least six feet tall in order to properly satisfy a discriminating man. A little muscle wouldn't hurt either, noodle-arms."

Alesta appeared to be on a slow, but steady burn. "Well, I believe my lord likes me just as I am. And, I shall ask as I can no longer tolerate it, but why is your face lighting up in such a peculiar manner?" Alesta put her hands on her hips and awaited an answer.

"Flash-Ons, from Waam. Xaphan men just love them; they're all the rage this year. You like it, Joe?"

A-Ram opened his mouth to respond. Alesta cut him off. "Such curiosities do not interest him."

Melazarr ignored her and looked around. "Well, I can't say I'm disappointed about this development. I mean, I've come all this way, and you two appear to be the only people out here tonight. And I meant it when I said I thought you were cute, Joe. You are cute, and I like those things on your face. So, Alesta, you sure you don't want to fight it out with me over Joe? I'll give you a free shot to start off with."

Alesta appeared rather conflicted. She looked like she was angry enough to take Melazarr up on her challenge, but she was too much of a lady to engage in such things.

"You're clearly joking again," A-Ram said.

"Actually, this time I'm not. I mean, what am I going to do now? Just sit out here and wait for somebody else to show? I could be here for days. I mean where am I going to go? You don't expect me to *walk* to civilization, do you?"

She flopped down on a stone and looked a bit forlorn, her flashing now intermittent and uncertain.

"Lady Caroline, we're sorry about this. Please, if we may offer a suggestion?" A-Ram said. "We would be honored to have you accompany us to our ship. Ladies of Caroline are considered visiting dignitaries, and you would be most welcome. Once there, we'll introduce you to the captain and we can come up with a suitable course of action for you. He's a good man, a wise man, and I'm happy to say he's my friend as well. Perhaps we can take you somewhere. Please, it's a chilly night; you'll freeze yourself to the bone."

"Rammy, I'm certain this woman has other arrangements more to her liking available."

"A ship?" Melazarr said. "What kind of ship do you have, Joe?"

"Please ma'am, call me 'A-Ram', all my friends do. And I am the master helmsman of the *Seeker*, a *Straylight*-class warbird."

Alesta interrupted. "Please, Rammy, we needn't inconvenience this woman by asking her to come away with us. I'm certain she has much to review and think about."

Melazarr's flashing took on a spot-light like strength. She was impressed. "Now, just hold on a second there, toots. A Warbird? A League battleship? Wow, you just scored lots of points, Joe, lots of points. I've never been on one of those. You might have just earned yourself the coveted fourth sex-roll with me! You talked me into it. Let's go."

Alesta gave an exasperated huff. Melazarr suddenly stopped. "Wait, you two sure you don't want something a little quick and easy while we're down here? I could teach you a few things, Alesta. You want to make Joe here happy, don't you? I could teach you all sorts of things."

Alesta fumed. "Ma'am, my Lord has said he prefers to be called 'A-Ram', and, additionally, I believe I know all that I need to regarding such matters."

"That true, Joe? Does this little string-bean make you happy?"

A-Ram stuttered. "Yes, yes indeed. I have no complaints."

Melazarr shrugged. "Suit yourself. But you really don't know what you're missing out on. Now, where's this ship of yours?"

2—PRIVATEERS

The usual clicking and officious sounds of the bridge wandered in through the open door of Stenstrom's office. A veil of stars glittered through the large windows, as well as the vast aft structure of the ship with its wings and tower and the hazy green/blue mass of Kana off to the right. Late in the service day, the night bell would sound soon. The Lord of Belmont-South Tyrol was rather tired. He planned to head off to his quarters, have a nightcap with his lady, Gwendolyn, and turn in for the evening.

His triangle hat and his great HRN coat hung from their pegs nearby. His pistols sat in their plush depressions in the wooden box atop the credenza. His office was, for the most part, as it was in the heady days of years past, when Captain Davage and Countess Sygillis commanded the ship; the one notable exception—his framed family crest, the black stars of Belmont and the green and white stripes of Tyrol hanging behind his desk.

Lord Stenstrom was a civilian appointed to the captain's chair of the *Seeker*, an old ship that had barely survived the scuttleman's yard. His appointment, contentious and costly, was a minor scandal in the hidden halls of the Fleet, and he had nearly been paneled over it, nearly been killed over it. He had paid for the *Seeker's* extensive refitting out of his own pocket and it had taken months to complete in a high-orbiting dry-dock over Kana's southern pole. Oh, the daily arguing with engineers, including his own Lady Gwendolyn of Prentiss, his chief engineer and full-time lover, the ancillary costs, the comings and goings of the craftsmen, the daily uploading/downloading of fixtures and specialty machinery, the drafts, the designs, the fussing over every detail, the re-acquisition of the crew: some days, it seemed too much.

But now, the refits done, the *Seeker* was once again a fully commissioned, fully functioning Warbird, ready for anything, bustling with crew and life, and all under his command. Through his windows, the whole of the ship unfolded in lengthening shadows, wings outstretched, lights blinking, scanning cones like searchlights moving back and forth in thoughtful arcs. He had been captain for just over a Kanan year. His official duty assignment: Privateer of the Third Fleet. His overall ongoing mission: interdict the Xaphans and take as many assets as would fit in his holds. He was, for lack of better terms, a Fleet and League sanctioned raider, pirate, and mercenary for hire, complete with a yearly assets quota and tally sheet of Xaphan vessels plundered, robbed, and sunk. The Fleet needed its coin, and the Privateers were tasked with taking it off the backs of their enemies, the Xaphans.

"Captain, you have a visitor," Private Taara de la Anderson said in her most formal voice. Taara never called him "captain" except when guests were around, and even then she didn't do it well. Today, though, she was on her best behavior.

The woman shown in by Private Taara was beautiful in the extreme and walked in the center of an elegant halo where everything around her was made better by her presence, made perfect. She wore a fine elaborate gown of teal, reds, and yellows inlaid with pearl and faceted stones encrusted in the fabric. He'd never seen a design quite like it. Her shoulders and toned arms were bare, revealing milky, pristine skin. Stacked high, her blonde hair was set in place with a great many jeweled pins. She wore a complicated wheeled timepiece around her neck that ticked in a pleasing, somewhat seductive fashion. She had baggage with her, a medium-sized box that tiny Taara, sideburns bobbing, lugged in behind her. Taara was like a veritable carpenter ant: little, but able move around big things with apparent ease. He had always marveled at that.

Extraordinarily tall, the lady had to stoop to enter the office. Taara was little more than half her size in comparison. Stenstrom was a towering 6-foot-7; nobody was taller, not even his mentor, Captain Davage of Blanchefort. In all the photos and group vids, Stenstrom always stuck up over the group like a lamp post. Not today, though. Her hair almost touched the ceiling, eleven-and-a-half-feet up. She seemed decidedly elongated in scale; very up and down while not being very left or right.

Stenstrom greeted her, looking up into her serene face. He came around his old Vith desk where the great Captain Davage had once sat and bowed to her, as all fine gentlemen of Esther and Tyrol did in the presence of a lady. He seated her in the padded baroque chair, the vastness of her gown filling it up. Taara set her box down nearby and took her place at the side of the desk, clearly wanting to stay. But with well-practiced hand gestures and general body language, Stenstrom whisked her out of the room. Taara left, but gave him a dirty look as she passed. When they were alone, Stenstrom introduced himself.

"Good evening, my lady. I'm Paymaster Stenstrom, Lord of Belmont-South Tyrol and captain of this vessel."

"My Lord," she said, lifting her hand. Her voice bore an odd accent, foreign and somewhat familiar, though Stenstrom couldn't quite place it. It had a singularly unusual sound to it; ancient, like how people centuries past might have spoken. Perhaps she was from Hoban, or some other exotic place about the League. He wished to hear more; her voice pleased him, rather like the troupe of VoiceBoxers he and Gwendolyn had seen in Saga, people whose melodious voices induced pleasure in those listening. He took her hand and kissed it above the knuckle, then seated himself.

"Well met," he said. "It's not often we have such a distinguished visitor aboard our humble ship. May I offer you a coffee?"

The woman thought a moment. "A coffee?" The notion seemed to perplex her. She adjusted a small wheel on her necklace. Something odd happened in the space of a moment, like those dreams that unfold and conclude in the blink of an eye. He thought he saw himself standing by the old silver coffee service making a hearty cup for her; he recalled numerous questions she had regarding its make and history. He had a distinct memory of her holding her cup and saucer, then taking a tentative first sip. He recalled being elated as she smiled and took another sip. And then it was gone, the whole sequence fading fast from his memory, then forgotten.

"Perhaps later, as we conclude our business," she said. "I like coffee."

"Of course. Well then, how may I serve you?"

She settled into her chair, the fabrics of her gown rustling. "You have offered me your name, sir, and I shall offer mine in return. I am Queen Wendilnight, co-proprietor of the Library of Time."

"The Library of Time? Your pardon, I've not heard of it before."

She smiled. "No pardon is required, sir. I wouldn't have expected you to be aware of it. Few are."

"Thank you. And, a queen, you say? You are royalty then?"

She blushed a bit. "Yes, after a fashion."

Stenstrom was interested and he pressed her for more. "May I ask where you hold title?"

"You may, sir. Asana Mons-Eagle, Solfid Castle, region of Armyak. Cammara."

Stenstrom had never heard of it. Cammara had a familiar ring, but he'd never been very interested in geography. He knew Kana and parts of Onaris, Bazz and the Gold Coast area of Hoban, but that was all. Gwendolyn would certainly know, but she was down at Fleet attending to her duties as engineer and would not return until the morning bell. He politely nodded, though he was lost and felt ashamed.

She continued. "You are a Privateer, sir, available for hire should the agreed upon price be met? Have I understood that correctly? I hope I haven't imposed upon your time fruitlessly today. Being of the Library of Time, I understand how important time is."

Queen Wendilnight had a good feel to her. The hand he had kissed tasted good, like a frosted dessert. Stenstrom considered himself a decent judge of character, and that he could trust everything she said and that it was important to listen to her.

"Aye," he said. "A Privateer in the service of the League. We do sometimes lend our sword, at captain's discretion, to those seeking to procure our services provided certain criteria are met. I'm afraid I don't offer my services often. I always meet my monthly Fleet quotas and more without resorting to side ventures. I feel it important to make that plain from the outset."

Queen Wendilnight smiled. "My goal today is not to extract a service from you; rather, it is to give you something, and to offer advice. I hope the things I tell you today will be understood."

"You wish to give me something, my lady?"

"I do. And you must listen to what I tell you."

"I thank you. I'll do my best to give ear and to properly understand."

She held her hand out, expecting him to offer her a cigarette, a custom in posh League Society circles. Stenstrom didn't smoke, but Gwendolyn liked to on quiet evenings and he had a case of hand-rolled cigarettes in the woodsy blend she favored in a desk drawer. He got the case out, selected a cigarette, then offered it to her. She pulled a stick from her bag and mounted the cigarette. Stenstrom took a golden lighter from his drawer and lit it. She had a pull and savored the smoke.

"You mentioned you have something you wish to give me, my lady?"

She lowered her cigarette. "Yes, I do." Smoke drifted out of her mouth in delicate feathers. "I must ask, may I see you in your proper uniform?"

"Pardon? I have no uniform, Great Lady, as I'm not actually a member of the Fleet. I'm a civilian."

"I remember your coat, so lush and green. I had been eaten by a great frog-like creature and you rescued me. I remember your coat and hat, your amazing pistols. I would like to see you in them again, please."

Stenstrom was perplexed. "Your pardon, ma'am, I don't believe I've had the pleasure before today." Perhaps the smoke from her cigarette was making her delusional. He pointed to the wall and his long green coat hanging from its peg. "There is my coat, Great Lady."

"May I ask you to put it on, please?"

"I'm not a show pony, Great Lady."

"Of course not, however, I would like to see you in it, simply for nostalgia's sake."

He sat there and considered her odd request; she didn't appear to be joking. Had she come to gawk at the eccentric man from Tyrol? He considered disregarding her request as this was his ship, the hour was late, and he wanted to be comfortable. However, this woman, this Queen Wendilnight, carried a serene and commanding presence, and her blue-eyed gaze was almost as potent as that of a Sister, though more benign. He supposed he could engage in a battle of wills with her over his attire and the clock would tick and the meeting would go bells deep into the evening; or he could simply comply with her request. It wasn't too unreasonable, just a little odd and a bit demeaning. And, he wondered, if the situation came down to a battle of wills, who would win out?

He sighed, stood, and pulled his HRN coat from its peg. It was a wonderful, embroidered dark green coat that went down to his ankles, heavy and creaky with Hoban fabrics. He stocked various arcane items in the many hidden pockets lining the interior. It had a proud "HRN" riveted in silver on the stiff collar. A mystical coat, the Sisters had done something to it and it could do amazing things, the whole of which he was still discovering. He slid his arms in. Despite its size and bulk, the HRN was never too hot to wear, nor too chilly. It was always just right. He could sleep in it nice and cozy if he wanted.

Queen Wendilnight watched him as he straightened his shirt and went to the box to get his pistols. "I assume you wish me to put my weapons on as well," he said.

"You assume correctly. Thank you, sir."

He opened the box and there were his pistols, the NTHs, the LosCapricos weapons of his father's line. Though appearing as simple flintlock pistols, the NTH fired a mystical green ball of energy that could slay virtually anything. He pulled them out of the velvet-lined box and slid them into his sash, allowing the lazy-S wooden stocks to stick out.

He picked up his black triangle hat and placed it on his head. There he stood, Stenstrom, Lord of Belmont-South Tyrol kitted out in full array: silk shirt, black knee britches, a pair of Tyrol boots, partially leather, partially metal, his green sash around his waist with the two pistols sticking out and his Barbary HRN coat. "Is this what you were hoping to see?"

"It is. How handsome and dashing. Exactly how I remembered it when you came to rescue me from the frog's mouth."

"Great lady, I have no recollection of such a thing. A frog's mouth, you say? I would think such an occasion would stick in my memory."

Queen Wendilnight reached up and turned a wheel on her necklace. Sudden flashes of memory pelted him.

Driving rain.

Mud and a stand of fernlike trees withering in the rain.

Debris from fallen shipping stuck in the mud, some of it flaming.

Dead bodies in the mud.

His hands clamped on the two halves of a great, warty mouth, desperately forcing them open like a clamshell.

Inside, resting in a pool of slime, was Queen Wendilnight, frozen in place. Wait! Queen Wendilnight! What was wrong with her body? It was . . .

She turned the wheel again and the memories faded, falling out of his thoughts as quickly as they had come in with only a flicker of notice on his part. "I have great cause to be thankful for you, sir," she said.

Stenstrom returned to his desk and sat down, feeling somewhat confused. "So, how may I assist you, Great Lady?"

She turned to the box Taara had lugged in. "I have come to give you this . . ."

She retrieved an odd item, then held it out framed in the lattice-work of her fingers. For a moment, he thought the device glowed, for it seemed to illuminate her hands, lighting her fingers up in red so that her bones shown through. But, on second glance, it wasn't glowing at all.

It was an ochre object, round, with a smooth sunk-in top portion and a flat bottom; it reminded him of a squatty bell. Queen Wendilnight held it aloft with both hands, offering it to him. Stenstrom took it; it didn't weigh much. His hand brushed hers as he did so, and the brief touch was magical, electric.

He set the device on his desk. It sat there, innocuous, like a loaf of bread illuminated in a pool of dim lighting from overhead. It seemed to be made of smooth, polished stone, or possibly an opaque crystal, he wasn't certain. It was featureless, with the exception of a small knob on top in the center.

Frankly, he was underwhelmed. "And what do you need done with this, Great lady?"

"I need it transported."

"Only this? Nothing more?"

"Yes, this is all."

"A League ship is costly, my lady. When tasked, we move freight in bulk, enough to fill a hold or two. This is a trifle, a keepsake, no offense intended. A smaller civilian ship, a bark, or a small private yacht would, no doubt, serve you better, If you had a large consignment of these items, several thousand, then I would understand, but for only one . . ."

"This one device is made just for you."

"Pardon?"

"We made it just for you."

"But consider the cost, it will be several thousand Fleet Solaris at minimum."

"It must be you, sir. Cost does not concern me."

"I see. Then I'll need further information." He gestured at the device. "What is this?"

"It's known as an Anatameter. My husband made it. Only he and a handful of others have the essential skills to create them."

"Is it dangerous?"

"Very dangerous."

Dangerous? Stenstrom stared at it, not seeing or detecting anything particularly threatening about it in any way, and none of his various devices he carried for detecting the arcane gave him insight. "We have the usual screening procedures to reject entry of any items that might pose a hazard to Fleet shipping and personnel. Were this device dangerous it would not have made it off the docks."

"It's not dangerous until it is activated."

"And then?"

"And then you might wish you had never set eyes upon it."

"I see. Perhaps I should ask my engineering team to have a look at it. I have my ship and crew to consider."

"Your engineering team would find nothing but a hollow stone. As I said, this Anatameter has not yet been activated."

"What is its function?"

"It is, for lack of better terms, a key. In its most basic form it guards the threshold between one plane of reality and the next."

The key from one plane of reality to another? Stenstrom sat back and allowed himself a slight laugh. He wondered what other ship captains would do in such a situation. Queen Wendilnight was, quite possibly, mad. Prudence and station demanded he politely hear her out, smile, seem supportive and interested, then, at a later time, berate his subordinates for allowing this crazy woman and her lump of stone into his office in the first place. Certainly few other captains would consider committing their assets in service of such a fantasy. It would be a scandal.

Yet . . .

As a trained sorcerer, a graduate of his late mother's underground school of Tyrol herbalism and black magic, he knew not to summarily reject the odd and the bizarre; he'd seen plenty of it in his lifetime. Queen Wendilnight had the air of the arcane about her. And, despite himself, he was curious; if anything, he enjoyed a good story. He decided to open his ears and listen. What could it hurt?

"Please, go on," he said.

"Thank you. For each reality, there is an Anatameter guarding the gates. There are always those seeking to cross from one reality to the next, and that can be very dangerous to the well-being of the universe. The Anatameter prevents these crossings. It works infallibly and the universe is much safer for it. My husband has made thousands."

"He's a skilled craftsman, then, your husband?"

"He is. Occasionally, and by sanction of the gods, he is tasked to custom build an Anatameter, and such is the case here. This example here is made just for you."

"You've mentioned that. I don't understand what import that has."

Queen Wendilnight stared at Stenstrom, then her expression softened. She seemed genuinely sad. "What import? It means this device, once activated, will transform you. You'll have knowledge that spans the universes. You'll have power as well, and all the troubles that come with such power. Demented, extra-planar creatures will be drawn to you, and evil men and women will seek its power, too. And, I'm so sorry, once you activate it, the Anatameter will, at least for a while, cause you nothing but misery. I have seen it.

"A hideous, reviled creature will steal it from you, and in your efforts to recover it, that is where you rescue me in a place not seen in thousands of millennia, if not in this universe, then another. In the process some of your loved ones will die, some will be sent off on a long journey, and others will be transformed without hope of ever returning to what they once were. Most changed of all, will be you, sir. The Anatameter will transform you into a new man, but not without a great crucible first."

Stenstrom had heard enough. "Taara," he said into the air.

"Ya', Bel," came the reply over the Com.

"I believe Queen Wendilnight is all finished up here. Will you prepare her arraignments back to the shore, please?"

"Two shakes, Bel."

"Thank you."

Queen Wendilnight smiled. "So," she said, "I assume you are declining the Anatameter."

He pushed it away, sliding it across the top of the desk. "How could I not? I'm sorry, you're an enchanting lady, and I truly don't wish to disappoint you. However, your description of this device, if it's to be believed, is horrifying. Frankly, I want no part of it, not only for myself, but for those whom I love. I must think of them as well. I suppose I like things as they are."

Queen Wendilnight's expression softened. "I know that . . ." She turned a dial on her necklace. ". . . and I am sorry."

"You realize the costs for engaging Fleet transport are not deferred by tonnage, or, as in this case, lack of tonnage. The transport shall be costly," Stenstrom said.

"Cost does not concern me," Queen Wendilnight said. She cleared her throat and flushed a little.

Stenstrom shrugged. "Be it so. And where do you need your tiny device taken?"

"The Cistern of the Shadow tech Goddess."

Stenstrom laughed. "Great Lady, if you've a task for me and my ship to undertake, to transport this device as you say, I will consider it, however I pray you be plain."

"I'm speaking as plainly as I can. There is a place not far, where you may take it: the Cistern of the Shadow tech Goddess. In the next day you shall encounter a daffy young *Merten* named Melazarr of Caroline. Does that name sound familiar to you?"

"No, should it? And she is a what? A *Merten* did you say?"

"Melazarr of Caroline carries a wealth of information, though she knows it not herself—that makes her a *Merten*. She will mention something about an entity known as the Shadow tech Goddess, and you will discover where the device needs to be taken."

"What is the Shadow tech Goddess?"

"A woman who does not exist." Queen Wendilnight reached into her box and pulled out a shining bar of brilliant metal. Stenstrom raised an eyebrow. "Is that Mithrilcyte?"

"It is. Your payment." She placed it on the desk. Stenstrom picked it up, amazed by its considerable weight. "This is quite a bounty."

"Will you accept it as payment? I offer it all to you, and in advance."

He guessed the bar was worth, conservatively, five million sesterces, several years quota. He glanced back at the odd Anatameter sitting on his desk.

"What is your answer, sir?" she asked, pressing him.

He placed the heavy bar of Mithrilcyte in a drawer. "I feel a tad guilty for taking so much for such a negligible task."

"Don't lose it, sir, please," she said, her gaze wandering to the floor.

"Oh, no, no. I won't lose it. I swear."

"Don't forget, when you put it in place, turn the knob eight times."

"Thank you, I won't forget. Turn the knob."

Queen Wendilnight smiled a little, but said nothing more.

3—A Visiting Dignitary

They led Melazarr down the bluff near the coast where a small Ripcar waited. A-Ram seated Alesta and wrapped her green robe around her like a blanket as he strapped her in. He then strapped Melazarr into her seat. She made large eyes at him the whole time; her flashing face lit up the interior of the craft.

Alesta, normally such a demure woman, turned red with anger. She crossed her arms and stewed. "Will you please cease that infernal blinking? It's giving me a headache."

"Well, we can't have that, can we?" Melazarr replied. She opened her mouth and drew out a surprisingly large round disk form-fitted to her upper pallet. She manipulated it in an odd fashion, then hid it within the metal structure of her gown. "Happy?" Alesta didn't respond.

A-Ram then piled into his seat and fired the Ripcar up. Soon, they were blasting high over the quiet Hala landscape.

✶　✶　✶　✶　✶

Stenstrom couldn't help but smile as he looked at the odd woman sitting at the far end of the table.

They were sitting in the *Seeker's* large main conference room, the lovely green and blue ball of Kana rolling past the window every so often as the ship orbited the equator.

Stenstrom, decked out in his usual dark green HRN coat and white shirt, sat at the head of the table. He was sans his once ubiquitous mask; he hadn't worn it in some time. Seated next to him in her well-cared for Fleet uniform was Lt. Gwendolyn, Lady of Prentiss and the ship's chief engineer. Farther down the table, Morgan-Jeterix, Lady of Thompson and the ship's Hospitaler, sat reviewing scrolling information on her pad. She wore her usual black and silver uniform topped off by her winged silver helmet which she kept pushing away from her nose, her blonde hair tightly braided and interwoven with beads, as always. Sitting on the other side of the table was Private Taara de la Anderson of the 110th Marines, the ship's first officer. Sitting next to Taara was Lady Alesta of Dare, 10th order, one of the contingent of the Pilgrims of Merian, who had taken permanent residency aboard the ship. Lady Alesta, as Pilgrims of Merian usually went, was a kind, winsome presence, always smiling and bursting with optimism.

Alesta wasn't smiling now; in fact, she looked rather put off. She cast a deadly gaze at the woman seated at the end of the table and loudly eating a plate of mirandasloss freshly made by the chef, Lord Rump.

The woman ate with relish. She didn't use the knife and fork provided, but moved the food around with her stubby knife, spearing the pieces, then popping them in.

Stenstrom smiled. "My good friend, Lord A-Ram told me you were hungry, and I can clearly see that."

She looked up from her plate. "Ohhh, I *love* League food." She looked around. "Where's Joe?" she asked as she ate.

"If you're referring to Lord A-Ram, he's standing at the helm," Stenstrom said.

"So, he really does fly the ship? That's great. I thought he was just trying to impress me."

Alesta narrowed her eyes and hunched up a little in her seat. "As was stated before, Lord A-Ram is *my* betrothed and impressing you is irrelevant. Perhaps you weren't listening. I would appreciate it if you could pay both he, and myself, the proper respect."

The woman shrugged. "Want to fight about it?"

Alesta didn't answer, but given her expression and shade of hue, clearly her internal response was a resounding "yes".

In the brightly lit interior of the ship, the woman's appearance could be fully appreciated at last. She was a long, lank woman wearing a confoundedly odd gown, partially made of black cloth, partially of bare metal and wire with a black undergarment hugging her chest, keeping her covered up. The wire harness about her torso appeared to be somewhat sharp, and she held a posture which appeared suited to prevent herself from being cut by it. The fabric portion of her gown was a tarnished green color, stained in black. She was wearing form-fitting black gloves that went up to her elbows. On her legs she wore a sultry pair of netted stockings ended with a pair of stiletto-heeled shoes, which looked very much like what was the fashion in the south of Hoban. The shoes added several inches to her already impressive height.

As before on the surface, her face was heavily made up, a thick base-coating of white with red and blue designs painted in at her cheekbones and deeply rouged cheeks. Her long hair was painted a metallic olive green and was held in place over her head in a towering, bunched-up mass. Her hair appeared stiffly teased or starched, so much so it almost looked like a hat or enameled shell instead of hair. There was a silver rivet stamped into the side of her nose. The woman also appeared rail thin and gangly, though her lean body was canvassed in cut, defined muscle.

She finished the last morsels of food. "That was good. I want some more."

Gwendolyn, sitting next to Stenstrom, raised an eyebrow. "You would like some more, *please* . . ." she said. "We follow rules of basic courtesy aboard this ship."

The woman pointed at her with her knife. "Does she have to be here? I don't think I like her much." She pointed at Alesta. "Her neither."

Stenstrom shook his head. "Com."

"Com here, sir," came a reply from above.

"Com, please ask Lord Rump for another helping of mirandasloss, along with refreshments all around. I'm thinking coffee for everyone here."

"*Coffee!*" she shouted. "We're going to have coffee?"

"That we are," Stenstrom said.

"Oh, this keeps getting better and better! I haven't had coffee in forever. Grown here on Kana, right? Not that crap-assed stuff from Midas that Xaphans call coffee?"

"No, well, actually the best coffee comes from Onaris," he said. "It's good Onaris Calvertland coffee we serve."

"Well, where is it? Let's get on with it."

A few minutes later another plate of mirandasloss came, along with several cups of coffee. Gwendolyn sat properly as Stenstrom prepared her cup; she then smiled and accepted it.

Regardless of the heat, the woman slurped her cup down. "Ahhh, that was good."

Gwendolyn took a sip from her cup, then folded her hands together. "So, do you by chance have a name? It's customary for one to properly introduce one's self."

"Is it? Not where I come from." She pointed at Alesta with her knife. "You, you know my name. Tell them what it is."

Alesta fumed. Stenstrom couldn't help but chuckle; it was so odd seeing the normally calm and reserved Alesta on the verge of a fit of temper. She ground her teeth: "This . . . 'creature' is Melazarr, and she also claims to be a Maiden of Caroline."

Melazarr . . .

Stenstrom's smile faded. "Melazarr? Your name is Melazarr?"

She turned her gaze to him. "Yeah . . ." she said slowly. "That's my name."

He stared at her. "I was told to expect you."

"Yeah? Well, here I am."

Stenstrom rubbed his chin. "Do you have any information for me?"

Melazarr stopped eating and rolled her eyes up. "Information? Ummm, you're sort of handsome, I guess. How's that for information?"

"And you are a *Merten*?" Stenstrom asked.

She looked perplexed. "Yes, no . . . what am I? What's a *Merten*?"

Gwendolyn jumped in. "And you claim to be a Lady of Caroline, is that correct?"

Melazarr speared more food. "I don't claim to be anything. I am a Caroline, but I'm no lady. 'Lady' is a League term that we don't use. I'm no lady."

"That is obvious."

Alesta sat there, her coffee steaming and untouched. "I cannot believe that this *person* is a Lady of Caroline. Everyone here knows that I always strive to see the good in people; however, in this case I see very little. I think of all those poor gentlemen going out to those dangerous ruins every night, hoping to encounter love, and instead ending up saddled with a bizarre creature like this."

"Oh, come on, 'A', let's hear how you really feel," Melazarr said.

"I believe that any who choose to go Carofab are doing those gentlemen a grand favor by saving them from the disappointment—and horror—of the real thing," Alesta threw in.

"I have no idea what a 'Carofab' is, therefore I forgive you," Melazarr said.

Gwendolyn spoke up. "A 'Carofab' is a woman who sneaks out to the Caroline ruins, pretending to be a Lady of Caroline. There's an extensive spy network here on Kana that makes it its business to know exactly who is going out to the ruins and when. When someone promising is expected, hopeful local ladies are made aware of it and attempt to pass themselves off as Ladies of Caroline. That is a Carofab."

Melazarr nodded. "I see, well goody for them. I guess, 'A', that makes you a Carofab then, doesn't it? Isn't that what you were doing down there tonight? Trying to sink your hooks into Joe's tiny shoulders?"

Alesta was outraged. "No! How dare you! A-Ram is *my* Lord, and *my* beloved future husband! He knew full well we were playing a simple game!"

Stenstrom spoke up. "Being a Carofab isn't a bad thing. My sister Constance went Carofab many years ago, and ended up with a fine husband to whom she is devoted. Lord A-Ram's brother too, paired off with a Carofab, though she still won't admit it."

Gwendolyn said, "I don't think this woman is a Caroline. I think she's a castoff from some low-level or downtrodden Xaphan House and was hoping to change her situation in the ruins. I think you, Lady Melazarr, are a Carofab too and would like for you to admit it, please."

Melazarr winked at Gwendolyn and blew her a kiss.

Morgan-Jeterix jumped in. "Gwen, per standard procedures, I examined the DNA sample Lady Melazarr offered up upon boarding. Her genetic markers do match the trace samples contained in the House of Caroline's ancient patent. Additionally, her genetics show a red flag for paternal Giantism, which is passed down from male to daughter, and Giantism is another feature of Caroline females. She also has a pierced nose and the somewhat patchy skin pigmentation we know Carolines have; thus her reliance on heavy makeup and gloves to cover it up."

"Easy now," Melazarr said.

"So," Morgan continued, "I am forced to conclude that Lady Melazarr is, in fact, a Maiden of Caroline."

"Again, a tragedy for any reputable young man going out there," Alesta said.

Melazarr smiled. "So, 'A', how are we going to do this? Knives, clubs, or plain old fists?"

Alesta, completely out-of-character, looked like she was going to stand up and accept Melazarr's challenge. Stenstrom quickly rose and hurried to her side. He placed his hands on her shoulders and she calmed down a little. Melazarr looked him up and down. Her gaze followed him as he returned to his seat.

"So, let's get down to it," Gwendolyn said. "What were you doing out there amid the ruins tonight?"

Melazarr continued looking at Stenstrom. "First, who is he?"

Taara, for the first time, spoke. "I don't think we've properly introduced ourselves. He is Stenstrom, Lord of Belmont and the captain of this ship."

Melazarr's gaze never left him. "He's not wearing a uniform. I thought she was the captain." She pointed at Gwendolyn with her knife. "What's his rank?"

"He's a Paymaster by title, a civilian," Taara said.

"A civilian is in charge of a Fleet battleship?" Melazarr said. "So she's second in command then, right?"

"Nope," Taara said. "I am. Private Taara de la Anderson, 110th Marines, and first officer of the ship."

"A private?"

"Yep, although my paperwork is coming down from Command, I'm soon to be promoted to P-Lt."

"Congrats. Would you like a roll in the sack to celebrate?"

"Thanks, and maybe later, `kay?"

Gwendolyn appeared to tire of the banter. "I am the chief engineer. I have the Paymaster's ear and—"

"Yeah?" Melazarr said. "What else of his do you have?"

Gwendolyn flushed and didn't answer. As usual when Gwen clammed up, Morgan-Jeterix spoke up for her, saying what was on Gwendolyn's mind. It was an annoying talent and once she got started, she rolled with it.

"We asked you a question earlier, so how about it?" Morgan said. "What were you doing down there in the ruins? As the legend goes, Caroline maidens only show up down there when in mortal peril. So, what happened?"

Melazarr resumed eating. "I was on a date."

"A date? You were on an outing?"

"Whatever you want to call it. I was having dinner with Rodrigo of Burgon."

Stenstrom thought a moment. "If I'm current on my knowledge of Xaphan society, Rodrigo of Burgon is a member of a high-ranking House."

"I guess so, sure."

"The House of Burgon are cannibals, if the rumors hold true," Morgan said. "Did he try to eat you? Is that what happened?"

"No, he tried to ply me with drink and then sacrifice me. Maybe he might have eaten me after that, I don't know. You know, Sten, you've got awesome eyes," she said, winking at him.

Both Gwendolyn and Lady Alesta fumed as though they wished she had been eaten or sacrificed. "His name, to you, is Paymaster Stenstrom, if you would be so kind," Morgan said, again channeling Gwendolyn's thoughts.

Stenstrom tired of this silly chatter. "Ma'am, you may call me 'Bel.' All my friends call me that."

She leaned over her plate and gazed at him. "I see . . . and am I your friend, Bel?"

"Absolutely."

"So then, why don't you—"

"Rodrigo of Burgon? Do you know him well?" he said. He was not going to let her control the conversation the way she had with Alesta and Gwendolyn.

She leaned back and smiled. "Not at all, actually."

"So how did you end up on an outing with him?"

"He inquired at our ancestral compound in Wilhelmina. He offered an impressive sum to been seen in public with a Caroline, and he inquired about me personally. I have certain Tropist talents that I'm well known for, so my father appointed me. It was a big deal, so here I am, all done up—gown, *caratina,* up-do, flash-ons, the works. Want to see it?"

"Don't you dare put that thing back into your mouth," Alesta cried.

"My Lady, please," Stenstrom said. "You didn't feel worried about being in such close quarters with a cannibal?"

She raised her eyebrows. "Should I have felt worried?"

Alesta spoke up. "Of course not. What should one, such as yourself, have to fear from a mere cannibal? I should think it was he who was in a greater bit of peril in your reckless presence."

"I'm getting the distinct impression you don't like me much, 'A'. I'm sure Joe likes me. I'm sure he likes me just fine."

"It's not in my nature to dislike anyone, I simply do not appreciate the manner in which you have treated both myself and the man whom I love."

"Ah, you mean Joe, the little guy I'm going to fu—"

"Madam, may we please stick to the topic at hand?" Stenstrom said. "So, tell us about your encounter with Rodrigo of Burgon."

Melazarr wanted more coffee and Stenstrom called for a fresh pot to be brought in. When it came, she drank down a piping hot cup or two and continued. "He came to Wilhelmina in a grand procession and took me away, to Burgon. Burgon's really not a bad place, and the Burgons don't eat man-flesh as often as you think. Mostly, they sell man-flesh to other beings. I don't know who buys it, but there it is.

"He took me to a fine restaurant in Berlinson at the edge of a vast forest. The date was kind of boring and I didn't care much for Rodrigo. There was this nasty woman all wrapped up in black sitting in the wings, watching us. I thought she might be his mom or something. Anyway, I could tell early on he was trying to get me drunk. He ordered bottle after bottle of sour-grape wine and seemed a touch put off when I didn't soften up as quickly as he wanted. The bad thing for him, I can drink. I could probably drink the lot of you under the table before I'm half-warmed up."

"Ha!" Taara replied.

Melazarr continued. "Anyway, when I got tired of the wine and the company, I pretended to pass out. I was sort of curious what would happen. That's when all the people in robes showed up."

"Robes?"

"That's right. They came out of everywhere. They picked me up and dragged me outside, cutting their fingers on my *caratina* here." She flicked her wire harness with her finger. "And complaining the whole time how heavy I was, which I rather took offense to. Then they stuffed me into a floater and took me out to the woods."

"And nobody in the restaurant cared to assist you while all this was happening?"

"Nope," she replied. "Xaphans . . . remember? They just kept on eating."

Stenstrom thought a moment. "So, you pretended to pass out, and they dragged you out to the woods. Is that when you disappeared? Is that when your VERY MARY spirited you away to safety?"

"Not hardly. The VERY MARY doesn't crash me out until the very last second. So, they took me out to the woods, still complaining about how heavy I was and how bad my *caratina's* messing them up. They lugged me out to a clearing with a fire. That's when Rodrigo showed up, dressed in robes just like the others. He mentioned something about burning me and reading my guts, I don't know."

"They wanted to burn you alive?" Stenstrom asked.

"That's what he said, and he was going to summon some sort of Goddess, then he pulled a knife and made to slice off my VERY MARY to keep me from getting away."

"Goddess?" Stenstrom asked. "You mean the Shadow tech Goddess?"

Melazarr thought back. "Yep, that's the one. That's when I clobbered him with my feet, and he fell back into the fire. He got up burning and ran into the woods like a flaming marshmallow. I got up and the others all drew knives and made to stick me. Though they really weren't all that tough. That's when the others arrived with a monster."

Stenstrom frowned. "A monster?"

"Yep. The fire turned black, lots of white smoke like fog, and something big was moving around inside the fog. I saw a bright pair of eyes like headlights on a C-Loader and it made this funny clicking sound. Before I knew it, a big pair of claws came out of the fog, like crab claws, and they came down to get me, and that was when the VERY MARY zapped me out of there. That's when I showed up in the ruins for the fifty-seventh time. And what did I find waiting there for me? Chocolates, and a little guy who's already hooked up to a hung-up, hit-out bitch."

Alesta bounced up. "Those chocolates were for me, not you, and I happen to like them very much! And, if you wish to toss names about, I'm certain I can respond in kind, you electro-plated Xaphan harlot! You miserable slut!"

"Bring it on, A!"

Stenstrom laughed. "Lady Alesta, please. Need I remind that you are in the Star's light, and it would certainly not approve of you fighting and cat-calling with a visiting guest."

She sat down and caught her breath. "My Lord, thank you for reminding me of my responsibilities. Madam Caroline, please accept my apologies for my rude behavior."

Melazarr smiled. "It's ok. Besides, it's not Joe I'm planning on taking anymore, so you needn't worry, It's him I'm going to have." She pointed at Stenstrom.

Stenstrom was a tad shocked. "That's . . . quite a story," he said. "And I'm certain all present are relieved you escaped your ordeal unharmed. So, madam, is that all? Do you have anything further to tell me?"

Melazarr pursed her lips and blinked. "No. I can make something up if that would make you feel better."

"Thank you, no. I suppose the next move is up to you. Where would you like to go? Your status as a visiting dignitary obliges us to be at your disposal for a short time. We can arrange to take you anywhere in the League you might want to visit if you wish to stay, or we can return you home."

"Bel," Gwendolyn said, "it's not the mission of a Main Fleet Warbird to ferry wayward Xaphan women home. We shall summon a transport to take her to Xandarr, where she may then make her way from there as she will."

"Assuming she wants to return to Caroline. Is that what you want, ma'am?" Stenstrom asked.

Melazarr looked at him hard, her eyes smoldering. "Why don't you tell me what I want, Bel?"

Gwendolyn spoke up. "So, it's settled then. Tomorrow, you're on the transport and safely on your way home. You'll have top-rated passage, I assure you."

"Well, gee, Gwen, what's the matter? Can't take a little competition? I just got here and I'm not ready to leave yet. Want to show me around, Bel? I just *love* League ships."

Stenstrom stood. "Certainly. Come on, Gwen, let's show our guest around."

"No, no," Melazarr said. "Not her. Just me and you."

"Fat chance of that happening," Morgan said.

"So, Bel, you promised me a tour."

"Indeed I did. First, however, I've duties to attend. I'll order quarters made available to you at once, and when you're refreshed, we shall have the tour."

"I'd rather stay with you," she said, making eyes at him.

Gwendolyn spoke for herself this time. "Ma'am, it is not appropriate for a visiting guest to speak to the commander of a Fleet vessel in such a manner. Rest assured you shall be accommodated in the best we have to offer."

Melazarr ignored her. "So, what do you say, Bel? Do I have a chance or not?"

"You do not," Gwendolyn replied.

"Yeah? What do you have to say about that, Bel?"

Gwendolyn rose and leaned on her hands on the table. "He has nothing to say to you. You've done nothing but tread on our good will and behave in a scandalous manner since you set foot aboard. I am growing tired of your constant stream of quips, both toward our helmsman and our commander."

"And what's it to you, ice-twat?"

Gwendolyn reached for her FEDULA. "My relationship with Paymaster Stenstrom is none of your concern!" she spat. "However, if you insist on antagonizing me, you can bet that you'll be losing a mouthful of teeth before I'm finished with you!" Stenstrom grabbed the hand holding the FEDULA.

"Well, let's go, babe, you and me. Right now!"

Taara joined Stenstrom in restraining Gwendolyn while Melazarr laughed.

4—The Shadow tech Goddess

L ater that evening, after removing his HRN coat and placing his NTH pistols in their box, Stenstrom slumped on the couch in his quarters. He was worn out after showing Melazarr around the ship. Both Gwendolyn and Lady Alesta had looked like they wanted to put her out an air-lock. For most of the tour, Melazarr was well-behaved, apparently enthralled with the ship. But when they got to the bridge, the trouble started. Melazarr, seeing A-Ram standing at the helm, was all over him, flirting relentlessly. Lady Alesta, naturally took exception and a scene was very nearly made, but Stenstrom managed to keep order.

They showed Melazarr to her quarters and left; though it wasn't long before he began hearing her voice in his head.

<*Bel . . . Bel!*>

He tried to keep her out of his thoughts.

Queen Wendilnight had predicted her coming.

And Melazarr had mentioned the Shadow tech Goddess. Also predicted.

He recalled the device Queen Wendilnight had given him, the Anatameter sitting in his wardrobe in the next room, and all the money she had paid to deliver it somewhere. If the Queen's predictions continued to be accurate, then he would soon know where to take it.

Several minutes later, his door opened and Gwendolyn, carrying a small over-night case, slipped inside. She set her case on the table, then embraced him.

"What a horrible day," she said after they kissed.

"Are you referring to our guest?"

Gwendolyn laid her head on his shoulder. "I have never seen Lady Alesta get so angry. I think that foul woman was intentionally antagonizing her, and me, as well."

"Probably. You two were making it easy for her. Just don't react; that's probably all she's looking for."

GWENDOLYN, LADY OF PRENTISS

"Let's hope."

Queen Wendilnight . . . had predicted her coming. Called her a "Merten".

Gwendolyn kissed him on the cheek, then took her over-night case into the bedroom. Stenstrom made a pot of coffee. A small, steady voice again invaded his thoughts.

<Bel . . .>

Melazarr hitting his thoughts with telepathy, something the Carolines were reputed to be masters at.

<Bel . . . I'm sitting here all alone . . . Nice room. It's missing a little something though . . .>

He pushed the voice from his head. Gwendolyn emerged from the bedroom, shoeless, dressed in a pink floral nightgown. She sat down and took her coffee cup. "It feels so good to get out of my uniform," she said, then took a sip.

Stenstrom settled next to her on the couch. "Why don't you go and get comfortable?" she said. "Our usual Airenet programming is on soon. I just want to spend a nice, lovely evening with you, all alone."

Gwen was such a homebody.

<I'm waiting for you, Bel . . . Guess where my hand is right now . . .>

"I've already taken the liberty of summoning a fine transport to take her to Xandarr, the *Hoban Night*. They'll take her to Xandarr or wherever she wants to go—and good riddance."

<I'm coming for you, Bel . . .>

Stenstrom winced. The voice in his head took on a savage note.

A knock came at the door.

Gwendolyn rolled her eyes. "Who in Creation could that be?" She rose and headed for the bedroom. "Don't answer it. It could be *her.*"

<You can do anything to want to me . . . and I am aching to do certain things to you . . . The things I could do to your flesh . . . Let me show you.>

Stenstrom went to the door. "Who is it?"

"Bel, it's Morgan. Can you let me in?"

He opened the door to find Morgan-Jeterix, still in her black Hospitaler uniform. "This is a surprise."

He stepped back to let her enter. He offered her a cup of coffee and she accepted, seating herself on the couch.

Morgan-Jeterix. Stenstrom had a very strange relationship with the Samaritan-class Hospitaler, and a member of the Ephysians, a sub-order within the Hospitalers.

He often wondered what might happen if he and Morgan were left in a room alone for too long. He wondered.

He wondered.

Such thoughts were unbearable.

The Sisters were in him this evening and he saw see the flowing details of her 4-D tattoo. The Sisters golden crest on her face, marking her as a Certified Empath, floated prim and proper over a turbid sea of passion and desire.

On days when he could see her tattoo, he wanted her like nothing else.

"So, what's the deal?" he asked Morgan. "Something on your mind?"

"Yes, as always. Got a visitor, Bel? Somebody's in your head with you, right?"

"I believe so."

"I can guess who it is. She's probably whispering sweet to-do's in your ear or worse, right?" Morgan reached into her pocket, fished around, then held out a small wooden carving. "Here you go, this should help."

When Stenstrom accepted the carving, Morgan ran her finger across his palm as he took it.

His palm lit up from the momentary touch. "A bolabung. Very nice," he said, looking at the carving.

"I should have known you'd be up on all your esoteric trinkets. With that in your hand she's not going to be able to get in and you'll have some peace and quiet. She's probably tearing her quarters apart in frustration right now. I kind of know how she feels. I'm surprised you don't already have one on you."

"Not a whole lot of highly telepathic people on this ship, but you're right, I do have one here somewhere, just have to dig it out." He gazed at her sturdy body sitting on his couch.

She met his gaze and bit her lip.

"So . . ."

She put her hand up and hushed him. "Wait," she whispered, then she leaned forward and gave him a brief kiss, running the tips of her fingers across his upper thigh.

His thigh jolted, his lips swam with her warmth and sweetness.

They both took a moment to compose themselves. "So, Morgan, what's on your mind?"

"I was hoping for a nice evening with you and she's ruining it."

"Is that you talking, or Gwen?"

"Both, I guess. In any event, I need to talk you, and to Gwen about something important, so it's good that she's here." Morgan glanced towards the bedroom. "Come on out, Gwen, there's no need to hide. I know you're here. Everybody on this ship knows you and Bel are seeing each other. What's the big secret? You're an adult, he's an adult. You act oh-so-professionally when you're out and about. I don't see what the problem is. Everyone also thinks you make a fine picture of a couple, almost everyone, anyhow."

There was no reply from the bedroom. Morgan sighed. "Well, okay then, I think, since nobody's here, I'll just make myself comfortable."

She slid close to Stenstrom, then laid her braided head across his collarbone. Without thinking about it, Stenstrom laid his arm over her chest where she took his hand. "Gwen, you've got ten seconds. Otherwise, I'm just going to pop my boots off, and if my boots come off, it's on out here—"

The door abruptly opened and out came Gwendolyn, a sheet draped over her shoulders. With perfect posture, she approached the couch. "Good evening, Morgan. I apologize for being out of dress." She properly seated herself on the couch some distance away from Stenstrom.

Morgan smiled and sat up. "Well, drat. Apology accepted. We're all friends here; there's really no need to sit at the other end of the couch."

Stenstrom scooted over and put his arm around Gwen. She kept her posture for a few moments more, then allowed herself to curl up next to him.

"So, what can we do for you, Morgan?" Gwendolyn asked.

Morgan darkened a little. "I wanted to go over some of the points our Xaphan guest made this evening."

"Melazarr?" Gwendolyn said.

"Yes, the tall lady who's been whispering nasty little things into Bel's head all evening."

Gwendolyn straightened. "Telepathy? She's hitting you with telepathy? That is extremely rude! I'm going to have a nice chat with her, right now!"

"Gwen, there's time enough for that later. I'm more concerned about what she said this evening," Morgan said.

"Concerned about what?"

Morgan considered where to begin. "I am a Hospitaler, but I'm also an Ephysian. Because of the Ephysian's willingness to work with the likes of the Ming Moorlands, the Xaphan Cabalists, and even the Hertogs we have a knowledge and understanding of certain things even the Sisters lack."

Gwen closed her eyes and relaxed into Stenstrom's embrace once again. "Hertogs? That could lead to a great deal of trouble should the Sisters find out," she said softly.

"Yes, but they're not going to find out, are they? We're all friends here, remember? So, to my point, Madam Caroline—who, incidentally, is a great deal creepier than I ever thought a Caroline would be—said some troubling things this evening."

"She most certainly did," Gwen replied.

"I'm serious, Gwen. I'm not talking about puerile quips uttered by an immature girl clearly starved for attention. I'm talking about the other things she said in passing—things she couldn't possibly be making up. The Shadow tech Goddess, the information stored in her innards Burgon wanted to burn her up for."

"What about the Shadow tech Goddess?" Stenstrom asked.

"Ah, see, I thought I noticed you reacting to that name earlier. What do you know about her?"

Stenstrom sighed. "Recently, I had an odd visitor come aboard named Queen Wendilnight who wished to hire the ship."

"I don't remember such a person coming aboard," Gwendolyn said.

"You were ashore at the Fleet. She not only mentioned the Shadow tech Goddess, she predicted the coming of Melazarr of Caroline and that she carried some sort of information within her. She called her a *Merten*."

Gwendolyn was perturbed. "Bel, you know I like to be informed when a possible hire comes aboard so that I can be there to help you properly vet them. What task was she presenting?"

"To perform an errand, to transport a device called an Anatameter."

"Transport it where?"

"The Cistern of the Shadow tech Goddess, wherever that is. She didn't tell me its specific location. Queen Wendilnight did say that when Melazarr of Caroline appeared, then I would know where to take it."

Gwendolyn shook her head. "You see, Bel, this is why I need to be present when there's a potential client. You're too easily swayed by the odd and the bizarre. That's not becoming of a flagged Fleet Warbird."

Morgan rolled her eyes.

"What was she offering in bounty?" Gwen demanded.

"About five million sesterces in Mithrilcyte. All in advance."

"Mithrilcyte?? To haul a . . . what did you call it?"

"An Anatameter."

"All right, I'll be glad to inspect this Anatameter myself. What is its tonnage? What hold is it in?"

Stenstrom laughed. "Tonnage? It weighs about three pounds, perhaps two-and-a-half, and is small enough to fit in my coat. It's currently sitting in my wardrobe."

Gwen was livid. "Oh Creation, it's an arcane device, isn't it? What have I told you about this, Bel? Go get it, please?"

As Morgan snickered, Stenstrom went to his wardrobe. He pulled out a small round item wrapped up in a linen cloth, returned to the couch, then set it down on the table.

"What is that?" Gwen asked.

Stenstrom unwrapped it. "This is the device. This is the Anatameter."

Gwen picked it up and examined it. "It looks like a polished rock to me, possibly a common chalcedony or moganite." She tinkered with the knob on top and couldn't turn it. "Seems like nothing, and you were given five million in Mithrylcite for this?"

"Aye. The funds have already been submitted to the Fleet. Seems a rich bounty for a mere fantasy, doesn't it? That will fill our quotas for years to come."

Gwen set it back down on the table. "It's not warm. It doesn't make my fingers tingle, and it's not setting off any of the shipboard detectors, therefore I assume it's not radioactive. We shall run it over with a fine tooth comb in engineering. Honestly, Bel, you should have given me this to look at straight away."

"Any thoughts, Morgan?" Stenstrom asked, feeling reproached.

She shrugged and picked it up. She toyed with it, as Gwendolyn had, turning the knob back and forth. "No, I've not seen anything like this before. It could be a model or mock up of something. It seems to have a purpose." She gazed at its smooth surface. "It's very pretty. I fancy it."

"Really?" Stenstrom said, looking at its drab, rather featureless form. "Is it related to the Shadow tech Goddess, do you think?"

Morgan set it back down on the table. "Now that's an interesting question. Do you know who the Shadow tech Goddess is?"

"No."

"To properly explain the Shadow tech Goddess, I must first introduce you to an obscure term. Do either of you know what a *Wvulgrom* is?"

Stenstrom and Gwendolyn thought a moment. Outside, stars glittered through the windows.

"A doppelganger?" Gwendolyn asked.

"Not a doppelganger, so much," Morgan said. "A doppelganger is an entity that has made a conscious effort to replicate your physical aspect and might try to replace you if it can. Though it may look and sound like you, a doppelganger is not *you*. A Wvulgrom, however, *is you*, from a theoretical alternate plane of existence. In theory, this reality we inhabit is merely one of many—the Hospitalers call it the Opposing Mirror theory. When you place two mirrors opposite each other, they create an endless re-reflection of each other down to infinity. In this regard, we are merely mirror images of our other-selves all the way to infinity. Your Wvulgrom occupies the same space you do, and is made up of the same atomic material—it is you, just in an alternate reality."

"You're saying a Wvulgrom is an opposite, possibly evil twin?" Gwendolyn said.

Morgan shook her head. "There are no positive or negative connotations with a Wvulgrom—they are as they are. They can be evil, I suppose. The variation lies in their differing experiences. Take myself, for example. I am, as you currently see me, the result of the choices I've made throughout my life. I'm a Hospitaler, but I am also a Lady of Thompson and a Hala by birth. Perhaps my Wvulgrom, out there somewhere, didn't choose to become a Hospitaler; perhaps she chose to remain a lady of the House, like my mother so desperately wanted. When I was a girl, there was a terrible fire that engulfed our manor; my father barely saved me. Perhaps other Wvulgroms of myself didn't survive that fire." Morgan's voice became dreamy. "I sometimes dream that I am all alone in the universe, like the Gallian Torr of Bazz, facing extinction.

That's how I feel sometimes."

She paused a moment. Stenstrom thought she might fall into tears, but then she blinked and regained her usual humor. "Or, perhaps there was no fire at all in other universes. Perhaps my Wvulgrom chooses not to be as . . . free . . . with her desires as I do. I see something beautiful, and therefore I love it. I love both of you . . . desperately; you know that, yes?"

"Yes, thank you, Morgan . . ." Gwendolyn said. "But while an interesting metaphysical topic, it can't be proved."

"The Hospitalers have confirmed the existence of these beings. Ask any reputable sage and they'll tell you. It's supposedly very difficult to cross the planes. However, should certain steps be taken, a Wvulgrom may be given lease to enter another plane of reality—and hence, the Shadow tech Goddess, and hence my concern."

"Go on," Stenstrom said.

Morgan picked the Anatameter back up again. She seemed to enjoy holding it. "The Ephysians know, from our association with Xaphan Cabalists, of a being called the Shadow tech Goddess. This being is a Wvulgrom and doesn't exist on this plane of reality, at least, not as the Shadow tech Goddess.

"The Black Abbess has dreaded her *possible* coming for centuries. As the Cabalists tell it, in a different reality, the Shadow tech Goddess was born of the Shadowmark and taken into the Shade Church and made a Black Hat. However, her power was beyond compare. She rose through the ranks and eventually challenged the Black Abbess herself—killing her in an alternate reality. This woman didn't stop there. She was driven, tortured . . . spiteful. She killed everything and plunged her universe into the darkness of a Shadow tech night until she was the only living being left, wallowing in her loneliness. Thus, the Black Abbess has ever been wary of her coming, watching for the signs to prevent it at all costs. She has spies roving the heavens, looking for traces of this woman who exists but doesn't exist, possibly here in League space as well. The Shadow tech Goddess is, most probably, one of the more well-known Wvulgroms. She's been venerated and worshipped frequently in the past by various cults. Obviously, her mundane identity is unknown."

Gwendolyn stirred. "You said she doesn't exist on this plane."

"I said the Shadow tech Goddess doesn't exist on this plane. However, the woman who *could be* her exists, and that's what's got the Black Abbess' knickers in a bunch. The possibility that this woman could become this goddess."

"If that's the case, why would a crass Xaphan man with Vith heritage like Rodrigo of Burgon endeavor to bring such a being here? He would be putting himself to the sword."

"I can't accurately answer that question, Gwen. I have no idea why he would want to do that, or how. But, he and others in his sect seem to be trying, don't they?"

"The Burgons are a bizarre lot, even for Xaphans," Stenstrom said. "I've heard they've practiced nihilist rites in the past, with the stated goal of bringing about the end of the universe."

"Good Creation, why?" Gwen asked. "Gods! Are the Vith all a pack of lunatics?"

"I recall my mentor, Captain Davage, who is most certainly *not* a lunatic, said about the Burgons. He said they had a history of erratic behavior and were censured by the Sisterhood of Light many times prior to their going to the Xaphans."

"For what?"

"For something near to my heart—practicing forbidden rites."

Gwendolyn stirred. "Sounds like more Vith foolishness to me; no offence to Captain Davage, of course. What credence could these Burgons possibly have?"

Morgan spoke up. "Again, I don't have the answer to that question." She held up the Anatameter. "But, we do have this. These odd little devices are sort of like keys; they guard the gateway from one plane of reality to another."

"I thought you said you knew nothing about this device," Gwendolyn stated flatly.

Morgan's eyes grew distant for a moment. "Did I say that?"

"Yes, you did."

She blinked once or twice and put the Anatameter back on the table. "Well, I was wrong. It's been a long evening and I'm tired. I know all about it. This device is a key meant to protect the well-being of the universe. With it in place, no passage between the realms can happen, no

Shadow tech Goddess. Perhaps that's why it was given to you, Bel, to plug up a hole."

Gwendolyn shook her head. "What drivel. Such a thing cannot exist; it violates every law of physics that I care to quote."

"Yet, here it is."

"So, what are you suggesting, Morgan?" Gwendolyn asked.

"I'm saying we take it to where it needs to go and put it in place. If you're right, Gwen, then doing so will amount to nothing more than a wasted afternoon. If I'm right, however, then taking the Anatameter to where it needs to go might help save us all."

"From what?"

"From Rodrigo of Burgon and his cult of nihilists. From the Shadow tech Goddess."

Gwendolyn's scholarly sensibilities were outraged and Stenstrom felt a lecture coming on. "Gwen, Morgan brings up a good point; actually she brings up two good points. In any event, we were paid handsomely to take this device somewhere, and I don't intend to cheat Queen Wendilnight out of her money. We'll take it to where it needs to go and that'll be the end of it. And if by doing so we casually manage to safeguard the universe, then so much the better."

"Very well," Gwen said. "After I certify it safe, we'll do what we were paid to do. The question is, where do we take it? Morgan, any thoughts on the matter?"

Morgan stood and rolled up her sleeves. "No, but I think I know where to get the information. So, I'll just leave you to it then, I get the feeling Gwen wants me gone. Too bad. You two truly don't understand what you're missing. Good night. I should have what we need by morning. The things I do for you two." She headed out the door.

Stenstrom and Gwendolyn watched her depart.

"What in Creation was all that about?" Gwen asked.

"I've no idea."

"I like Morgan, but I don't approve of some of her caprices."

"Morgan is a good friend," Stenstrom replied, his thigh still aching from her touch.

"If she had her way, all three of us would be in the bedroom right now. It makes me uncomfortable. She's nearly as bad as our Xaphan nymphomaniac on the other side of the ship."

"She's nothing of the sort. She's simply honest with her feelings and isn't afraid to make them known, in a polite and non-threatening manner."

Stenstrom tightly squeezed her and she settled back into his arms. "I wish you would be a little more open with your feelings sometimes."

"Bel. I know I can seem a little distant when we're about, and I'm trying to allow myself the luxury of being more open with my feelings in public. I simply feel our relationship is private, between you and me and nobody else needs to be involved. You know how I feel, Bel. You know that I love you."

"Do you think Lady Alesta acts inappropriately with Lord A-Ram in public?"

"No, absolutely not. I admire their relationship and find it rather endearing."

"Well then, why not act like she does?"

Gwendolyn thought about it for a moment. "I'm trying. I'm trying."

5—An Encoded Message

The next morning at eight bells, the *Hoban Night* appeared abeam the *Seeker*. The ship hailed and Melazarr was put off via Ripcar. Stenstrom, being the ship's Paymaster, wrangled out and observed the payment to the ship for her service before Melazarr boarded.

She didn't go without a struggle, and was salty to the point of being violent. She had put her Flash-ons back in and was lighting up hard. "So, Bel," she hissed as they entered the Ripcar bay, "when next we meet, you going to hide in your room again like you did this time, you rotten muck-spine!" In her Hoban heels, she was eye-to-eye with him at six feet, seven inches.

"Next time?" Gwendolyn said. "By tomorrow morning, you shall be several light years away, sweating it out on Xandarr. I bid you a pleasant trip, and I'm certain the dry, roasting climate will do wonders for your pores."

Melazarr scowled at her with lit-up eyes. "If you're all I have to worry about . . . babe . . . then I'm not worried."

She turned back to Stenstrom. "You Slag!! Next time you and me are going to be on the floor, wrapped up. I promise you!"

Gwendolyn tried to step between them. "Your Ripcar is waiting, madam," she said icily.

Melazarr got very close, her breath moistening Stenstrom's ear. "Let me clue you into something: you never meet a Caroline just once. You're going to see me again. I'll be back to save you from this frosty piece of rump you've been attempting to pleasure yourself with, and I'll show you what a real woman can do."

He felt the heat from the light coming out of her mouth. The tip of her tongue touched his earlobe. She then pulled away and climbed onto the Ripcar. "Ta!" she said giving him a wide-eyed harlequin stare as the hatch closed, her eyes shining and face lighting up through the glass.

They watched the Ripcar pull away and out of the containment field.

Gwendolyn sighed. "Well, thank the Elders that's over."

Morgan stood there and watched the Ripcar soar away. She leaned toward Stenstrom. "Hey Bel?" she whispered, "She wasn't kidding; she's no dunce in the sack. I could barely get up this morning."

Stenstrom and Taara walked onto the bridge. A-Ram stood at the helm. "Our friend gone?" he asked, hanging onto the pegs.

"She is, and heading to Xandarr in first-class comfort," Taara said.

"Alesta will be glad to hear it. I've never seen her so un-nerved before. She was nearly inconsolable at breakfast this morning."

Stenstrom approached A-Ram. "Madam Caroline was that off-putting?"

"Off-putting?" He thought a moment and turned the wheel a peg or two. "I wouldn't say that. I thought she was intriguing. If I didn't have Alesta, I might have taken her up on her offers."

Taara smiled. "Me, too. I heard Morgan took the plunge."

Stenstrom put his finger to his lips. "Shhh, not so loud."

He headed for his office, Taara following. He plopped down behind his desk and took his hat off. Taara seated herself in her usual spot.

"So, how did Gwen respond to Melazarr?" she asked.

"Not well."

There was a knock and Morgan entered.

"Rough night?" he asked.

"More than you can know." She seated herself and gave Taara a wink. "I've got the information. I know where the Anatameter should be taken."

Stenstrom was surprised. "That was fast. Gwendolyn has the Anatameter down in engineering right now, doing Creation knows what to it. So, where did you get the info from?"

"From our guest, Melazarr of Caroline. You told me Queen Wendilnight had mentioned Melazarr is a *Merten*. I checked, a *Merten* is a 'herald' of sorts, and Rodrigo of Burgon was going to slice her open and burn her to get information of some sort. Sure enough, she is carrying a message within her."

"In her guts?" Taara squealed. "That's really gross."

"Various people, these *Mertens* from time to time, carry information within their vitals," Morgan said. "We call them 'EV's', for 'Encoded Vitals'. We don't know how the information gets there, or why a particular person has it while others don't, but sure enough, it's there. We suspected the Sisters of doing it, selecting people as unwitting messengers to convey information without fear of it being intercepted or detected."

"But you found out wrong, right?" Taara asked. "You found out the Sisters weren't doing that?"

"Did we, Taara? We're still investigating. In any event, there was a whole litany of information inside Melazarr's body, and Burgon was going to kill her for it."

"So, what did you do? How do you extract such information?" Stenstrom asked.

"Various ways. Sometimes it's a simple matter of reading bumps and tick marks, usually found on the anterior of the small bowel, that sort of thing. Sometimes sex does it with a controlled release of pheromones; that seems to be what the Sisters favor. And, as in Melazarr's case, burning will do it, too. So, what did I do? After we finished our nasty little business, I slipped her a malek and went to work. I made a small incision in her abdomen and inserted an othroscope. I discovered that her encoding is triggered by heat. I used pin-point intense heat and then immediately healed the damage. And there it was, the whole story in bits and pieces. Rather remarkable to see first-hand. After I was done, I closed the incision. She never knew a thing had happened."

"What did you discover?" Stenstrom asked.

"Now remember, I was reading everything in bits and pieces, and I probably missed a lot. Burning her would actually have been a much more efficient method of reading the information.

"Hidden in the Clovis ruins in Kana's Vithland region is a secret complex that was once used as some sort of dimensional gateway to a secret place free of the Sisters' influence. Apparently many Vith strongholds have something similar. The gateway no longer functions; the Sisters did away with it long ago. According to Melazarr, the Clovis once stumbled upon a place of evil inhabited by a being they called the Shadow tech Goddess. They were very afraid of this being, so much so they sought help from the Gods of Cammara, of all places. The Gods came and corrected the problem with an Anatameter. Not your Anatameter, a different one. There are lots of Anatameters, most inaccessible."

"Queen Wendilnight said she was from Cammara."

"Yes? Then she might even be a God. The old Vith spoke in secret of these tall and beautiful people from far away who 'safeguarded' the universe and seemed to have mastery over death and time. In the Clovis ruins is a place where the Anatameter once sat, a 'socket', if you will. When the Sisters shut down the Vith's pocket dimension, the Anatameter residing there was no longer needed and was removed by persons unknown, though probably by the Gods. So, that's where your's goes, in the ruins of Clovis in the old socket. It's still there."

Stenstrom shrugged. "All right, that doesn't sound too difficult, assuming I can find this socket and install my Anatameter. We'll do it this very day. We don't have anything on the boards today, do we, Taara?"

"Nope."

Morgan looked concerned. "But, Bel, some of the other things I read trouble me."

"What things?"

"Like I said, I didn't get it all, but much of what I read concerned old cults and pagan shrines and Shadow tech and human sacrifice. It also mentioned places like Punt, Cammara, and Eng. I don't know what 'Punt' is, but Cammara and Eng, those places were once our home worlds many millennia ago. Those places are lost to us, Bel, ask Gwen. We don't know where Cammara and Eng are anymore; like Lemmuria, they're places of legend. Too much time has passed. And, there was mention of monsters that follow this device around, hoping to make use of it."

Taara, who had been day-dreaming, came back to attention. "Monsters? What sort of monsters?"

"Demons, extra-planars, cursed entities, old gods that pursue devices like these hoping to make use of them for their own ends. According to mythology, an Anatameter is very powerful. The most frightening entity was something called a *Tempus Findal*, a sort of wandering zombie. It's all alone in the universe, seeking its opposite; and it destroys and ruins everything in its path. It's immune to the Anatameter's power and can cross the planes at will. It's some sort of chaos-bringer."

"That sounds cool, actually," Taara said.

Stenstrom laughed. "Well then, we'll fulfill our part of the bargain; we'll take it to Clovis and that'll be all."

Morgan got up, pushed past Taara, and got in close with Stenstrom. "But what about the *Tempus Findal*?"

"What about it?"

"Don't underestimate it." Morgan's eyes grew large and intense.

"All right, all right. I'll research it and devise defenses. This creature, whatever it is, won't be a factor."

6—"Kat"

"So, why didn't Morgan want to come with us today?" Gwendolyn asked. "She's always keen to tag along on these shore missions."

"She said she wasn't feeling well," Stenstrom said.

"Ah well. Then I get you two handsome gentlemen all to myself."

It was a wonderful, chilly morning as the Ripcar came down through the high clouds, the vast carpet of grayish mountains stretching off into the north as far as one could see.

A-Ram flew the Ripcar, with Gwendolyn and Stenstrom sitting in the passenger seats. Morgan's usual seat was empty, occupied instead by a wooden lunch basket prepared by Lady Alesta. The three of them, all good friends, were laughing and chatting. Gwendolyn, feeling at ease, let her usual guard down and hung all over Stenstrom. She noted A-Ram's stylish glasses. "Have I told you how handsome you look in these, A-Ram? They very-much suit you."

"Thanks," he said, blushing.

"Does Lady Alesta favor them, too?"

"She does, but she says she also favors the old black things I used to wear. Sentimental, I suppose, since I was wearing them when we met. She keeps them in a box on her nightstand."

"Oh, my . . ." Gwendolyn said, pinching his cheeks.

She sniffed the basket. "Smells good, A-Ram; what did Alesta pack for you this time?" Lady Alesta always packed A-Ram a basket of lunch when he went down to the shore.

"Chicken, I think, and as usual there's enough for all of us."

"What would we do without Lady Alesta?" Stenstrom said as he watched the gray, mountainous land far below come into focus.

"Go hungry," Gwen replied.

A-Ram laughed. "Oh, that's my lady. After we finish up, can we take some time out and eat it before heading back, Bel?"

"Sure, A-Ram, sure. I love Alesta's cooking."

Whenever Stenstrom wanted to go somewhere, A-Ram, the Master Helmsman, usually took him, leaving the ship in the care of Crewman Joles, the junior Helmsman. A-Ram had tried to teach Stenstrom how to fly on several occasions, but he had no feel it, couldn't generate any harmony of control; so better to just let A-Ram do it.

A complex of ruddy buildings, scrabbled into the side of a mountain like a wrecked train, came into focus.

Stenstrom leaned his head over as far as he could, brushing the containment field. "That looks like it down there, A-Ram. Clovis, or what's left of it anyways, abandoned since the Great Betrayal centuries ago."

"Bel!" Gwen said. "I'm amazed you know that."

"Yeah, yeah. Find a suitable spot and bring us down," he said.

Stenstrom thought he saw somebody moving about in the ruins; from this altitude, just a black dot. It felt sinister, just a hunch, though. Morgan's talk of old gods and extra-planar creatures was firing his imagination.

A-Ram circled the area and found a flat spot several hundred yards to the south of the ruins. After they landed, he dropped containment and they all climbed out, their breath steaming in the chilly Vithland air.

Stenstrom hoisted his Megaeye and peered into the forlorn ruins. He spied black, darting movement in the distance and clearly saw the figure he'd spotted from above moving towards the stony hills. "Look there," he said. The figure glided away like liquid.

"What?" Gwen asked,

"You see that?"

Gwendolyn and A-Ram looked around. "See what?" A-Ram asked.

"Movement. Out there," Stenstrom said, pointing.

Gwendolyn grabbed his Megaeye and hoisted it to her face. "I don't see anything," she said, panning about. Snatching Stenstrom's Megaeye without warning was a bad habit Gwen had acquired. "Probably a mountain goat."

"I doubt that. Never mind."

All three of them straightened their coats and popped their hats on; A-Ram wearing a handsome Fleet triangle hat, replacing the huge, plumed, broad-brimmed adjutant's hat he once wore. Stenstrom checked his NTHs, then slid them back into their sash. Gwendolyn hung the Megaeye around her neck and clipped on her FEDULA, a long, rapier-like sword. She also pulled her MiMs pistol, checked her clip, then cocked the pistol. She was very particular about her MiMs, even though the gun had such a small caliber and grain size per slug it was virtually useless, more for show than anything.

Stenstrom reached into the Ripcar and picked up the Anatameter. He held it gingerly in his hands, wondering how he was supposed to fit it into the 'socket'.

"We couldn't find anything during our investigation," Gwendolyn said, waving a hand at the Anatameter. "It's just a rock, and an ugly, uninteresting one at that."

"Well good. We shan't miss it then, once we figure out where it's supposed to go." He slipped it into one of the larger pockets inside his HRN.

Off in the distance was a line of fallen stone structures of old Clovis, gray, just like the towering mountains all around. A-Ram leaned into the crew compartment and hit the Ripcar's Com.

"Com," he said.

"Com here."

"Please let Private Taara know we're down. We'll check-in again when we depart."

"Aye. Safe shores."

"Out." He then powered down the Ripcar.

A-Ram pulled a small red and green scarf from the Ripcar and put it on along with a pair of black gloves.

"Did Lady Alesta give you that scarf?" Stenstrom asked, noting the familiar Merian colors and symbols.

"She made it for me."

"Aww," Gwendolyn said, "you two are so cute."

Fully kitted out, they crunched through the stiff grass, the somber ruins quickly approaching.

Ahead, before the perimeter of the ruins, was a small bronze statue mounted on a granite plinth. "What's this statue here?" Gwen asked. "Looks like a Vith female, fairly new. Perhaps that's the figure you saw, Bel?"

"I doubt it."

The statue depicted a slender woman in a gown, her head up, shoulders back, and holding a system glyph. Her dainty arms were molded in a demure, yet dramatic pose. A plaque bolted to the plinth read:

THE RUINS OF CLOVIS ABANDONED IN 000000AX
A SCHOLARLY EXPEDITION WAS CONDUCTED HERE IN
003720AX BY
GRAND DAME HANNAH-BEN SHURLAMP, EVOR,
UNIVERSITY OF DEE
AND HER ESTEEMED PARTY.
ALL HAS BEEN REVEALED AS A RESULT OF THIS
EXPEDITION
THERE IS NOTHING FURTHER TO BE LEARNED.
PLEASE SEE PROFESSOR SHURLAMP'S PUBLISHED WORKS
FOR
FURTHER INFORMATION.

"Can you believe the nerve of this person?" Gwen asked. "Apparently there's no need for us to search about, for Hannah-Ben Shurlamp, EVoR, has discovered all. Phah!"

"Perhaps she knows where this device needs to go," A-Ram quietly offered.

"Unlikely."

Stenstrom laughed. "Come along, Gwen, you know how scholars are. Let the lady bask in whatever glory she may." They moved past the statue, Gwendolyn giving it the evil eye.

"Hey, Bel," A-Ram said. "Do the thing . . . come on, do the thing."

"Oh, please, A-Ram . . ."

"Come on."

Stenstrom had learned quite a bit in the last year. He'd discovered that he, as the Sisters Fist, could do pretty much everything the Sisters could—including using TK at a hyper level. He lifted A-Ram gently into the air. A-Ram spread his arms like a bird in flight and savored the feel, his scarf fluttering.

"I love this!" he said as Bel drifted him toward the ruins.

The Ruins of Clovis were stout and fairly intact. A number of smaller structures surrounded a larger, more fallen-down one in the center. The architecture was typical Vith, ornate and splendid.

They heard only their steady footfalls and the somber cry of the wind. Occasionally, they caught sight of a massive Parafly buzzing about. The party sorted through several of the outlying structures. Lined with leaf-litter and other nesting materials, the hollowed out buildings had been inhabited only by successive generations of various wildlife.

Gwendolyn peered into one of the empty windows. "Do we have any idea at all what we should be looking for?"

Stenstrom peered in next to her and she leaned her head on his shoulder. "Some sort of secret area where this Anatameter goes. Probably underground somewhere."

Gwendolyn smiled brightly. "Fortunately, I took the time to perform a bit of study on these wretched Vith ruins. Somebody has to do the intellectual legwork. This building here is the wheel house. That one over there is the cistern."

All three headed for the cistern. "We're looking for the Shadow tech Goddess' cistern," Stenstrom said. The building was just a hollow shell with a depth of dank standing water waiting at the bottom.

"Doesn't look promising to me," A-Ram said, "unless the area we need is underwater."

They moved on. Eventually, they made their way into the fallen structure of the main manor house, mostly a pile of shifting rubble. It hadn't survived the centuries as well as the other smaller buildings had. Gwen and Stenstrom sat down, their legs getting tired from all the rummaging around. Stenstrom gently set A-Ram down.

"Well, I'm stumped," Stenstrom said. "Any thoughts?"

"These ruins have only been here for centuries, Bel," Gwendolyn said, placing her cold hands into Stenstrom's pockets. "Wow, is it cold."

"We're going to have to dig in our heels and search a bit harder." He pointed north. "I do see a chapel in that direction. Let's have a look."

"Oh, Bel, must we? My feet are killing me," Gwendolyn said, pointing at her boots. "There's nothing up there, except more of the same."

"Mine are hurting, too," A-Ram said, sitting next to Gwendolyn. "Come on, let's head back to the Ripcar and eat."

Gwendolyn put her arms around A-Ram and rubbed his shoulders to warm him up. "How is it that your feet are hurting, A-Ram? You've been flying around this whole time."

"I don't know, but they are. Must be sympathy pains."

Stenstrom rose and dusted himself off. "All right, come on, let's go."

"You could just toss that silly thing and anywhere it lands is as good as any," Gwendolyn said.

With a fuss, they trudged north through the central section of the ruins. Stenstrom noticed something. He froze. "Wait . . . wait! Stop!"

They both looked back at him. "Bel, what is it?" Gwendolyn asked.

He was just becoming acquainted with the Sisters' Gifts. When he visited them in their distant temple, they were remarkably mum as to just what exactly he could and could not do; they were too busy giggling and touching him on the shoulder. He'd figured out the TK thing on his own, and he found himself speaking with his mind every so often. He struggled against that. He didn't want to speak with his mind.

And, he could apparently detect Shadow tech, just like the Sisters could. All around the ruins, plain as day, he saw an impossibly dense amount of Cloaked Shadow tech Traps, like a plague of insects.

Invisible StT's were favorite calling cards of the Black Hats. Black Hat assassins loved leaving them behind to create chaos and mayhem. The Sisters were usually very good about discovering and clearing them out. But here in Clovis they were everywhere.

"I see StT's, all over the place!"

Gwendolyn was alarmed. "Shadow tech Traps? Here?"

"Yes. A-Ram!" he said, turning to him. "Don't move!"

A-Ram swallowed. "W-why?"

"Because there is a particularly large one crawling up your back." He turned white. "A-Ram, don't panic. Just stay still."

"Where . . . where is it?"

"It's right by your head; it has its legs around your neck right now."

In his "Sister-Sight" the StT looked like a black robotic cockroach with an ovoid body and a small head rotating on a thin neck. Its Shadow tech legs were fastened around A-Ram's shoulders.

He was on the verge of panic. "What . . . what's it doing?" he whispered.

Although Stenstrom could see the StT, he couldn't determine what it was pre-programmed to do. An StT could be set to do any number of things. It could attach itself to a victim and immediately explode in searing Shadow tech fire. It could slice a person's head off. It could infest machinery and cause malfunctions. It could cling there and covertly spy on the person or create misfortune or kill loved ones. The possibilities were endless.

The trap suddenly expanded, enveloping A-Ram in a black film of Shadow tech. A-Ram collapsed to the ground.

"A-Ram!" Stenstrom shot forward, Gwendolyn joining him. He quickly lifted her into the air with TK, so that StT's couldn't attach to her as well.

"Bel, it's suffocating him!" She struggled as she floated.

The Shadow tech was forcing its way into A-Ram's mouth and down his throat. Stenstrom waved his hands, trying to dispel it like the Sisters did.

Nothing happened.

Just for once he wished the Sisters might share techniques with him, train him. They expected much, but it was all on the job training.

A-Ram didn't have time for him to learn by trial and error.

He concentrated and waved his hands again. The StT smoked, as if it were on fire.

Another wave and it was gone. A-Ram instantly sputtered and gagged for breath.

"Bel!" Gwendolyn cried from above. "There's a Black Hat! To the north!" She drew her MiMs and fired.

The StT's laying about the ruins came to life like a plague of locusts. They surged forward, some climbing into the air to attack Gwendolyn, others diving for the two men.

With a swipe, Stenstrom managed to get rid of quite a few of them; but others attached themselves to his legs and arms. A-Ram was fully covered after just a moment, as was Gwen.

Stenstrom picked A-Ram up, StT's and all, and TK'ed out of the area, coming to a landing near the Ripcar. A-Ram was in some sort of suspended animation, his cheerful red and green scarf smeared in black.

He brought Gwendolyn down. She too, seemed to be in a Shadow tech induced stasis.

The StT's around them were complicated and deep-rooted. Without knowing how they were programmed, he could cause more harm than good if he tried to disperse them. It could kill them right off.

He had to try. Gwen and A-Ram could be dying.

He set to work.

<*I wouldn't do that . . . if I were you . . .*> a sneering voice said in his mind.

He turned.

On the roof of the wheel house, a Black Hat crouched on all fours, like a cat ready to spring. He sensed her gazing at him for a few moments, before she gracefully launched herself into the air and landed on all fours on the scholarly statue of Hannah-Ben Shurlamp a few feet in front of him.

She wore black with bits of scarlet mixed in. A little black shirt, with baggy sleeves down to her elbows, was laced up to her neck. Her forearms were wrapped with black bandage-like strips all the way to her wrists. Her hands were bare; her fingernails, painted black, were long and curved like a bear's. A baggy pair of black pantaloons went down to her knees. Her calves and ankles were wrapped in black strips, just like her arms. Her feet were partially wrapped up, though they were mostly bare. A tight-fitting black head mask had a large hole cut out for her eyes, which were a sparkling green. He could see the bridge of her nose and hints of her Shadowmark dancing around her right eye.

Enemies of the Sisters, the Black Hats had an unrivaled command of Shadow tech. They were always fierce, of an evil disposition, and a constant threat to the League, though, several had been "tamed" in recent history. His friend, Countess Sygillis of Blanchefort, was an ex-Black Hat.

She reminded him of a cat, ready to fight or pounce on a mouse. She even had a "tail" of Shadow tech that moved slowly around over her head, ready to strike.

"Well . . . well . . . well . . . look what we have here. A male Sister. Who would have ever imagined such a thing?"she said, her voice a gravely crawl.

She jumped down from the statue, still crouching, and they slowly circled one another. "What have you done to my companions?" he demanded.

"I've got them in my little web; yes I do . . ." Her voice stretched into a demonic shriek. *"And they're never getting out!!"*

Morgan had warned him that monsters followed the Anatameter. And now he was face to face with one: a Black Hat assassin. He side-stepped to his left. She uncoiled and sprang, taking a swipe at his face.

He caught her hand in mid-air. Her nails were danced in micro-point Shadow tech, sharp at an atomic level, they could slice through anything.

She must be Knife; the Black Hat the Sisters had intended him to follow. But she didn't look like the Knife he remembered. This woman dressed differently and was a different size and shape. She seemed taller than Knife had been. Still . . .

"Knife," he said, still holding her hand. "Release my companions, immediately."

Her leg lashed out and she kicked him square across the face with her heel. He threw her down to the stone.

She made to spring again, and he belted her across the cheek. She fell against the base of the statue, dazed for a moment, then recovered, her Shadow tech tail flicking wildly.

Again they circled. "Your companions belong to me," she said, rubbing her chin. "As do you."

She swiped at the statue of Hannah-Ben Shurlamp with a laser claw of micro-fine Shadow tech, cutting it clean from the base. She lifted it with her tail and threw it at Stenstrom. He caught it and held it aloft like a club.

She was very mobile for a Black Hat, and willing to engage in a hand-to-hand encounter, something most Black Hats avoided.

Her eyes flicked to the silver HRN letterings on his collar. Then she attacked, slashing and kicking, trying to climb on top of his shoulders.

He shoved her off and tried to hit her with the statue. She raked it with her claws, sending it raining down in small, cube-like bronze bits.

So much for Professor Shurlamp's nice statue.

She spun around and landed a solid back-fist on the side of his face. She then tried to hook his legs and fall on top of him, but he held firm and pushed her away.

They stood there panting. The Black Hat seemed to be enjoying herself. She made a trilling sort of purring sound through her mask. "What is your name?" she asked.

"You know who I am, Knife! Release my companions; they have nothing to do with this!"

She straightened a little, and spoke. It was strange hearing her speak. Knife had sworn she would never speak to him again. "You speak as if I should know you. I don't know you," she whispered.

"You do know me. Your name is Knife."

She snickered. "My name is not Knife. If I were to tell you my name, you'd have to take me home with you and . . ." She loosed a small ball of Shadow tech that quickly formed into a cinder-black cat. ". . . you don't want that!"

Stenstrom wasted no time and vanished it.

She was on him. Holding on with her legs, she put her claws against his chest and raked them upward, hoping to gut him.

His shirt shredded into ribbons, but no blood came. She hadn't been able to cut him.

Stenstrom seized her by the throat and slammed her down to the stone. She tried to pull his hand away. She flailed and kicked, but he held her firm.

She smoked, the beginnings of a Waft to teleport away.

"No, no, no," he said, "you're not going anywhere." He squeezed a little tighter and she recoiled, her Waft falling apart. "I suppose I'm just going to have to save my friends on my own."

She spoke in a choking whisper. "Got a hand on their souls, I do. Take it off, and they die. Kill me and they . . . die."

He picked her up and threw her against the granite plinth. She coughed a little, trying to clear her throat. "That . . . wasn't nice." she rasped.

"My friends—release them! I'll not ask again!"

She composed herself. "Your friends are fine as long as I wish them to be fine. First, I have questions for you. Not . . . negotiable."

"Ask your questions, Knife, and be done with them."

She locked eyes with him. "My name is not Knife. Let us make that crystal-clear."

She reached up and pulled her mask off. There was a girl with whitish blonde hair and a pleasing, somewhat heart-shaped face underneath. Nice teeth. Interesting Shadowmark.

She was not Knife.

"Who are you?" he asked.

"We do not say our names. What is your name? That is my first question and I demand you answer it."

"You might place a curse on it."

"Your name! Answer, now!"

"Stenstrom, Lord of Belmont-South Tyrol."

She puzzled for a moment and reformed her Shadow tech tail. It flicked about her head. "How is it that you can do what the Sisters do?"

"If I knew for certain, I'd tell you."

She glanced at the Ripcar and pointed. "Do you have any food?"

"Why, are you hungry?"

"Yes or no?"

"I think A-Ram bought down something for lunch. His fiancée usually packs him something."

"Well then, shall we? It'll be our first meal together."

Careful to keep his eye on her, Stenstrom reached into the Ripcar and pulled A-Ram's basket out. A few feet away, the Black Hat seated herself, sitting cross-legged on the cold ground. Her tail flicked by her head in a hypnotic fashion.

All they were missing was a tablecloth and a violinist, he mused.

"Come now, HAF, we've not all day," she said. "I'm hungry." She pushed her messy blonde hair out of her face and smacked her lips.

Stenstrom set the basket down and opened it; the scent of chicken drifted out. Inside, wrapped in a cloth, was a loaf of chewy Merian bread, along with a covered ceramic bowl filled with baked chicken, a bottle of sweet raspberry wine from Calvert that A-Ram was partial to, and Stenstrom secretly hated, silverware, and a little folded note on homemade paper from Alesta. He tried not to look at it, but he glimpsed a heart drawn on the folded interior of the paper.

A-Ram and Alesta, so in love.

And there A-Ram lay, locked in a Black Hat's StT, his life and his soul in jeopardy.

He set the food out. The Black Hat seized the loaf and tore into it; devouring it as if she hadn't eaten in some time. She seized the wine bottle by the neck and chugged down the contents. He removed the cover off the bowl of chicken and she pulled out several pieces, eating them bones and all.

"Are you not taught manners in all those places of darkness you inhabit, Black Hat?" he asked, a bit disgusted.

She looked at him and made a kissing motion with her greasy lips. "Care to teach me some, HAF?"

"Why are you calling me HAF? What is HAF?"

"You are HAF. I call you HAF because you have H, A, F on your collar."

"HAF? No, no, that's H-R-N. Do they not teach you to read, either?"

She seemed to take exception to that and chugged another swig of wine. She finished eating and wiped her hands on her sleeves. She reared back and loosed a satisfied, juicy belch.

"Yes, well done," he said with disgust. "Right, you have eaten. Now release my friends."

The Black Hat stood, rubbing her full belly. "First, you and I are going to take a short walk. Yes, we are."

"Where are we going?"

"There's a hidden place, just up those mountains." She pointed off into the distance.

"I am going nowhere with you."

"Then both your friends are going to die."

"Kill my friends, then I kill you."

The Black Hat was smug. "So much killing, Mr. H-R-N. Seems to me everybody's going to die today, and all could be avoided with a simple walk. I thought you League fellows were supposed to be reasonable." She got up in his face. She smelt of devoured chicken and Calvert wine.

"Will you swear to release my friends afterward?"

"I swear to nothing." She pointed to the north. "Come now, just a short walk, and you may *possibly* have your friends back, unharmed."

They began walking, Stenstrom re-tracing his steps through the ruins, only this time the Black Hat walked at his side.

"What does H-R-N mean?" She seemed remarkably eager to talk—something he'd heard Black Hats were loathe to do. "I don't understand. I looked at the letters; they are H-A-F."

"The letters are H-R-N. Did the Black Abbess not bother teaching you to read?"

Again, she seemed stung a bit. "And what does H-R-N stand for?"

"I'm really not interested in sharing a conversation with you, Black Hat."

They trudged through the central ruins. He looked back every so often, seeing the blackened masses of Gwendolyn and A-Ram sitting by the Ripcar near the ruins of the statue. The Black Hat moved at his side, her Shadow tech tail flicking as she walked.

Ahead was a disused trail heading up a steep mountain face. Nimbly, using her hands, legs, and her tail, the Black Hat bounded up the side passing him. "Come along."

Stenstrom, not being much of a mountain goat, carefully stumbled up. "Are you having difficulties, HRN?" she called down.

"I'm not a cat like you. I could TK myself up, but that would be a disgusting use of power."

The Black Hat, waiting for him on all fours, laughed. "Cat . . . that is spelled: K, A, T, Correct?"

He didn't answer. As he made his way up the side, he marveled at her. Similar to Countess Sygillis of Blanchefort, her hands and bare feet seemed impervious to pain or damage. She had traveled up over a broken trail of sharp, unyielding rock and her feet seemed neither troubled nor dirty. They looked clean and fresh, like she had just emerged from a wash. She was also limber to the point of being rubbery, making him feel like a stiff, immovable doll in comparison.

"Aren't your feet hurting you on this terrain?"

She took her left foot and pulled it back, up and over her head and placed it on the small of her back. "No."

One-legged, she bounded up the side of the mountain a bit more and then stopped. If he didn't know better, he'd say the Black Hat was showing off. She seemed eager to impress him. She pointed down at the ground. "Here we are." She waved her arms and two hidden doors opened, rock, moss, and dirt sliding off them.

A stony stairwell led into the earthy dark.

Kat used her Shadow tech in a very odd way. Stenstrom couldn't see it. Black Hats normally made a grand show of it, having Shadow tech in vast black waves covering the sky. Not this one—not Kat, she used hers in an effective but invisible manner; except for her tail, which moved about like a living thing.

"Now, you shall go down these steps and enter the room beyond. Within is said to be a face carved on the wall, the face of the Destroyer we've been informed. You will make an impression of the face with this . . ."

She held out a small packet of Shadow tech. "You will then return and give it to me. I'll then release your friends and take my leave."

He gazed down into the hole. Stairs went down about a hundred feet to where a stout set of wooden doors waited. Laid out on the steps were the torn remains of two bodies, flattened, twisted.

"My associates," Kat said. "They didn't make it. Somebody's rigged this place, made it very dangerous. Poor you. Now go, do be a good boy and get me what I need. Remember, your friend's lives count on you emerging with my stamp."

Stenstrom took the ball of Shadow tech and went down the stairs, musing on what horrors awaited beyond.

He stopped. "Are you, by chance, here to investigate the possible coming of the Shadow tech Goddess?"

He could see her smile under her mask. "We are always investigating such a thing. It's always a concern."

"Who is concerned?"

She crouched down, tail flicking. "Who do you think? Now, you have your assignment, fulfill it and your friends shall live. Go on."

He neared the bottom. She followed a step or two and then stopped, crouched on all fours. "If you survive, perhaps we can fight some more. We can find a nice place where the ground is soft and we can fight. I found it rather enjoyable. Did you enjoy fighting me?"

He didn't answer and continued down the stairs.

When he got to the bottom, he turned to her. "What killed your companions? It might be helpful to know."

"I don't know. There is . . . something . . . guarding that room. Something that's killed many of my predecessors, as you can see. I was about to go in there and face the peril, whatever it might be, when you showed up. Better your skin than mine."

He turned back to the waiting doors. "Why don't you come with me? Perhaps, the two of us with our combined might more easily prevail."

The Black Hat shrieked with laughter. "What? Team-up? Me and you? KAT and HRN? I'm fine where I am. Now, sir, time is wasting. You're dying friends aren't getting any healthier."

He examined the doors and noted a round, Vith-style lock. He tried the doors and they rattled in their frame.

"Wait!" she cried. She produced a folded slip of paper. "What does this say?" She bounded down the stairs and held it out by the tip of her Shadow tech tail. "Read it to me."

It was the note Lady Alesta had left for A-Ram in his lunch basket. He took it from her.

It read:

Rammy

I've packed your favorite. It will be cold in the north of Kana and your lunch will help to keep you warm. Be sure to share with Bel, Gwen and Morgan.

I'll expect to hear all about your adventures when you return.

I love you.

—Bear-Bear

Ah, Lady Alesta and A-Ram, such an endearing couple. He thought of A-Ram out there in the cold engulfed in an StT—his life in the balance. He wondered what he would say to Alesta should A-Ram be hurt or killed.

And what about Gwen?

"Well, what does it say?" she demanded as she bounded back up the stairs.

"It's a private note to my friend whom you have on ice. It's a personal matter, full of love and warmth. Nothing that would interest you in the slightest."

Stenstrom took the note, put it into his coat and reached for the door again.

"Have you really any thoughts as to what interests me, and what does not?" she said, tail flicking.

"Locked."

"I can blow the doors down for you, if you like?" Kat said from the top.

Stenstrom glared at her and thought for a moment. He shook his hands and produced a set of lock picks.

"And so, you're a magician as well as a male Sister, HRN?"

Stenstrom pushed the picks into the lock and felt them latch. He expertly worked the lock and the door opened without resistance. He carefully swung the heavy door out, revealing a quiet pitch dark space within. With a shake he returned the lock picks to his HRN.

Before entering, Stenstrom smiled and did his fade into the shadows, a skill taught him by his mother long ago. He allowed her to watch him fade from sight. Kat looked sideways, trying to see him.

"HRN?" she said.

He plunged into the darkness.

"HRN?" she said again from beyond.

7—THE HALL OF MIRRORS

Though darkness engulfed him, he sensed a vast space all around him, a great cool emptiness. Slowly, he got used to the murk. His eyes, aided by the Sisters' power, soon adjusted to the gloom.

He was in a vast, underground amphitheater. The walls and ceiling were squared-off and lofty. The ceiling was a heavy slab about twenty feet off the floor. The setup reminded him of the old culvert running under the hill at home where his mother had taught him the ways of Tyrol sorcery.

The central area was roped off by several lengths of shiny, wound-up wire. Tiny charms hung dangled from the wire at irregular intervals. Dust and sandy grit covered the floor.

He froze. That wire, he knew what it was. It was one of those arcane LosCapricos weapons that each Great House of Kana and Hoban possessed. He carried his own, his father's NTH's and his mother's MARZABLE; and he was familiar with his mentor Captain Davage's CARG weapon. Lord Davage had always tried to impress upon him the importance of knowing each LosCapricos weapon and understanding what it did in battle; that was key. Not knowing was very dangerous, as they could do virtually anything.

He thought of his many rousing dinners in the Capricos Hall at Castle Blanchefort where all the LosCapricos weapons were boldly displayed on the wall. Captain Davage was a LosCapricos master; he knew them all by heart. Stenstrom, Lt. Kilos, and Countess Sygillis were always stumped.

The wire gleamed at him, silent and ominous. He thought of the two dead Black Hats killed at the doorway, of how their bodies had been mangled. This wire must have killed them.

It seemed inert at the moment. Fading into the shadows must have defeated its defenses. He had to have information; he had to know how it worked.

He produced a green Holystone from a hidden pocket, then tossed it across the floor. A sizzling red beam shot out from the wire and incinerated the Holystone on the spot. The flash revealed the remains of more bodies scattered on the floor. More previous victims.

He noticed minute ant-like activity coursing back and forth on the wire. Tiny pewter pendants, shaped like unblinking eyeballs, hung from the wire. The eyeball pendants moved left and right across its taut length. When two eyeballs bumped into each other they reversed direction and went back the other way. There were also strange pendants shaped like noses and ears, possibly sniffing and listening for intruders. Mouth pendants smiled. *"Anybody there?"* they whispered.

He produced another green Holystone and tossed it. Instantly, one of the eyeball pendants stopped moving, along with an ear. A cannon pendant hanging from the wire came up and blasted the Holystone with a withering red beam. It was quite the thing to see.

As his fade into the shadows appeared to be effective against this weapon, he thought it safe to continue. The walls of the room were covered in dusty murals depicting the old days of the Vith when their power was in ascendance, matching and possibly exceeding that of the Sisters. The murals told of rare items and wondrous treasure guarded by fanciful beasts, of faraway places where the Sisters could not reach and wondrous people of great height with whom the Vith communed.

The Gods of Cammara? Queen Wendilnight? Her head had nearly touched the ceiling in his office, eleven feet above the floor. And look, there was a drawing of a tall fair-haired lady sitting in a throne next to a stately gentleman. Was that her? It seemed like her. This chamber was several centuries old, built by the Clovis before they left the League in 000000AX. So, if that representation was indeed Queen Wendilnight, then she was, at minimum, nearly four thousand years old.

Nearby he found a setback in the wall marked with a stone frame carved in Vith writing. This must be the gateway to the Vith's private world and the Gods of Cammara before the Sisters put an end to it.

He found a face at last painted on the stone. A somber, fair-haired girl of a tragic bearing. He stared at the face. Was this the Shadow tech Goddess? No, the face had a familiar bearing. Morgan had mentioned something about Melazarr of Caroline, how Rodrigo of Burgon had seen her face in the ruins of Clovis.

This was Melazarr's face placed here thousands of years ago, unpainted, vulnerable and sad, carrying the universe's messages.

And that was all, just a silent forgotten place in the dark. He got out the Black Hat's Shadow tech ball and rolled it along several murals, including Melazarr's, but he didn't see anything relating to the Shadow tech Goddess.

He looked further. In a corner was a rough stone protrusion with a flat top, like a stump for an anvil. He produced the Anatameter from within his coat. It seemed to be of the same general size and width; perhaps it went on top. He leaned down to place the Anatameter.

He noticed something scratched into the surface of the stump:

BEWARE THE SHADOW TECH GODDESS

He set the Anatameter on the stump and slid it around until he felt it drop into place; then he gave it a slight clockwise turn and it locked solidly. It dug in so tight he couldn't get it back out.

He stepped away, his duty to Queen Wendilnight done. Now to look to his own and find something to appease the Black Hat outside.

Oh, wait, he was supposed to turn the knob. Queen Wendilnight had said to turn the knob. It hadn't ever shown signs that it would turn before. He reached down and, surprisingly, it turned with an easy, ratchet movement.

CLICK!

He heard a voice from behind.

"*Bel . . . !*"

The eyeballs, ears and noses roving back and forth on the wire took no notice. He wondered if he'd heard it at all. It might have been his imagination.

But, then, it came again.

"*Bel . . . hmmmmmmhehehehe . . .*"

He turned and discovered the chamber around him had changed. No longer a drab square room, there was now a corridor at the far end leading to the left and the right. Another change: the wire with its floating eyeballs was gone.

The Anatameter itself was different. It was now mounted on a central pedestal carved of delicate fluted columns. Its previous dull ochre hue and half-baked bread appearance was gone, replaced by a spiky jewel-like sheen, dancing with color, emitting a sapphire light.

The eerie bluish pall from the Anatameter illuminated the corridor with ghost light. The corridor ran perfectly straight and went down in either direction as far as he could see. On the right-hand side were a series of spacious alcoves that were dark and mysterious. They were evenly set into the wall about every hundred feet.

The tittering voice he'd heard came again. *"I'm awake! I'm going to kill her, Bel. Do you hear?? I'm going to kill her."*

He drew his NTH and cocked the hammer. He couldn't place where the voice had come from, possibly somewhere down the right hand side of the corridor.

He took a few steps, then noticed a scrawl on the stone, drawn in chalk. It read:

THE SHADOW TECH GODDESS

He stopped and stared down the corridor, straining to see. Far off, as his eyes adjusted, he saw a faint blue smudge, like a patch of moonlight. Something down there waited for him. And it filled him with a wave of fear that cut deep, past his natural courage, past the Sisters protections. He'd never felt anything like it. He couldn't take another step. He couldn't level his gun and fire it. He couldn't do anything. Everything felt so heavy, he just wanted to fall down and lay there. Why was he here? How had he arrived? It was all so confusing.

"Bel!"

A pair of hands gripped him at either shoulder and spun him around.

A fair-haired woman stood there, her lips pulled back in fear. Her eyes were wide. She was quite tall, nearly as tall as he was, wearing a gray piloting suit complete with hoses and straps dangling past her waist, a belt of many pockets and compartments, and a sturdy pair of strapped trudging boots. The butt of a gun jutted from a shoulder holster.

"Who are you?" he managed to say. "Where did you come from?"

"I'm your wife, Bel! Your countess!"

He blinked and took a hard look at her face. It seemed familiar, but he couldn't place it. He was having trouble thinking, putting things together.

He might know her and he might not. "I don't know you," he finally said.

She lost her composure for a moment, half laughing, half groaning. She tightened her grip on his shoulder and shook him. "Bel, she's coming! She's coming, do you understand? I know you're feeling the effects of her proximity. That fear you're feeling, that confusion, it's from her!"

She pulled in close. She smelled of sweat and stale fear. "Did you turn the knob?"

His mind was numb, like he was asleep or only partially awake. "The what?"

"The knob, Bel, the knob! Did you turn it?"

Through the dull, clouded passes of his mind he recalled the Anatameter and its innocuous little knob. "Yes . . ."

"How many times?"

"One, I think . . ."

The woman shrieked and shook him. "EIGHT TIMES, BEL!!! EIGHT TIMES, NOT ONE!!!"

Something approached down the corridor. ". . . *heeheheeheheeeeeee . . .*"

The woman reacted with stark terror. She hauled Stenstrom around and shoved him up the corridor toward the chamber. He fell to the ground. Panting with terror, she drew her gun. "Gh-go. Tu, tu, turn the knob. Seven more times. I'll hold her here. Do it, Bel!"

Stenstrom, his mind clouded with fear and confusion, crawled toward the chamber as he was told, his limbs heavy, his head hanging toward the ground.

Behind him came a ruckus of gunfire and screaming. *"Die, die, why won't you die??"* said a terror-filled voice.

He sucked in his breath and kept moving. Where was his courage, his valor? Why wasn't he standing fast helping this woman who claimed to be his wife, though he had no wife? It didn't matter who she claimed to be, she needed his help; yet all he could do was continue on one drag at a time.

He reached the chamber; behind him was a dreadful commotion of bodies struggling in the grit, of cloth tearing and bones breaking. There came hideous, glee-filled laughing and an agony-choked scream he couldn't bear to listen to.

There was the Anatameter atop its pedestal, gleaming like a forgotten gem. He reached up, it was too high. Panting, straining to stand, to raise himself up, he leaned against the pedestal.

Too much, he couldn't do it. He was bewitched.

"I'm your wife, Bel! Your countess!"

The woman's words ran through his mind. He allowed his guilt and shame for not helping her to fuel him, to give him strength. He pushed himself up and reached out to turn the knob at the top of the Anatameter. She had thought it important enough to sacrifice herself.

"BELLLLLLL!!!" came a blaring ugly voice.

The fear and the weight he'd felt before was ten-fold now, a palpable, crushing force and he crashed back down into the grit. He struggled to raise his NTH.

A hand appeared from the corridor, gripping the edge. The hand was pasty white with hints of greenish veins running beneath the skin. The fingernails were cracked and broken, a distinct green color.

A head and shoulder appeared around the edge. The demented face of a woman hovered there, mouth open in delight, eyes wide and lamp-like, and they fixed on him, burning into his soul. "There you are . . ." she rasped. She emerged from behind the edge. She wore a black, form-fitting suit of some kind, her sleeves pushed up to her elbows. Her hair was a rope-like green tangle. She approached, holding her hands at chest-level, her crab-like fingers snapping.

He raised his NTH's with all the strength he had and fired two shots; the woman tittered and kicked them away. She dove down and he felt the life drain out of him with her touch.

"Been waiting for thissss."

She stood and grasped the Anatameter with both hands. With a twist it came away from the pedestal; the woman held it aloft in triumph. "Gotcha . . . hhhhhhehehehehehheeee . . ."

She squeezed his cheeks together with her pale hand which smelled of the grave and was smeared with blood. Blood? He feared for the woman in the corridor. Was she hurt? Was she dead?

The creature then pulled him up and kissed him. The kiss was frigid and dank; his heart failed and skipped several beats. She released him and walked back into the corridor carrying her prize with her.

"Come and get it . . . hhhhhhhhhhehehehhe . . . I'll be waiting . . . ."

The corridor shimmered, then vanished.

<Come and get it . . .> came the echo of her ghastly voice.

The hand of fear that had rendered him helpless diminished with her passing and he was himself again. The chamber reverted to what it had been, just a dusty stone room. He sat up; his NTHs lay on the ground an arm's length away. He picked them up and tucked them into his sash.

The woman's voice ran through his thoughts. *I'm your wife, Bel! Your countess!*

Who was she? What was he to her and what was she to him? His wife, his Countess? He had so many questions. All he knew for certain was that, though terrified, she had stood and faced her fear, hoping to give him time, and he had failed her.

"Hey," came a voice.

The eyeballs on the wire were all staring at him. Noses, ears and a laughing mouth were there too, forming a dangling rudimentary face.

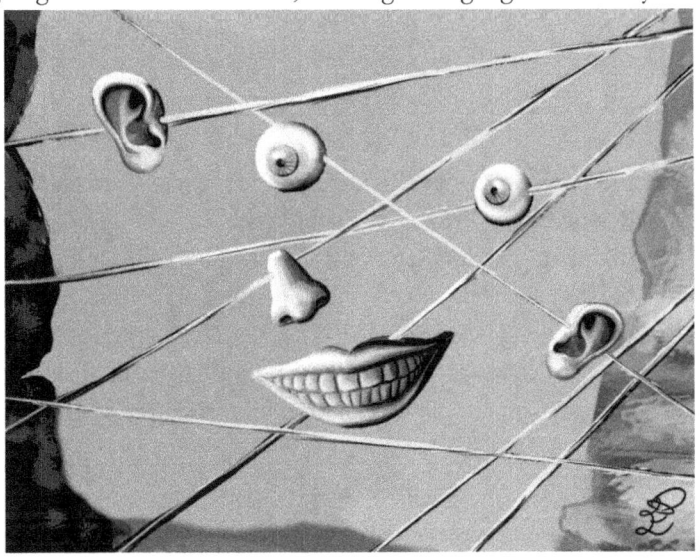

He was not faded into the Shadows and they could see him, hear him, smell him. They blinked with indignation. A cannon charm took aim.

The chamber exploded.

"Bel? Bel!" came a frantic voice.

He opened his eyes. A terrified Gwendolyn and A-Ram stared down at him.

"Gwen . . . A-Ram . . ." He sat up. He was lying on the cold ground near the Ripcar. Gwendolyn and A-Ram were leaning over him. His clothes, with the exception of his HRN, were in blackened tatters. "Are you two all right?"

"We're fine," A-Ram said, holding his hand. "I recall seeing something black coming toward me, then, before I knew it, I was sitting by the Ripcar next to Gwen. You were lying here as well."

"Bel, your clothes? What happened to you?" Gwen asked, having trouble masking her concern.

He started to speak, then stopped. Rummaging through his thoughts he found a blank spot; most of the afternoon was gone. He remembered the ruins and the Black Hat, and something about someone calling out to him, someone who had needed him and he had abandoned.

Did that happen? The thought troubled him.

"I don't know. My head . . ." He looked around. "Where's Kat?"

"Who's Kat?"

"The Black Hat."

Gwendolyn and A-Ram scanned the area. "We haven't seen the Black Hat. She must be gone, thank Creation."

A-Ram pointed at the open basket and the clutter of crumbs and the overturned wine bottle. "You had lunch, I see."

"She had lunch. She was famished; like she hadn't eaten in days. She demanded to be fed, otherwise she wouldn't release you two. She locked both of you in a complex set of StT's." Stenstrom struggled to recall what had happened. "Then . . . she made me go up the path and into a secret room deep underground. She was afraid of something inside that room. And then . . ."

"I am your wife . . . ."

He sat there and tried to clear his head. "I don't remember much about what happened after that. I must have . . . I don't know. I seem to have lost the Anatameter."

"Oh, to blazes with that ruddy little nothing, Bel. It's gone and we needn't worry about it any further. I'm just elated the three of us didn't get killed in the process of losing it. Just rest, darling. Don't strain yourself," Gwen said, hugging him. "You've been through a lot."

He slowly stood and looked around. Most, if not all of the StT's once strewn about the ruins were gone. He remembered something about being in the dark, and an ugly laugh.

". . . hhhhehehhhehehhehhe . . . Come and get it . . ."

A-Ram leaned over, looking at the side of the Ripcar. "Bel, what's this?"

Stenstrom approached. "What is it?"

"Look."

Scratched in the Ripcar's sturdy frame in a handwritten scrawl was: KAT.

He couldn't shake the feeling he'd just let somebody down.

8—The Woman with the Gun

A-Ram woke with a start. A week after the incident at the Clovis ruins he still dreamed of the Black Hat and her StTs. Still dreamed of things going down his throat and eating him from the inside out. Still dreamed of being smothered.

But he was snug in his quarters on the *Seeker's* starboard side, Deck 3, and only a few doors down from Taara's quarters. Alesta was asleep, tightly hugging him. Her nude body still slightly lubricated from their recent lovemaking. She was supposed to sleep on Deck 6 with the rest of her Merian congregation, but she was rarely there in her little room that contained nothing but a bed, a chair, and a picture of him. Most nights she spent with A-Ram.

She'd loved him from the beginning; with porcelain skin and, black hair,she could have courted most any fellow she wanted. True to her Merian teachings, she had followed her heart and proudly given her love to him. Coy about her age, he knew she was approaching two-hundred, though she never said the exact number. In true Elder fashion, Alesta's age and A-Ram's being in his forties was a non-issue; they both appeared young and rosy. They planned on a spring wedding; probably in a quiet meadow or grassy clearing far away from the bustle and confusion of the League.

A-Ram, jostled a bit after his nightmare wanted to get up and fetch a glass of water, but Alesta gripped him tightly. He normally kept a glass at his bedside because Alesta had a habit of getting him in a death grip and not letting go until morning, but he had forgotten to pour one this night.

He settled and tried to go back to sleep. Alesta was snoring ever so slightly. "Oh, so thirsty," he mumbled. No matter, he'd be comfortably asleep again in minutes. As he waited, he toyed with the idea of waking Alesta and making love to her again. He found sex in the early morning smashing fun: the hot skin from the blankets, the mussed hair, strange smells, bad breath. He loved the whole experience, though Alesta wasn't a great fan of it.

"Are you thirsty?" a stranger's voice said.

He tried to sit up, but Alesta protested. He dismissed the voice as a fantasy and fell back, his mouth dry.

A few moments later, a soft hand touched his face and gently guided a glass of cold water to his lips. The glass came away. He felt around for his Dragons, found them on the nightstand and popped them on. He was near blind without them.

Across the room, a figure stood near the chair. It was dark, he couldn't see clearly, but he was certain it was there. Seeing it woke him up fully.

"Alesta? Alesta! Wake up!"

She stirred. "Rammy . . . what is it?" She peeled herself away from him and rubbed the sleep out of her eyes. "Really, darling, I'm a mess, I don't want to make love right now."

"Alesta, over there, I see something!"

"What?"

They sat up, Alesta holding the sheets over her breasts.

"Who's there?" Alesta asked.

A quiet voice answered. "Hello Lord A-Ram, Lady Alesta. How I've longed to meet you."

"Do I know you?" A-Ram asked. "I don't recognize your voice."

The figure sighed. "You gave me my heart."

"What? What do you want?"

"I will tell you, but, please, not here. If you would be so kind as to meet me down the hall."

"We'll call security," Alesta said.

"You both have nothing to fear from me."

The figure opened the door. Light spilled in from the corridor, and the stranger glided out.

They came out of bed. While Alesta squirmed into her robes A-Ram pulled on his pants, slippers, and a robe. "We should call security right now," she said.

A-Ram thought about it. "I want to go see."

"What? Why?"

"I don't know; I just do. I don't think we're in any danger. Are you coming?"

A-Ram and Alesta hurried into the corridor. It was long after night bell and the corridor outside was empty of the usual crew traffic coming and going. One person stood toward the aft of the ship, a female. She smiled.

"A-Ram!" she cried, overjoyed, holding her arms out, inviting them to come forward. She was quite tall, towering over both A-Ram and Alesta. She wore some sort of jumpsuit, similar to what a Marine pilot would wear, only hers was gray instead of vivid red. She even had on a life support harness dangling with hoses and cords, a compartmented belt, and a pair of knee-high boots with a thick tread. The pugnacious butt of a gun jutted out of a shoulder holster. Despite the utilitarian look of her gear and footwear, her blonde hair was elaborately set, as if she were heading out to a ball. She radiated beauty.

She smiled and put her arms around the both of them at once. "Oh, you two!" she cried in delight. "Look at you; you have that glow of young love. Not even married yet probably."

"In a few months," A-Ram said. "I'm sorry, Great Lady, do we know you?"

She considered his question for a moment. "Of course you do, in a manner of speaking."

Alesta held her robe shut. "What does that mean?"

"It means that I know you very well, though we've never met in person."

"What do you want?" Alesta asked.

"The same thing you do. I'm hoping you'll come with me, for I have things to show you."

"What things?" A-Ram asked.

A-Ram and Alesta stood there holding each other.

"I realize how strange this is," the woman said. "You don't know me at present, but I know you and what good friends you both are. Please, I'll explain everything in a few minutes."

A-Ram and Alesta cautiously relented. The three of them made their way down the hallway. Doors marked the corridor at regular intervals as it went about two hundred feet forward in a slow curve and then turned sharply, following the articulation of the ship. The woman walked serenely at their side, her hoses and cords knocking together.

They arrived at the bend in the corridor. The woman stopped them. "Before we continue on, you, A-Ram and Alesta, have a decision to make. Continue on with me and you two will begin a long journey. You will see amazing things and go to unusual places, and I can't promise you will be back in time for your wedding. You might have to postpone it for awhile."

A-Ram and Alesta stood there arm-in-arm. "And if we go back, return to bed and pretend this never happened?" he asked.

The woman flushed. "Then, Bel, and Gwen, and Taara, and . . . and me, will be lost and without guidance. All of us, myself most of all, need you. I have come to you because, in all these worlds, you two are most commonly the same. You always find each other. Do you know how rare and wonderful that is? I beseech your love and wisdom." A tear fell down the woman's beautiful face. "In all honesty, were I in your position, I think I might turn around and go back to bed. The choice is yours."

A-Ram and Alesta turned to each other and silently debated the matter. The woman watched them, her concern showing in her face.

"Well, then," A-Ram said, "if we can be of help to those we love and count as dear friends, then we can put off our wedding for a bit. What is a wedding but a day? We've our whole life together after all."

The woman smiled and placed her hand on her heart, "Oh, such true friends. Come with me, then. I promise, when this is done, you'll have such stories to tell your children someday."

Hand in hand, she led A-Ram and Alesta around the corner and disappeared.

9—Old Friends Returned

Paymaster Stenstrom was concerned. A-Ram was late for his shift at the helm. He was never late, and he was never early, either. He was always right on time; stepping onto the bridge at six bells without fail, always in his dapper fleet uniform and his Dragons. Junior Helmsman Fidamer, a lady of the House of Widmark, was rousted from her rack by Ops to man the helm in A-Ram's absence. Then, Ops informed the captain of his helmsman's missing status.

Stenstrom and Gwendolyn immediately went down to A-Ram's quarters. On the way, they passed Taara's quarters. Stenstrom banged on her door.

". . . What?" came a sleepy voice from the other side. Taara didn't usually rise for another three bells.

"Get your butt up, Taara. We can't find A-Ram."

"I'll be there in a second," she said, knocking around on the other side.

They continued down the corridor and knocked on A-Ram's door. There was no answer.

Stenstrom banged his fist on the door. "A-Ram, you all right?"

No reply.

"I'm concerned," Gwendolyn said. "Perhaps he's suffering ill effects from his encounter with the StT's in Clovis. I know I've had some odd dreams since then."

Clovis. Stenstrom hadn't said anything, but he hadn't fully recovered from Clovis: the ruins, the StT's, the fight with the Black Hat, the hole in the ground he dimly remembered venturing into, and the missing Anatameter. Something happened in that hole, something important, something undone. Two words stuck out in his head—*wife, countess*—and those words taunted and stung him.

Gwendolyn nervously toyed with her FEDULA. "Com," she said, looking up at the ceiling.

"Com here, ma'am."

"Check the dispensary. Please inquire if Lt. A-Ram is there."

"Aye, ma'am.". There was a momentary pause. "He is not there, ma'am. His MAGGA locator indicates he is in his quarters."

Gwendolyn reddened. "Thank you."

Stenstrom shook his hands and set to work on A-Ram's door. A moment later, the lock picked, he swung it open. "A-Ram, you in here?"

Again, no reply.

They went in. A-Ram's room was tidy and well-organized, as always. His abstract metal and paint creations hung on the wall in their usual spots. There was a metal relief work near his bed; A-Ram had claimed it was a rendering of Alesta, though Stenstrom couldn't make a face or form out of it. Surprisingly his bed was unmade—not something often seen with A-Ram. On a nearby chair, Lady Alesta's green brocade Merian robe hung innocently from an arm. Her slippers sat by the foot of the bed. One of A-Ram's uniforms was laid out nearby. Gwendolyn checked it. "Here's his MAGGA locator. Bel, I'm really worried."

A yawning Taara appeared in the doorway a few moments later, her black hair messy from sleep. "Did you find him?"

"No," Stenstrom replied. "His bed's unmade and here are a few of Alesta's things."

"Ohhhh, she's being naughty again," Taara said. "She's up here all the time wrestling with A-Ram. She actually makes a fair amount of noise when they're having sex. I was going to say something, but never got around to it. I didn't think Merians were allowed to hop into the sack with guys."

"I'm not aware of Merians observing any sort of vow of chastity," Stenstrom said. "I'm going to call for security."

Taara approached A-Ram's bed. "Don't bother. He's not on the ship."

"What makes you say that?" Gwen asked.

Taara pointed at her head. "What do you think? MOLLY says he's not here. Maybe they cut out on the Merian's Road; you know how they come and go."

"But without telling us?"

"I don't think he and Alesta are in any danger. Why don't we cut them some slack for a day or two. I'm certain they'll turn up and A-Ram will be all full of apologies why he missed his shifts."

Two days later, A-Ram and Lady Alesta still hadn't turned up. Taara allayed Stenstrom's concerns. "They'll show up. They're fine I'm telling you."

Their disappearance only added to his general feelings of loss and woe since Clovis.

Preoccupied, Stenstrom finished his shift, brooding out the day on the bridge watching Kana slowly spin through the viewing cone and half-listening to the muted chatter around him. The ship wasn't due out for several weeks so there wasn't much to occupy his time except fret and worry. As the bell sounded and the crew changed shifts he decided to return to his quarters and get ready for dinner in the mess with Gwen and maybe Morgan. He hoped they might raise his spirits. He shuffled into the lift and went down to his deck. As he passed the *Seeker's* main conference room he heard his name whispered from within.

"*Bel!*"

He stopped, wondering if he'd imagined it.

"*In here!*"

Full of dread, he opened the door and entered.

The conference room was lit up and comforting, the clean Nadine-wood table, the smell of rich, fresh-brewed coffee tickling the air. He rarely used the room. He didn't like formal meetings and get-togethers, thought they were a waste of time, talk about talking. Captain Davage taught him the best place to sort out and pass along information was in the mess hall; that's where people listened and things got done. Gwendolyn, though, made use of the conference room often in her various engineering duties. She usually had it booked well in advance, leaving little time for anybody else to get a turn.

There, seated at the long table, were A-Ram and Lady Alesta, all smiles, with two steaming coffees on saucers sitting in front of them.

"A-Ram, for Creation's sake!" Stenstrom cried, his heart jumping. "We were worried sick!"

They stood and greeted him. A-Ram was oddly dressed. Instead of his usual Fleet uniform and hat, he wore a dark blue Calvert suit. Alesta was in her usual Merian robes; however, she was wearing a pair of buttoned up traveling boots, a strange sight on her normally unshod feet.

"Hey, Bel, I'm sorry. I offer my apologies for missing my shift these past few days; I hope I didn't let you down," A-Ram said.

Stenstrom embraced them both. "Just been worried about the pair of you is all. What happened to you?"

A-Ram flushed. "We had an odd visit a few nights ago."

"From whom?"

A-Ram and Alesta turned to each other as if debating what to say to him and what to exclude. Alesta took the lead. "We . . . were contacted and asked to go on a long journey. We couldn't refuse."

Stenstrom felt something tug on his heart. "You're leaving? Leaving the *Seeker?*"

Alesta laughed. "No! No, of course not. The *Seeker* is our home. A new friend of ours asked us to help her, and we intend to do just that. Our task here today is to provide you with crucial information and guidance, and we have to make certain we properly relay it to you. It's an oath we made."

"Who asked you to relay this information?"

Alesta reached down and rubbed her feet. Then she removed her boots and kicked them aside. "I used to love shoes, then I became a Merian and, after a hundred and fifty years of bare feet, I hate them." A-Ram wandered into the kitchenette. "Want some coffee before we get started, Bel? We might be here for awhile."

"I suppose so, thanks."

As A-Ram worked, Stenstrom turned to Alesta and took her hand. "So, what's all this about?"

"We know what happened at Clovis, Bel. All of it. We know you've been beset by feelings of guilt and remorse. You don't know why you feel that way, but we do and we're here to tell you what happened and that it's not your fault. You couldn't have been prepared."

"Prepared for what? What happened?"

Alesta closed her eyes. "Your Countess died there."

Deep inside, Stenstrom winced, but outwardly he remained unmoved and cheerful. "I wasn't aware I had a wife."

"You do, Bel. I . . ." She struggled for words.

"As a trained sorcerer, I'm no stranger to the arcane and bizarre. I'm certain I'll be able to listen objectively."

Alesta squeezed his hand. "Of course, but it's . . . difficult to know where to begin."

They sat down at the table, still holding hands. "Well then, let's start with the basics. Who set you to this?" Stenstrom asked.

"Your countess did."

"My countess?"

"Does that surprise or shock you?"

"Of course it does, but I'm well-suited to hear odd news, as I said." Stenstrom then asked the question whose answer he dreaded. "Did you learn what happened to me at Clovis?"

"We did."

"Then tell me. Please. I need to know."

Alesta began. "You entered a place the Old Clovis called their 'cistern' because they wished to keep it hidden from the gaze of the Sisters. In actuality, the chamber was the Clovis' gateway to another world, a secret world that many Vith Households maintained at that time. The Clovis, however, claimed that their gateway was plagued by a demon of death and destruction they called the Shadow tech Goddess and that they were unable to free themselves of this troublesome entity."

A-Ram spoke up. "The Clovis solved the Shadow tech Goddess problem with the addition of an Anatameter. They got it from the Gods of Cammara—whoever they are—and it worked for centuries until the Sisters eventually deactivated the Clovis' gateway and the Anatameter was removed. You, Bel, placed your Anatameter into the old socket where the original once resided and a dimensional doorway called the Hall of Mirrors was opened. That's where you met your countess, and that's also where you encountered the Shadow tech Goddess."

"What happened to my Countess?"

Alesta bit her lip. "She died. The Shadow tech Goddess killed her."

Stenstrom was crushed. "Why didn't I stand and fight with her? How could I have left her there? Why wasn't I killed too?"

"Before I answer that," Alesta said, "tell me . . . how do you feel about this person? This woman who said she was your countess? You knew her only for a moment, and know nothing about her other than that she claimed to be your wife and that she was brave. You don't remember her, do you? How does me telling you this make you feel?"

Stenstrom thought about it. "I suppose I feel confused, but I also feel loss and regret. This is a woman I have no memory of, whose face I don't recall, whose voice I wouldn't recognize. Yet, I know what you're telling me is true. I wish I could have had a moment to speak to her and ask her name, to perhaps have held her hand and know her heart. If an alternate version of myself loved her, then certainly I could have and I feel that loss. I wish I could have assisted her. I failed this woman."

Alesta gave a bright smile. "I knew it. You have this light about you, Bel, I feel it. You care for a woman you can't even remember. That's why we agreed to postpone our wedding and go on this odd journey, because you deserve our help."

He tried to assimilate what Alesta and A-Ram had just told him. "So, I went to Clovis under the pretext of delivering an apparently mundane and inert stone trinket, and instead met up with a woman whom I married in another reality and a planar demon who killed her for no apparent reason. So why am I not also dead? And what happened to the Anatameter?"

"As for why the Shadow tech Goddess didn't kill you too, we're not certain. We do know she stole the Anatameter,"she said.

"Stole it? Then good riddance. She's welcome to it."

"But that's the whole problem. That Anatameter was built for you. It has a knob at the top that takes eight clicks to make a full revolution," Alesta said.

"Why was it made for me?"

"We're not sure. We don't know who made it, either. We were told you were supposed to turn the knob at Clovis eight times, doing so would have rendered it inert. We think you only turned it once," A-Ram said.

"Gwen checked it over. She dismissed it as an uninteresting rock, and all of my arcane instrumentality took no notice of it either." He felt defeated, negligent and culpable. He should have known better, been better prepared. "It was just a bloody trinket."

A-Ram reached into his coat pocket and pulled out a folded piece of paper.

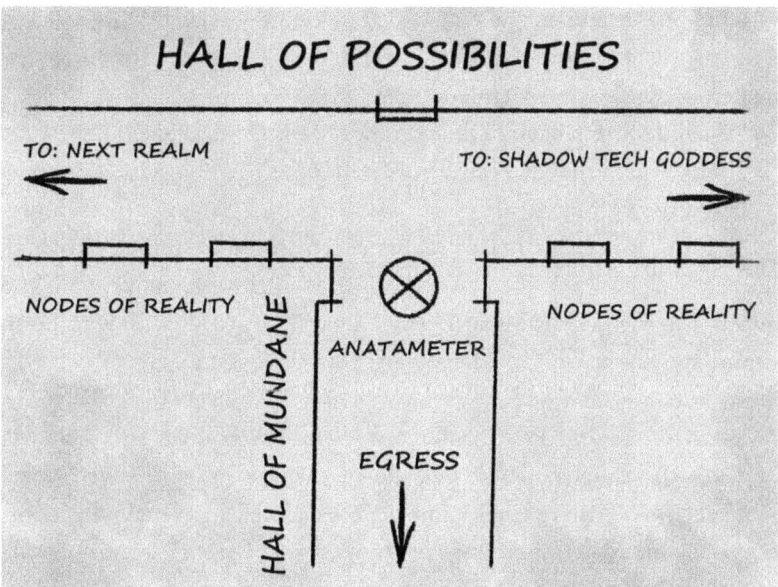

"The Anatameter is the centerpiece of a place scholars call the Hall of Mirrors. The Hall of Mirrors is the access point from one plane of reality to another. It's like the pressure hatch between two cars in a land train. Have you ever ridden one of those?"

Stenstrom shook his head. Great Lords did not ride land trains.

"Ok, look, you have Plane of Reality A and Plane of Reality B, and the only way to get from one to the other is through the Hall of Mirrors. It has general characteristics, but no set appearance. It can look like anything. I guess that's why it's called the Hall of Mirrors."

"We've been through one," Alesta said. "To us it looks like a plain stone corridor."

A stone corridor? That jogged his memory a bit. He remembered something about a dark corridor, and someone standing there in the dark with him and the wall of fear that filled it. He remembered trying to raise his NTH's. He remembered screaming.

"Look here. It has two distinct regions, sort of like in a 'T' shape, that's how I think of it," A-Ram said, pointing at the picture on the paper. "The Hall of Mundane is the stick of the 'T'. That's where you came from, the safe hall. The top part of the 'T' is the Hall of Possibilities. That's the dangerous one." A-Ram tapped the page again. "There's the Anatameter, in the junction between the stick and the top. We have been told that people and, in some cases, various extra-planar entities, attempt to cross the planes of reality. I guess that's supposed to be pretty dangerous. With the Anatameter there, they can't cross."

"What does this have to do with me?" Stenstrom asked.

"Bel, we're in the Hall of Mirrors right now," A-Ram said.

"Right now? Why?"

"Because you placed your Anatameter and didn't turn the knob all the way, and, until you do, you and everyone in close proximity with you are stuck in the Hall of Mirrors. The only way to get out of it is to finish turning the knob. Until then it's going to follow you wherever you go," Alesta said.

Stenstrom scanned the conference room. It was quiet and secluded, far from the usual noise and bustle of the ship, save the occasional muffled passing of crewmen outside. The far wall was lined with floor-to-ceiling windows admitting cheery starlight. On the opposite wall, several paintings hung: one of Captain Davage, Countess Sygillis, and Lt. Kilos, the previous commanders of the ship and dear friends of Stenstrom, one of Lord Milos of Probert, the ship's designer, and a smaller, dour one of Captain Gona of St. Paris, the most recent captain. At the far end of the room was a small parallel corridor with a bathroom to the right and a service door to the left for orderlies to come and go. Nothing seemed out of the ordinary. The usual retinue of arcane protections he always carried in his HRN didn't indicate anything out-of-sorts., But they had failed him with the Anatameter, so perhaps they couldn't be counted on now. He would have to rework them.

He rose and went to the corridor at the far end of the room and peered in. It was dimly lit and smelled of fresh coffee from the nearby pot sitting on the sideboard. To the left, behind a door several paces down, was a small kitchen used by the orderlies when a formal conference was in progress.

"So, right now, we're in the Hall of Mirrors?"

"Yes," Alesta said.

"According to the drawing, to the left is the next plane of existence, correct?"

"Yes."

To the left was an innocuous door. Light peeked through the crack.

He turned to the right. The bathroom door was closed. "And what if I go to the right?"

A-Ram's face darkened. "The Shadow tech Goddess awaits. She's always at the right-hand of the Hall of Possibilities. She's like a watch dog; or an attack dog if you will. Those who dally too long in the Hall of Mirrors will stir her up, attract her attention, and then that's it. If you go in there, she'll awaken."

"And she'll destroy me?"

"Yes," A-Ram said.

"So, you're saying the Shadow tech Goddess is in the bathroom?" Despite himself, he chuckled.

"We're probably not correctly explaining it," Alesta said. "We were told she's always at the end of the right-hand passage. Does that mean she's in the bathroom right now? Maybe, and maybe not. Your guess is as good as mine, and, remember, the Hall of Mirrors can look like anything; so, yes, it could look like a bathroom, I suppose."

Stenstrom stood there, the bathroom door mere feet away. He reached for the doorknob. He knew behind the door was a toilet and vanity. A small picture of the *Seeker* hung on the wall and the vanity might hold a vase of flowers. He'd been in it many times. He and Gwen once had uncomfortable sex in it.

There's nothing but a bathroom behind this door.

A-Ram stood up. "I wouldn't test it, Bel. If she is in there, she destroys everything."

Stenstrom mulled it over, then returned to the table.

Alesta took his hand again. "At Clovis, when you put the Anatameter in place, it activated and the Hall of Mirrors came to you. We're told this is a unique situation; normally, an Anatameter wouldn't let you get as far as you did. It would have turned you around and you would have been none the wiser. But, in this case, the one you put in place was made specifically for you, so you may pass without resistance. You unknowingly made it into the Hall of Possibilities and there you encountered the Shadow tech Goddess."

A-Ram jumped in. "And you're still in it, in a meta-physical sort of sense. Being in the Hall of Mirrors for a protracted length of time is very dangerous; not just for you, but for all of us as well. If the Shadow tech Goddess is stirred up again, there's nothing to stop her from continuing on down the Hall of Mundane and having a field day. She's is very powerful . . . and chaotic. She can be a raving lunatic who destroys everything around her with Shadow tech; other times she's rational and full of remorse. She can generate a zone of crushing fear all around her, has the strength of twenty men, unrivaled command of the arcane, and is essentially immortal. There could be nothing left when she's done."

"Apparently that would make Rodrigo of Burgon very happy," Stenstrom said.

"We're serious, Bel. You have to return to the Anatameter and turn the knob. Once you do that, everything will be fine. You'll be out of the Hall of Mirrors," Alesta said.

"So, if we're in the Hall of Mirrors at this very moment, then shouldn't I be able to access the Anatameter and finish turning the knob? I see it here on the drawing."

Alesta shook her head. "No, unfortunately. You can only access it from areas with a socket, like Clovis. It would be great if we could do it from here, but we can't."

"All right. So, we return to Clovis then?"

"It's not there anymore," A-Ram said. "The Shadow tech Goddess moved it or stole it or whatever. There's nothing at Clovis now but a blasted-out underground chamber."

"So, where is it?"

"That's what we're going to find out." A-Ram reached into his jacket and pulled out a small ceramic disk of an ochre hue. "We were given this. It's a guide to help us instruct you in getting to the Anatameter. We would give it over to you, but we have to help *the others* as well, so it was left in our care."

"What others?"

"Other versions of you. This affects not only you, but a number of alternate versions of you, one for each click of the knob. We're helping them too."

"You've met other versions of me, then?"

"We have," A-Ram said.

"And how was I?"

A-Ram smiled. "They're you. Some are a little different; one is really different . . . I–"

Alesta cut him off. "Suffice to say, they all have your light, Bel, and we're glad we can provide them guidance."

Stenstrom nodded. "Then they're in safe hands. Back to this disk here, tell me what it does?"

A-Ram scratched his head. "Well, from what we understand, two things can come out of the Hall of Mirrors besides the Shadow tech Goddess: your love and your enemy." A-Ram referred to his map. "See these little rooms in the Hall of Possibilities, here . . . and here? Those are called the Nodes of Reality. Your loves and your enemies in this particular plane come out of them. Once you've discovered those nodes, then the location of the Anatameter in this plane of reality will be revealed."

His love came to him in Clovis.

"I am your wife!"

And then the enemy.

<heheheheheheheheeeehhee . . . >

"That makes no sense."

A-Ram and Alesta exchanged unsure glances. "Well, we're still trying to puzzle this out ourselves. This is new to us, too. I'm sure as this goes on, we'll get better at it."

Alesta shuffled in her seat. "Actually, Bel, despite this situation, I've rather been looking forward to this. In the next hour or so, we're going to find out who your loves are; their names will appear on Rammy's disk and then we'll know where to go next." She tapped her fingers against the table, betraying excitement. "And, what's more, the first person who walks in here will be your love in this plane of reality."

"Let me see that, please?"

A-Ram laid it on the table and Stenstrom picked up the saucer-sized ceramic disk that was mostly plain and unadorned. It looked like a similar construction to the Anatameter. "This disk is going to reveal all of that?"

"Yes."

Stenstrom's first inclination was to be rather skeptical; however, after Clovis, he knew not to disregard anything, no matter how innocuous. He noticed a line of tiny printing.

DECK 6 CONFERENCE ROOM, *SEEKER*

"I take it this means that, at this moment, the conference room is where we discover where the Anatameter is located."

A-Ram nodded. "As we understand it, yes, after your love and your enemy have been revealed."

10—Waiting for a Lady

Stenstrom looked at the disk again. "So, how long are we to wait?" "We don't know," Alesta said. "The waiting will last until it's done. We should see eight names appear on the disk. I think it's sort of exciting, don't you?" Alesta glanced back at the door.

"You are a vivid romantic, Alesta," Stenstrom said.

"Yes, yes, I am." She giggled. Alesta took A-Ram by the arm. "So, now we wait."

The stars drifted past the windows as the *Seeker* steadily orbited Kana. A-Ram finished a cup of coffee, then another and wanted to visit the bathroom. He remembered who might be waiting there, had a change of heart, and stayed where he was. Outside, whenever someone passed by, Alesta excitedly craned her neck to see out into the hallway. Nobody came into the conference room.

The Com overhead chattered. "Bel!" came Gwendolyn's voice. She sounded upset.

"Aye, Gwen, I'm here."

"Where is my damn consignment form? I submitted it to you two weeks ago. Are you the bloody Paymaster of this vessel or not?"

"I am, and I'm also your commander, Gwendolyn. Please keep your temper in check."

"I'll *'check'* you into unconsciousness, Bel. I want my damn form, tonight!" The Com buzzed off.

Alesta peeked at the disk and burst into a smile. "Look, Bel!" She showed it to him and, sure enough, Gwendolyn's name was printed there, lengthwise in clear letters.

"So, Gwendolyn yelling at me over the Com is her pronouncement of love?"

Alesta laughed. "Oh, you know how she is. She doesn't mean anything."

The Com buzzed from overhead again. All three of them hushed;

Alesta listened with relish.

"Com," Stenstrom said, feeling a bit uneasy. The prospect of discovering his soul-mate was a bit nerve-wracking.

"Com here, sir. You have an incoming message."

"From whom, please?"

"A civilian via League liner ship. Her name is Madam Melazarr of Caroline. She doesn't have an authorization code; however, she insists on speaking with you."

Alesta recoiled. "Oh, Bel, not her! Don't answer it. I was dreading dealing with her again and don't feel up to it at this time."

Stenstrom spoke into the air. "Fine then, I'll take the message."

"Aye, sir."

The Com clicked, and the harsh, rather wiry voice of Melazarr of Caroline crackled in.

"So, you had the guts to take my call, did you, you son-of-a-bitch!"

Alesta frowned and turned red as she listened. She clearly disliked the woman.

"Madam Caroline, what can I do for you?"

"What can you do for me? For starters you can send a ship or something and get me back over there. I don't want to be here—I want to be there! I've decided to forgive and forget and offer you a second chance to get properly fucked!"

Alesta covered her ears.

"I'm sorry, Madam. You are on-course for Xandarr. I'm not sending a Ripcar for you. I shan't think we'll have further occasion to enjoy each other's company, ever."

"No? No? You'll be seeing me again, fancy boy, and when I get my hands on you, watch out!"

"I see, well, sorry about that."

"And, you know what?"

Stenstrom rubbed his forehead. "What?"

"I put a curse on you. A bad one. You're going to have to come to me to be rid of it and I can't wait to see you. You're going to be begging me. Ohhhh, it's going to be good."

"I see. In any event, I bid you good day."

"No, wait!" she cried. "What's that ship I see coming in? I see a big old white ship out there all lit up. Is that you coming to get me? It is, isn't it? I knew it! The curse works every time!"

"No, madam, it's not us. Now, if you'll excuse me I must return to my duties."

Melazarr gave a parting snort. "See ya', soon . . ."

He cut the link.

"Oh, thank Creation that's over," Alesta said. "How I hate . . . I'm sorry, I don't hate anybody; it's not in my calling. How I *pity* that bizarre woman." She checked the disk, gripping it so hard with both hands her knuckles stuck out, then she closed her eyes and sighed. Stenstrom checked the disk. Sure enough, Melazarr's name was now next to Gwendolyn's. She muttered something and shook her head. A-Ram laughed.

"So, this means that Melazarr of Caroline is my love?"

Alesta nodded. "In a demented and pitiful alternate reality, no doubt. I cannot believe that I'll have to deal with this woman again."

"I didn't mind Melazarr. I sort of liked her," A-Ram said, cutting her off. Alesta shot him a deadly look and he returned to his coffee.

Stenstrom laughed and took a sip of his coffee. Despite himself, he was enjoying this session as much as Alesta.

Com clicked on again. "Bel," came Gwendolyn's voice. "I didn't mean to yell at you, and I apologize. I just wish that, on occasion, you behaved a bit more professionally."

"Is that a fact?" Stenstrom answered. "I suppose, Gwendolyn, that giving jaw to your commander over an open Com is a professional method of handling things, then? We shall discuss your issues with courtesy and insubordination at a later time. Out."

He cut the Com link. "Well, that ought to stir her up. Is her name on the disk again?"

Alesta checked the disk, smiled, and nodded. Gwendolyn's name was now etched on the disk twice, with Melazarr's name sandwiched between.

The afternoon continued on in nervous starts and stops. People passing by outside was maddening, and Alesta got up and closed the door so that the sounds of passersby wouldn't alert her. They went through several more cups of coffee. A-Ram's need to visit the bathroom increased; however, he was not going to use *that* bathroom in the conference room. The afternoon dragged on; the odd disk sat on the table with three names etched on its face.

The Com came on again and the three of them sucked in their collective breath. "Bel?" came Taara's voice.

Alesta smiled and listened.

Stenstrom was open-mouthed in shock. "I'm right here, Taara," he said, somewhat breathless.

"Where are you? I was getting a little hungry and wanted to know if you guys wanted to hit the Mess or something? Where's my gang? Where's my crew?"

"I'm a little busy at the moment, Taara. I'll eat with you later, though I can't promise when that will be."

"You're in the conference room on Deck 6, right?"

Stenstrom muted the Com. Alesta fidgeted with excitement. He sighed. "I think of Taara as one of my dear sisters. We've showered together for Creation's sake, but we showered like men do. I didn't think twice about it and I certainly wasn't peeking at her tiny naked body in any sort of amorous way. I'm not comfortable with the idea of Taara being my soul-mate."

"Oh, but Bel," Alesta said, "Taara's confessed to me that she likes you. She's always liked you a little past being just friends. Don't let her odd Bazz bravado fool you. Deep down she's pretty shy about these things and she didn't want to get in Gwen's way. She was content to just be your friend, but, as the disk now shows . . ." She held it up for him to see, and there was Taara's name next to Gwen's, ". . . in at least one instance, she is much more than just that. She is the woman at your side. Maybe it's this one."

Taara's voice came down from the Com again. "Bel, you still there?"

He unpaused the Com. "Yep, I'm here. And, you're right, I'm in the conference room with A-Ram and Alesta."

"They're back? I knew it! Are you guys coming to the Mess? Why didn't you get me?"

"We will later, but we can't promise the time."

"Ok, stay put, I'll be right there." The Com clicked off.

Stenstrom shook his head. "Wait, Alesta, you said the first person to enter this room would be my love and soul-mate on this plane of reality, correct?"

"Yes."

"Well, Taara's on her way. I don't know if I'm square with this, truly. I love Taara, but as a sister, as a friend. Maybe elsewhere in the universe it's different, but here I think it would be too odd for me. I like things as they are, with Taara as my right hand."

Alesta shrugged her shoulders. "We'll see."

Stenstrom opened a pad on the tabletop and keyed in several sentences.

"What's that?" A-Ram asked.

"Nothing. Just a quick note to the Com officer on the bridge."

Alesta was cross. "What did you just do? Did you divert Taara somehow? Bel, that's cheating."

Stenstrom leaned back in his chair. "We'll see." He opened the Com. "Gwendolyn?" he said into the air. There was a silence, and then an answer.

"Yes . . . *commander?*" Her voice had the usual sound of Gwendolyn mad, Gwendolyn pouting. He could imagine her sitting down in Engineering, arms crossed, jaw sticking out, Gwen in a full temper.

"Gwen, don't be silly. Can you please come right away to the conference room on deck 6 and we can discuss this face to face? It's rather urgent."

"I will consider it when my duties allo*w* . . . *sir,*" and she Comm'ed off.

"Good Creation, a fine time for her to be in a temper. Has her name been logged onto the disk?"

Alesta held it up. "No, just the previous ones. Wait . . . there it is! We now have Gwen, Melazarr, Gwen again, Taara, and now Gwen a third time."

Stenstrom had a thought. With this latest Gwendolyn entry, he seemed able to manipulate the outcome of this name-gathering session. He Comm'ed Gwen again, but his Com was refused. What a terrible time for her to be mad at him. He had another thought and opened the Com again.

"Morgan? Are you there?"

Nothing. "Where's Morgan?" he asked.

"We don't know," A-Ram said. "She should be here, or perhaps she was called away for a Hospitaler function."

"Com, where is Morgan-Jeterix?" Stenstrom asked.

The Com officer on the bridge answered. "Sir, Hospitaler Morgan-Jeterix does not carry a Fleet MAGGA transponder."

"I see, thank you." Stenstrom checked the pockets of his HRN. "I think I have her personal Com on me here somewhere. She gave it to me once."

"You wish a relationship with Morgan?" Alesta asked.

"Yes, I do, if not here, then elsewhere."

He pulled out a surprisingly large volume of items from the depths of his HRN: vellum, writing implements, small wooden boxes containing powders and oils, a mortar and pestle, a handful of Holystones colored like gumballs, some glass beakers and other such bits. He pulled a large black ball from his coat and set it on the table. It was smooth and glinted in the light.

"What's that?" A-Ram asked.

"This? This is a ball of Shadow tech given to me by Kat, the Black Hat we encountered at Clovis. I was supposed to record some information on it and return it to her, but she didn't wait around to collect. I'd forgotten it was still in my coat."

The ball of Shadow tech oscillated about on the table.

"Why is it moving like that?" Alesta asked.

"It's Shadow tech. it always rumbles around."

"Can you be rid of it? It troubles me," she said.

Stenstrom reached out to dispel the ball and it reacted. It hopped off the table and grew in front of them into a life-sized replica of Kat. She was small and lithe, wearing her baggy black suit with wrappings and bare feet, her delicate fingers wreathed in Shadow tech claws and a black, cat-like tail that flicked about her head. She glanced at Stenstrom a moment, then dispersed apart into a fine cloud of dust and vanished.

"What was that?" A-Ram asked.

Alesta glanced at the disk. "Bel, look!"

On the disk next to Gwendolyn's name was: KAT

"Her, too? So, according to this device, some aspect of me chooses *her* as his soul-mate?"

"Well, yeah, I guess so," A-Ram said, recovering, "though I find the prospect of that rather chilling as, sooner or later, Alesta and I will be encountering her as well." He took a sip of coffee and swallowed with dread. Stenstrom thought about it and laughed.

Did you enjoy fighting me? he remembered her asking.

Yes, yes he had.

Alesta, on the other hand, after coming to terms with the idea, seemed enchanted. A memento from Kat the Black Hat, even a sinister one of toxic Shadow tech, seemed to place her stamp on the proceedings, to validate them for her.

"Oh, Bel, that sounds so romantic," she said. "To meet as enemies in the forlorn mountains, only to find love later on. I'm actually looking forward to meeting her. I imagine she must be an amazing woman, once the Black Hat in her has been properly dealt with, of course. We'll leave that process up to you." Alesta closed her eyes and took a deep, dreamy breath. "I'm sorry, I do enjoy reveling in these sorts of things; I have a weakness for improbable romantic situations and happy outcomes. Imagine if Rammy and I had met in such a fashion." She balled up her fist and gave A-Ram a playful tap on the cheek. "I think it would have been fun, you know, to have engaged in some sort of barbaric situation mano-y-mano and then to have fallen into each other's arms after it was over to tend to our wounds. That would have been something to tell our children."

A-Ram adjusted his collar. "You certainly have some novel ideas pertaining to romance, Bear-Bear." She smiled and nodded.

Listening to Alesta ruminate on improbable and possibly violent romance, Stenstrom laughed softly. He must share Alesta's passions to some degree, because the thought of courting a deadly Black Hat, as Captain Davage had done with Countess Sygillis when she was known as Sygillis of Metatron, intrigued him. It intrigued him very much.

The three sat there drinking their coffee. Time crawled by. The afternoon was nearly over and the evening bell would soon sound. "I really need to get back to my duties." Stenstrom said. "How long have we been in here?"

"You can't leave until this business is concluded, Bel," Alesta said, pointing at the disk. "You have two slots remaining. I wonder what happened to Taara?"

"Don't know." Of course, Stenstrom knew full well what had happened to Taara; he just wasn't saying.

A ruckus came from outside the conference room. Alesta cracked the door. Taara was yelling at somebody far down the hallway, by the lift. Taara had a bad habit of yelling and her voice carried. It was the Bazz in her and he'd talked to her about it several times. There was no need to yell at anybody.

Taara, his dear friend . . . Laughing with her in the mess, snapping her naked butt with a towel after a shower . . .

His soul-mate . . . possibly.

"She's probably on her way here, Bel," Alesta said, excited. "That means . . ."

"I know what that means and it horrifies me."

He hit the Com again. "Gwen, are you there?" The Com opened and hissed in silence. "Gwen, if you're there, please say something. It's urgent."

To his relief she responded. "I'm here, Bel, and I'm sorry. I suppose my behavior this afternoon has been quite childish."

"It's fine. I have A-Ram and Alesta here with me. Come on down and we'll head to the mess, and fill you in on certain things."

"Oh, why didn't you say so? Let me grab my things and I'll be right there."

"Hurry," he said, still hearing Taara rant and rave in the corridor.

Alesta checked the disk and nodded. Gwendolyn's name was now on the disk four times, along with Melazarr, Taara, and Kat the Black Hat, all the names arranged evenly around the radius of the disk in a pie-slice manner.

One slot left.

He tried Morgan one more time. The Com opened but it was distorted, full of static. "Morgan?" he asked.

A garbled voice responded.

"Morgan, I can't hear you."

Outside, in the corridor, Taara called his name. "Bel? You still in the conference room?"

He poked his head out the door and spotted her down by the lift in her red Marine uniform. "I'm here! Hey, can you look at the Com node for the conference room? It seems to be acting up."

"Sure." She walked to the starboard wall and removed a panel. She stuck her head in. "Looks ok to me."

"Adjust it a little, we have bad garble."

Taara reached in. Overhead the Com surged and went in and out. Stenstrom thought he heard many voices superimposed together followed by a singular, empty silence. "Morgan?" he asked again.

". . . *I'm here,*" came a cloudy, ghost-like response. *"I'm awake."*

"Morgan?"

The Com went out. Outside, he heard the wall panel clang as Taara put it back into place. "Alesta, did you get anything?" he asked.

She checked the disk. "Yes, well, I don't see a name, just an odd sort of cloud there." She handed the disk to Stenstrom. In the spot where the final name should go was a faint black cloud that changed shape. He didn't know what to make of it. Hungry and a little irritated, all of this weighed him down, making him feel tired. He'd had enough. "Come on, let's head to the Mess and get some dinner. I think it's pot roast this evening. Feeling hungry?"

"I am," A-Ram said. "And I really need to visit the bathroom—just not that one over there."

"Well, yes, of course, but . . ." Alesta said, not wanting to leave the room.

"No 'buts', come on. The disk is full, I'm hungry, you're hungry, let's go."

Reluctantly, Alesta put her boots back on and A-Ram cleaned up their cups. Stenstrom waited by the door. "Taara, we're going to the mess."

"'Bout time," she said, still standing in the hallway.

A-Ram and Alesta were ready and they turned to exit.

Noise at the far end of the conference room startled them. Light from the service hallway on the left shown through the corridor, and there was Gwendolyn holding an armful of papers. "Oh, there you are Bel, I was checking the pantry as I want to use this room later today for a maintenance conference with the boatswain."

She saw A-Ram and Alesta. "And there you two are! We have been worried sick! You didn't hear the two of us fighting today, did you?"

Alesta squealed with delight and charged across the room, throwing her arms around Gwen causing her to drop her papers.

"Oh, Gwen, Gwen . . . it's so good to see you!"

"And it's good to see you too. You can tell me all about where you've been; I'm dying to hear it."

Stenstrom collected Gwen's things. A-Ram picked up the disk sitting on the table. He glanced at it and then showed it to Stenstrom. The names were still there, etched in. On the reverse, it read:

GWENDOLYN, LADY OF PRENTISS

At the perimeter of the disk, more lettering had appeared. It read:

RUINS OF CAROLINE

"That's where we need to go next," A-Ram whispered. He put the disk away just as Taara met them at the door of the conference room.

"Hey!" she cried. "Sorry I'm late, guys, I got hung up on the bridge. The damn Com wanted me for something, I don't know. Anyway, while I was there, we got a wire out of Xandarr, and I thought you would want to know about it right away." She gave A-Ram a rough hug.

Despite himself, Stenstrom was relieved. "A wire out of Xandarr? Tell me?"

Taara released A-Ram. "The *Hoban Night*, the transport that linked up with us yesterday . . ."

"What about it?"

"She was just destroyed, 6AM of the Tammarack Cluster."

"Destroyed?"

"Yep. The details are still unclear, but it appears she was jumped by a group of Xaphan *Ghome* ships."

A-Ram went to a terminal to call up information on the ship's destruction. Melazarr had been on that ship. He had just spoken to her. "Survivors?"

"Don't know. The *Jackalwere* and the *Woodyard* of the 5th Fleet are proceeding to the area from The Kills to investigate, so looks like they've got it covered. I just thought you'd like to know, since that creepy chick was here with us. Looks like Raiders are at it again. Maybe we should head over there and jump on the Raiders. Might be good prizes for the taking, and there's always revenge to consider."

Gwendolyn adjusted her FEDULA. "Well, we can only hope everyone aboard, including that miscreant from Caroline, made it out into a life boat before the ship was breached. The 5th Fleet will handle it."

"Nah," Taara said. "I'll bet she's right back down there in the Caroline ruins. Can't kill her with that thing she's wearing."

"Pity to whomever stumbles into her path," Gwendolyn added. "Come, dinner awaits."

"What do you think, Bel? Should we head over and get the Raiders? If we make full sail we can be there before Bells-Out," Taara said.

A-Ram called up the information, and seemed taken aback. "Bel . . . look at this."

Stenstrom turned. "What is it?"

"Before she was destroyed, the *Hoban Night* sent out a last signal. Quote: *Comes the Shadow tech Goddess* . . ."

11—The Hunt for the Anatameter Begins

A-Ram landed the Ripcar in the tall grass. Gwendolyn hopped out first, her blue coattails fluttering as her boots dug into the soft ground.

It was mid-day at the Ruins of Caroline. The emerald-green Halalands stretched out bumpy and low to the north for as far as Stenstrom could see. To the south was the craggy shoreline. The choppy waters of the Straights of Elder scraped against the land. To the north-east, situated squarely in the water, was the tall spire of the Sisters' Lighthouse of Caroline. The light from its blue lens, visible even in broad daylight, panned about in a never-ending revolution.

Stenstrom checked his NTHs and jumped out. Gwendolyn took in the sights with an empirical Zenon eye. "So, what are we doing here again, please?"

"We're here to locate Madam Melazarr and gather information pertaining to the attack and destruction of her vessel."

A-Ram helped Alesta out of the Ripcar, she very lady-like in her Merian robes and buttoned up boots.

Gwendolyn wrapped her hand around the hilt of her FEDULA. "I still don't see why our personal intervention is required. The local magistrate is more than capable of handling this matter."

Stenstrom smiled. "Would you like to tell her, Alesta, or should I?"

Alesta scowled.

"Tell me what?" Gwen asked, elbowing Stenstrom in the ribs.

"That final message the *Hoban Night* broadcast pertaining to the Shadow tech Goddess has me curious, and, as Melazarr was a witness to the whole event, I want to interview her."

"That mythical creature again?" Gwen asked. "Why such interest in this, Bel? Are we Privateers or a Warbird full of scholars pursuing a quaint research project? We ought to be making sail in pursuit of the raiders who sank the *Hoban Night*. That is how we can best serve that harlequin slut from Caroline. Right, Alesta?"

Alesta held her robes and flushed. "Normally I wouldn't agree with you, Gwen; however, that crazed woman could use time praying in a proper convent." She turned to A-Ram. "Rammy, are you certain this is the correct place?"

He discreetly pulled the disk out of his coat and consulted it. "Yes." He slipped it back into his pocket. Alesta sighed in frustration.

As before, the Ruins of Caroline lay like pieces of charcoal scattered about a vast grassy patch. The place seemed very still and abandoned. Stenstrom put his hand to his mouth. "Melazarr! We're from the *Seeker*, here to take you to safety! We have questions about the attack on your transport! Melazarr!"

Nothing.

He turned to A-Ram and Alesta. "Have you any guidance or insight regarding this development?"

A-Ram, still in his blue Calvert suit, shrugged. "No, only that this is the correct place to be."

Stenstrom lowered his voice so that Gwen, browsing through the ruins some distance away, wouldn't hear. "But do you agree that being here is the appropriate course of action, given the clue on your device and the Shadow tech Goddess connection?"

"I would say so, yes," A-Ram replied. "Sorry we're not more help, Bel. Perhaps we'll get some insight here. What do you think, Bear-Bear?"

"I think if she's here she might receive something sure enough . . . a black eye and a kick in the rear," Alesta said.

Gwendolyn laughed and examined some faded flowers at the base of a nearby stone. "You want to know what I think, Bel?"

"I believe I can imagine what you think at the moment, Gwen." Stenstrom waded further into the ruins with Gwendolyn, pausing when he came to a crossroads. To the left were the remains of a parlor or antechamber, to the right, down a ways, was the old Caroline chapel, the most intact structure remaining on the grounds. "You know, Gwen, the light here gives your scar the slightest shade of rose."

She winced and covered the scar running across her cheek with her hand. "You know I'm sensitive about that, Bel."

"Why? I think it gives your face character," he said. "So, where's

Melazarr? When that ship was attacked she should have been zapped back down here as usual; and I want to know what happened."

"Well, perhaps the unthinkable occurred and some poor soul was here waiting when she arrived and they've gone off to an evening of illegal activity. I pity that person, whoever he or she might be," Gwen said.

Some distance away, Lady Alesta found a stone adorned with a colorful assortment of flowers and cards left by gentlemen past. She picked up a few cards, seated herself, then read them. She was touched. "Oh, these poor gentlemen. They come out here seeking love, their hearts on full display, and look what might await them—a debauched harlequin in a wire gown and a glowing face, ready to waylay and mangle."

"Lady Alesta, that was not at all nice," Stenstrom called to her.

She continued reading. She did not take back her words.

"She's got a point, Bel!" Gwendolyn said, standing tall on a rock. She put her hand to her mouth. "Biiiitch . . . I mean, Melazarr! Come out from whatever sleazy nest you're currently naked in, you walking, talking hell-hole!"

A-Ram and Alesta laughed.

Stenstrom couldn't help but chuckle. If A-Ram and Alesta were correct, Gwen was destined to be his countess, the matter decided for him by Universal Fate, despite his feelings for Morgan and fascination for Kat.

"Gwendolyn," Stenstrom replied. "That woman could have been killed in space."

"Perhaps next time, then," she said.

A-Ram reached into his coat and pulled out the device again and consulted it.

"Still the same?" Stenstrom asked.

A-Ram nodded.

Stenstrom looked around the craggy ruins. "So, I take it we're in the Hall of Mirrors again?"

"Probably so. And, this time, we're expecting your enemy to come out," A-Ram said.

"My enemy?"

"That's what we were told. Out of the Nodes of Reality, first your love, then your enemy. We have your love, Gwen, now we await your enemy. Then the location of the Anatameter will be revealed," A-Ram said.

"If that's the case then I want you, Alesta, and Gwen to get in the Ripcar and go. I want you gone from here."

"But, Bel, you might need our help,"

"The Sisters are with me, and what I need most is peace of mind that you three are safe. Ok? That's how you can help."

A-Ram wanted to argue but saw the wisdom in leaving Stenstrom alone with the unknown. "Bear-Bear, we're going!"

Gwendolyn emerged from the rocks. "We're leaving?" she asked.

"Not me. A-Ram and Alesta are leaving, and so are you, Gwen," Stenstrom said.

"I'm not leaving you here alone with that giant-sized trollop!"

Stenstrom was in no humor to argue. "Gwendolyn, you're vacating the area, and that's an order."

She turned beet red and showed all the signs of becoming fiercely insubordinate and having a frosty row with him right then and there. But, after glancing at A-Ram and Alesta, Gwen restrained herself. "Why am I leaving, please?" she asked in an enraged calm.

"Because it's come to my attention this ruin might not be safe and I would feel better knowing the three of you are out of harm's way for the time being. Honestly, Gwen, I can handle a wayward Xaphan girl."

"Can you?"

Stenstrom escorted them back to the Ripcar sitting lonely near the sea. A-Ram helped Alesta get seated and Gwen climbed in, her FEDULA rattling. "We shall discuss this in further detail later, *Paymaster*," Gwen said as A-Ram strapped her in.

"I look forward to it, Gwen. All right, don't forget about me."

"We'll be back for you in two bells," A-Ram said, climbing in. "We'll fly west to Feren and get some lunch to pass the time. Want us to bring you anything?"

"I'm good, thank you."

Stenstrom tapped the hood of the Ripcar with his fist for luck and walked away. As he re-entered the perimeter of the ruins he heard the small ship climb into the sky and move safely away to the west.

He felt rather alone and missed their presence as the Ripcar sailed past the horizon. If A-Ram and Alesta were correct, then he could expect his enemy to appear in these ruins. What sort of enemy he could only guess.

Old Gods.

Extra-Planar creatures.

Demented entities drawn to the Antameter.

Who knows? And, furthermore, if they were correct, then the Shadow tech Goddess was here somewhere as well, waiting to come out and lay waste to anything in her path.

The Sisters were with him; he could feel their power tucked up inside. The Sisters' power came and went; they gave it to him when they wished and they took it away just as easily. The easiest way to know if had their power was to look at Morgan. If she appeared "painted," then the power was with him; to see her normal meant it was gone. The Sisters, though, were reliable enough to always give it to him when he needed it. With it, he should be able to handle whatever was to come; and he had his weapons and his skills. He hoped he was ready.

The ruins were quiet. The grass was still a bit dewy from morning. So far, there was no sign of Melazarr, just the level green and tumbled stones. He moved past broken shards of blackened rock littered with the colorful and hopeful detritus of past loves, coming at last to a crossroads. To the left was a long retaining wall leaning to one side in the grass, while to the right was the remains of the Caroline's old chapel.

Left and right: the Hall of Possibilities and the danger that lurked within.

A dash of movement caught his eye. Off to the north a figure in black crouched in chest-high grass. He pulled out his Megaeye and hoisted it to his face. The figure was small and lithe, seemingly female in shape. He saw the stitching in her black clothing and her green eyes peeking through her tight-fitting mask. A black tail flicked.

Was that Kat, the Black Hat he had encountered in Clovis? The one he'd fought with?

The same Kat who would be his soul-mate in another reality according to A-Ram's disk?

Despite himself, he called out to her. "Kat!!"

The figure moved slightly on hearing the name.

"Who's Kat?" said a slightly annoyed voice from behind. He whirled around and there, standing in the sun tall and proud, was Gwendolyn.

He was enraged. "What in the Name of Creation are you still doing here?"

"Well, don't sound so glad to see me or anything, Bel."

"You're supposed to be in the Ripcar with A-Ram and Alesta!"

Gwendolyn got fully in his face. "I didn't want to be on the Ripcar! I want to be here with you!"

"I gave you an order."

"You know I don't much like being ordered around!"

He glanced back to the green north of the ruins where Kat had been. She was gone. "Things could get dangerous here and I don't want to have to worry about you. I was thinking of your best interests."

Gwen looked incredulous. "Dangerous? How so?"

He seethed in frustration. He had to remember Gwen didn't know about what Alesta and A-Ram had told him. But her natural courage and home-grown Zenon stubborn streak were working against him. "Will you do me the courtesy then, of waiting by the shore?"

"I will not. Who's Kat?"

"The Black Hat who nearly killed you and A-Ram in Clovis; that's who. I saw her."

Gwendolyn took his Megaeye. "Wants a rematch, does she?" She scanned about to the north.

"I don't see anything."

Stenstrom TK'ed into the air and had a good look about. He saw nothing. "Nor do I." *Where did she go?*

A small part of him wanted to seek her out, to talk. Her name on A-Ram's disk stuck in his mind.

Kat: soul-mate.

I enjoyed fighting you. Did you enjoy fighting me? she had asked.

Yes. Yes, he had.

A chilly wind blew in from the sea. Gwendolyn hugged herself.

"When we find this person, I've got a few things I'd like to say to her. Zenons can fight Black Hats just as well as the Vith," Gwen said, then headed off in the direction of the chapel.

The Chapel!!

If they were in the Hall of Mirrors and A-Ram's description of it was correct, then Gwen, moving to the right of the intersection, was unknowingly walking down the Hall of Possibilities toward the Shadow tech Goddess.

"Gwen, wait!" She stopped and looked back.

What good was it to be the Sisters' Fist, to be nearly invulnerable, when there was a very vulnerable, very mortal person standing nearby? Small wonder most of the previous Fists employed by the Sisters operated alone—it was easier that way.

He took off his HRN coat, then held it out. "Gwen, take your coat off."

Gwen cracked an ear-to-ear smile. She took off her Fleet coat, folded it neatly, then set it on a building stone. "So, you do love me!"

"Of course I love you."

She allowed him to drape the HRN around her. The coat had a number of arcane properties, one of which seemed to be invulnerability. No matter what damaging hell or misadventure he put the coat through, it survived unscathed. It didn't even get dirty. He had a thought it might also protect the wearer in such a fashion.

"I love how this feels," she said, sliding her arms into the spacious sleeves. The coat was slightly too big for her, especially in the tails. "Takes the bloody chill right out of the air. Alesta told me you'd be offering me your coat."

"That right? Just before you decided to hop out, correct?"

"Yep. She said in the Ripcar that if you loved me, you'd give me your coat. I love you, too, Bel. She also said 'congratulations'." She gave him a kiss. "What is that all about? What did I win?"

Stenstrom looked her over; the long coat suited her, the dark green fabric, the glinting HRN on the collar enveloping the frills of her white Fleet shirt. "You won a trip for two to the Ruins of Caroline in Hala." He straightened the collar for her. "Now, do me a favor. See the chapel over there?"

Gwen glanced at it. "What about it?"

"Please stay away from it. I've heard it's structurally unsafe. That a gentleman injured himself there recently." He had heard no such thing, of course.

"Fine by me," she said, slipping the megaeye into one of the hidden pocktets.

Gwendolyn adjusted her FEDULA to account for the length of the HRN and threw her arms around him. "Perhaps this wasn't a waste of a trip after all. How fortunate for you that you needn't resort to a fad or gimmick to find love. Your love is before you, sir."

Stenstrom could smell Gwen's fine perfume and feel her loving arms around him.

Still, a tiny, distracting voice rang from somewhere deep: *Where was Kat?*

"All right, since you're here, please cover the north grounds. And, remember, stay away from the chapel."

Stenstrom watched her as she drifted north through the maze of old masonry, thoughts of Anatameters and inscrutable Halls of Mirrors vexing his thoughts. He wished Gwen wasn't here. He wished she was on the damn Ripcar heading west.

"Next, you will meet your enemy," A-Ram had said.

Gwendolyn froze in her tracks. "Bel! Bel come here!"

He sprinted towards her and came upon a horrific sight. Ahead, standing upright against a tall shard of stone was Melazarr of Caroline. She appeared to be unconscious; her head lolled against her shoulder and her face was swollen, as if she'd been beaten. She was tied to the shard by a coiled-up length of wire wound so tightly around her chest and shoulders she was bleeding where the wire cut into her skin. A fire burned nearby and she was red in some places, black in others. Wisps of cloying yellow smoke drifted up around her head. The hard green lacquer she had painted her hair with was cracked, revealing a bird's nest of fawn-colored hair within. Long strands drifted around her neck and shoulders. Some distance away, her VERY MARY garter belt, ripped and torn like a mangled snake, hung from a stone.

Gwendolyn drew her FEDULA. "Gods, look at her; she's trussed up like a Nether Day goose and she's badly burned. I'm going to cut her free. She needs Morgan to look her over immediately."

Stenstrom put his hand out and stopped her. "Wait!"

"Bel, what are you doing? She needs help." She raised her voice. "Melazarr, we're going to free you!"

Gwen's voice carried around the ruins in a loud echo. Two large objects hanging from the wire like festive ornaments fell free and clattered to the ground.

He pulled her around the corner of a nearby stone. "Gwen, look at that wire binding her. Look at it carefully and keep your voice down."

She peeked around the stone, then pulled out the Megaeye. She focused in on Melazarr. "I see the wire; it's metallic, a fairly fine gauge, like piano wire or something." She was puzzled. "Hmm, There's a methodical movement along the length of the wire, like insects or . . ." She adjusted the lens. "The movement is coming from a number of silvery charms traveling along the length of the wire. Some of them are emitting that yellowish gas hovering around her head." She lowered the Megaeye. "Looks like Vith mysticism to me."

Stenstrom whispered. "I think this exact contrivance is what blasted me out of the Clovis vault the other day. I remember something like that there. Those pendants on the wire maintain some sort of constant vigilance, and, not only that, they can unleash hell in any number of ways."

"So, what are we going to do? She can't remain there."

Stenstrom peeked around the corner. The two objects that had fallen off of the wire were creating rising pillars of greasy black smoke. He thought they might explode. He flopped on top of Gwen and waited for several long seconds as she noisily struggled beneath him.

"Shhhhh!" he said. "Be quiet!"

Nothing happened.

Cautiously, he got back up and peered around the corner.

The pillars of black smoke were gone, replaced by two people: a gentleman and a lady. They were dressed in black, expensive-looking garments. The gentleman wore a dapper coat with a buttoned up vest and a tiny, near brimless hat. The lady was in a long lacy gown of a style and taste Stenstrom didn't recognize. Her lanky, boney arms were wrapped up in black gauze or bandages that extended all the way to her wrists, revealing her pale spidery hands. Her wrappings reminded Stenstrom of the white wrappings the Sisters wore. She had shiny, walnut brown hair piled up in coiled braids and pushed into a vast, fancy hat that sat on her head like a manhole cover. She squinted behind a tiny pair of lenses similar to the ones A-Ram wore; though much smaller and clinging precariously to the end of her nose. She carried a large black handbag. Her face was remarkable for the fact that it was so unremarkable, neither ugly nor pretty. She did, however, bear a crazed, rather insensate look, particularly in her eyes—like a nightmarishly dark nanny, an insane librarian or a tax accountant from the pit of hell. A smoldering cigarette on a long stick hung out of her mouth.

The man looked annoyed. "And who are you, please?" he said in a nasally voice with a Xaphan accent. "You've interrupted my dinner."

Stenstrom drew his pistols. "I'm Paymaster Stenstrom, Lord of Belmont-South Tyrol, captain of the Fleet Privateer *Seeker*. With me is Lt. Gwendolyn, Lady of Prentiss, and Chief Engineer of the *Seeker*."

"What is your business here?" the man asked.

Stenstrom leveled his NTH's "We are here to effect the rescue of Melazarr, Lady of Caroline."

The man glanced at the woman in black, and they both snickered.

"Ya'?" the woman said in an odd, childlike voice. "Well, here she is!" She reached out with her stork-like arm and seized Melazarr by the hair. She wrenched her head up, placed her other hand on Melazarr's mouth and pushed her cheeks in and out, causing her mouth to move as if she were speaking.

"Hi," the woman said, attempting to imitate Melazarr's voice. "I'm Melazarr and I'm a slut and a dumb bitch." The woman fixed her gaze on Stenstrom and he felt raw malice and chaos pouring out of her.

"She cooked enough yet? This fire's hot," she said to her companion.

The man checked over Melazarr with a dark device. "Ah yes, it's here at last. Let me see . . ."

The woman glanced at the fire and it went out cold, as if it had been stomped dead and doused.

The man held his device. "You did say you are Paymaster Stenstrom of the Fleet Privateer *Seeker*, correct?"

"Correct."

"How convenient. Then, per my information here you are coming with us." He turned to the woman in black. "Kill this Caroline woman; she's no longer needed, and kill Paymaster Stenstrom's companion as well."

Stenstrom cocked his pistols and Gwendolyn drew her FEDULA. "Turn around and place your hands on the stone where I can see them. The pair of you are Deposed to Panel."

"Huh?" the woman asked. "We're what?"

"You're under arrest per authority of the Fleet and the Sisterhood of Light."

The woman pushed her lenses up and laughed. Nonplussed, the man opened his coat and drew out a tiny item. Stenstrom had to squint to see it properly. It was a toy hammer, about two and a half inches long and mounted on a ruddy length of wood serving as a handle. The man had to pinch it between his thumb and forefinger to hold it. He drew a telescoping stick from his coat and mounted the toy hammer to the end.

"All right, enough of this," Stenstrom said. "Drop what you're carrying, step away from Melazarr, and place your hands on the rocks, or I shall put the two of you down right here and now. I'll not ask again."

The man glanced at the woman. "Well, go on, kill the woman, incapacitate the Paymaster, and let us return to dinner."

Stenstrom fired a green NTH shot globe at each of them.

The man had time to scream and drop his hammer as the NTH shot sizzled into his chest. He fell to the ground in a heap of newly dead flesh, his mouth locked into a distended "O" shape.

The woman gritted her teeth and watched the shot come in. To Stenstrom's horror, the NTH shot stopped in mid-air and burned like a tiny green sun before her. He felt TK pouring out of her; only a Sister had such power.

She gasped in wicked delight. "Huh? You like that? Huh?"

She sent the NTH shot back at them. "This is yours, I think! Here!" she cried as the speeding shot hit Gwendolyn square in the chest. She fell backward and dropped her FEDULA as she crashed to the ground.

"Gwendolyn!!" He stared at her stupidly for a moment.

Gwendolyn?

Gwendolyn!!

Dead!!

The woman in black leaned down and casually reached into her bag, her back and rear-end exposed. He aimed his guns and fired.

She swatted the shots aside, sending them in random directions. Some shots hit the ground, killing the grass in a neat circle. She never stopped what she was doing during Stenstrom's fusillade. She stood and pulled a black watch fob with a long chain out of the bag, then walked over to the dead man. Hoisting his rotund dead body into the air with one arm, she wound the chain around his neck several times and then moved the hands on the watch face back about an hour.

The man gasped and kicked, sputtering to life. "Dammit, woman!" he cried. "Go get him! Kill him if you want, but make sure it's a nice clean killing so we can bring him back later. We need his Anatameter!"

Nonplussed, she lit a fresh cigarette. "Ya', ok." She took a long drag. "Hear that, fella'? I'm coming to kill you!"

His NTH's useless, he faded into the Shadows and moved off to the right, trying to get around them.

That watch she was carrying had brought the man back from the dead. It would work for Gwendolyn too. He had to get that watch.

"Where did he go?" the man cried, picking his hammer back up.

"Dunno'," the woman replied. She held out the watch fob. "Hey, mister! You looking for this, huh? Trying to fix your lady over there? Time's a-wasting. Come and get it!"

Stenstrom moved east, thinking out a method of attack to get the arcane watch fob from her grasp.

As he moved into position, the woman seemed to float off the ground, rising higher and higher and letting the watch fob dangle from its chain between her thumb and forefinger. She hung in the air like a skinny black doorstop. She wasn't actually floating; she was being lifted into the air on three, black metallic appendages sprouting out from within her gown like a tripod of articulated legs. He'd seen such a thing before, metallic appendages strapped to the waist and hidden under long coats and gowns, under full control of the wearer like a prehensile monkey tail. VUNKULA, the LosCapricos weapon of the House of Grenville. A person skilled in using the VUNKULA had precise control over it and could move the tail with remarkable speed. VUNKULAs usually sported only one tail; this one the woman was wearing had three and she was standing on them like a set of stilts.

Meanwhile, the man prowled about, holding his tiny hammer like a bat. "Lord Belmont, let's be reasonable here. You have something we want, something we will kill for, obviously. May I suggest a simple transaction, a swap of goods? We can bring your companion back from the dead; wouldn't that be nice? In exchange, you give us what we want: the Anatameter." He looked around. "What do you say? One piece of goods for another?"

Stenstrom produced a MARZABLE dagger, lined him up, and threw.

One of the metallic appendages snaked out of the folds of the woman's gown and punched the dagger out of the way before it could hit. The man gasped in surprise and swung his hammer, clipping a nearby stone and hacking out a huge jagged piece as if it were a full-sized warhammer. "You are overmatched here. You must know that!"

Stenstrom, still faded into the shadows, attacked. The man squealed in surprise when Stenstrom seized and cuffed him across the cheek. The man swung wildly with his hammer. A lucky blow caught Stenstrom in the midsection. The hammer hit with the bludgeoning power of a weapon many times its volume and weight. Only the Sisters' Power flowing through him kept him from being shattered.

Stenstrom subdued the man and wrenched his arm behind his back, causing him to squeal.

He appeared from the shadows.

"I have your man here!" he yelled. The woman grinned and spun the watch fob around her finger.

"So?" she said.

"I'll burn him into ashes so there shall be nothing left to reanimate. Now, give me the—"

The woman belted him across the jaw with one of her three VUNKULA tails. It had moved with uncanny speed. The blow hit with the force of a small grenade and knocked Stenstrom to the ground.

"Ha!" the woman cried with glee.

Her companion scrambled away, grabbed his hammer, then fell upon Stenstrom, beating him across the back and shoulders, each blow thundering into him.

"Now, the deal is off! Your woman stays dead and you too will be dead! Then, we bring you back and we torture you dead again and again until you feel inclined to hand over the Anatameter!"

A lithe figure in black appeared, crouching in the grass.

"Oh, who's this now?" the man cried, panting from his exertion. Before he could say another word the figure attacked and raked its claws across his chest. For the second time, the man fell dead, this time in a pile of horrific cubes of sundered flesh. The figure turned to Stenstrom and seized him by the shirt with bloody hands, then pulled him around a stone.

It was Kat; her green eyes fixed on him. She spoke close in a growl. "Second time I save you, HRN. Second time! How lucky for you I'm here." She formed an StT in her hand and threw it into the pile. The man's remains burst into red and green flames.

Kat put her bloody hand on Stenstrom's chin. "Now," she said, "I . . ."

A metal tentacle came down and tore into Kat's neck and shoulder, jerking her into the air. Kat struggled like a fish on the line and lashed out with laser-like points of Shadow tech. The woman in black cast them aside, turning them to ash.

The woman brought Kat close to her face and, with a burst of TK, reduced Kat's brain to jelly. Stenstrom felt the force of it.

Kat went limp in her grasp.

The woman reared back with the tentacle and flung Kat across the ruins into the tied-up, burned body of Melazarr. The pendants hanging from the wire exploded; no doubt killing both Kat and Melazarr.

The woman strode over to Stenstrom and drove him into the ground with a metal tentacle. She glanced at the ashy pile of her former companion flickering in Shadow tech fire. "Now, what the fuck am I going to do with you? Huh?"

PART 2

THE LOVES OF
PAYMASTER STENSTROM

THE FIRST TURN

1—T̶ʜᴇ HRN

S tenstrom lay there, partially dug into the ground, the woman in black standing over him, victorious.

There was a metal on metal RING! and the woman toppled to the ground where she landed with a dramatic arms and legs thud.

Someone rushed past him.

Gwendolyn, it was Gwendolyn! She had chopped through the metal VUNKULA tentacles with her FEDULA, bisecting all three.

Painfully, Stenstrom stood, trying to collect his wits. Somehow, beyond all hope, Gwen was alive.

A few feet away, Gwendolyn and the woman in black were locked in a clashing sword fight. Two long, saber-like blades had sprouted from her wrapped-up wrists and she was skillfully matching Gwendolyn cut for cut.

"Ca'mon, honey, let me look at you!" she said, trying to fix Gwendolyn in her gaze and lock on with TK.

"Gwen! Don't look at her!" Stenstrom cried, recalling what had happened to Kat. Gwen sidestepped, expertly staying out of her direct gaze. The woman quickly became frustrated, as if she was used to having her way with her opponents with minimal effort.

"Will ya' stand still, will ya', bitch!" she roared.

"Bel!" Gwen cried, desperate. "Bel, help me!" The woman was breaking through her defenses.

He thought fast. So far the woman in black had shown incredible power and foiled all of his attacks. Time to use her own weapons against her. He grabbed her bag sitting in the grass and dug through it. There were things inside that couldn't possibly fit: weapons, trinkets, jewelry, and other such things. Seemed to be a collection of LosCapricos weapons; he even found a spool of wire and a velvet bag full of pewter eyeball charms, though they seemed to be asleep. He found the butt of a rifle and pulled it out. It was impossibly long and coal black.

DEATHLOCK. Stenstrom wasn't an aficionado of the LosCapricos weapons like Captain Davage, but the DEATHLOCK was a well-known instance. It was a rifle that, when fired, would zero in on the intended target no matter how far away they might be. All one had to do was have a victim in mind. And he had a victim in mind. He pointed the barrel skyward and fired.

BOOM!

The woman had almost worn Gwen down. Stenstrom jumped in and, with all his might, punched her square across the jaw, snapping her head around. She grinned and cracked her knuckles. "Now, I'm going to have to get . . ."

The bullet from the DEATHLOCK plummeted down from above and hit her between the shoulder blades, knocking her down. Stenstrom didn't see a bullet hole, just a scorch mark from where the shell exploded.

He shook his hands and produced three green Holystones. He rolled into position for a clear shot and threw them.

"Cheatin' Jo-boy!" she screamed as the severed tail came up from the folds of her black gown and blocked them.

They exploded in a confusion of webs, burying her deep within. She struggled.

He threw a red Holystone and the tangle burst into flames.

Stenstrom and Gwendolyn fell into each other's arms. "Dear Creation, Gwendolyn, I thought you were dead!" He kissed her face and held her.

She squeezed back. "I thought I was dead for a moment," she said returning his kisses. "Your coat saved me, Bel. She got me fair and square right in the chest with an NTH shot. Gods . . ."

They turned to the mass of flaming webbing which rustled as the woman struggled within. They heard her mumbling insults and threats over the flames. "Jo-boy! Jo-boy!!" Stenstrom heard.

The struggling stopped. Stenstrom and Gwendolyn let the fire and molten webbing burn down. The red Holystone burned hot and there probably wouldn't be much left of the woman other than a charred mass. The fire soon lost strength and the burning mass rapidly cooled. They dug through. "She's gone!" Gwendolyn cried rummaging through the ashes with her FEDULA.

There was nothing, just a husk of burned webbing. Elsewhere her handbag had vanished as well. They went to the other side of the ruins looking for the bodies of Melazarr and Kat. They found little if anything; the explosion had consumed them.

2—Proposal in Bed

Stenstrom had never felt closer to Gwendolyn then he did after the ordeal at Caroline. His moments of vacillation with Morgan, Kat, and others were gone. Seeing what he thought was Gwen's dead body lying on the green grass had shocked him. He'd learned a vital lesson; he'd underestimated his feelings for Gwen, had taken her for granted. Perhaps it was her matronly aspect that stirred his soul; that seeing her, apparently dead, was like experiencing his mother's death afresh. Perhaps it was the bravery she displayed afterward.

Either way, feeling her loss had been devastating. He clung to her, determined not to let this second chance be wasted.

As promised, A-Ram and Alesta returned shortly afterward. Eyes wide with delight, Alesta bounded out of the Ripcar and threw her arms around Gwendolyn. A-Ram also was all smiles. He noted Stenstrom's ruined clothing and patted him on the back. "I assume you met your enemy."

"And how. Consult your device, A-Ram. What does it say now?"

A-Ram got the disk out of his pocket. "It says:"

SHRINE OF BORASTER

"What's that?"

"I don't know. We'll look it up later."

They returned to the ship and briefed Taara on what happened. She informed Fleet and they promised to send a follow-up team to the Caroline ruins.

"I'd like Melazarr's remains gathered and returned to her home as decency demands. Kat's as well."

"The Black Hat? She was there?"

"She was."

Stenstrom returned to his quarters to change. Gwendolyn soon knocked on the door, waiting outside with her usual overnight bag. He opened the door and pulled her inside.

Her dead body lying in the grass. Such loss. Such emptiness.

He put her against the wall with a crash and knocked her over-night bag aside, spilling its contents onto the floor. Normally, Gwen was rather tight about showing her love, keeping it private and well hidden behind closed doors. She resisted at first, trying to remain impassive and demure before finally giving in and opening herself to the moment. She climbed up and put her legs around him, the door to his quarters still open.

He dragged her into the bedroom and made love to her as never before.

That night, as they lay in bed in the aftermath, he gently shook her.

"Bel?" she responded, sleepy.

"Gwen, wake up please."

"I'm tired, darling. We'll make love again in the morning, alright?"

He felt the smooth fabric of her night gown and the heat of her sturdy body. She always put a night gown on after they finished making love. Why he didn't know; it was a ritual she had.

"Gwen."

She jostled about, her hair all over the place. "What are you doing, Bel? I'm tired. I was almost killed today, and so were you."

"I thought I'd lost you," he whispered

"I'm fine."

"I—I've taken you for granted, Gwen. I've allowed the familiarity of our relationship to get the better of me. My thoughts . . . have been straying recently."

Gwen paused a moment. "You mean Morgan? I was hoping you might come to me and discuss the matter. I thought you were tiring of me. I know . . . I know I can be a stiff . . ."

"I thought Morgan was fascinating, and seductive. I admit that. But, seeing you, apparently dead, I realized what I had and what I almost lost. I put my coat on you on a whim. If you hadn't been wearing it you'd be gone. And that thought was—is—devastating for me."

Gwen maneuvered around and took him into her arms. Their bodies fit together well. "What are you trying to say, Bel?"

"I'm saying that I love you. You, Gwen—not the stuffy person you force yourself to be during the day. You, that magnificent brave woman who fought at my side today. This afternoon, before you arrived in the conference room, A-Ram and Alesta told me the next person to enter the room would be my soul-mate—and there you were carrying your armload of things."

"How would A-Ram and Alesta know that?"

"It's a long story. So, I'm hoping if I extend you my hand, you might put that stuffy Lt. Gwendolyn away for good and be at ease to be the true Gwendolyn, whom I love."

"Bel, are you asking me to marry you?"

"I am. I wish you as the first Countess of Belmont-South Tyrol."

Gwendolyn didn't say yes or no as they lay in bed, but her actions, kissing him about the face and neck and holding him tightly and weeping, spoke for her.

"I have something I'd like to give you, Gwen. I've had it for awhile."

"A present for me? I don't have anything for you."

Stenstrom slipped out of bed and went to his bureau. He opened a drawer and took out a small box. He returned to the bed, Gwen sitting up in her nightgown.

"Your beating heart and warm breath is gift enough. Take this as a symbol of my love."

Gwen opened the box. Inside was an intricate, finely crafted ladies watch resting on a cushioned backing, its silvery face gleaming under an exquisite crystal. "Ohhh," Gwen exclaimed.

She took it out of the box and held it up to the starlight.

"I know the Zenon custom for a man to purchase a special gift for his lady when he extends her his hand. I got it some time ago on the Gold Coast of Hoban at a fine jeweler's make. It tells time in standard Kanan bells and in Hoban hours. It has both an analog display and a holographic one if you prefer a more modern treatment."

"I fancy watches with an analog face and I love silver," she said, putting it on.

"It's not silver; it's platinum. I wanted to get you something I thought would last, something I thought you could use every day."

Gwen pulled off her nightgown and took Stenstrom into her. He felt the cold metal of the watch around her wrist as they made love again and again.

★ ★ ★ ★ ★

A few hours later, deep into the night bell, there was a knock at the door. Already acting with more regal confidence, Gwendolyn got up to see who it was—shoeless and in her nightgown, something she had never done previously. She had always hid when in his room.

Stenstrom, mostly asleep, saw the light come on in the living area of his quarters and drift through the door. He heard the muffled sound of Gwen talking to someone.

"Bel, wake up. Come out here," she said from the other room.

After easing out of bed, he pulled on a pair of bottoms, then went out into the living room.

A-Ram and Alesta sat on the couch. Alesta was all smiles.

"Congratulations, Bel! Gwen just told me!" She got up and gave Stenstrom a gigantic hug.

Gwendolyn went into the kitchenette. "I'd always envisioned my wedding announcement taking place in some grand Zenon ballroom, but being here in close quarters with the people I love most, I'd not have it any other way. The only person we're missing is Taara, but there's no possibility of getting her out of her rack at this hour. We'll bring her up-to-date first thing in the morning. Anyone for coffee? I'm going to make a celebratory pot."

"Me!" A-Ram said.

"Me, too!" Alesta said. "Bel, do you mind?" she said, pointing to her traveling boots.

"No, no, be comfortable."

She sighed and undid the buttons, then set her boots aside.

It suddenly hit him he was wearing nothing but a pair of bottoms. "I need to get changed."

"Ah, the hour is late and we're all friends here, Bel," A-Ram said.

Everyone was all smiles as they waited for Gwendolyn to finish with the coffee. "You've made Gwen very happy, Bel. And, you'll see the change in her for the better now that you're formal. You will!" Alesta said, beaming. "The watch looks beautiful on her."

Gwendolyn joined them with a coffee service.

"So," Stenstrom said. "I'm assuming this early morning visit has to do with the events at the Ruins of Caroline today."

"That it does, Bel," A-Ram said, taking a drink. "Great coffee, Gwen."

"It's nothing like yours."

A-Ram laughed and finished his cup.

Gwen seated herself next to Stenstrom. "So, we're all friends here, and as I am now the Countess-in-waiting to the House of Belmont-South Tyrol, I feel that I should by privy to all. Is there anything I should know here?"

"N-N-No," Alesta stammered, she being a poor liar. "What makes you say that?"

Gwen grabbed a sheet of paper and a marker. She settled next to Stenstrom and began drawing. "While I was flat on my back in Caroline wondering how and why I was still alive, I had a vision. I saw this . . ." She showed them what she had drawn.

"This? What is this? I'm fairly well certain you know what it is?"

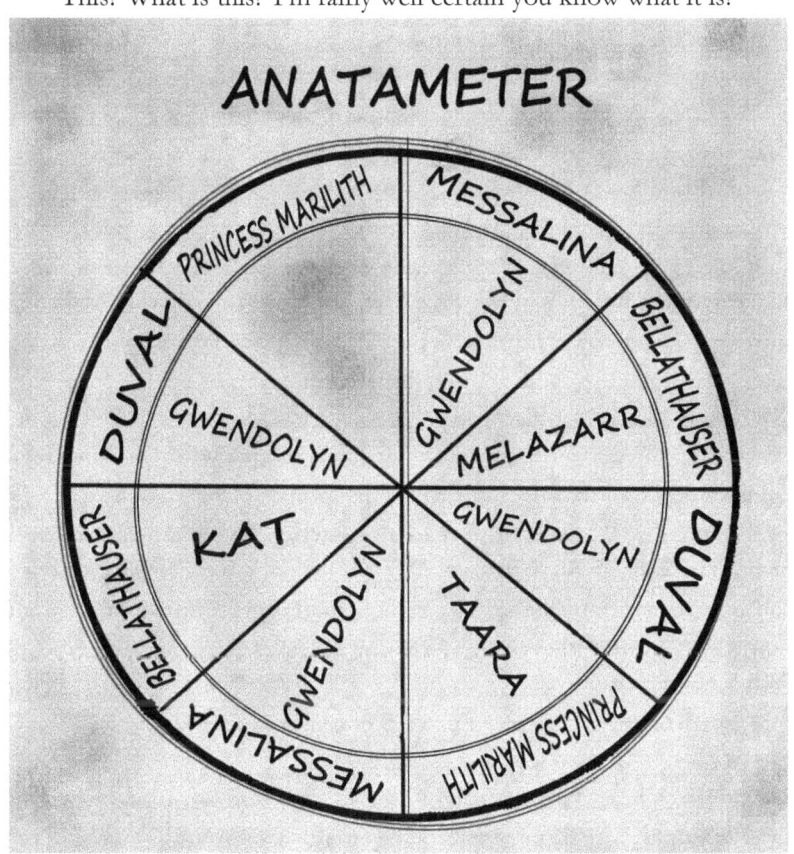

Stenstrom looked at the paper and told Gwendolyn everything. He told her about Anatameters and Halls of Mirrors and differing planes of reality. Gwendolyn, sitting there in her nightgown, took it all in with remarkable calm. He wasn't certain how long he talked, but he noticed the same distinctive spit of land in Esther pass by the window several times, so it had to have taken at least a bell or two.

"So, if I understand correctly, you're saying these eight portions represent different versions of Bel and these names here signify the woman he is with?"

"That's right, Gwen," Alesta said. "His soul-mate."

Gwendolyn looked a bit perturbed. She pushed the paper away. "I don't understand. Why isn't my name there all eight times?"

Alesta shrugged. "Different places, different choices. Look, you're listed four times, more than anybody else. You might have had more if you hadn't been angry with Bel today."

Gwen didn't accept that as an answer. "I should be Bel's soul-mate in all places; he would certainly be mine. Look at these names: Morgan, *Melazarr of Caroline* for Creation's sake! Kat, I don't know who Kat is . . . Taara? Taara is our friend and nothing more."

"Not as we see here," Alesta said.

Gwendolyn stared at the drawing and stewed a bit. Alesta finished her cup and snuggled into A-Ram's shoulder. "Things are now well in motion. Today was a turning point of sorts, for a number of reasons. You confirmed Gwen as your soul-mate in this realm of existence. You saw what tends to happen to the also-rans, to Madam Melazarr, to the Black Hat, the women who could have been your soul-mate. They tend to die. I don't know why, but that seems to be the case."

He considered the prospect of not having Gwen and felt her loss again. He glanced at her. There she was, drinking her coffee, sitting on the couch, wearing her watch, bathed in the greenish glow of Kana coming in through the window. He quickly tried to dismiss the thought of her dying.

"But what about Taara? I'm very concerned. I certainly don't want her to die."

"I don't know. If she can avoid the Hall of Mirrors, I think she'll be fine. Might be wise to keep a distance from her until this is concluded. I shall pray to the Star that nothing happens to her. Taara's our friend too."

A-Ram jumped in. "Let's move on, please. Taara's not going to die. We haven't seen her dead yet. We also learned today who your enemy is, Bel," A-Ram said. "The gentlemen who got killed in Caroline is—or was—Rodrigo of Burgon. I believe Madam Caroline mentioned him and his Nihilists of Punt."

"Who are they?" Stenstrom asked.

A-Ram continued. "A non-League sect whose stated purpose is to bring about the end of the universe; and, before you ask, we have no idea why anyone or any group affiliation would want to do such a thing. From what we've been told, there's a mythical place called Punt and there they worship an entity whom we have become quite familiar with as of late."

Stenstrom knew. "The Shadow tech Goddess?"

"Correct. The Punts seek her out hoping to entice her to destroy the universe. They seek her by way of the Hall of Mirrors and the Anatameter; and now that they've locked onto yours we can expect to be seeing them again. Now, the woman in black, her name is Messalina and she was his paid bodyguard. She's your enemy in this realm, as her name now appears on the disk," A-Ram said.

"This 'Messalina' person was incredibly powerful. She stopped an NTH shot cold and had mastery over TK only the Sisters display," Stenstrom said.

"She is a Sister, Bel, or, more precisely, she *was* a Sister. She's fallen Sister—a member of the Order of Lacerta," Alesta added.

"The what?"

She continued. "The Sisters aren't perfect. Sometimes they tire of the stern life they're expected to live. It's not something the Sisters like to discuss much, but sometimes they fall and become one of the Order of Lacerta. They are formidable foes. They have all of the Sisters abilities and none of their inhibitions. They are hedonists, freely indulging in what was once forbidden to them: good food, nice clothing. Sex, oh, they are ravenous for sex, and drugs too."

"She talked a lot and had a foul mouth," Gwen added.

A-Ram agreed. "Lacertas like to talk as well. They re-learn how to use their mouths and enjoy swearing, so we're told."

"That much is confirmed. So, now what?" Stenstrom asked. "We've followed the steps, and I'm eager to rid myself of this Anatameter device once and for all."

A-Ram pulled the disk from his coat. "The word that formed on the disk as the battle concluded, 'SHRINE OF BORASTER', is the key to moving forward."

Gwen's ears pricked up. "Boraster?" she repeated. "Boraster was one of the Elders, yes?"

"Yes," A-Ram said.

Gwen puzzled over it. "I know of no such shrine. Boraster was virtually unknown. His name is simply listed as one of the twenty-five Elders. There are no stories that I recall where he was installed as a featured eminence, no associated lore. His name was simply listed along with the rest."

A-Ram finished his coffee while Alesta spoke.

"We are told that the Elders took turns holding sway over us prior to their death during the EX time epoch. Each time we moved from one planet to another, a different group of Elders came to the front, while the previous fell into obscurity. Here on Kana Nylax, Va, Faquil, Terfall, Auld, and Selax were the predominate Elders. However, in a different time epoch on a previous home world, Boraster held supreme power. And from what we've discovered, he was rather more heavy-handed and apt to indulge in god-worship than Nylax ever was."

"That was a long time ago, and clearly it's been forgotten. So, where is this shrine located?" Gwendolyn asked.

A-Ram shook his head. "Unknown. That was over a hundred thousand years ago and the location of his shrine is lost to the ages. However that is where your Anatameter is currently located. You must go there and turn the dial."

Gwendolyn turned on the Holonet. Brilliant images spun about the room as she accessed data. "It seems our search might be extensive. I'm not finding any data pertaining to the location of the Shine of Boraster. It's mentioned here in the database, and that various scholars agree that such a place once existed in the ancient past, but there's nothing more." She read the data and flushed. "Oh, well, look who it is, I see a certain scholar, EVoR Hannah-Ben Shurlamp, professor emeritus, University of Dee, has written several papers on the subject. Remember her, the woman with the arrogant statue out at Clovis? She seems to think the Shrine is located on Eng, our ancient home world."

"Perhaps she has the information we need," Stenstrom said.

"Oh, please. Eng, just like Cammara, Emmira, Lemmuria, and Earth, all former home worlds, is lost to the ages. Nobody, including this corseted tea-drinker from the University of Dee, knows where Eng is, and, therefore, nobody knows where the Shrine is as well," Gwen said. She turned to A-Ram and Alesta. "Seems like a dead end."

Alesta smiled. "We are told our contact might soon have some promising information regarding the location of Eng. We should know more tomorrow."

"How so?" Gwen asked, her curiosity rising.

"Even as we speak, an alternate version of Bel is questing for the location of Eng. We should have it soon."

"Well then, I hope I find success," Stenstrom said. "In the meantime, we'll try to contact this Professor Shurlamp in the morning and possibly learn more. If the Shrine is located on Eng, then we'll need some idea of where on Eng it is. An entire planet is a lot of territory to cover."

A-Ram finished his coffee. "I've been told professors can be a bit of a handful."

Gwen powered down the terminal. "Can they? I'm certain we can handle one dyspeptic bookworm from Calvert. We'll feed her some information and take what we need. If she starts asking too many questions, we'll turn to stone on her and let her twist."

A-Ram and Alesta stood up. "We're going to be in and out a lot over the next few days; we've other places to visit as well. When you see us next, we should know where Eng is located. Good night, and once again, congratulations."

3—Hannah-Ben Shurlamp

First thing in the morning, Stenstrom and Gwendolyn got up and looked for A-Ram and Alesta. As promised, they were gone—missing from the ship. Not surprising, yet a bit disappointing.

They then had breakfast with Taara, who chattered on about nothing for the whole meal. They attended to their various duties and then reconvened in the conference room to contact Professor Shurlamp. It took a great deal of doing—Gwendolyn performing most of the work—to maneuver through a bewildering avenues of data and reach her sprawling Data Temple. Gwendolyn knew a little about hacking a Data Temple; however Professor Shurlamp's was devilishly complex and well beyond Gwen's means to crack it.

"Oh look at this, she's charging a fee to get out of the public levels of her Data-Temple, Bel," Gwendolyn said with dismay. "We're not going to get anywhere unless we pay."

"How much?"

Gwendolyn gasped. "Seven thousand solaris? Is this woman insane?"

Stenstrom shrugged. "Fine, we'll pay it."

"Seven thousand solaris? I say we jack-out and consult a library or simply wait for this 'other you' to gather the data. All I know is that 'other' you better have an 'other' version of me there at your side."

"Who knows how long that will take. Gwen, let's do it. If this professor has useful information, it will be worth it."

She reluctantly uploaded the money from the ship's stores and got into the higher levels of the Data Temple where the Holoflashes, real people lined-in to the Professor's Temple, resided in rooms full of data. She got routed from one Holoflash to the next, answering an endless retinue of questions. "No, I do not have an appointment!" she shouted over and over.

"Please hold," was the dry response and Gwendolyn stewed as they waited.

"I have little patience for Holonet nonsense," she said.

"Nor do I, that's why I'm letting you do it."

Eventually, after a lengthy wait, the holoscreen switched to a somber header advising their connection to EVoR Hannah-Ben Shurlamp would begin within the minute and to have all necessary materials ready.

A connection opened to a vast office filled with wonderful baroque furnishings and padded silk-papered walls of stately red. Sitting at a dragonball desk of dark cherry wood was a slender woman. She wore a frothy white gown of lacy complexity, her arms, hands, and delicate face were powdered a stunning shade of white and she wore a towering wig of tight white curls. Dancing around her head in a steady orbit was a dizzying array of holo-screens blasting out images, data, reports, codes, charts, and graphs. She held a wand-like control glyph in her slender hand, flicking it here and there.

She spoke with a steady, cultured accent. "Paymaster Stenstrom, captain of the Fleet Privateer *Seeker*, 3rd Wing, greetings. I am Hannah-Ben Shurlamp, EVoR. I believe congratulations are in order."

"For what, Professor?"

"For your engagement."

Both Stenstrom and Gwendolyn puzzled over how she could have known about that since it was only hours old; then Gwen recalled the watch sitting on her wrist, an obscure give-away. Hannah-Ben Shurlamp had a fast eye for detail and a fertile head for putting together connections.

Before Stenstrom could answer, she spoke again. "I will advise you to make haste. Your initial fee is not unlimited and my time is short."

"Thank you," he replied. "I have a question pertaining to the Elder Boraster. I'm told you are the premier authority on the subject."

She nodded. "I have written a number of well-received treatments regarding the Elder Boraster. They are all published and a matter of public domain. I will thank you to carefully study them."

Stenstrom went on. "Specifically, we seek information regarding a certain shrine or temple ascribed to him: the Shrine of Boraster."

"And why, sir, does a place not seen by Elder eyes in over one hundred thousand years interest the likes of you; if it exists at all?"

"My reasoning is my own, Madam."

She shrugged. "I see. Here is some public-knowledge for you. In days long past, Boraster was the chief of all Elders in various matters. By himself he brought the Haitathe of old to Kana from parts unknown. He had hoped to interbreed our two species and create a heartier, larger Elder-Kind. Now then, this particular shrine was built by the Sisters in tribute to Boraster two-hundred and fifty-seven thousand years ago. A demon is said to live there, and there is also the persistent story of a trapped woman, a goddess, requiring rescue. A fanciful tale that has survived the centuries."

"We understand the Shrine is possibly located on the planet Eng, and . . ."

"Not possibly, sir. If it exists, it is located on Eng. There can be no doubt. Now, my question to you is why? Why ask such a thing, the pair of you are no scholars. You are Privateers. What profit is in it?"

Stenstrom and Gwendolyn sat there and felt interrogated. "We need to go there; and we need some idea where on Eng it might be located."

"Go there? To Eng? Eng's stellar positioning is unknown."

"We might have some information," Stenstrom proffered.

That seemed to get the professor's full attention. She moved the floating holo screens aside with a flick of her glyph and stared hard at them. While she, at first, appeared to be a white seraph, on second glance hints of raven danced all about her. Her pool-like eyes were deep brown and her skin under the powder appeared olive in hue. From beneath her wig, tendrils of coal-dark hair lay on her shoulders. "Information? On Eng? Tell me."

"We are performing research, nothing more," Gwen said, jumping in before Stenstrom could answer. "It's a passing hobby of mine."

"A hobby? You previously said you might have information regarding Eng's stellar positioning; now you say you're merely performing research to satisfy a hobby, of which you paid seven thousand solaris to entertain? So, which is it to be? Tell me the information and I will attest to its merits or point out its shortcomings. What do you know?"

"We paid to ask you questions, Professor, not the other way around," Gwendolyn said.

"Well then, here, I have refunded your solaris, plus a little extra as payment for your time. My interest in this matter comes not necessarily for the Shrine and its charming stories of demons and dames in need of rescue, but for Eng itself. Eng's stellar positioning has been lost and has been a topic of great scholarly debate for some time. To the scholar who can re-discover it will come recognition and accolades which are very important to a person such as myself, but would mean little to a pair of spacefarers such as you—no insult intended. After all, what are scholarly dreams, but just that? Being spacefarers, perhaps you've heard something in your travels? Some rumor or piece of gossip, in Xaphan space, maybe, where you ply your Privateering trade. Starfaring vessels are a treasure trove of information, and I would be happy to pay for such assistance."

"Professor, give us a moment, please, Gwen asked.

"Of course."

Gwendolyn muted the Com and disabled the screen. "What should we do, Bel? I don't know if I trust this woman."

"She just spelled out her intentions. All she wants to do is take credit for re-discovering Eng. If she'll help us find the Shrine, then so much the better, at least she'll be motivated."

The door to the conference room opened and A-Ram and Alesta rushed in.

"You're back!" Stenstrom said.

A-Ram was a bit out of breath. "We are, we are!! Oh, some of the things we've seen."

"Did I win?" Stenstrom asked. "Was I successful?"

"Oh yes. We have new information, Bel, and we're glad we caught you," Alesta said. "First, did you attempt to contact Professor Shurlamp?"

"We did, in fact she's on the Com even as we speak." A-Ram and Alesta gave a start.

"Don't worry, she's muted and the screen's disabled."

"Did you tell her much?"

"Not really."

"We have the information as we promised, you did succeed, Bel, but we made a bad mistake previously. We thought that the name Messalina on our disk referred to the Lacerta you encountered in Caroline. It seemed only natural, but we were wrong."

A-Ram jumped in. "Were we ever. Listen, 'Messalina' is actually a code name. In the Hertogs, Messalina is a name referring to none other than Hannah-Ben Shurlamp, EVoR herself. In this reality she is your main enemy, Bel."

"And how so?" Gwendolyn asked. "She's just a professor sitting in a room of padded silk paper watching her trades go spinning by. What's she going to do, egg-head us to death?"

"Gwen, this Professor . . . she's into everything, and she is pulling all the strings. The Lacerta with Rodrigo, she was actually working for Professor Shurlamp."

"Why?"

A slight noise came from the Com. All eyes turned to the monitor. The screen was back on and the mute feature had been disabled. Somehow Hannah-Ben Shurlamp had done it from remote. She had heard every word they had just said.

She spoke. "Burgon does happen upon interesting finds every so often. As I said, re-discovering the location of Eng is quite important to me. Rodrigo of Burgon was said to have access to information on the subject, and so my paid associate kept tabs on him. And, in fact, she mentioned your name. You said you had additional information. What is it? Whomever you are working for, be it known I am an interested buyer and will better their offer, plus one thousand solaris. I am here now and I am willing to bid sight unseen."

"Bel!" Alesta cried.

Gwendolyn tried to cut the Com link, but it would not go out.

"Two thousand solaris, then," Hannah-Ben said.

A-Ram ran to the Com monitor and pulled the cabling from the wall.

"Ten thousand sol—," came her voice as the connection faded.

"Good Creation, Bel, we're sorry we didn't get here sooner!" A-Ram cried.

The overhead shipboard Com crackled to life. The smooth, accented voice of Hannah-Ben Shurlamp rained down on them. "Twenty-five thousand solaris. That is my top offer. Understand, Paymaster, you do not want me as an enemy. You would do much better with me as your benefactor, your ally; I can assure you of that." Gwendolyn killed the connection.

"Come," Alesta cried. "Let's away from here where we may speak in peace."

Immediately, the Com buzzed, demanding to be answered.

"Let's go!" A-Ram said as they exited the room.

As they left, the Com buzzed relentlessly after them down the hallway.

They traded the well-lit splendor of the upper-reaches of the ship for the chilly, pitch-dark hold at the bottom where the Merians lived shielded from power and technology, as was their way. Stenstrom, having become fond of the Pilgrims of Merian after the Drury Incident, gave them the spacious hold and a good part of Deck 10 to do with as they would. Using mismatched and donated materials, they created a primitive world in miniature. Alesta allowed them in and lit a candle. In the flickering orange light, she led them through the zig-zag of make-shift wooden structures the Merians had built to her small room in a wooden dormitory in the center of the hold immediately adjacent to a barn full of cows. Here in this technology-free soak there seemed no way Professor Shurlamp could get to them.

They pulled up chairs as A-Ram built a fire in the small grate. Alesta's room was quite plain, just a few chairs, a spindle, a closet full of Merian clothes, and a bed with a nightstand. A picture of A-Ram sat on her nightstand. Gwendolyn sat down next to Stenstrom and took his hand. "I'm not certain what all the fuss is. Professor Shurlamp is just that, a professor. How dangerous can she possibly be?"

Alesta allowed A-Ram to seat her and she adjusted her robes. "Her role, from what we've seen so far, is rather changeable. She can be a great help and a valuable alley, or she is a very dangerous and ruthless foe. I think she's a Bloodstein by birth . . ."

Gwendolyn sighed. "Oh dear, not another Vith lunatic."

"Her brilliance has never been called into question; it's her methods that have people in the learned circles talking. She's been accused of stealing other people's work and taking credit for them. They say she has money all over the place, in the Ex-Commons, the Science Ministry, even the Fleet; and she employs an army of thugs to carry out her bidding. We've also heard she'll step on anybody who gets in her way, and, something like this, the re-discovery of one of our former home worlds is a ripe prize for a scholar. If she thinks information like that is to be had, then she won't rest."

"None of this is proved," A-Ram said, "and it sounds a little ridiculous to me, actually."

"It seems her only interest in this matter lies with taking credit for the re-discovery of Eng. Why don't we simply give her what we know and eliminate her from the proceedings?" Stenstrom asked.

Gwendolyn answered. "Because, Bel, *we* are going to re-discover Eng, not *her*."

"Come again?"

"The Professor said it herself, the quest to re-discover Eng has been a key topic of scholarly debate for centuries. I recall attending several lectures on the subject when I attended the University of Arden, and the topic became a passing hobby of mine. Though the subject is simply a matter of scholarly prestige, I think that prestige should be ours. We'll prove Eng's location. It would be a great piece of notoriety for our House, something we can hang our hat on."

"I appreciate your enthusiasm, Gwen, but if we can appease the Professor, it will be one less thing to worry about."

"I honestly cannot fathom how a powdered, wig-wearing professor sitting behind her desk in Calvert could be any nuisance going forward. Now that we know of her interest we simply keep her out of the loop. She obviously has various technological tricks to force her way into our Com system; I've seen such a thing before and I'll change the codes immediately. That will be the end of her."

"Gwen, are you certain?" Alesta asked. "What about the Lacerta in her employ?"

"What about her? I shan't think we'll see her again. Now, let us speak no more of this boorish woman. Our first clear task is to locate Eng. What information do you have, Alesta?"

"According to our source, and thanks to Bel's efforts in another reality, the Grand Abbess of Magravine knew where Eng was. She recorded its location."

"The Grand Abbess of Magravine?" Stenstrom repeated with a bit of shock. "You mean the Black Abbess, the leader of the Black Hats? Is that what you meant to say?"

"She eventually became the Black Abbess, yes," Alesta said quietly.

A-Ram jumped in. "But, before that—before the Black Abbess—she was said to have kept lore alive regarding the location of Eng at her old temple at Magravine."

"And I figured this out in another universe?" Stenstrom asked.

"You did. You fought hard for that information."

"Well, perhaps somebody should have knocked me upside the head."

Gwendolyn's fertile mind was beginning to percolate. "Magravine was destroyed ages ago by the old Vith. There's nothing left of it but a crack in the ground. My University of Arden performed an extensive series of excavations there some years back, and I recall attending a display where many of the artifacts and collected materials from Magravine were publically presented for viewing; it was quite fascinating. If the location of Eng had been discovered at Magravine, then that would have caused a sensation."

Alesta agreed. "It would have, yes. However, there are things at work at Magravine that have escaped scholarly notice. There is much there, yet to be discovered. And danger is there as well."

"How so?" Gwendolyn asked, skeptical.

"We've learned there is a Grand Animalium located at Magravine."

"A what?" Stenstrom asked.

"Grand Animalium," Alesta said. "The Elders made an extensive collection of various wild DNA as our ancestors traveled with them across the cosmos in ages past. This goes back nearly half a million years, starting at mythical Earth where we all supposedly came from. Then, through the Epochs of Time, we traveled across the cosmos with the Elders, to forgotten Lemmuria, to Emmira of golden light, to Cammara where we were made young and healthy, to Eng where the Elders began to fade, and then to Kana where we are now. Through our travels, the Elders collected complete samples of local flora and fauna and saved them in stasis in a vast library. When we arrived here at Kana 100,000 years ago at the beginning of the EX Epoch, the planet was bare of native life; as if it had been scoured away. The Sisters now believe that the Kestrals, who occupied the planet at the time, had wiped it clean, except for the Monama peoples to the south leaving us a largely empty, yet fruitful world. Seeing the planet bereft of life, the Elders created several automated 'stations' and buried them deep in the ground. There, nurtured by vast technology, they placed the various collected samples they had gathered through the ages—a mix of animal and plant life from Earth, Lemmuria, Emmira, Cammara, and Eng. At a measured pace, animals came forth from these stations, these 'Grand Animaliums' as the Sisters call them. Plant life was seeded on the wind. Life spread out and filled the empty spaces of Kana."

A-Ram jumped in. "The Elders didn't want to share this technology with us so they guarded these Grand Animaliums."

"How many of these facilities are there?" Gwendolyn asked.

"Seven," A-Ram said. "There's one deep underneath the Sisters' stronghold of Valenhelm to the north. Another is suspected to be located near the Hazards of the Old Ones in the Tartanlands. One in Esther, two in the foothills of Remnath, one in the Great Armenelos forest, and the final one is at Magravine at the bottom of the chasm."

Gwendolyn was unconvinced. "Not possible. The scholarly studies would have uncovered such an oddity."

"The Animaliums are Elder tech of a potent kind and veiled in secrecy. They are keyed right into your senses and your Gifts as well. You could be looking right at one and not see it. You could be standing in one and never know it," A-Ram said.

"Illusions can be defeated," Gwen said.

A-Ram disagreed. "It's not an illusion. It's a matter of altered perception that cuts deep."

Stenstrom closed his eyes and felt tired. "So what's to be done, then?"

Alesta continued. "There is a bit of hope. You're familiar with Blanchefort village, correct?"

"Certainly, I've been there many times."

"There is a small college there. Do you know it?"

Stenstrom opened his eyes. "Sarfortnim College, just a little place. My friend, Lt. Kilos, is a big fan of the college's brandtball team; the 'Forties' they're called."

A-Ram clapped his hands. "Oh, I love brandtball! The St. Edmunds Tarpons are my team, the old Greenbacks. Brandtball is in my blood. St. Edmunds rules, unlike bowling that I'm not too keen on."

Alesta took immediate exception. "Well, Rammy, I thought you liked to bowl."

"Oh, Bear-Bear, I like to watch you bowl, you know that. But when you're not around, I really don't like bowling."

She glared at him, and Gwendolyn laughed. "You two are simply too cute."

Alesta gave A-Ram another dubious stare. "We shall discuss this further later, Rammy. Meanwhile, back to the topic at hand. At

Sarfortnim College, there's an odd set of artifacts in their displayed collection. They're not much to look at—basically a set of rough-hewn stone helmets going back to the early EX days, making them approximately ninety thousand years old. They're relics from the old temple at Magravine, one of the few items to survive the Vith attack there. They're considered interesting if unremarkable museum pieces. What's not commonly known is that these two helmets contain Elder tech. When wearing these helmets, the many defenses exhibited by the Grand Animaliums are rendered ineffective. You'll then be able to see what is really at the bottom of the chasm at Magravine. There you will find the location of lost Eng."

Stenstrom shook his head. "So, let me make sure I've properly absorbed all of this: we are to go to Sarfortnim College, borrow a set of Elder artifacts, go to Magravine chasm and determine the long, lost location of Eng, then go to Eng and finish turning the dial of the Anatameter. Have I got that?"

"You have, Bel," Alesta answered. "And don't think we've seen the last of Professor Hannah-Ben Shurlamp. If she overheard us talking in the conference room and she believes the stellar location of Eng is to be had, then you can bet she won't give up until that information is hers, by means fair or foul."

After that, they sat there on their respective couches before the crackling fire in Alesta's room, no one saying anything.

4—Sarfortnim College

A-Ram put the Ripcar down at the ship park at the far southern end of the Blanchefort village docks. Stenstrom and Gwendolyn jumped out, their boots making a pounding hollow sound on the wooden planks of the dock. A-Ram and Alesta remained within.

"We must leave," A-Ram said. "But don't worry, we'll be back at the correct time."

With that, they sealed containment and A-Ram lifted the little craft away, moving to the south along the edge of the coast past the Elephant swim.

Gwen and Bel stood there for a moment and took everything in.

Blanchefort village. From the south-side docks, the place looked bewildering, a tumbled collection of huddled wooden buildings and taut narrow streets following the long natural curve of the bay. At first glance it might be considered a salty Barbary city, like those found in Calvert. However, the buildings past the docks were all perfectly straight up and down, and the architecture was distinctly Vith in precision and design. A few Vith domes of stone and copper peeked above the rooftops. Beyond the buildings was a steep shelf of impressive mountains that climbed into the heights. Perched at the top was Castle Blanchefort, elegant and dominating as always. Behind the castle was the low-hanging green fog of the Telmus Grove.

Gwendolyn felt the cold wind blowing in from the bay and closed her coat. "It is freezing." She placed a protective hand on her scar. "It's making my face hurt." Her long brown hair caught the breeze and took flight. "How can these Vith stand it here?"

Stenstrom, in his HRN, felt just right. "Dav's never admitted it to me, but I'm pretty sure the Vith are impervious to cold; doesn't bother them in the least. You'll get used to it, Gwen."

Holding her coat shut, she looked around and didn't seem overly taken with the place. "Yes," she said in a somewhat haughty tone. "Very Vith."

"Gwen, what is your continued dislike for the Vith? I think this place is breathtaking; especially Dav's castle up there." He pointed up into the mountains.

"Proper Zenons prefer more subdued surroundings."

"Gwen, you promised not to fall into your Zenon shell again, remember? Take a look around and enjoy what you see."

She considered his words a moment, then laughed, her breath coming out in a cloud. "You're right; you're right." She sighed and looked around, this time with a less stern eye. "It is pretty, and as the castle belongs to your friend, the great Captain Davage, it's a place to be respected."

"That'll do, I guess." He looked at the dock. The permanent moorings for the *New Faith*, Captain Davage's *Triumph*-class ship, were empty. The captain and his countess, Sygillis, were gone again, faring the stars no doubt with several of their children. Dotting the dock and the street corners were five-foot tall plaster statues of Countess Sygillis, each painted in bright, fanciful colors.

"What are these statues?" Gwen asked.

"I think they were donated by the Captain and Countess. They placed them all over the village and invited the children from Cyantown to paint them. They then personally judged each one and invited the artists of their favorites to their castle for dinner and a tour."

"Interesting thought," Gwen remarked. "The statues would be better life-sized."

Stenstrom chuckled. "These are life-sized, Gwen, the Countess is not a tall woman. I wish Dav and Syg were here today. I'd love to see them and properly introduce you."

"Perhaps next time," Gwen replied, taking note of a statue painted bright green. "Of course we're not really here for fun and visiting, are we?"

The dock wasn't completely empty. A few berthings down several merchant vessels were lined up innocuously in the water, as well as a Fleet Sprint ship. Long, twelve decks high, and slightly tubular in shape, the medium-sized vessel with its tiny wings placed well aft reminded Stenstrom of a capital "T".

"I had an opportunity to board a Sprint ship," Gwen said, admiring the sleek lines of the vessel. "Not long ago. My uncle suggested it."

"Why didn't you?"

"Need you ask? I'll just stay an engineer aboard an old Warbird turned privateer with the man I love."

He took her arm and they strolled north. Gwen became accustomed to the cold and let her coat fall open.

"Where's this college?" she asked, holding his arm.

"At the northern end of the village. We've a ways to walk."

They'd gone a few more blocks, the village deceptively spread out and vast. They passed a ramshackle pub that was a little crooked in relation to the buildings around it. A sweet-smelling cloud drifted out into the cold air. "Smells good," Gwendolyn said, taking it in.

A wooden sign swinging on a chain announced the pub as the 'Drunken Eel'.

"It's honey ale," he said. "Oh, this pub is a favorite of my friend, Lt. Kilos. I wonder if she's in there right now."

"The Marine? Isn't she pregnant?"

"Ex-Marine. She is, but that's not going to stop her from tossing back."

He went to the doors and looked in. "Lots of people in there; let's see."

Gwendolyn put her arms around his waist and pulled him away from the door. "Come on, Bel. We can look for your friends later."

Moving on they passed the massive dome of St. Vith cathedral and entered the tree-lined outskirts of the college area.

Sarfortnim College was built in a classic configuration with the main buildings situated around a central green featuring a Vith Fox Shrine and radiating outward several blocks in a confined but orderly manner. Twenty brownstone buildings huddled here and there off the green, and many more dormitories and ancillary structures spread out farther to the north. Even the ever-skeptical Gwendolyn had to suck in her breath a little at the stone, horse-shoe shaped pitch where brandtball games were frequently played. Columned and buttressed, the arena was a true masterpiece of Vith design.

They wandered about a bit, getting the lay of the land. "If I were an ancient Elder artifact, where would I hide?" he asked, looking around.

"A-Ram and Alesta didn't say they were hidden. They said they were on full display. Let's find the administrative building. I'll wager they've got a small museum within, or perhaps a series of display cases set up for viewing. I am highly skilled at locating museums."

"Good to know," he replied, not quite sure what to make of that.

They found the Venslarr Science & Administrative building at the north end of the campus, a handsome edifice with a large Sarfortnim eagle carved over the entryway. Gwendolyn, positively giddy, pulled him inside. Apparently, she was an avid museum enthusiast.

Inside, they found a confusion of corridors and wood-paneled rooms. They passed a large room marked AMPHITHEATRE populated by many people in magenta-colored robes; Gwendolyn couldn't help but open the door and pop her head in to see what was going on. It was some sort of medical seminar presided over by several Hospitalers in their black and silver robes. They were dissecting a cadaver as the audience of scholars looked on.

Rather squeamish, Gwen closed the door and continued on, pulling Stenstrom with her.

"Ah!" she cried, pointing ahead. "Here!"

A small sign promising a collection of artifacts discovered in the north Vithland area pointed down a flight of steps.

They descended and entered a small but inviting setup with a number of softly lit cases and stands lined with shelves loaded with various-sized trinkets.

The place was quiet: somber lighting, red carpeting. Few people browsed the displays. The whole place was rather sedate and forlorn. Stenstrom just wanted to run through the displays and locate their objective, but Gwen took his arm, deliberately slow in her search. She took her time, leaning over and carefully examining each displayed item, reading the placards, even the ones that couldn't possibly be what they were looking for.

"Gwen, we don't have time for this."

"I won't hear of it," she said. "A visit to a museum isn't a race, Bel. When I enter a museum, I make it a point to appreciate everything. Ah, yes, these are lovely pieces. I believe I'm beginning to take an interest in Vith artifacts, despite myself."

"Fine time for it."

Moving at a snail's crawl, they advanced from one case to another, Gwendolyn not continuing on until she had fully taken in everything. It was maddening.

"Quite a collection, isn't it?" came a voice from behind. They turned.

Standing there and holding a brochure was a male Fleet captain and a blue-haired female lieutenant wearing a large hat. Gwendolyn stood up straight, her FEDULA clinking against the glass. "Captain, good day to you, sir."

"Good day, Lt." he replied. "I wasn't expecting to see any Fleet personnel here this afternoon, as we're the only League ship berthed at present."

"Our ship is in orbit, sir. Greetings. I am Lt. Gwendolyn, Lady of Prentiss, chief engineer of the Fleet Warbird *Seeker*."

The captain studied Bel's face a moment, then slapped the brochure to his leg. "Ah, the *Seeker,* our celebrated new Privateer! If that's the case, by chance are you sir Paymaster Stenstrom, the ship's appointed captain? You must be. I'd heard you wear an old HRN coat, and here it is sure enough. Very striking."

"Stenstrom, Lord of Belmont-South Tyrol at your service. Lt. Gwendolyn is my countess-in-waiting."

They shook hands. "Ah, congratulations. Please allow me, I am Captain Duval, Lord of Willshire, commander of the Fleet Sprint ship *George Parr*. Perhaps you saw her parked in the bay. And this is my first officer, Lt. Remm Deckard."

Gwendolyn thought a moment. "Captain Duval . . . I've heard your name. Weren't you decorated for bravery at—"

"At the Battle of Mirendra I, aye,"

Hiding under her hat and a curtain of blue bangs, Remm Deckard offered a vague smile and held out her hand. Stenstrom saw hints of complex tattoos on her hand as he shook it. Her hand was warm and electric.

Captain Duval smiled warmly. "It's always good to become acquainted with our fellow Fleet; especially those brave heroes in the privateer service providing the much needed funds the Fleet requires to survive. Very unappreciated lot, the privateers. Have you lunched?

Perhaps we might sit a spell and get up-to-date."

Gwendolyn wanted to accept their offer, but waited for Stenstrom to give his confirmation. He pondered for a moment, then said, "Sure, why not."

Captain Duval was elated. "Wonderful. Shall we? We saw a lovely café just a short walk away that claims to specialize in classic Remnath fare. I could do with a taste of home so far north."

They all left the museum and headed to the cafe.

After they finished lunch, Bel and Gwen waved goodbye to their new acquaintances and walked several blocks away, twisting and turning through the streets, eventually ending up in a small, smoky tavern-inn near the cathedral. Stenstrom paid for a room for the night and they clambered up the narrow stairs, located their room, and went in.

"Bel, what are we doing? Shouldn't we press on our search?" She went to the window to throw open the curtains and admit some sunshine. Greenish light from the terragrin sign outside lit up her face in an emerald hue.

"Leave those closed," he said. He locked the door, and, with rapid shakes of his hands, produced Holystones and silver holders resembling small candlesticks. Gwendolyn, always fascinated by Stenstrom's Tyrol sorcery, sat down on the bed and watched.

"What are you doing?" she asked, unclipping her FEDULA and leaning it against the wall. She removed her Fleet hat and fluffed her hair in the mirror.

Stenstrom was busy at his arcane work. He placed the silver holders in a triangular configuration on the floor and carefully set a blue, dark green, and mottled yellow Holystone into the cup of each one. "Try not to move around too much, Gwen. The vibration could knock the stones loose."

Fascinated, she smiled, removed her coat and took her boots off, setting them aside. "All right, I'll be careful." She flopped onto her stomach to watch, and the green Holystone fell to the wooden floor.

"Gwen, what did I just say?" He picked it back up and returned it to the cup.

"Sorry. You are going to teach me this field of study once we're married, yes?" she said, holding her arm out and admiring her watch.

"If you want to learn, I'll teach you. Now, watch your movements, please."

She lifted her feet and slowly bobbed them back and forth. "I will. So, again, what are we doing? If we're staying here, we need to contact the ship and give them an update. Taara's going to be getting worried, and I didn't bring an overnight bag."

"We'll update the ship in a bit."

He pulled a purple Holystone from his coat. He placed it on one of his silver candlestick holders and set it alight. It belched bluish, aromatic smoke that quickly drifted around the room.

He set his pistols down and inspected his work with the Holystones. He then joined her on the bed, the springs squeaking.

"What's all this smoke?" Gwen asked.

"We shall be able to temporarily speak freely; the smoke will jam any technological ears that might be listening, and these additional Holystones will warn us if we are being spied upon. I've a distinct feeling our new friends are not what they seem."

"The captain and his first? I thought they were enchanting." She slid him out of his HRN and set it on the floor. "You and all your stuff, Bel." She coiled around him and they lay back, getting comfortable.

"You didn't find it odd that we'd meet a pair of Fleet personnel in an out-of-the-way museum in the Science & Administration building of Sarfortnim College?"

"Well, why not? I was enjoying the displays."

"Gwen, I've been to Blanchefort village enough times to know that Fleet personnel on shore leave don't spend their off-hours browsing in museums when other, more primal pursuits beckon. I have a distinct suspicion Professor Shurlamp is afoot."

"Oh, please," she sighed.

"You're not giving this woman her proper due."

"So, what are you suggesting? That a Professor from Calvert counts under her employ a Fleet captain and his first officer?"

"That is exactly what I am suggesting. Line a man's pocket with enough silver and he'll try anything."

Gwendolyn considered the notion. "Captain Duval is a hero."

"Heroes can be bought too."

"How then, if you are correct, did they track our movements?"

"We filed a flight plan with Fleetcom when we came down in the Ripcar. They knew where we were headed."

"How would Professor Shurlamp have access to that information?"

"I would say it's quite easy for a well-connected person of means and intelligence to hack the Fleet's Low Rent traffic. Lt. Kilos' husband does it all the time. Therefore, I think it best the two of us fall off the grid for the time being. We must assume any standardized traffic to the Fleet is being scrutinized."

"Ok, Bel, assuming your logic is correct, what do you think we should do?" she whispered.

"We wait until nightfall, then we sneak back to the college and fetch the objects in question."

"But we didn't locate them."

"I did, just as the captain arrived. I think I saw them in a corner case. So, we'll break in, borrow them, and then sneak back."

Gwendolyn checked her watch again. "Night fall's a few bells away. Let's get comfortable." In the green terragrin light, she unbuckled her belt and slid out of her pants, letting them fall to the floor. She was down to her shirt, knickers, socks, and watch. She began undoing Stenstrom's clothes, setting them aside until he was down to the same.

"Gwen, are you certain you don't wish to simply toss in and give Professor Shurlamp what she wants? It probably isn't too late. None of this sneaking around is really necessary."

Gwen absently watched the smoke dance around the room. "Oh, I'm positive, now more than ever. The day we allow a tenured brat to intimidate us shall be a cold one indeed." Gwendolyn smiled and got on top of him, kissing his neck. "Besides, I think this is kind of romantic, don't you? You and me, here in this village, in a contest with a ridiculous scholar from Calvert." They lay on the bed in the quiet first stages of making careful but passionate love. A Sub-Orbital rumbled down the street. One of the Holystones came out of the silver holder and fell to the floor. Then, a second fell, and finally the third.

They both stopped and stared at them.

✳   ✳   ✳   ✳   ✳

They discovered the sophisticated bugs placed on their coats later that afternoon. Tiny, barely thicker than a hair and made of tacky synthetic material splayed out in a network of vein-like conductors, they found four on Stenstrom's HRN and three on Gwendolyn's Fleet coat.

Gwendolyn fumed. They decided to not deactivate them as that would further prod Professor Shurlamp. Instead, they spent the afternoon in their room, keeping their conversations to a minimum and throwing out fake clues as they worked out their plan to grab the artifacts. Stenstrom contacted the ship and informed them they were enjoying the sights and would call for a Ripcar in the morning. Taara, as expected, put up a fuss, but Stenstrom calmed her. They then ordered dinner in from the tavern downstairs, ate, and worked out a plan.

The smoke from the Holystone began to give out. "Looks like we need a fresh Holystone," Gwen said.

"I don't have any more of these purple ones. We'll need to mind our words."

And then, Gwen laid a bombshell on him. Without opening her mouth, she spoke to him loud and clear.

<Well, since we're now formal, and no husband and wife should maintain secrets, I'll tell you. Zenons are quite widely telepathic, much more so than the Remnaths and Esthers, even more than the Vith. The Sisters often put us through various tests to gauge our abilities, and if you score up, they paint you red and stamp you with the word 'Cordra' for telepath. It's all kept private, but I never wanted to be examined in such a fashion and painted up like Morgan is. I deliberately softened my abilities and so got a low score and was forgotten. I make it a point to keep it bottled up when away from Prentiss, though Morgan could often tap my thoughts with her empathic tendencies.>

<Always full of surprises,> he responded.

<And, one more thing. My family can perform something we seldom speak of. I call it 'The Pop'. I can focus my thoughts to the point that I can disable an individual from a great distance. I thought to use it on you during our little chase way back when, but decided not to as I wished everything to be above board. It wouldn't have been fair.>

The Holystone crumbled into ash. "Pretty place, isn't it Gwen? I suppose in the morning we'll head out to Hoban." he said, making a show for the ears listening in from afar. *<Thanks for that. Come dark, I'll*

head back to the campus to collect the artifacts. You stay here, I can hide in the shadows and not be seen,>

"It's growing on me, I must admit." *<I actually agree with you. I cannot believe those two would dare place rigs on us, and smile while doing so. I think what I'll do is stay here in our room and cover you.>*

<So, you'll cover me from afar and 'Pop' any unfriendlies who might happen by. Can you really knock a person out with your thoughts?>

<I've never tried before, but I know I can generate enough force to do some good.>

When the sun went down, he quietly exited their room and went downstairs. He stayed to the shadows, following the narrow stairwell down into the noisy tavern unseen. He moved through the crowded room, past all the people deep into their cups and their games, wondering if any were spies from Hannah-Ben Shurlamp. If she was invested enough to secure the services of a Fleet Captain and load him out with ruinously expensive rigs, then nothing could be put past her.

And, sure enough, there she was in bold 3-D on a for-rent Holocone near the bar: wigged, powdered, frothy white, all smiles. She spoke in a hypnotic fashion in her regal accent: *"And, remember, it is never too late to seek out advice and proper counsel. A new day has dawned and all accounts are clean. Nothing is beyond my reach. All one need do is seek me out . . . ."*

He was certain the message was intended for him and Gwen alone. He moved out unnoticed into the cold night air.

<Can you hear me, Bel?> came Gwen's thoughts. He winced a little at the force of it.

<Loud and clear. Wow, you really do have some skill.>

<As I said, I am Zenon after all. It feels so good to finally allow myself to let loose in your presence. We are the most telepathic of the seven tribes.>

<Eight, you're forgetting Tyrol.>

<Tyrol's not a tribe, Bel.>

How his mother would be turning over in her grave at that one. *<A discussion for another time. Professor Shurlamp is sparing no expense in seeking us out. She wants us to know there's no hard feelings and we may come to her at any time.>*

<Let her waste her coin, Bel. She is not an issue here.>

<Fine then. I'm heading north.>

Passing the unsuspecting people strolling down the street, he moved north, past the shoppers crowding Rundle Way, past the cathedral into the college campus area. It was dark and fairly empty of people when he arrived.

He quickly vaulted to the top of a nearby building and looked around. He crept to the Science & Administration building and dropped down. <*I'm here, Gwen.*>

<*Kay.*>

The doors were locked and held shut with a fairly sophisticated maglock system. A few moments later, with the correct tools from his coat, he was in, encountering several more locked doors as he went.

He passed the amphitheatre that had spooked Gwen and located the stairs leading down to the museum and took them.

When he got to the bottom he discovered the museum had been cleaned out, the cases emptied, glass doors swinging ajar. A sign sat off to the side of the entrance reading:

THE EMBRY-VITH DISPLAY HAS BEEN TEMPORARILY CLOSED BY ORDER OF THE STELLAR FLEET. SARFORTNIM COLLEGE ADMINISTRATORS APPOLOGIZE FOR THE INCONVENIENCE.
THE MUSEUM WILL REOPEN SOON.

Stenstrom stood there and shook his head. <*Gwen, the museum is gone.*> <*Gone?*> Her telepathic voice had a distinctly tinny sound to it.

<*The viewing area has been cleaned out. The display cases are empty. A sign says the items on display have been seized by order of the Fleet, and will be returned at a later date.*>

<*Oh, that little powdered weasel. I must hand it to her, there's no quit in that woman.*>

<*So, with this current development in mind, are you certain you don't wish to amend your position, dine on a bit of crow, and admit the Professor into our plans?*>

<*Absolutely not, especially after this development. We shall not be bullied about by these harassing antics. It's clear she has no direction in which to turn and is hoping to glean some sort of clue from the artifacts themselves. I'll wager, if our hypothesis is correct, that the pieces are, at this moment, under lock and key in Captain Duval's Sprint ship.*>

Stenstrom quickly made his way up the stairs. *<I agree. I'm heading there now.>*

He passed the amphitheatre and paused. The door now stood wide open.

<Bel . . .> came a voice. It wasn't Gwendolyn's mental voice, it was someone else. *< . . . In here . . .>*

Curious, he looked in. There were several rows of comfortable elevated seats and a flat platform at the bottom.

A gurney and a silent form covered with a sheet sat in the center of the platform. He wondered what was the cadaver still doing there?

"Who's there?" he asked.

The form on the gurney sat up with deathly slowness and turned its head to look at him. The sheet came away. A pale, diabolical face came to light, eyes glinting, teeth showing in a graveyard smile.

Stenstrom was filled with an unearthly feeling of fear, total fear. He'd felt it before, in Clovis. He was certain of it.

What had Alesta said? *"The Shadow tech Goddess came and filled you with fear. She killed your Countess."*

The figure stood and eased forward, holding its clawed hands up. *<Can't get away from me, Bel . . .>*

Summoning what strength he had left, he TK'ed out of the building, into the night air, grim laughter following him. He soared to the top of a nearby building and took up a defensive position, NTH's at the ready.

Nothing came out of the building. The campus was still and peaceful. The overwhelming coffin of fear that had taken him faded and was replaced by a rush of endorphins, giving him a minor euphoric feeling.

<Bel, what are you doing?> came Gwen's telepathic voice.

<I thought I saw someone in the building.>

<Who?>

<I don't know, a corpse. A demon.>

<A corpse? I'm not picking anybody else up in your vicinity. Perhaps that smoke you breathed in all afternoon got into your head. It made me feel a bit dizzy. Get moving. We don't have all night.>

He tore across the darkened campus, past St. Vith's and south along the edge of the bay near where the elephants crossed the water.

The crowds of people strolling about in the chilly night air increased as he neared the heart of the village. He TK'ed above the rooftops to be clear.

Ahead, floating on its pylons like a winged serpent and lit-up in panning lights was the *George Parr*, Captain Duval's Sprint ship. The gangways were sealed and a detail of Marines guarded the entrance points at the docks.

<The ship is closed off and sealed with Marines prowling the gangways,> he sent to Gwendolyn.

<So, they've got their booty on lockdown, do they?> Gwendolyn sent back. *<That won't stop us. Check the aft dorsal area near the wings. Sprint ships have blow port that they routinely open to vent their life support systems when they're grounded. You should be able to get in that way.>*

Stenstrom drifted over the ship, marveling at its ram-rod straight design, which was quite a departure from the flowing, swan-like shape of the *Seeker* orbiting high above.

Farther back, near the wing assembly, he spotted the open port Gwen had mentioned. It was hissing and steaming slightly in the chilly night air. He crawled in down a narrow tube until he reached a locked grate. He produced a lock picking set and had it open after just a few moments.

<I'm in, Gwen.>

<Good! Head down to the cargo area on Deck 4. I'll wager that's where the artifacts are being kept.>

Still faded into the shadows, he drifted down through the ship's corridors, passing numerous crewmen and officers along the way—none aware of his presence. Reaching Deck 4 with ease, he heard activity coming from Cargo Bay 2. He drifted to the entrance.

Sure enough, inside, arranged on row after row of temporary tables, were the contents of the museum, all the artifacts carefully laid out. A black-haired female crewman took vids of each object with a floating holo-camera and scribbled notes on a pad. A male crewman laid out more objects, shuttling back and forth from the tables to an open crate. Watching the two of them work was Lt. Remm Deckard, Captain Duval's first officer, still hiding under her huge hat and blue hair.

"I want these items inventoried and cataloged as quickly as possible and report back to me when the task is complete, understand?" she said in a stern voice.

"Yes, ma'am," the female crewman answered. The first officer looked the bay over one last time with a critical eye and then walked out, mere feet away from Stenstrom. He drifted in undetected.

As soon as the first officer left the area, the two crewmen stopped what they were doing and started flirting, hugging and giggling.

"Lessa, come here, Lessa," the male said as he put his arms around her. Stenstrom paid them no mind and searched the area. He immediately saw what he was looking for: two large helmets made of rough-hewn stone laid out on a table in the second row. They seemed primitive and poorly made. If they were wondrous Elder-tech as Alesta had said, then they hid their secrets well.

The two crewmen were becoming intimate. "Gordon . . ." the female purred as he kissed her neck, "she might come back. Hehehhe . . . Gordon . . ." The male crewman picked her up and set her down on the table. Stenstrom, wishing to give them privacy, took the two helmets and exited the bay. He encountered no one along the way and was out of the ship with prizes in hand in no time.

5—Spun Around

After Taara sent down a fast, unregistered Ripcar, Stenstrom and Gwendolyn were back on the *Seeker*.

"These things don't look like much to me," Taara said, gazing at the stone helmets sitting on Stenstrom's desk. She tentatively tested their weight. "Elders Balls! These things are heavy."

"Taara, don't play around with those; it's not safe," he said.

She kept fooling around with them.

Stenstrom sat quiet in his seat. Morgan-Jeterix was leaning over him checking for any remaining rigs that might still be present. Gwen sat nearby.

Morgan finished her work. She appeared rather testy. "You're clear, Bel. I can't say much for your mental state, however."

"What?" he asked.

"I heard you and Gwendolyn are engaged to be married, the ship is just abuzz with the news. Is that true?"

"Yes, it's true."

Morgan put her tools and scanners away. "When were you planning on telling me?"

"It just happened, Morgan," Gwen said.

"Well, if I may speak frankly, I think you two are being rather premature. I mean, there's a whole world of possibilities out there you both have failed to properly explore."

She pulled a tincture from her bag, popped it open, and handed it to him. "Drink this."

"What is it?" he asked.

"Your dopamine is elevated. You could be on the verge of a significant psychotic episode." He drank it. It tasted terrible.

Morgan stomped to the door and made to leave, her braids moving as if alive under her silver helmet. "If either one of you have any guts, you'll make an appearance at my quarters this evening. Come one or come both. I'm tired of this fooling around."

"Morgan, where are you going?" he asked.

"Someplace where I'm wanted!"

She stormed out and Taara laughed. "I wonder if that's a clothing-optional meeting she's talking about? Can I come too, Morgan?"

Gwendolyn blushed. "Please, Taara, it's really not funny. She seems genuinely upset."

"Well sure she's upset. Wouldn't you be? I would."

For a moment, Stenstrom wanted to go after Morgan, but he held firm and the moment passed. He had made his decision. Gwen had won, and he wasn't regretful. His passions for Morgan were quickly fading in his thoughts. "Morgan's our friend. She'll be fine. Let's focus on the matter at hand."

Taara, using both hands, lugged one of the helmets up. "Have we tried putting one of these things on yet to see what they do?"

"No."

Taara wrestled it onto her head. "I'm going to put it on."

"Don't, Taara!"

"Relax, Bel, will you?" she yelled as she popped it on, the thing rather huge on her tiny shoulders. Her little face appeared in the square stone opening. She looked around, pawed at her head and screamed, then slumped to her knees.

"Taara!" Stenstrom plunged to her side. He yanked the helmet off, and there was Taara, winking and laughing.

"Gotcha!" she piped.

"Taara, I've a mind to take you to the gym and mess you up! That wasn't funny!"

"I know, and I'm sorry. Couldn't help it. And I didn't see a thing, just you guy's ugly faces."

Stenstrom put the helmet back on the desk.

"Perhaps they only work if a Sister looks through, Bel?" Gwen added. "Here, put it on my head." He picked it up and gently paced it over her head, helping to situate in on her shoulders. She slumped under the weight a little. Her face emerged in the blank visor. "No, Taara's right, I don't see anything. Take it off me, please, it's not comfortable."

Stenstrom pulled it off her head.

Taara was impatient. "You want to try, Bel?"

He readied to put it on, and then stopped. "I've always had a bit of fear of the Sight. To see things best left unseen. The things Captain Davage has told me, I'm not at all certain how he managed his sanity through it all. I'll take a look later."

Wanting nothing further to do with Magravine and the bloody helmets, Stenstrom decided to wait until breakfast to determine his next course of action; perhaps sleeping on it might provide him with clarity of thought. Unfortunately, he and Gwendolyn bickered about it all morning as they took breakfast in his office. He wanted to wait and try something indirect, while Gwendolyn favored a rapid, immediate shore mission to Magravine. The prospect of discovering the stellar location of long forgotten Eng had taken flight in her head and she was keen to discover it. Once Eng was rediscovered, then certainly Cammara and Emmira would be rediscovered as well. A new age of exploration into the past was possibly at hand. She sat up all night at the holo-terminal, reading about Eng, the home world of the Elder-kind in the DX time epoch, a place abandoned as the Elders drive for sustenance forced them to continue across the heavens, to lovely Kana where they'd been ever since. She's also read the various scholarly debates, arguing Eng's possible stellar position.

She chattered at breakfast about discovery, about publishing a paper, about speaking at symposiums and having their names indelibly etched into the learned history of the League. And, she spoke of actually setting their boots down on Eng—for the first time in one hundred thousand years. She sounded like Grand Dame Miranda of Rosel when she spoke of such things, and, probably like Professor Shurlamp as well, where the quest for knowledge was every bit as fierce and consuming as that for the pursuit of wealth or conquest. He felt a bit of her enthusiasm, and he had to admit he was curious, but at the end of the day, it wasn't Gwen who was going to have to plunge into Magravine chasm and put the helmet on—it was him. Seeing all there was to see, and he didn't want to. He dreaded it.

Taara joined them as they finished up their meal and what she told them didn't help matters. The *George Parr* had returned the Vith artifacts to Sarfortnim College, then departed Blanchefort village and was currently high in orbital Zone D, directly over Magravine.

Stenstrom and Gwendolyn were stumped. "Their presence there can't be a coincidence. How do they know that's where we were headed? I don't understand," Gwendolyn muttered.

As they wondered over the matter, the Com rang in. "Sir, you have an incoming message," the Com officer said from the nearby bridge.

"Source?" he asked.

"Ship of the line. It's Captain Duval of the 7th Fleet."

They all looked at each other a moment. "Fine, Com, I'll take it here." His terminal began flashing. The captain was waiting.

"I can guess what he wants," Stenstrom said.

"Let's keep things close to the vest, Bel. Give him nothing even if we have to play the fool," Gwen added, nervous, pushing her plate aside.

"Shouldn't be too hard," Taara added.

"Taara," he said. "It's been a while since we've practiced basic seamanship. Let's Beat to Quarters, all right?"

"Now?" she squeaked. "But I want to listen."

"Now. Hop to it."

She walked out the door to the bridge. The claxons went off a moment later as the crew began jostling around.

"I want us ready, Gwen; just in case the good captain chooses to jump us."

"Here, over Kana? It would be a scandal. The Fleet would be all over him."

"We'll see." He pressed the button.

On the small holo-screen, the dapper form of Captain Duval appeared. He was seated behind his desk. A coffee sat on the table in front of him. Floating on a secondary terminal were the morning posts.

"Paymaster, Lt., thank you for receiving my transmission," he said in his cultured Remnath accent. "It is good to see you again."

"Our pleasure, sir," Stenstrom replied. "What can we do for you this morning?"

Duval sipped his coffee. "For one, we can drop the droll cat and mouse game. I'm quite certain you're not as stumblingly stupid as you appear. It seems to me that the two of us are involved in a race, one of particular importance."

"So," Gwendolyn said, jumping in and not bothering to deny anything, "how much is Professor Shurlamp paying you?"

Captain Duval shrugged. "Quite a bit, actually. She is a driven personage, isn't she?"

Stenstrom replied. "How much is 'quite a bit'? If Professor Shurlamp has bought you, then name your price and I shall trump her bid and relieve you from further participation in this situation."

Captain Duval laughed. "Allow me to show you something." The Com image panned away from the Captain to the other side of his office. Sitting in two chairs were the black-haired female and the male crewmen he'd seen in the hold yesterday. They looked frightened, their eyes darting about.

"Do you recall these two, Paymaster?" Duval asked. "You should; you stole several artifacts right under their noses. Isn't that right Crewman Lessa and Crewman Gordon?" Duval reached into his pocket and placed his tiny blue MiMs pistol on the desktop. Crewman Lessa drew her breath in a panic.

"What are you planning on doing with that weapon?" Stenstrom asked.

"This?" Duval picked it up, showed it to the screen, aimed and shot Crewman Gordon through the chest. He slumped to the floor. Lessa stood and screamed.

"That's just to show you how serious I am, Paymaster."

"You just murdered that man!" Stenstrom cried. "And you did it over an open Com. I will have you off your chair and on your way to a stockade before the sun sets."

"Will you? Check your archives; you'll find no record of this transmission."

Gwendolyn turned to the console and scanned through the Com archives. She nodded at Stenstrom,. Somehow, their transmission was not being archived.

"Yes, Professor Shurlamp has her uses. However, make no mistake, I am not in this simply for her coin. I have a grander purpose in mind."

"And what is that?" Stenstrom asked.

"To return to St. Mary's Axe and kneel at the feet of the Shadow tech Goddess."

Stenstrom frowned. That name again. "What is St. Mary's Axe?"

"A portal. In St. Mary's Axe I walked at her side and I sampled the wild fruits of her garden. I saw a table of past loves, and loves that never were. In a place of Shadow tech, I slept in her bed and I walked on tilled earth awaiting seed, any seed I desired to place there. I saw genius and godhood, and she awaits my return even now."

"Captain, are you saying you are in love with the Shadow tech Goddess, and that she loves you in return? You are deluded, sir," Stenstrom said.

Duval scowled. "In that distant Shrine on a forgotten planet, is St. Mary's Axe, my pathway back to her at last, and I'll not be denied any further. Look at my work, look at this dead man on the floor."

Gwen stood. "Captain Duval, you were a hero. What has happened to you?"

"A hero is nothing more than the larval stage of a full-winged failure, Lt. Now that you understand the lengths I'm willing to go to, you will hand over those artifacts you stole immediately; otherwise, this poor girl here won't live long, will she? I've a whole ship full of souls to kill. My goddess demands it."

"Then I shall inform the Fleet immediately of your murder!" Stenstrom cried.

"Please do. Without any sort of proof, your request will be duly noted and investigated in two, perhaps three months. Please, Paymaster, you are a Privateer; a pirate barely tolerated in the mud room of the Fleet's grand hall. I have been a Fleet captain for over forty years. I'm a hero, remember? I've friends all over the Admiralty. I've dined in their homes and I've tasted their grape. Who will be believed? You or me?"

"And when the murdered man goes missing?" Stenstrom asked.

"Ah, blood poisoning. Came upon him fast. Burial at sea." Duval smirked and pushed Lessa's terrified face close to the Com screen, the barrel of his MiMs resting on her cheek. "You have five bells." The screen went dead.

Stenstrom and Gwendolyn were beside themselves. "The man is clearly insane. So, now what? We can't allow him to murder his crew, all the while laughing in our faces," Gwendolyn said. "He's got us by the hip. Without proof, the Fleet will not take immediate action."

"You know, Gwen, I think I've opted to take the hard way around things far too many times, you've said as much yourself."

"How do you mean?"

"I mean, perhaps it's a flaw in my character, but I never seem to want to use the resources that are around me in a proper fashion. I always want to do things the hard way. Perhaps it was my upbringing, always wanting to outdo my mother all on my own. If I'm going to be the captain of this ship, I'm going to have to jettison that way of thinking. I think I'm going to do something I normally never do. I'm going to call my father."

Gwen laughed. "You're going to call your father? What for?"

"What for? We're faced with a unique foe who exists within our own fold and laughs in our face as he commits cold-blooded murder with impunity. We've been toiling with this problem wholly wrong-footed so far. Captain Duval has used his position in the Fleet to his advantage and I think it's time to use the shield of the Fleet against him for a change. Remember a week back when my father wanted us to accompany him on his quest for dantimony in Heart's Field?"

"Oh, Feature, yes."

"He was very keen that we come with him, wasn't he? I don't get to see my father very often and he's proud of my current station aboard the ship. He laughingly suggested that he *entreat* our presence in his entourage to Heart's Field."

"You mean he was going to order us to come with him?"

"Order is too strong a word, I think. Since my father sits on the chair of a *Triumph*-class Warbird, his vessel holds precedence over ours. He has decades more prestige and a superior class of ship, therefore his wishes hold great weight, not only with the Fleet and the Admiralty, but with the Captaincy as well. It's not a written rule; however, centuries of Fleet tradition demand compliance. So, if my father made it generally known that he wanted us to go with him to Heart's Field, then we'd pretty much have had no choice but to go. I think he's still looking for that fourth ship to go with him, and I believe I have the perfect candidate in mind."

"You mean the *George Parr*?"

"Most definitely I mean the *George Parr*. Captain Duval's mounting a Sprint ship. That means, should my father come calling in his Warbird, then he'd have little choice but to go. My father is a Fleet hero, too. Honor would demand such."

Gwendolyn agreed. "We tell your father what we witnessed and I would suggest he send a well-armed party aboard the *George Parr* as an on-board liaison. I should think their presence will help protect the crew from further wanton acts from Captain Duval."

"My thoughts exactly. We'll see how he reacts when summoned."

Stenstrom punched in the code to raise his father on the grand Warbird *Caroline*.

Soon the image of his smiling father appeared on the Com.

They spent the remainder of the afternoon watching a tactical map of Fleet traffic coming and going from a computerized model of Kana. It was like watching a well-coordinated ballet: the innumerable white dots of satellites orbiting the planet in a geo-synched cloud, the stationary yellow dots of Fleet Dry-Docks, the rising and descending green blips of smaller Fleet ships, transports, frigates, and scouting vessels, the blue blips of intermediate-sized vessels, then the mighty red dots of the heavy ships clearing a path wherever they went. Stenstrom was proud the *Seeker* was one of the red blips, while the *George Parr*, parked by itself over Magravine, was a smaller blue one.

Taara came in, then pulled up a chair. "So, what are we looking at?"

"The *George Parr*."

Taara squinted at the screen. "Oh, you mean that one right there over Vithland? What for?"

Stenstrom and Gwendolyn decided to tell Taara what was going on. They gave her the full story, taking over half a bell to lay it all out.

They even told her about the Anatameter, and how Taara's name had been on it along with Gwen's. Taara usually took things in stride, with a smile. Nothing surprised her, who was by far the oldest of the three of them. But now, as she contemplated what they said, she seemed, just for a moment, to be sad and full of helpless angst.

And then it was gone and the usual Taara was back. "Well, two things. You should have clued me in sooner; and you've totally gone about this wrong."

"How so?" Stenstrom asked.

"How? I'll tell you how. You two are smart and brave and all that, but you're too nice. You play fair and by the rules, even when your opponent probably isn't. I'll tell you, anything we do here on the ship is monitored. We make a Com in or out, it's logged at Fleetcom. You give an order, it's logged; the navigator sets a course, it's logged, and so on. All that info is encrypted, but anything can be hacked. And if your lady, the Professor, has a Fleet Captain in her hip pocket, then she doesn't even need to hack the data; she can use his codes to get in. She's going to know everything we do as we do it; and I wouldn't put anything past her."

"The *George Parr* is hanging over Magravine, the very place we need to go. We aren't certain how she made that connection," Gwendolyn said.

Taara shrugged. "Probably something you guys did that she picked up on. It wouldn't surprise me if she took that stuff from the museum with the sole purpose of hoping you'd come and steal the ones you needed, giving her a clue as to where to go next. Those helmets probably have some old connection to Magravine or something. Look, if she's an EVoR, then obviously she's incredibly smart, and knows how to follow subtle clues to get info out of people, right?"

Stenstrom knew Taara was correct. Alesta and A-Ram had even said the helmets were taken from old Magravine. He had been played for a fool yet again.

As they watched the model of Kana, a procession of three red blips came down from the shipping lanes.

"Ah, look!" Stenstrom cried. "Our first bit of luck. My father's procession has arrived."

The blips orbited in a box formation and, sure enough, the blue blip of the *George Parr* came away from Magravine and joined them in the rear. The four ships then left orbit and headed off toward Heart's Field.

"See, Taara, we can be devious as well. My father just swooped in and fetched Captain Duval. So much for him. Now, Magravine is open."

The Com buzzed. "Sir, message for you from the *Caroline*."

"Aye, thank you. I'll take it here." He got up to put his coat on and be presentable. "It's probably my father." Gwen scooted over and answered the Com.

On the screen, a face appeared, but it wasn't Captain Stenstrom the

Older. It was a mousey female, clad in black.

It was *Her*, the lanky woman in black from the Ruins of Caroline. Her brown hair was loosely braided and coiled into a bun as before. A cigarette mounted in a long stick quietly burned. She gave a wry, crooked smile, lifted her gloved hand and waved. "I've missed you two assholes," she said.

"You!" Stenstrom cried. "You look no worse for your adventures, burning up in my webs, you filthy harlot!"

She snorted. "Aw, sticks and stones, buddy boy!" she said in her child-like voice. "Hope I didn't bust you up too bad." She glanced at Gwendolyn. "Guess the next time I shoot you down, Jo-girl, I better stomp on ya' once or twice to make sure you're good and dead. Let's fix that . . ."

She leaned forward and flared her eyes. The Com screen flickered and exploded. Alarms on the bridge sounded. Gwendolyn cried out, grasping her head. Stenstrom caught and held her fast.

"What the hell just happened?" Taara cried.

"Morgan!" Stenstrom said to the Com. "Morgan, Gwen needs your help, quickly!"

No answer. "Morgan!"

Gwen's eyes rolled back in her head and her body convulsed.

The door opened and two figures rushed in.

"Gwen, oh Gwen!" Alesta cried, running to her side.

A-Ram came in as well. He pulled a handkerchief from his coat and held it to Gwendolyn's head. She was bleeding through her ears. "Gods! She's been Buzzed!"

"Bel," Alesta cried. "Where is Morgan?"

"I don't know. She's not answering."

Alesta pulled Stenstrom to the door. "Bel, let's get her to our Merian hold! We can help! I promise you we can!"

Stenstrom didn't argue as he didn't have a better thought. Carrying Gwen, he raced out the door to the lift to Deck 10.

6—BUZZED

It was like plunging into a cave, going into the Merian's area. Triple bulkheads, no lights, and no tech made it unnaturally quiet. One would never know one was deep in the bowels of a starfaring ship.

Following Alesta, Stenstrom shuffled through the flickering, lantern-lit confines of what was once Cargo Hold 3. They moved quickly through the narrow "streets". As they went along Alesta pulled various people from what they were doing and bade them to follow. Soon, a small, shuffling gaggle followed them through the hold.

They got to a small barn and entered. Stenstrom lay Gwendolyn down in the soft straw and backed away. The Merians Alesta had gathered assembled around her.

"I'm sorry, Bel, you'll need to wait outside. You, too, Rammy. I love you, but you must give us space," she said, then knelt down.

Stenstrom and A-Ram backed out of the barn and a Merian lady slid the door shut with a grating clunk. The handkerchief A-Ram had been holding to Gwendolyn's ear dripped with blood, deep red. He dropped the bloody thing, and it lay there on the metal floor dusted with straw; ominous.

* * * * *

They waited outside the barn in the semi-lit dark. It seemed like they waited a long time, sitting on the straw. At last, the barn door slid open and a Merian lady came bustling out. "Ma'am?" Stenstrom asked. "Ma'am!" But the lady just hurried along, not answering. She disappeared around a corner. A few minutes later, she returned with two other ladies. They were carrying several large baskets.

"Ma'am, please," Stenstrom said, but again she and the others ignored him and went in, sliding the door shut behind them.

More time passed in the flickering dark of the hold. Eventually, Taara emerged in the lantern-lit gloom, escorted by a Merian. "Bel, how's Gwen?" she asked.

"Don't know. They're in there."

Taara looked at the rough wooden planks of the barn. "I think she's all right."

Stenstrom took heart. "The MOLLY tell you that?"

"Nope, just a feeling."

She flopped down next to him on the straw.

"It's sure peaceful in here," Taara said looking around. "Like being in a cave." She sighed. "I've got a little bad news, Bel."

"Seems the day for it. What is it?"

"Morgan, she's gone."

"Gone? Where did she go?"

"She left the ship this morning. She packed a few things and took a Ripcar off. I guess she was pretty mad finding out about you and Gwen. Guess where she went."

"Please tell me she's safely down at the Fleet, or at a Hospitaler sanctum somewhere."

"She went to the *George Parr*, before they broke orbit. I don't know why; but that's where she is."

Stenstrom felt a headache coming on and a wave of worry for Morgan. He rubbed his forehead. "I'm sorry she felt that way. Morgan is loved here; she knows that. I just . . ." He took a breath. "I had to make a choice; what was I supposed to do? That certainly doesn't mean I don't want her here."

Taara turned to A-Ram. "That device you have, the one with all our names on it. Is that really how it is? That there are really lots of different Bels and lots of different Gwens and Me's too?"

A-Ram nodded. "I've seen it myself. There are probably many, many more out there that didn't make the list. These eight are important, for whatever reason."

"And me, did you see me out there somewhere, with Bel?"

A-Ram hesitated and then nodded. "I did. You're very different, Taara, you're . . ."

"What? I'm what?"

"Do you really want to know such things?"

"I do."

"Then walk with me." A-Ram and Taara got up and walked off into the gloom, leaving Stenstrom alone by the barn door with his troubled thoughts.

When they returned several minutes later Taara was all smiles. She sat down next to Stenstrom and seemed rather giddy. She gave him a pat on the cheek. "It sounds like fun. I'm good with it."

"Good with what?"

"All the sex we're having out there in an alternate universe. You and me like a pair of monkeys doing it left and right."

"And that prospect doesn't trouble you?"

"No, no, I'm good."

"Fine. Taara, I want to break orbit. File a flight plan to The Kills with the Fleet and begin a standard patrol. I want some distance from Kana and Professor Shurlamp. That ought to keep her puzzled."

She stood and brushed herself off. "I'll bet we haven't seen the last of that crazy Lacerta woman. She's going to be tough to deal with, Bel."

Stenstrom agreed. "Good. I'm not done with her either. Go on, Taara, let's get underway. I'll inform you of Gwen's progress as I find out more, ok?"

"'Kay." She gave him an affectionate pat on the head, then turned and walked away.

"What did you tell her, A-Ram?" Stenstrom asked.

"I told her some strange things, Bel, all true."

Before Stenstrom could ask more, the door slid open; a Merian girl peeked out. "My Lord, please, come in. Please . . ." she said.

Stenstrom felt his heart beating with dread now that the moment of discovery was upon him. Was Gwen alive or dead? The girl's tone had given away nothing. And, if she was alive, was she hopelessly brain-scrambled? Mouth dry, he entered with A-Ram following close behind.

Gwen lay on the straw at the far side of the barn. Several Merians leaned over her. They had removed her uniform; she was in a white Merian night shirt that went down to her knees. Her uniform, boots, and other small garments, like socks and knickers, were neatly folded and stacked in a corner. Her watch sat atop the stack. Gwen's FEDULA was leaning in its scabbard against the barn wall. He glanced at it, noticing fingerprints on the scabbard.

Gwen's fingers left those marks. Gwen, whole and unharmed . . .

She must be incapacitated; she would never allow herself to be removed of her uniform and boots in a public setting. Gwen was such a proud woman.

Alesta sat by Gwen's head, holding her hand by the wrist.

Wait—where's her head? Stenstrom was shocked. For a moment, he thought she had no head. It seemed replaced with some sort of . . . empty space where a head should be. As he neared, he discovered her head was actually submerged in a deep glass bowl filled with a slightly bluish fluid. The bowl was recessed on one side, allowing Gwen's head and neck to recline easily into the depths of the bowl without tipping it over.

And Gwen's entire head was submerged; mouth, nose, everything. Her rich, chestnut brown hair flowed out in a mass.

Alesta turned and reached out. "Bel, come here." She sounded serious. He sank to his knees, then sat next to her. She took his hand. "That was a real lick the Lacerta put on her, Bel. She was going to die sure enough."

He looked at Gwen's still form, unused to seeing her in a Merian nightgown. The future countess of Belmont-South Tyrol—here she was, her head in a bowl. He took her limp hand and choked up a little, feeling suddenly hot in his HRN. "Is . . . she going to be all right, Alesta? What's her prognosis?"

"I don't know. The next few hours will tell the story, Bel. This water comes from a place that we know of, far away on Trimble. It has amazing properties. It can be breathed in without fear of drowning. It speeds healing and aids in recovery. She'll need to stay like this all night to allow the water to perform its work. Then, once she begins stirring, we'll know how much damage the Lacerta did to her." A-Ram sat down next to Alesta. "There's really not much more we can do, except wait it out."

He glanced over at her watch. "May I put her watch back on? She's not taken it off since I gave it to her; perhaps it'll help at a spiritual level."

"Certainly."

He got the watch and gently put it back on her wrist, fussing with the clasp, trying not to make it too tight. "There, Gwen, I've given you your watch back." He sat there holding her hand.

Alesta gave a bright smile. "Why don't we go get some lunch. It's Macon day in the mess, and that's not to be missed. There's nothing more to be done here except wait. My friends, Marlah and Zemmala, will look to Gwen. She'll be safe."

Stenstrom didn't want to go.

"Come on, Bel. Gwen needs her rest. Let's get something to eat. You'll feel better, then we'll return."

"So, let's share with you some of the things we've seen," A-Ram said as he leaned over his lunch in the Mess. "This adventure has been remarkable to say the least."

"All right, let's hear it," Stenstrom said.

"Captain Duval, in many of the places we've seen, is a madman. He was once a promising officer in the Fleet, a hero even. Then, he changed, the light about him seemed to fade and he went mad—it had something to do with his wife dying in an accident. Very tragic, actually. He wears a very convincing mask covering that fact, a father of ten and a church-go'er. He's also a sociopath, a murderer, and an inner-circle member of the Nihilists of Punt, an ancient order. They exist outside the League into Xaphan space and beyond. Their stated goal is the destruction of the universe so that a better, more perfect one can be created from the ashes of the old."

"He made frequent mention of something called St. Mary's Axe. I wasn't certain what he was talking about," Stenstrom said.

"It's his name for the Hall of Mirrors. That's where he encountered the Shadow tech Goddess," A-Ram said. "As a boy and a younger man, he had the ability to summon it to him whenever he wished; an ability he lost after the death of his wife."

"Captain Duval seems to think the Shadow tech Goddess loves him."

"That he does. We've seen that a lot, and he hitches his wagon to anybody he thinks can help get him to her side, in this case the Nillists of Punt and Hannah-Ben Shurlamp," Alesta said.

"Therefore, time is of the essence," Stenstrom said. "I suppose I could off the ship and double back to Kana while the *Seeker*, under Taara's command, continues onto The Kills. Perhaps the Professor won't expect that."

Alesta smiled; the first time she'd smiled in a while. "No need, Bel. We're going to get you down."

"How?"

"How do you think?"

"You mean the Merian's Road? Am I invited to walk your Road?" He was dumbfounded. He hadn't considered daring to ask to walk the Merian's Road. He didn't believe it was his place to do so.

"Always, Bel. Our Star favors you, as do we. As Rammy said, it's best if we proceed as covertly and as quickly as possible. We have access to a wondrous method of travel that's completely undetectable, so why not use it? Our Star acknowledges a good cause, and you have never pressed me to use it for your personal gain. So, why don't we get started?"

Alesta took them through the hold and the Merians treated her with reverence as they passed, stopping what they were doing and honoring her with a silent nod. They also bowed to Stenstrom, who had given them this space, and at his home in Tyrol. Mixed in here and there were some of his crew who had become involved with members of their order, just as Alesta had become involved with A-Ram.

They returned to the barn to check on Gwen. "Wait here for a moment," Alesta said. She gave A-Ram a loving kiss on the cheek, then went in. She returned a moment later, her blue eyes wide with delight. "Bel, come in here!"

He came in and there was Gwendolyn, sitting up, coughing water out of her lungs. The Merians sat beside her, drying her off.

"Gwen!" Stenstrom cried, rushing to her side. She looked at him for a moment, groggy, mouth open, without recognition, and then she smiled and put her hand on his cheek. "Hey, Bel," she whispered. "Looks like I'm out of uniform, huh?" She coughed again.

He took her hand and kissed it. "Gods, Gwen, I thought you were gone!"

She winced. "Oww, not so loud, please. My head. I don't remember much. I recall having breakfast with you in your office. I recall discussing Eng, and . . . and a call came in. I don't remember much after that, except for a funny child's laughter coming from somewhere. That's mostly what I remember, a child laughing. Was there a child someplace, Bel?"

"No, Gwen, it was just a dream."

She held her forehead. "Creation, my head hurts."

"You've had a severe trauma. You're going to need to rest."

Stenstrom leaned down and took her into his arms. She hugged him back weakly. "Let me . . . let me get up and get dressed for you. I'm a— I'm a mess. Where are my clothes?"

Weak, she tried to stand but Stenstrom gently held her down. "You're fine, Gwen. Just rest, all right? Will you do that for me?"

She lay back and relaxed a little. She took Stenstrom's hand. "What's happening with Eng, Bel? Have you already discovered its location? Did I miss it?"

"I haven't been down to Magravine yet. I've been a touch preoccupied."

Gwen spoke, a little desperately. "Well, I'm back, and I'm all right; though I'm probably not much help right now. Not feeling overly energetic."

"Gwen, don't worry about Magravine."

"Don't worry? I'm dying to learn where Eng is located. I've been . . . I've been doing research and . . . and all sorts of things like that. I can picture it, even now . . ."

Gwen's eyes glazed over. A-Ram fetched a coarse blanket and draped it over her. Gwen was falling into delirium. "And . . . I . . . I want to be introduced as Countess Gwendolyn of Belmont-South . . ." She fumbled with her watch.

She drifted back into shallow sleep.

Alesta adjusted her cover. "I think she's going to be fine, Bel. Just fine. How the Star has blessed us. She just needs rest."

"I owe you much, Alesta. For this."

"You don't owe me anything, Bel. You two are my friends."

A-Ram chimed in. "Just promise to stand with her at our wedding, once we finally get to it."

"A promise easily kept," Stenstrom replied. He stood and brushed the straw off his knees. "Well then, I better go get a helmet and do this task at Magravine. Eng awaits. I don't want to disappoint her."

Gwen babbled slightly as Alesta and A-Ram patiently listened. "He . . . he asked me to marry him. Me. I . . . I have to make a better effort to show him how I love him. He's not a Zenon, he . . . . He wishes that I display my love for him more openly. I must accommodate him. I have to . . ." She began to tear up a little. "I wish I were you, Alesta, the way you are with A-Ram. That's how I am with Bel in my heart. I . . ." She faded back into restless sleep.

He took a last look and left the barn, venturing through the ship back to his office. Taara was there. "How's Gwen?"

"Good, and getting better. I think she's going to be fine. Just needs a little time to rest. Let's make sure Lt. Zemitin is up to performing Gwen's duties while she recovers."

"'Kay," Taara replied.

"What's our position?"

"9 am of the Tammarack Cluster, about halfway to The Kills."

He picked up one of the Elder helmets. He dreaded the thought of putting it on. He didn't want to see what it might show him.

"Oh, you're going to do it, down at Magravine?"

"I am," he replied. "I don't want to, but what choice have I?"

He waited for Taara to protest or offer up a piece of unsolicited Bazz common sense.

She did not. He found that a bit odd. "Aren't you going to try and stop me?"

"Nope."

"Why not?"

She seated herself, put her feet up and gave him an odd look. "Because you need to get this done, so I can have my turn."

7—Magravine

Taara had rigged up a fake set of Com codes, making the *Seeker* appear as a completely different ship.

"How did you manage that?" Stenstrom asked, fumbling around with the helmet he'd selected. "The Com codes are hard-wired to the ship."

Taara loved shady operations. "I got my hands on the brainbox to the old frigate *Essex* before she got put down and smelted, and I installed it in the Missive's Panel. I figured, being Privateers out for plunder, it might be a good idea to send out fake signals every so often to fool the creeps. I threw some creds around, and I think I slept with somebody too somewhere. It wasn't all that hard if you're not afraid to muck about. So, I've got the *Essex* in there, and the crappy old growler *Bellowbus* too—that's really going low rent. The *Bellowbus* sucked. Who would even imagine the brains to the *Bellowbus* is actually mounted in a Warbird? That should put old H-B S off the hunt for awhile."

"Taara, you never fail to impress."

Using the fake headers, he sent a call out to his father, Stenstrom the Older and informed him of Morgan-Jeterix's presence aboard the *George Parr* and requested she be immediately removed to the safety of the *Caroline*. His father assured him he'd have her off as soon as possible, and that, so far, everything appeared to be normal aboard the *George Parr*.

Stenstrom picked up the helmet. "Now that I'm certain Morgan is safe, let's go to Magravine and do this."

He gave one of Taara's Mollock sideburns a quick tug for luck as was his habit. She slapped him on the rear as he exited.

He returned to the Merian's hold and rejoined Alesta. Gwen was sound asleep. He spent a moment with her, then allowed Alesta and A-Ram to lead him out of the barn and deeper into the hold. Behind the dormitories, they came to a wooden wall. Alesta produced a key and opened a door hidden along the wall's length. They entered a long, empty corridor, once the back end of the cargo hold. Lanterns were suspended from wires high overhead, creating a mock starry pattern. Forced air from the compressors on deck 4 bobbed the lanterns about.

"Here is the most shielded section of the ship," Alesta said, her voice oddly loud in the quiet of the corridor. "Here, we may call our Road."

Stenstrom inspected the surroundings. "Are you certain this is permitted, Alesta?"

"You are most welcome here," she said as A-Ram gathered a small pack.

With that, Alesta, arms outstretched and singing, called the Road, and it came in good time in a wall of silent fog.

The Merian's Star appeared at the end of the tunnel of fog, yellow, wreathed in red twisting cloud like an unblinking eye, and the corridor vanished. Seconds seemed like days as they stood there in the fog.

The still silence of the corridor was replaced with an equal, drafty silence all around. The lantern-lit softness of the hold gave way to the broad sunshine of a hazy afternoon.

They took a good look around. Stenstrom, A-Ram and Alesta stood on the lonely plains of Magravine in the central Vithland area of Kana. Amazing, Stenstrom thought. In just a moment or two, the three of them had traveled from 9am of the Tammarack Cluster to Kana—a distance of half a light year. What such a mode of transport could do for the Fleet, for the League—what possibilities. But no, he had to temper his thoughts. The Merian's Star was not to be taken for granted, nor was it to be pressed into service. He was honored to walk their Road.

Magravine was all alone in an uninhabited portion of central Vithland east of the Tartan foothills and west of the River Seven pocket; it was a place that invoked a great deal of thought and feeling. To the non-Vith tribes of Kana, like Stenstrom's, it was proof the Vith were a hard people living in a dangerous place. It was a place that stank of deeds done in the past. There wasn't much at Magravine; except the occasional herds of mis-matched animals migrating away from the area in various directions, thus lending credence to the notion that some sort of Elder "Animal-Factory" existed nearby.

The area was quiet. There was no wind and Stenstrom thought he heard the slow gurgling of the River Seven, lazy in its banks miles away.

Far to the northwest was the distant iron-hand of raw mountains Vithland was famous for.

A-Ram and Alesta got their bearings. "There, to the northeast," A-Ram said.

Stenstrom turned and spotted a low, grassy rise to the north, obscuring the valley beyond. Behind the rise, a small finger of mist slowly snaked into the sky like a fluffy cable hanging from the heavens. A-Ram opened his pack and pulled out Alesta's travelling boots. Leaning against him, she put the hated boots on and buttoned them up.

The ground was studded at regular intervals by small stone cairns mostly overgrown with weeds and grasses.

"These are old Vith markers warning the curious of danger," A-Ram said. "To the Sisters, this place is about as bad as it gets."

Stenstrom produced an odd, multicolored Holystone and held it in his palm. "They might be right. Don't move, you two."

They both turned to him. "What's wrong, Bel?" Alesta asked.

He examined the ground: low and mostly bare with tumbled stones and orderly Vith cairns. Lots of places to hide booby traps.

"I've been working on this chromatic Holystone. It's supposed to warn me of danger."

"What sort of danger?" A-Ram asked.

"Well, that's the whole thing, I'm not sure. It's trembling right now, which tells me that danger is nearby; but I don't know what the nature of the danger is. The *George Parr* had about a day to loiter over this area and do what they wished. There could be traps about, as you treated on in the mess, and, there's always the Lacerta to consider. She could be skulking about. Alesta, I would like you and A-Ram to return to the ship, please. I need to do this alone. I have my tregador here and will contact you when I'm ready."

"You never wear your tregador, Bel," A-Ram said, skeptical.

"I have it this time."

"Show it to me."

Stenstrom pulled his sleeve back and there was a fancy silver gauntlet with a fine agate encrusted in the center around his wrist. "See, it's here. It's got five stones within, so it should be completely untraceable. I'll contact you when I'm done."

Alesta looked worried. "You're probably right, Bel, but I hate leaving you here alone. In the first few moments after you put the helmet on you might feel overwhelmed and seriously believe that you are going mad. Just ride it out, all right?"

"Be careful, Bel," A-Ram said.

"I'll do my best."

Alesta reached into her pack. "Oh, Bel, take this." She pulled out a small bag pulled tight with a string. Stenstrom took the bag and opened it. Inside were a number of turquoise stones shaped roughly like a teardrop. They rattled in his hand like polished rocks. "What are these?"

"Holystones," Alesta replied. "We're told they're an effective counter-measure against LosCapricos weapons, should you encounter any."

Stenstrom closed the bag. "Thank you very much. I won't ask where you got them." As Alesta watched, he made the bag disappear with a wave of his hand.

She got up on her tiptoes and gave him a kiss on the check. "How I adore you, Bel. Such a good friend, in all places. I know you'll be fine. Yes, you'll be fine."

With that, she removed her boots and replaced them in the pack. A-Ram came up and shook Stenstrom's hand. "Safe shores, Bel. We'll be waiting to bring you back home."

Soon, a wall of fog rose around them and when it dispersed a minute or two later, they were gone.

<We're back on the ship, Bel,> came A-Ram's thoughts over the tregador.

<That was fast, though I shouldn't be surprised. How's Gwen?>

<We're on our way there now.>

<Keep me informed please.>

Though they were now about a light year away and getting farther all the time, the power of the tregador kept them always within reach. A technological sensation created by the departed House of Want, the interlinked power stones within the agate allowed his tregador to be connected covertly to A-Ram's, Gwen's, and Taara's matching ones, regardless of distance. Tregadors were fairly new aboard Fleet vessels, only recently having been approved for use by the Sisterhood of Light after decades of careful testing, replacing the old, unsteady J-Rasters. He didn't presume to remotely understand how they worked.

All right, now to it. He navigated up the rise, testing each step, wondering if some clever booby trap was about to be sprung at any moment. He'd come to respect Hannah-Ben Shurlamp enough not to put anything past her. Though he was apparently alone on the step, he faded in the shadows and took flight, the tails of the HRN spreading out around him as he TK'ed himself into the air, the Elder helmet tucked under his arm.

Gliding silent, he crested the small hill. Stretching off into the distance in the valley below him was a great crack in the ground, at least a mile long and about a quarter mile at its widest. The grasses covering the steps all around abruptly stopped near the crack, giving way to bare, hardened earth dotted with orderly Vith cairns arranged in a polka-dot pattern radiating away.

The warm afternoon air came to grips with the markedly cooler vapor issuing out of the chasm, creating the ever-present feather of cloud rising up. He had to steady himself as the updraft from the chasm spun the air a bit.

Magravine had a distinctly vaginal look to it, long and straight, a geographical nod to the evil woman who once lived there. Once a great Vith temple stood in the valley, spired and ornate, reaching into the sky, the stronghold of the Grand Abbess of Magravine. Then there was Shadow tech and madness. Then there was the Black Abbess and all those dead at her hands. Then there were the armies, the Vith, the Sisters arrayed against her. Now, there was nothing but a scar on the landscape that time had yet to heal.

He circled. Something was waiting for him down there; his trembling Chromatic Holystone was proof of that. At least Alesta and A-Ram were safe far away on the ship; one less thing to worry about.

Descending to near ground level, he surveyed the situation: apparently there was nothing more beneath him than hardened earth. He produced a black Holystone and rolled it along the ground toward the perimeter of the chasm.

Something moved; he thought he caught a glint of light. He veered away. A searing red beam blasted the Holystone to nothingness.

He hoisted his Megaeye and had a look. Moving with tiny, ant-like precision, were numerous muted pendants in the shape of eyeballs hanging from a wire that was slung about the chasm in a spider web fashion. They moved in a mechanical fashion, sliding smoothly in one direction until they bumped into each other, and then reversed course and slid back in the other. The wire was tightly slung all across the open face of the chasm, the eyeball charms moving slowly back and forth. There were other types of charms as well: ears, noses, cannons, odd, six-legged shapes, horned and tusked. He recoiled with hidden memory. He'd encountered something like this before, possibly at Clovis and at Caroline. The wire that had restrained Melazarr as she slowly roasted; he'd seen it there.

And here it was again.

<A-Ram?> he thought into the tregador.

<I'm right here, Bel,> came the quick reply.

<I'm encountering an odd weapon here at the chasm, a taut length of wire studded with moving charms and pendants. What can you tell me about it?>

<Hold on, let me get to a terminal.>

<Don't use Fleetnet. Our query could be observed. Use the shipboard archives.> There was a pause. *<Ok, ok, one sec. Guess who's sitting here with me, Bel?>*

He smiled. *<Hi Gwen.>*

Gwen's thoughts drifted into the tregador. *<Hey Bel.>*

<You should be resting.>

<I'm fine. How can I rest with you so far away? I want to help. Now, what are we looking up?>

He brought her up-to-date. There was a pause, then Gwen spoke. *<All right. The wire is a LosCapricos weapon called the ANGRY MISER, registered to the House of Sorranson. They took it with them when they went to the Xaphans in 00000ax. The Sorransons were noted businessmen and practitioners of Gellar magic. They used the ANGRY MISER to guard their cache of wealth. Though the Sorransons were officially Zenons at the time of their departure from the League, they were actually transplanted Remnaths, and . . .>*

<Thank you, Gwen. We'll discuss their tribe status later. So what can this thing do?>

There was another short pause. *<It's a length of wire studded with a variety of charms and other animated trinkets.>*

<I see that. Go on.>

<The charms do different things. There are the ones in the shape of a roving eyeball—those maintain a powerful vigilance. They 'move' about the wire, detecting anything that might come near. There are ear charms that can hear you and nose charms that can smell you too. Once a victim is determined, they can target it with any number of energy, gas, or projectile weaponry that look like cannons.>

<That's probably what blew me into oblivion at Clovis.>

<And that's not all. There are the sympathetic charms—those in the shape of animals and other monstrous creatures. If you trigger them, they'll drop off the wire and come to life, growing to full size and attacking. There are mouth charms also that can utter curses and cast spells.>

<What if I cut the wire?>

<Then they'll all drop off and you'll be stuck fighting the lot. And then there's the Guardian charms that are cast in the likeness of certain individuals. Remember how the Lacerta and Rodrigo of Burgon appeared from a pillar of smoke at Caroline—it was a Guardian Charm in their image that summoned them. With such charms, the Lacerta doesn't actually have to be there, she shall be summoned when needed.>

<Wonderful. How convenient.>

<And, another thing. The Lacerta was carrying an odd handbag at Caroline. I looked it up. That handbag is known as a GALVATAR. With it, she can pull out any other LosCapricos weapon. Obviously, she's all the more dangerous.>

<I'm fairly certain that my shadow movement defeats the notice of the seeing-eye charms. They don't seem to detect me.>

<You've promised to teach me how to do that, Bel,> Gwen replied.

<Indeed I have. The moment we're married I'll begin teaching you.>

Gwen giggled slightly. <I cannot wait. About that, I was preparing a letter to send home to my family in Prentiss announcing our intention to be wed. As per Zenon tradition, they're going to want to interview you at length and give their formal consent. Will you mind such a thing??>

<I'm sure I'll do fine.>

A-Ram's thoughts barged in. <This is heartwarming stuff here, Bel, but let's focus on the task at hand, please.>

Stenstrom surveyed the landscape. <I think I see an uncovered spot at the northern end of the chasm. I'm going to sneak past the MISER at that point and make my way down.> He veered to the north and dropped close to the ground.

Gwen came back on. <Bel, the chasm at Magravine is, at its deepest, one-

thousand, two-hundred, fifty feet. It's been pretty well surveyed over the years and is perfectly safe, though folklore and superstition keeps most people away. It's not exactly a tourist destination. Various scholarly expeditions at the site have installed level ramps and handrails all the way down. Do you see them?>

He looked around. Sure enough, at various points, ramps were dug into the side of the chasm with hand-rails—all level and safe for the un-athletic scholars to perform their work.

<I do, but the railing is entwined by ANGRY MISER—a very convenient place to anchor it.>

He approached a ramp. Numerous winds of wire were strung at intervals with dangling eyeball-shaped charms, noses and ears hanging here and there industriously going about their patrols. The mouth charms occasionally spoke in a dire voice: *"You there?"* He carefully dropped down between the runs of wire and went into the chasm. The air became cold, the afternoon light quickly swallowed up in darkness. He drew a yellow Holystone and shook it, creating a warm, orange glow. The stone around him was black and shiny, a remnant of the fiery attack that took place here centuries ago. Glancing at the stone as he went down, he thought he could occasionally see indications of the foundation and sublevels that the Temple of Magravine once rested on, home of the Grand Abbess of Magravine—the Black Abbess. The old Vith heroes had come to this place and extracted revenge on Magravine for her forbidden and sadistic experiments with Shadow tech.

The horrors this place had once seen were silent in black shiny stone.

<How are you doing, Bel?>

<About half way down, Gwen. I really don't want to put this thing on.>

<I know you don't. I wish I could be there with you, to offer comfort. I love you so . . .>

Hearing those words, something she didn't say often, gave him comfort. He wished she was here with him.

The ramp ended, and he still wasn't to the bottom. There was about fifty feet to go, murky and unsteady. His HRN spread out around him like a pair of dark green wings as he drifted down.

He touched bottom. *<I'm at the bottom, Gwen>* he thought into the wrist-bound tregador. *<The footing is terrible. No flat surfaces at all. No real place to stand.>*

He looked up. Far above, he caught a few small glimpses of light here and there, but not much. His Holystone held aloft threw the place into craggy relief.

He sighed and put the ancient stone helmet on before he could stop himself.

A nightmare of fantastical images hit him cold. He staggered. Odd planets spanned the sky in a blur and graveyard hands reached out from hidden places. There was no sky, just a gallery of the abstract spanning off into the paneled distance. He saw colors that couldn't exist and intersections of time and space that were not logical.

He was bewildered. He was unprepared. He fell to his knees.

He saw transcendent layers of reality. He saw himself remade over and over. He saw doorways opening and closing with horrid figures standing behind them. Just an arm's length away was a whole universe of black: a dead universe. There was a single person at the center of it: a lost, forlorn person.

The Shadow tech Goddess.

He saw a sandy tornado growing until it engulfed all.

He saw a Great Tree stretching out to infinity.

He saw hands reaching for him across time.

Stenstrom pawed at the helmet. Mad, he was going mad, and quickly.

He saw flashes of Gwen's face with its tiny scar, and Taara's face with its usual sideburns. He saw Morgan, in his room, and he was making love to her hard, their bodies twisted together.

And there was Taara—a giant-sized, massively endowed Taara with him at Belmont Manor. And they were . . . No! With Taara??

He looked in a mirror and saw himself as a woman. A woman???

And there he was in a mask again, shunned and laughed at, prowling the rooftops of Tyrol. Somebody bounded at his side; someone in black, small and quick.

Everything was a funnel pouring in unwanted information, and he was choking.

Alesta's face. *"Ride it out, Bel. You're such a dead friend . . ."*

Dear friend . . .

He saw Alesta as a used-up harlot trawling the streets for dimes. Coughing, withering away.

Lost in a pool.

Gwen's face: *"I love you . . ."*

Animals . . .

Morgan's face: *"I love you, too. What chance did I have? There are many of You, and only one of Me. Explode in me—you know you want it!"*

Hatches and reaching hands. *<You can't get away! Hehehehehehheeeehhhhhh!>*

Animals standing over him, nuzzling his face through the visor.

Forgotten colors and islands in the sky . . .

A warm, moist tongue licking his face . . .

He was lying on a metal floor, flat and precision machined.

You're falling through space.

No, no, you're at the bottom of the chasm of Magravine wearing an Elder helmet.

No, look, you're lying on a flat metal floor.

Things began to sort themselves out. He was lying on a metal floor covered with ages of animal droppings in varying degrees of freshness. Hoof prints were imprinted in the feces.

There was some sort of horned goat with a tufted white beard standing over him, browsing on the collar of his HRN, having no luck chewing off a piece.

Looked sort of familiar. Goats, where had he seen goats like this before? Oh! In the mountains near Castle Blanchefort. What were they called?

Quit trying to eat my coat . . . Get away!

He sat up and the goat skipped down the hallway, adding its hoof prints into the layers of feces.

Ibex! That's what they were called. The goat was an Ibex, a hearty mountain goat found in the north.

A whole herd of Ibexes rumbled down the corridor, their hooves creating a thunder of noise. He could smell their wild gaminess as they passed around him.

Where was he? Holding the helmet steady with his right hand, he took a hard look around. He was in a long corridor that rose up in a towering series of metal stacks or chimneys. The corridor he stood in was about a hundred feet wide and an undetermined length long. It was flanked with a dizzying array of glass and metal carousels that spun in unison, each joined to the others all around like an assemblage of cogs working in ageless precision. There were ten levels of carrousels with the smallest being situated at the top, getting progressively larger through the lower levels to three times the size of a man at the bottom, like an inverse series of church bells. Through the glass, the carrousels were filled with some sort of dark blue fluid. Floating forms of what looked like Spotted Tallups, a kind of medium-sized wild cat common in the Esther marshes, drifted around in the fluid like laundry in a washer.

The Tallups spun in the carrousels, asleep.

So, here, in a crack in the ground, completely undetectable, was a Grand Animalium as A-Ram had called it, built by the Elders, covered in dung, and functioning perfectly all these centuries spitting out random animals and sending them on their way.

He fought off the urge to explore. He had to remember what he was here to find: the stellar route to Eng.

Where could it be? Could be anywhere.

He thought he heard someone walking up behind him. Soft footsteps clicking on metal, moving at a quick walking cadence. He turned.

A woman approached wearing white Sisters' robes, missing the headdress. She had long black hair and a stunning face. Who was this? She carried a heavy arm-load of papers, scrolls, parchments, and a little, table-top telescope. She had her nose buried in a loose collection of parchments.

She walked up to him and gave a surprised start. "Your pardon," she said in a preoccupied voice as she moved past him.

Stenstrom was incredulous. Who was this woman? A Sister clearly, but . . .

"Sister, wait!"

The woman stopped and turned her head a little. "I am in a hurry."

"What are you doing at the bottom of Magravine chasm?"

"Chasm? This is my home," she said, continuing on. "It is a little remote, but I'd hardly call it a chasm."

Her home? He lifted the helmet and peeked under. He felt his brain recoil a little. The Grand Animalium disappeared, as did the woman. He was back in the unsteady, uneven bottom of the darkened chasm. He stumbled and fell down a few feet, wedging his foot.

He dropped the helmet back down. A fist of color and a film of disjointed images passed before his eyes and he was back in the Grand Animalium.

He moved down the corridor, following the woman. "Great Sister!"

Again she turned. "What may I help you with, sir?" she said in a hurried but reasonable voice. "It's not often I have visitors here."

"Are you the Grand Abbess of Magravine?"

"Who else would I be?"

"You're also the Black Abbess?"

She stopped and puzzled. "I don't know that name. Who is the Black Abbess?"

"You are. You're the Black Abbess."

"Again, I don't know that name. Not a very flattering one by the sound of it. Is that what they're calling me now in Valenhelm? I never wear black." She glanced at the stack of papers she carried. "I confess to being in a bit of a rush. Perhaps you might care for a spot of lunch as I attend to my duties. As I said, I don't often have visitors. Stay, please. Once concluded, I shall join you."

She turned and began walking away.

"Great Abbess, I'm looking for Eng!"

She stopped, her curiosity tweaked. "Eng? Why are you looking for Eng? It's not an overly pleasant place—very low troposphere, rather cold, and a little dark as well. I've been there several times myself, a tiresome, ghastly trip. I can't say I recommend it."

"I lost something there, and must recover it."

"A family heirloom perhaps? Many people left things behind on Eng. Quite a shame."

She produced some sort of time-keeping device and consulted it. "Well, I'm heading in that direction, walk with me and I'll show you. I've recorded Eng's location."

He came to her side, Stenstrom's six foot, seven inch height towering over her. She adjusted the stack of items she carried and held them out, expecting him to carry them for her. He reached out and took them. What she handed him, didn't have weight, per se, but it had substance of some sort. That done, she continued walking, Stenstrom at her side. "Please keep up, sir." Stenstrom quickened his pace.

This certainly wasn't at all what he had expected. The Grand Abbess of Magravine: the enemy, the inflictor of pain.

The Black Abbess.

And here she was, a perfectly reasonable and enchanting woman. But, what was she? A projection, a transaction of thought locked in time? That must be it. She had to be an after-image from ages past, probably before she became the Black Abbess.

A ghost stuck in a nether-reality, replaying past events, able to interact to some extent.

"Great Abbess?" he asked.

"Yes?"

"You mentioned you seldom have visitors; why is that?"

"I don't know, really. I suppose it's because the others are afraid of me, and what I know."

"The others?"

"The Grand Abbesses. I think in ways they often don't find palatable. I explore topics they are too afraid to. And, I suppose I have a rather obsessive nature. My sister, Subra, is also obsessive, but people love her. Everyone loves Subra and leaves Magravine to her books." She looked up at him and smiled. "But, you're here today, and I welcome your company."

He listened to her words—possibly spoken ages ago.

He wondered about something. "Have you ever heard of Shadow tech?"

"No, should I have?" She sounded intrigued. "I'm not often asked a question I don't know the answer to. What is 'Shadow tech'?"

"Nothing. My mistake."

"You are lying, sir. I know when lies are told, and when they are not. Yet another reason why they're afraid of me."

They walked a little bit further. She stopped and pointed. "The location of Eng, carved here in perpetuity. It's no great secret; however, the information might become lost to the ages with the passage of time, as with Cammara and Emmira. I intend to preserve the knowledge. There is nothing more tragic than something that is plainly known falling into oblivion."

"I agree, Great Abbess, and thank you." She held out her hands and Stenstrom gave her papers back.

"Do not forget; lunch shall be served in an hour. May I count on your dining with me? I do confess to sometimes being a bit lonely."

"Of course. I truly wish to have lunch with you."

She looked at his face and gave a smile. "And I have been remiss. What is your name, sir?"

"I am Stenstrom, Lord of Belmont-South Tyrol."

Magravine looked puzzled. "I don't know that name. You are full of information I don't know. I would be keen to learn more about your home, and about this 'Shadow tech' you mention. Sounds worthy of research."

The dead girls. The dead bodies. The torment. The Black Abbess. The Vith coming in force. The smoking hole in the ground they left behind. The Black Hats.

He studied her, and for a moment, her image changed. She became a hunched, terrifying figure, eyes glazed in utter evil, skin blackened, hands clenched and ready to mangle. Just for a second she appeared that way, then she was back as she was.

"Ooust is on the menu for today," she said, continuing down the corridor. "I hope you fancy it."

"Sounds . . . good," he said.

He watched her walk away and, for a moment, he grieved. She was such a lovely person, and then what had happened? Discovery, obsession, madness? Loneliness? Agony? If only she would have remained as she was, how things might have been different. The chasm of Magravine might never have been.

If only . . .

He turned to the area where she pointed. He saw nothing but the Elder tech carousel slowly spinning. He concentrated and rummaged around with the helmet's sight, passing through the layers of time and reality. A carved mural appeared before him, laid out as a celestial chart of bewildering complexity.

<Gwen!> he thought through the tregador.

No response. He produced a pen and folded ream of vellum with a wave of his hand and carefully copied what he was looking at, double and triple checking everything to ensure he got every detail right. He left nothing to chance; he copied everything: the symbols, the figures, even cracks and imperfections in the stone.

No, no—they weren't right. Copying by hand was too imprecise. The chart relied on angles and lines of intersection; any tiny deviation would put one off millions of stellar miles in the wrong direction. After several failed attempts, he decided to create a rubbing. He tacked up a sheet of fresh velum, and using a piece of graphite he made Holystones with, created a detailed rubbing, the lines and features of the chart coming out nicely.

When satisfied, he put his materials away, placed the rubbing in the center of the ream to protect it, then turned to leave. He was excited, his heart pounding. He'd done it! Here, before him was the location of long lost Eng. Gwen must be rubbing off on him. The moment of discovery was intoxicating.

Oh, what stories he'd have to tell Gwen and the rest. Would they believe that the Black Abbess was once a charming lady? Probably not.

He TK'ed himself up, past the magnificent carrousels made by the Elders and up into the heights. The view through the helmet began to flicker as, in his excitement, he wasn't controlling it as well as before. Lines of force passed in front of him, ages passed.

As he flew up, he heard a ghastly cackling coming from below. *"AHAHAHAHAAHHAHAHAHAHAHAHA!"* It was the ugliest laugh he'd ever heard.

"Where are you going?" he heard a diabolical, baritone voice cry out. *"You've only just arrived and I wish to show you wondrous things!"*

He thought he saw something black and veiled flying up from the depths after him, reaching and laughing, twisted and demented.

"LET ME SHOW YOU!!!"

The raw evil that radiated from the figure was overwhelming. Quickly, he pulled the helmet off and the shiny-black sides of the chasm returned, the laughing gone, though it echoed through his thoughts.

He crashed through the runs of ANGRY MISER wire, scattering the animated charms into the depths. The eyeball charms, fully alerted, didn't go down without a fight. Cannons turned in his direction. Hot beams of energy, buck shot, and explosive gases erupted in a fiery wall.

Stenstrom fell to the hard earth near the lip of the chasm. He pushed the helmet away from him, uncertain of where he was in space and time for a moment.

The rushing sounds of claws scrabbling up the side of the chasm brought him back.

Five Stoutbacks, large six-legged reptilian creatures from Onaris, clambered over the side. They were the Onaris version of an ox coming from the fierce mountains in the central continent, emerald green, tireless and strong, able to cling to near vertical surfaces with ease and, if Lt. Kilos was to be believed, as mean as a snake and packing a dirty bite that could put one into a bout of blood poisoning with the slightest nip. Many of Ki's brothers, sisters, and cousins were missing select body parts due to careless encounters with the bad-tempered Stoutback.

They tested the air with their flicking tongues and shambled off in various directions, most paying no attention to him. One, however, loped in his direction, head lowered, tongue darting out of its mouth. Its cow-like size and apparent power came clear as it closed the distance. Stenstrom took the helmet and tried to TK into the air.

He couldn't concentrate, his mind still addled from the ordeal of the helmet. He remained rooted to the ground.

The Stoutback opened its maw, dripping with sticky saliva, and attacked. Stenstrom raised his left arm to protect himself and the great lizard chomped down on his forearm with crushing force. His HRN held; the dagger-like teeth failed to penetrate. The creature thrashed about, trying to knock Stenstrom down where it could then rend him open with its claws.

The Sisters were with him. He had their power. He stood his ground. Stenstrom supposed he could kill it easily enough with his NTH's, but he found he had a kind heart for beasts no matter how huge or terrible, and he'd rather not kill if he could avoid it. He shook his hand; the bag Alesta had given him appeared from nowhere. He managed to reach in, drew a stone, then cast it at the Stoutback, hitting it in its haunches.

There was a flash and the great beast vanished, the others looking on impassively in the distance. The sleeve of his HRN was a mess with lizard slobber, but, as always, it resisted and was undamaged.

Lying on the ground was a shiny pewter charm in the shape of a six-legged Stoutback. The turquoise Holystone Alesta had given him worked. He picked the charm up and placed it into the depths of his HRN.

<Gwen, are you there?>

<Right here, Bel! What happened to you? We were getting worried.>

<I got cutoff when I put the helmet on. I have the data. Don't ask me to describe what it was like because I'm not up to it right now. I'll tell you later. I crashed through the ANGRY MISER, and now there are Stoutbacks from Onaris running around all over. I got attacked by one.>

<Are you all right?>

<I'm fine. My HRN will probably need a cleaning. I got rid of it with one of the Holystones Alesta gave me.>

<Those must have come from the sympathetic charms. According to our research, they won't last forever, give them ten or fifteen minutes and they'll return to where they came from.>

<I'm going to clear out of here. I'll head southeast toward the River Seven. If A-Ram and Alesta could come and get me, that would be great.>

A-Ram's thoughts came on. <No problem, Bel, We're on our way.>

Stenstrom gained some height and drifted away, moving east. He had a great deal of visibility and could see the distant river moving slowly in its banks. Before long he saw the familiar whirling column of white fog appear to the east and then fade just as quickly. There was A-Ram and Alesta! He hurried down to join them.

"Took you two long enough," he said jokingly as he emerged from the shadows.

A-Ram and Alesta were in distress.

The Lacerta was there, standing skinny in her black lace gown and her lenses, smoking her usual cigarette, and she had them both by the arm.

"Well, hi, buddy boy!" she said in her child-like voice. "Did you miss me, huh?"

"You!" Stenstrom spat as he drew his NTH's. "Have you been hiding here this entire time, you miserable git?"

"Yep! We'd figure you'd show sooner or later, and ya' didn't disappoint."

"I owe you a killing, Lacerta for what you did to Gwendolyn."

"Awwww . . . How's your lady? I buzzed her pretty good, didn't I? Right through the fuckin' terminal and all!" She tightened her grip and A-Ram whimpered a bit. "So, first thing's first, did you get the data you were looking for? Did ya', Jo-Boy? My employer wants ta' know."

"I found nothing."

"Aww, well, that's too bad. I guess I'll have to kill these two for nothing then."

"Harm my friends and you die seconds later."

The Lacerta's eyes flashed with delight; she was enjoying this standoff. "Oh! You know I'm supposed to play ya' this message, let's see." She tossed A-Ram aside like a rag doll and he flew through the air a considerable distance before landing hard.

"Rammy!" Alesta cried.

"Shaddaup, you scrawny little bitch!" She fished around in her handbag and got out a small holo-disk. She tossed it to the ground. The disk came to life and the holographic image of Hannah-Ben Shurlamp, seated behind her dragonball desk, appeared in withering color.

"Paymaster Stenstrom," she said, "well met . . . again."

"Are you not tired of these games, Professor? Haven't you anything better to occupy your time?"

"Absolutely not, Paymaster. Rest assured, you have my full attention. It needn't have come to this; I was willing to pay, handsomely so, for the information. Now, unfortunately, look where we are."

"You're going to allow your paid dog to harm my friends over a bit of meaningless information?"

"Yes, I am, and I'm certain you're aware it's not meaningless by this point. I believe your countess-in-waiting understands, pity. So, allow me to ask, and please note, the lives of your friends depend on the answer, did you locate the information? Did you locate Eng?"

Stenstrom paused. The Lacerta tightened her grip a bit. Alesta grimaced.

"Of course I did."

Hannah-Ben Shurlamp's brown eyes flared in anticipation. "I see. Well done. Well done, indeed. You have accomplished something not done in thousands of years. Unfortunately, none but those present will ever know that. You will give it to my associate, or both your friends shall die."

Stenstrom shook his hand and produced the roll of vellum. "You mean this?" he asked. "Is this what you want?"

Professor Shurlamp stood up. "Give it to my associate now and she will verify the contents, then your friends may go free. And they'd best watch their tongues in the days ahead, for they shall be watched."

He took a step forward and held out the roll of paper. The Lacerta let go of Alesta and TK'ed both her and A-Ram into the air. She reached out and took the paper, allowing her finger to gently run down Stenstrom's. They stood nose to nose.

"I'm aching to kill you," Stenstrom whispered.

"Ya', well, here I am, Jo Boy. Kill me, kill me up fine." She closed her eyes and took a deep breath in through her nose. "Know somethin', you smell good, fella'." She then TK'ed Stenstrom into the air as well. He felt the crushing vise of it constrict around him.

Hannah-Ben Shurlamp spoke again. "Unfortunately, we're at a place where I can't allow any of you to live. People might talk. And, remember, you've only yourself to blame for this." She turned to the Lacerta. "Open the scroll and show it to me, please."

The woman in black stared at Stenstrom, breathing in his scent deeply. She seemed captivated by his smell.

"Lacerta!" Shurlamp yelled.

"Huh?"

"The documents! Show them to me!"

She shook her head and gave Stenstrom a last wink. She opened the roll of paper and showed it to the hologram, the Professor's eyes livid with the moment.

"Yes, yes, I see!" she cried.

A pewter charm, nestled within the ream, fell to the ground. A gigantic Stoutback appeared, roaring and tongue flicking. It bit down on the Lacerta's wrist, slicing through her black wrappings and drawing blood. Stenstrom heard her bones crunch under the force. She screamed in agony and released the three of them from her TK. A-Ram and Alesta staggered away as the Stoutback, in a full killing frenzy, clawed the Lacerta's lace gown to shreds.

"For the love of Creation, Lacerta, control this situation immediately!" the holographic Hannah-Ben Shurlamp demanded. Stenstrom stomped on the disk, destroying it.

The Lacerta wrenched herself free of the Stoutback. Stenstrom slammed the stone helmet onto her head. Her gaunt, pale face shown through the visor, and as had happened to him, she was overwhelmed by the ferocity of what she saw. Her eyes went round. She screamed.

Stenstrom hauled back and haymakered her square in the face, shattering the stone helmet to innumerable bits. She fell and the Stoutback had her again. Stenstrom snatched up the vellum and several of the larger bits of the helmet, took A-Ram and Alesta into a light TK and bore them away. His last glance of the Lacerta: the Stoutback had her by the head, thrashing back and forth, her body shaking about like a doll.

8—Point of Light

He took them several miles east to the River Seven. There, Alesta called for the Merian's Road, and in a few minutes the three of them were safely back on the *Seeker*.

"Are you two all right?" he asked. embracing them both.

"We're fine, Bel," Alesta said, somewhat shaken. "That foul woman was nearly the death of us. Smart thinking with the Stoutback."

"I can be just as devious as Professor Shurlamp."

"Did you see what it was doing to her?" A-Ram asked. "I almost feel sorry for the woman."

"Any pain she endured before signing off was well earned."

A short time later, Stenstrom was reunited with Gwen who was resting in her quarters.

"Here it is, Gwen. Here's what Professor Shurlamp was ready to murder the three of us for." He handed her the rubbing.

Flush with excitement, Gwen kissed Stenstrom on the cheek, then got out of bed and took the paper to her terminal.

Stenstrom and Alesta pulled up some chairs while Gwendolyn and A-Ram fussed over the details of the chart. While Gwen entered the information into the embedded terminal, Alesta prepared coffee.

"You sure you're up to this, Gwen?" Stenstrom asked.

She nodded and continued working while sitting there in her nightgown. Gwen was taking this and running with it. She was absorbed. Rediscovering the location of Eng would be a scientific event of great acclaim.

There was a knock at the door and Taara came in. "How'd it go?"

Stenstrom tossed her a piece of the destroyed Elder helmet. "Here, Taara, for your window sill. Are we still on course?"

"Yep."

"Anybody out there hanging off our Six and Nine?"

"Nope, I checked." She pulled up a chair.

Stenstrom was troubled. He was still thinking about the Black Abbess. What a loss.

Alesta came out and served the coffee. "Taara, would you like some?"

"Nah, not enough sugar."

Gwendolyn took her cup and downed most of it in a gulp. Normally, with everybody dressed and she in a nightgown and shoeless, she would be very guarded and self-conscious. Now however, she was too absorbed to give it a thought. "I've got all the information entered into the terminal. Good thinking creating a rubbing, darling. The precise geometry of this chart is essential and I doubt you would have been able to re-create it by hand."

Darling? She's never called him that in mixed company before. "Darling" was for after a love-making session or late in the night in bed. Even Taara took notice.

A-Ram had a few passing thoughts and he tried to get at the keys. "But, Gwen . . ."

"Get away, will you," Gwen said, lightly slapping his hands. "It's good as is." She pressed a few buttons and the lights went down. She enlarged the holographic cone and a stellar chart appeared in mid-air, along with Stenstrom's rubbing.

"All right, it's obvious that this stellar object on the Black Abbess's chart is Kana," she said as one of the dots in the lower portion of the chart began blinking. "These bodies here appear to be Onaris and Bazz, adjusting for one-hundred thousand years of parallax."

"No, no, Gwen, you got too much . . ." A-Ram protested.

"It's fine," Gwen replied. "Drink your coffee, will you?"

Stenstrom's humor wasn't the best. "May we please get on with it? Fine, that's Kana, so what's next?"

Gwendolyn turned back to the map. "Following this line of intersection all the way to this point here, we end up, apparently, 6:00am of the Bell Nebula. It's big enough to be an acceptable stellar landmark. I imagine the Elders and our ancestors also used it as a one ages ago. Now, these symbolic calculations here appear to be an old form of trans-boolean, which provides crucial course correction information. They didn't use AM/PM back then. So, given that, and applying the correct calculations and converting the results to AM/PM, we make a radical adjustment at the Bell Nebula to 4:52AM mark 7:36PM, to this point here, going past Ming Mooreland and out into a long slog in open space." A-Ram commented. "It seems the Elders led our ancestors on a straight course from Eng to here without much deviation."

Gwendolyn came across a blip along the way. "It appears they stopped at this system for a time."

"That's Punt," A-Ram added. "That's where the Nillists of Punt came from initially. There's an open vortex of Shadow tech there."

"Good to know," Gwendolyn said. "The line continues on until we get to a twelve-planet solar system orbiting what appears to be a Type A Orange medium." She expanded the size of the solar system. The eighth planet began to blink. She looked at it for a moment, her eyes fixed and wide in the moment of discovery, on that little blinking dot. Without taking her eyes from the cone, she held her hand out to Stenstrom. He took it, and she squeezed hard. "That is Eng. Long lost Eng . . ."

Everybody looked at the blinking image.

"How far?" Stenstrom asked, adding a somewhat unwelcome edge of practicality to this rather ethereal moment.

"Twenty-two LU's. Roughly one hundred and forty light years."

"A-Ram, at full sail, how long will it take us to get there?"

A-Ram rubbed his chin. "Under full sail, with quite a number of Stellar Mach transverses in between, just under five weeks, assuming we don't have any great amount of sickness or breakdowns."

"Gonna' need at least ten SM's," Taara added. "That's lot for one crew shift."

"We shan't breakdown," Gwen said. "Not this ship."

Stenstrom looked at the map. "Five weeks through open space?"

Taara put her boots up on the table—a very bad habit of hers. "Aw, what's the big deal, Bel? Five weeks, we've been out for longer than that."

"In charted, patrolled space. But this—we'll be on our own. No resupply, no forage or safe harbor. No dry dock."

"How do you know there won't be any forage?" Taara asked. "What about that Punt place?"

"No way!" A-Ram cried.

"The *Seeker*'s fully serviced and more than up to the job, Bel," Gwen said. He turned to her. "What's the status of our coils?"

She gazed at the blinking holographic lights hovering over the table. "Gwen?"

She shook her head and pulled back from her thoughts. "Sorry, Darling. Fine. The coils are fine. They're not due a dry-docking for quite a few more set-tachs yet. We're good to go."

Stenstrom remembered being far from the League during the Kestral Affair with Captain Davage. The *New Faith*, Davage's ship, had been cast far out into Kestral space with a month-long journey ahead of them. He remembered it being a very lonely feeling, to be so far from home. And, the *New Faith* was a faster ship.

Everybody looked at him. "I'd say we should make sail for Planet Fall and load out for a long voyage then head off."

Alesta finished her coffee and lit up. "Why all this talk of long treks in virgin space, Bel? Again, you have our favor."

"You can go that far out, Alesta?"

"We can go anywhere we choose. We simply must have seen our destination with our own eyes. Anywhere we've seen, our Road can go."

Gwen stood. "There's the telescope in the tower. Would that count, seeing Eng as merely a point of magnified light?"

Alesta smiled. "Yes."

Gwen stood. "Please, give me a moment to dress."

After she dressed, they went up into the tower, the highest point in the rear section of the ship. Gwen walked a bit slowly, leaning on Stenstrom as she went along. The Tower also contained the ship's main mess hall and library and they encountered many crew coming and going. At the very top of the tower was the observatory, a place once used by the Sisters when they frequented the *Seeker*. It was a dome of clear dura-plas, and when the lights were turned down to the correct level, it appeared as if one were standing naked in space surrounded by layers of stars. In the center of the observatory was a large motorized telescope mounted on several gimbals.

Gwen went to the terminal and punched up her coordinates. A-Ram took the lights down and the place filled with starlight. Far below, the main bulk of the *Seeker* stretched off in one direction, lit up by running lights and the roving shaft of the main sensor light as it panned about in a regular arc.

Scrolling through her calculations, Gwendolyn went to the telescope. "Bel, we're not in the correct attitude to train the telescope properly. We need a Z-axis roll."

"How much?"

"52 degrees."

"Com," he said.

"Com here, sir," came the reply from the bridge.

"Com, send to helm. I need a 52 degree Z-axis roll."

"Aye, sir."

After a moment, the stars moved in unison as the ship rolled. Gwen stood by the telescope, her hands shaking a bit. When the roll completed, she finished entering her coordinates. The telescope came to life and glided around, its cylindrical tube pointing up and to the starboard side. She put her face into the view-finder and made small adjustments, moving the knobs with the pads of her fingers.

Gwen erupted into a smile. "There! There it is!" She checked her watch. "Sixteen bells, three-quarters—that's when we laid eyes on Eng once again." She took several pictures with the telescope's mounted camera. "Come, everybody, look." She stepped away and put her arms around Stenstrom as A-Ram and Alesta took turns peering through the view finder. He felt Gwen's heart racing.

"That's it?" Alesta said looking through the view finder. "You're sure?"

"Positive."

Alesta came away and Gwen pulled Stenstrom by the hand to the telescope. "Go on, Darling—take a look." He put his face into the view finder and saw a vast ocean of stars. Caged in the crosshairs was a small, nondescript orange point of light.

"That's Eng's star, Bel. Relax your eye and you'll see several smaller points of light appear at is axis. Eng is the eighth one out to its right."

He fussed with the view finder and tried to relax. "I don't see anything."

"Have patience."

He tried again. Several tiny points of light emerged. One of them was Eng—a long way off.

"So, Alesta, having seen Eng through the telescope, you believe we may use your Star's Road to go there?"

She was ecstatic. "Yes, we can go at our leisure. We can walk there this very day."

He shook his head. All that space and distance, meaningless. "Well then, if we are favored, then we are honored."

"Let's enjoy lunch, and then go. I need to rest up a bit," Gwen said.

"You're not going anywhere, Gwen. You're still recovering."

"I am coming, Bel. It will be said in posterity that Lord and Countess Belmont, along with Lord and Lady A-Ram and Taara de la Anderson of Bazz were the first to touch foot on Eng in over a hundred millennia. I don't care if you have to prop me up and carry my FEDULA, I will be there at your side. And if you have to work extra hard to preserve my life for some reason, then that is on you. Now, let's eat. I'm starving."

Stenstrom stared at his plate of beef and mashed potatoes in disbelief. "Com," he said. "Locate Lord A-Ram and Lady Alesta."

"Aye, sir," came the reply from the mess hall ceiling. "They are not aboard the ship, sir."

He ran a disgruntled hand through his hair. "I should have known it wouldn't be this easy."

"What happened," Gwen asked, holding her fork.

"A-Ram said he'd received an urgent private message, and they went to his quarters to take it. Now, 'poof', they're gone, and the Road is gone with them." A-Ram and Alesta's unfinished and abandoned lunches sat cold on the table.

Taara was nonplussed. "They're probably off helping you out in some other reality."

"Great good that does me here in this one."

Gwendolyn didn't seem bothered, either. "Then, if that's the case, we'll have to cut anchor and sail."

"We can't just cut anchor and sail, Gwen. We need provisions. We're not loaded out for a long trip. We're going to have to dock and the loading will take at least three days."

Gwendolyn sighed. "Three days, and I'm certain Professor Shurlamp will harass us the entire time." She looked at her hands. "I suppose I've been a bit selfish as of late. I got caught up in all the excitement. You and

A-Ram and Alesta could have been hurt or killed, and all because of me. I need to apologize to them, the moment they return."

"A day or two ago I would have been inclined to agree with you, but, after hearing Duval's ravings, this quest to Eng is a race we have to win. And I don't think Professor Shurlamp will be a problem for the next few days."

"Why not?"

"Because the rubbing I gave you wasn't the only drawing I did. I made several when I realized I couldn't get the details down accurately enough by copying freehand. The Lacerta showed one of the bad drawings to Professor Shurlamp; so right now she's spinning her wheels looking in the wrong direction."

"Bel, I love you!" Gwen cried.

"So, now is the time to act, before Shurlamp figures out what the deal is. Taara, let's come about and make sail for Planet Fall. We'll go low rent and make berth in a dock seldom used by Fleet traffic. We'll kit out there for a protracted voyage, taking on at least ten months worth of provisioning."

"Ten months is a bit excessive, wouldn't you say, Bel?"

"We'll fill an extra cargo hold if we have to. I want nothing left to chance."

"Ten months will exceed our Fleet rations."

"I'll pay for it personally, then. I have quite a few hidden cashes of money stashed about, as I'm certain Shurlamp is monitoring the Belmont coffers. While we're down, Gwendolyn, I want a complete inspection of the SM coils—tip to top."

"Bel, that will take days."

"Then let it take days."

She gruffed. "Fine. However, if I'm to be stuck in the Engineering bay performing a battery of pointless tests after I have already told you our engines are fully serviceable when I could be on the town with my betrothed, then you're going to be down there with me observing the procedure. I insist . . . Captain."

"Agreed. We'll have at least another two weeks before my father eases his grip on the *George Parr*. By then, we'll be gone into parts unknown leaving him and the professor well behind. Taara, if anyone gets curious, leak a rumor that our destination is the Hedgepeth."

"Ok, Bel."

They finished their lunch; Gwen happily chattering about their soon-to-be realized discovery and Taara talking about some clubs she knew on Planet Fall. Stenstrom gazed at A-Ram and Alesta's unfinished lunches. He had a feeling that this time they were going to be gone a while.

9—HOFFMAN PLATE

Three days later, with little fanfare, the *Seeker* made birth in a seedy dock in the western reaches of Hoffman Plate, one of the three man-made floating "continents" orbiting Planet Fall.

Planet Fall, a massive brown dwarf streaked with reds, whites, oranges and browns, was all alone in its vast orbit around lonely Rho-Procyon, far away from everything. The nearest neighboring star was forbidden Codis, the beak of the constellation Corvus, the Crow, as seen from Kana, was the largest gas-giant class planet in the League. Through the stellar millennia, Planet Fall had proved the death of its solar neighbors, either enslaving them as moons or devouring them with its wretched, ever-present gravity. The environs around Planet Fall were a shooting gallery of large, small, and medium sized moons in disorganized orbits coupled with deadly gravity wells and pools of hard, unshieldable radiation. It got its name in the days of the old Fleet from its habit of latching onto and pulling starcraft, even those at a fair distance, down into its dense, cloudy atmosphere. Even modern vessels had to be careful, though the most deadly gravitational regions around the planet were well mapped. Normally, such a hazardous planet would be marked and generally avoided. However, Planet Fall was rich in rare trace elements and exotic gasses; the spoils of previously devoured worlds floating in its high-speed winds, and the race was on to tame and inhabit this bucking bronco of a planet.

It was a certain testament to dogged persistence and ingenuity that the feat was accomplished in 000643ex.

Planet Fall was still a dangerous place, though, and its approach best left to the experts. A standard practice was to board a Tugger, a professional helmsman of the Order of the Tuggers who knew the pitfalls of navigating through Planet Fall's moon and rad field.

The Tug ship *Nifta* hailed for a boarding and the Tugger was admitted. Stenstrom's junior helmsman, Tennoen of Marx, was glad to step back and let the expert Tugger take over and pilot them in. Stenstrom had been to Planet Fall many times as paymaster for Captain Davage, and had never thought twice of it. But now, as captain of his own ship, seeing the massive gas giant with its coral-reef of moons, its iron-hand gravity and pockets of lethal radiation, he felt a bit apprehensive.

The Fore sensing station's rad meter squealed continuously, warning the bridge of unshielded radiation. The Tugger, a salty fellow in a midnight blue uniform, dirty hat, and an unkempt beard, didn't think anything of it. "What's tha' count on those rads, darlin'?"

"850 micro-rungens and climbing. That's what's getting through our shielding," the fearful Fore sensing crewman said, a hint of panic in her voice.

"Squelch that alarm, darlin'. 850's not worth worrying about," the Tugger said. "When it gets to an even gerback, you lemme' know."

"What is a 'gerback', sir?"

"A thousand, kid. A thousand. If yer' gonna' hang out in Planet Fall, you need to pick up the lingo. We don't get nothin' in a twist till we sees a gerback on the dial." He held onto the helm with one casual hand and pulled a gold pocket watch from his vest. "We gotta' wait fer Moedron to pass fore' we can settle into approach."

"What's Moedron?" Stenstrom asked.

"It's a moon, Chief, an' it's the hardest place you ever seen. Got swallowed up by Planet Fall's gravity ages ago; but, she ain't hit bottom yet. She's jus' spinnin' round an' round beneath the clouds, going faster an' faster, dropping down a few feet each passin' year. In a couple par-millennium, she'll hit bottom, and when she does, Planet Fall'll go up like a Hoban Fireball. When she passes, the gravity will spike. You'll feel it in yer' guts, then you'll know you been Moedroned."

"How long are we to wait?" Stenstrom asked from his chair.

The Tugger checked his watch. Stenstrom felt a slight, sickening tug in his stomach and the ship's nose dropped. The Tugger casually moved the helm to compensate. "`Bout now," he said. "You feel that? That's Moedron talkin' to ya'. Now that's over with, we can take a nice dive in."

He sank the nose and barreled into the Gallery, making small talk the whole time in his harsh Planet Fall burr. "So, you datin' anybody?" he asked the shocked girl at the sensing station as the rad meter started squealing again. "I could show you 'round, keep you from tha' tourist spots. I know where the good drinkin' grog is."

"1050 micro-rungens!" she cried. "You said to inform you when the meter spikes over a 1000!"

The Tugger wiped his nose. "Ahh, don' worry 'bout it."

Soon, swerving this way and that, the *Seeker* plunged into Planet Fall's upper atmosphere, the turbulence battering the ship. The bridge crew was on-edge and tense with gritted teeth; the Tugger, however, seemed to have to labor to stay awake during the whole ordeal. They descended and eventually a large object appeared in the distance, anchored in the clouds. Appearing small at first, it loomed larger until it filled their holo-cone, a great assemblage of metal and blinking lights.

"Hoffman Plate," the Tugger said. "A marvel, I tell ya'. Four gerbacks long, two gerbacks wide, all kinds of everything going on down there. You want it; it's going on in Hoffman Plate. Deckard is boring and Z-Encarr—I piss on it! Got the best joints and cricket shacks on Planet Fall right here on Hoffman Plate. You watch the Erynes, though. You see a lady with red eyes comin' at ya', you move in the other direction, hear?"

With a final jolt of heavy turbulence they entered Hoffman Plate's containment field and things became blissfully calm as the Tugger dove down toward the berthing docks at the southern end of the structure. A massive and continuous city emerged in a pincushion of spired towers as they got closer. buzzing with activity. Skillfully, the Tugger made berth and the *Seeker* was down.

The *Seeker* sat in port as the crew filtered out to take their shore leave, exploring deep into the wonders and temptations of Hoffman Plate. Stenstrom wondered about Professor Shurlamp and her spies. They must be here on the lookout even though the *Seeker* had been flying the old *Exeter*'s flag. Most of the crew had been tipped that they were heading to the Hedgepeth, so if prodded, they would deliver false information.

Gwendolyn wasn't kidding about making Stenstrom stay with her while she conducted tests on the coils. He just stood there in the bay not having any idea what was happening. He tried to sneak out several times and Gwen took immediate exception. One time he actually got down the hallway and:

<Get back in here, Bel, or I might forget that I love you and Pop you one!>

Gwen finally finished her tests on the ship's SM coils and certified the *Seeker* as well fit for travel. Feeling near fully recovered, she wanted to spend their last evening on Planet Fall and see the sights before take-off on the morrow. She literally dragged Stenstrom from the ship. As promised, her stiff Zenon demeanor had become much looser since his proposal. She'd take his arm and swing her hips a little. She'd even kiss him on the cheek; quite a change from the prim proper Gwendolyn of old, stiff as a piece of stale bread and utterly boring.

The great continuous city at the top level of Hoffman Plate was black and cavernous in the early evening against the ruddy orange, red, and white streaks of turbulent clouds roaring over the lofty containment bubble. The docks were crowded with Fleet and League shipping, bobbing slightly in the stray fields of counter gravity designed to keep Planet Fall's invisible hand from crushing man and machine alike. Every ten bells the sirens sounded and they felt the gut-churning passage of Moedron through the cloudy depths of Planet Fall below.

They plunged into the city, investigating the exotic shops and tasting the local fare. Occasionally they passed some of the crew wandering about. They gave the correct Fleet salute at first, but when they saw Gwen was in a less-formal state, they happily just waved.

"I feel guilty, Gwen," Stenstrom said often throughout the day.

"Guilty about what?"

"About dragging these people off into the unknown, so far from the League."

"These are Fleet crew members, Bel. They understand the risks, and if they're too yellow to perform a little exploring, then let Hoffman Plate be their safe harbor until a more sedate ship comes along. Exploration is part of the Fleet purview. You're acting like an old woman."

"Not in our case. We're privateers. We're supposed to march the tried and true and pick the Xaphan's pockets."

Gwen pulled him into an expensive shop that caught her eye. "You are this fabulous 'It Man', and you can do all these impossible things. Your crew and your betrothed are mere mortals—yet you might be surprised what we can do, too. Now, hold my bags, 'It Man'. I'm going to spend some money."

Later, loaded down with packages, they looked for a place to eat and found a nice cafe overlooking a large man-made river flowing the length of the continent. As they read their menus, trying to make sense of the Planet Fall dishes, a slight gentleman approached and stood over their table.

Stenstrom put his menu down. The man was wearing a black Remnath suit with a steckle tie, as was the Remnath tradition. "Pleasant evening," he said.

"Aye," Stenstrom replied, rather dubious. Gwen put her menu down and looked him over with a stern eye.

Without announcement, the man pulled a chair and sat down. "Your pardon," he said. "I don't mean to interrupt your dinner—oh, I recommend the Pullyap. It's a wonderful dish if you've not sampled it before. May I inquire, are you, by chance, Paymaster Stenstrom of the Fleet Privateer *Seeker?*"

"Aye," Stenstrom said again. "Are you looking for passage?"

The man smiled. "Ah, I thought so. Your coat announces your presence well. My name is Ottoman John Esquire, formerly of Bazz and associate of the famed Professor Com-Presor, professor emeritus at the University of Arden."

Gwen spoke up in an icy voice. "Professor Compressor?? And what can we do for you, Ottoman John of Bazz?"

"Yes, his name does arouse a bit of humor from time to time. I had heard that the *Seeker* is about to embark on a long voyage. I was hoping to earn passage and come along."

Civilians seeking passage wasn't uncommon and were generally welcome, provided they had the ready coin to pay their fare. However, Stenstrom and Gwendolyn were in no fit state to be trusting anybody, especially a scholar. Taara had been on the snoop for signs of their friend, Hannah-Ben Shurlamp; so far she hadn't made her presence felt. Both Stenstrom and Gwendolyn were on their guard.

"For what reason?" Gwen asked. "Is a mundane stellar curiosity such as the Hedgepeth of special interest to an un-athletic little man such as yourself?"

Ottoman John adjusted his tie. "Certainly not, my lady. I'm sorry, I did not get your name."

"My name was not offered."

Ottoman John was taken aback; to withhold one's name was the height of rudeness. "I see. Well then, to be direct, as I'm certain you are eager for your dinner, we have heard, through the grapevine, that Professor Hannah-Ben Shurlamp is on the verge of a remarkable discovery. My Professor . . ."

"Say his name," Gwen said in a commanding voice.

Ottoman John flushed, then continued. "Professor 'Compressor' has heard that the *Seeker*'s destination is not the Hedgepeth, but rather Eng, and that Professor Shurlamp has discovered Eng's location at long last and is questing to lay foot upon it by way of hired proxy. The entire learned community is simply buzzing about it. If that is the case, I must be aboard to properly document such a momentous event for posterity."

Gwen's eyes narrowed. "What was your name again, sir?"

"Ottoman John, of . . ."

"I am not certain where you get your information, sir, but we do not waste Fleet assets in search of lost dreams. Nor do we fly at the whim of a desk-bound, zip-head professor without proper channeling and payment. Do you understand me, sir?"

"I . . ."

"Our destination is the Hedgepeth and a dreary tour of measuring quarks. Also, if I'm not mistaken, we are full up. Isn't that right, captain?" she asked Stenstrom.

Before he could answer she cut him off. "There you see. And, sir, you might wish to inform your man, Professor Compressor, that Hannah-Ben Surcock . . ."

"Shurlamp, ma'am," he corrected.

"Whatever. Professor Surecock is most certainly 'half-cocked' in this situation. I'm certain whatever symposium she's planning will be an alcohol-fueled debacle of processed, catered food and starched shirts wishing they might someday kiss a member of the opposite sex. And, what's more, if Professor Compressor wishes a ride, tell him he should come here to Planet Fall and ask for himself; that is, if he can generate the courage to exit the safety of his office." Gwendolyn stood up to allow

Ottoman John to appreciate her size.

"Professor Compressor does not engage in such activities."

"Well then, Professor Compressor is clearly as big a loser as Professor Shurlamp, isn't he? Perhaps they should marry and asphyxiate each other while consummating their marriage."

"Professor Shurlamp is already married, to a teetotaler in . . ."

"*Who . . . cares*?" Gwen said.

Ottoman John blushed and cleared his throat. He turned to Stenstrom. "Paymaster, I would dearly . . ."

"I said we are full up, sir," Gwen said again, jumping in, her eyes on fire.

Ottoman John sighed and stood. "Aye then, well. Thank you. I apologize for interrupting your dinner." He stood, pushed in his chair, then walked away.

Stenstrom watched him depart. "Gwen, you . . ."

<shhhh,> she responded telepathically. *<Read your menu, Bel.>*

He picked it up. *<What is wrong with you?>*

<What's wrong with me? WE are discovering, Eng, Bel—not some idiotic associate professor from Arden. 'Professor Compressor'. I've never heard of such a silly name. And I am enraged Shurlamp would try to claim credit for Eng's discovery so fast. I'm simply dying to attend her symposium, stand up and shout 'You are looking in the wrong place, you wig-wearing, powder-faced bitch!' There will be no doubt, and no confusion, as to who re-discovered Eng—it's you and me. Those pasty-faced Shocktytes may take their diplomas and their wigs and stow them!>

<Shocktyte?? Bitch?? Such language.>

<He should consider himself lucky I didn't take him to the ground right here in the cafe for all to see and make him cry out in submission like a schoolgirl.>

<Well, I suppose you told him, then.>

<I suppose I did!> Gwen put her menu down and tried to change the subject. "Doesn't one of your old girlfriends live here on Hoffman Plate?" She posed the question in a light-hearted manner, but with a bit of teeth waiting to bite should the answer not be to her liking.

"If you're referring to Lady Christiana, you've got the wrong continent, Gwen. She lives on Z-Encarr."

"I see, and what is she to you?"

"A good friend."

"Ah. You might want to clarify that with her in writing. In fact, I insist."

He thought to commence a spirited debate with her on the subject when his tregador interrupted.

<Bel!> came Taara's frenzied thoughts.

"It's Taara over the treg," he said. *<Taara? What's going on? You're not in jail, are you?>*

<Bel!> she responded. *<There's a bomb on the ship! . . . It's . . .>* Taara's thoughts cut out.

"Bel, what's wrong?" Gwen asked, sensing his concern.

"Taara just said the ship's rigged with a bomb!"

"How did a bomb get on the ship?"

"Feature if I know!" *<Taara!>* he thought. *<Taara!>*

The tregador came to a scratchy sort of life in his head. There was a long, static-laced pause. *<Heya', Jo-boy . . .>* came an eventual icy response.

The Lacerta! He tensed up. *<Gave that Stoutback a stomachache, did you?>* he thought, trying to be bold.

<So, where were we? When we left off, you tried to feed me to a big-assed lizard out there in the middle of nowhere. At least I got a new handbag and a nice pair of shoes out of it. So listen, here's the score, I'm getting paid an awful lot of money to kill you and your crew, ok? It's nothing personal, that's just how it is. I should be pretty pissed, that lizard tore up my clothes and I had to get injections to keep my arm from falling off; but, we'll let bygones be bygones, right?>

He rose from his seat. "Gwen, stay here!" He then TK'ed himself into the air at speed, the people at the cafe gasping.

Gwen was furious. *<By the Elders, Bel—I will knuckle you up! Come back here and get me this instant!>*

He sped through the canyons of buildings, his HRN flapping like a sail. Soon, the waiting mass of the *Seeker* at dock appeared in the distance.

Somewhere in the ship was the Lacerta and a bomb.

<Where did you come from, Lacerta!> he thought back, trying to get her talking to grant him time to act.

<Got a Sister Priory, don't `cha?> she replied over the tregador. *<I used it. Took awhile to get my bearings and sniff you out, but, here I am.>*

<This is between you and me, Lacerta! Let us mix and spare the bystanders.>

<Nope, nope. I've got to kill you and everybody else as well. Too bad, you smell really good, boy. Yeah, like a fuckin' steak dinner. I had a good whiff of you out there at Magravine. That's what really gets a Sister going, you know, a person's smell, and you smell just great. If I had my way, I'd drag you to Valenhelm and do you right in the Sisters' front yard so they could watch. But, maybe I'll just paint their wall with your brains. I need money, you know, and lots of it. I love fine fabrics and rich foods, and those damn sex robots cost a fortune to keep running. I keep breaking them.>

He reached the ship and flew in through the open main hatch.

<Lacerta!> he thought as he rounded a corner and sped down the main corridor. *<Lacerta, I'm warning you!! I have command of a host of crawling things from the unlit bowers of the League unknown to the Sisterhood and, therefore, to you as well! I have creatures from your deepest nightmares available for immediate summoning!! By Elder's End, I can sit down to a ritual and fix demons to your soul that will give you no peace from here on out until your life blessedly comes to an end!! You claim to enjoy good food and rich clothing—my demons can turn every bite you take into spoonful of dust before it falls upon your eager tongue and rot your clothing into a musty grave shroud falling off your lank, disgusting body. And sex—they'll line a brick wall in your foul works where you'll not feel the touch of a man, woman or child ever again!! By mouth, by cardinal, by rear—you'll enjoy nothing! The harder you try for relief, the more numb you shall get and the roar for it you'll feel always; a fire unquenchable!! All this and more is in store for you!! Light that bomb and you'll walk the League at my command: insensate, famished, naked, ravenous, debauched, aching, celibate, and pitiful—I promise you!>*

Silence was his response. From the strumming of the tregador, he knew she was still there. Probably trying to come up with a suitably threatening reply.

<Lacerta! Answer me!>

She responded in a mental shriek. *<My name is not Lacerta, Belmont! I have fought hard to have a name, would you like to hear it?>*

<Your name does not interest me, Lacerta, only that bomb you've planted on my ship.>

<Say my name. It's . . .>

<Your name is irrelevant.>

<SAY MY NAME, YOU SLAG!!> she shrieked into his tregador. *<MY NAME IS . . .>* She then wailed over the tregador. *<AAAAAAAAAAAAAAAAAAAAAA!!!>*

His tregador blew out and he spiraled into the floor, his brain ringing. He got up and ran, tearing down a lift and out onto Deck 6 near the Priory.

Someone stood at the Priory gates. It had to be her. He put his head down and charged.

Bam! He plowed into the figure and tumbled to the floor with it beneath him. He reared back to hit it with all his strength.

"Bel!" the figure said. "Bel wait!"

It was Taara. He couldn't stop his blow, but he managed to deflect it. He hit the floor and his fist made a noticeable depression. He pulled her up.

"What in Creation happened?"

"I really don't know. The Lacerta came out of the Priory with a Wet-Head bomb."

"A Wet-Head bomb?"

Taara sat up. "Yeah, it's a Xaphan type of bomb using submerged chromatium. It's a pretty dirty device and not overly inventive, but it would have taken not only the ship, but probably several square miles of Hoffman Plate along with it."

"Where is it?"

"Right here." She pulled a tiny metallic device out of her coat pocket, a disk no bigger than a large coin.

"That's it?"

"Yep. Don't worry about it. It's disarmed."

"How did you find it so fast?"

"She hid it in J-45. Just tossed it in and figured we'd never find it. I zeroed right in with the MOLLY and had it disarmed in no time. Then, I was going to try and sneak up on her and let her have it with my SK, and all of a sudden I hear this scream and my brain catches on fire."

"Taara, where is she? Where's the Lacerta?"

She pointed to the Priory. "When I recovered, I saw her crawling in there."

"Crawling?"

"Yeah, she was crawling and making whimpering noises. Sounded like a dying bunny."

"And she went into the Priory?"

"Yep."

"What happened?"

Gwendolyn appeared around the bend, holding her drawn FEDULA. "I happened, Bel. I Popped her—the arrogant cow. I Popped her a good one. Creation, that felt sweet. She didn't even raise a defense." She turned to Stenstrom and pointed the tip of her FEDULA at him. "By the way, Lord Belmont—you leave me stranded ever again and I'm Popping you next!"

He couldn't believe what he was hearing. What he thought would be a horrific one to one battle with the Lacerta was utterly disarmed by Taara and Gwen.

"I hit her hard enough to kill just about anybody." She shook her FEDULA. "Now that I've taken the grand tour of the tawdry innards of her brain, I want her head to go along with it."

Stenstrom drew his NTH's and went into the Priory. "Come on."

They entered. Taara drew her SK and held it in a shaking hand. Gwen brandished her FEDULA and Stenstrom cocked the hammers of his NTHs. Their search was futile. The Lacerta was gone. "Here's her shoe," Gwen said, reaching down and picking up a fine, Conwell-style button shoe lying on the floor. It was still vaguely warm from her foot.

"And here's a bit of blood," Taara said, pointing out a clear trail of blood dribbles dotting the floor. "Probably leaking out of her shattered ears."

Pressing on, they found a lacy bag of fine black material held shut with a clasp. Taara picked it up. "She must have dropped this." Taara opened it. "It's full of candy. She must have a sweet tooth, the rotten trollbag. There's a box of cigarettes, too."

They reached the end of the Priory. The trail of blood went to the stone wall at the far end and stopped. The gate was sealed.

"Looks like she high-tailed it out of here."

"She should be dead, Bel," Gwen added.

"She's not an ex-Sister for nothing," Stenstrom said. "You caught her arrogant and unprepared, but she obviously can take a lot more mental abuse than the regular person. I'll have to do something about this gateway to prevent her using it again."

Taara came to his side while Gwen inspected the wall.

"I'm getting a headache, Gwen," Taara said rubbing her ears. "Watch what you're doing next time, or give me a warning or something."

"Sorry," she replied.

They spent the rest of the evening looking for more bombs and found nothing. The ship was clean. The next morning, fully complimented and provisioned, the *Seeker* blasted off from Hoffman Plate and headed to the Bell Nebula to begin its long trek into virgin space. The non-encounter with the Lacerta had taught him an important lesson. Taara and Gwen had easily handled what he thought was going to be the last battle of his life aboard his doomed ship. He didn't worry about them and his crew as much after that. As Gwen said, they could take care of themselves.

10—The Shadow tech Goddess?

Five weeks into the journey to Eng is when it happened.
The ship was holding up well—*Straylights* being tough birds and the engines were responding normally. The crew, allowed extra rations, entertained themselves with bowling in the hold and a little grog, were also doing well; mitigating Stenstrom's initial fears. He fully admitted he hadn't given them their proper due.

Gwendolyn and several crew from the ship's navigation, made careful maps, finding little but far-flung systems populated with gas giants and other inhospitable worlds along the way. Every day Stenstrom went to the observatory and looked through the telescope, now auto-caged on Eng, seeing the tiny blue speck of light grow into a progressively bigger speck as time went by. Another week or two and they should be able to make out surface details. That would be something to see.

They performed Stellar Mach intersections several times a week, bringing the huge SM coils to bear and "blinking" out of existence for up to ninety seconds, then re-appearing vast distances ahead. The ravages of SM travel upon mind and body prevented longer forays. The body could be preserved in compression tanks, but the mind would be left behind. People would emerge insane, possessed, or "Blanked" with no consciousness left to them. Even the short intersections they entered into created problems—the mysterious sickness known as Gift-Valve being a severe issue. Fortunately, nobody had yet come down with it.

Stellar Mach was a must, though, as Gwen calculated without it their five or six week trip to Eng would take, at standard sail, 10,000 years.

Gwen had dropped the demure pretense of hiding and had moved into his quarters full-time. He was surprised how many personal things she had; his quarters now almost unrecognizable from before. She had begun a slow but steady process of integrating him into her thoughts; the "Stop-Over" she called it. She told him, as a girl, she and her sisters often went for long stretches of time in the Prentiss household connected to the minds of her parents, sharing their deepest thoughts and feelings. Gwen said it wasn't unusual for them to go months without hearing each other's voices; their minds did all the talking for them.

The sensation of Gwen entering his mind was akin to a tiny fist sliding into his skull, pushing his brain aside, and then the hand slowly opening, the fingers spreading out. The loving tapestry of Gwen's mind radiated away from the hand, filling him up. He'd try to speak, and always she'd gently put her fingers to his lips. "Shhhh," she'd say.

Always, he was saturated with information. The new and unfamiliar landscape of Gwen's mind moved around him like a vast art gallery of paintings and relief sculptures just waiting to be discovered. At the perimeter of the gallery were the blaring minds and chatter of the other people on the ship being forcibly kept out by Gwen.

He'd be inside her body, and, he assumed, she was in his as well. So odd, the shape and extra weight of her breasts, the way her clothes hung on her smaller frame, the sizzle of estrogen in her blood, and the distinct void between her legs, no penis and the strange plumbing of her vagina. Wow—that, that was . . .

She liked to kiss him on the cheek at such times. He'd feel her lips on his cheek and endure the effect of the kiss moving throughout her body, registering as a slight itch in her womb.

Sometimes they'd retire to bed, minds hooked together. He'd have his own dreams, and share hers as well, the two mixing into a thick mental paste. He'd always assumed her dreams might be a bit more pugilistic, perhaps of fighting tournaments and boxing. But no, her dreams were modest and down to the ground. She dreamed of him quite often, of sitting in the parlor of their manor, playing the dulcimer or sitting down to an evening of cards. She dreamed of someday carrying their child. Being a mother was very important to her.

His dreams, on the other hand, were frenzied, either by design or by the unfamiliar mental openness with Gwen he was placed in. His dreams bordered on the psychedelic.

He dreamed often of the Hall of Mirrors, a place that was all around him and full of danger, soaked in darkness. And, once or twice he dreamt of Morgan. He dreamt once that he woke up in bed and she was in bed with him, fully dressed, just staring at him. Another time he dreamt that

Morgan was there performing an autopsy on Gwen while in bed. That was the most horrific dream he'd ever had.

Other times he dreamt of someone laughing in the darkness.

"So, we're well on schedule," Gwen said, giving Stenstrom a debriefing in the conference room. She had, up on the holocone, the Black Abbess' stellar chart. A blinking dot marked their progress. It was well past halfway. Taara sat at the end of the table with her feet up as usual, her red Marine coat thrown open.

"What is the status of our engines?" Stenstrom asked.

"The engines are fine, as I said," Gwen answered. <*I have a whole databank of telemetry if you want to see it,*> she happily sent to him.

<*No, thank you.*> "And provisioning?"

Taara answered. "Fine, fine. Ship's pantries are still brimming with provision."

"How many Stellar Mach intersections have we accomplished so far?"

"Twelve."

Stenstrom raised his eyebrows. "Twelve? That's quite a lot. Have we had any crew go down with sickness?"

Taara answered. "A few. One was injured in the run up to Mach Steady; and we've few small cases of Gift-Valve. Nothing to worry about."

"How many is 'a few', exactly?"

"Eight."

"All right, eight. And are these eight cases are being properly dealt with?"

"They are. Not having Morgan here is a hindrance, but our Chancellor Hospitalers are doing fine."

Stenstrom rubbed his chin.

"Honestly, Bel, eight cases of Gift-Valve is not a hefty butcher's bill," Gwen said. "I've seen more than that come down with it after only one SM. You never know how people are going to react. Those who are profiled as susceptible to Gift-Valve are usually screened out of ship duty."

"How many more Stellar Mach transverses will we need before we arrive at Eng?"

Gwen answered. "Three, maybe four. Our next one is due in fifteen hours."

"I've never had Gift-Valve before," Stenstrom said. "What are the symptoms?"

Taara answered. "It varies. In mild cases, you get a bit of nausea and paranoia, accompanied by bouts of confusion and hallucination. In severe cases, a person stricken with it can become catatonic with minimal brain function and have to be kept alive in an espersion tank."

Stenstrom felt a twinge in his stomach. "Do we have any cases like that right now?"

"No," Taara said.

"Well, thank Creation for that. What is the treatment for this condition?"

"Rest and removal from ship duty is the best treatment. Pharmaceuticals can also help."

"Do we have any habitable planets nearby where we can make berth if need be?"

Gwen drew Stenstrom's attention to a system not far ahead of the ship's present course. "Well, that's the odd thing. To date, our Magravine chart has been startlingly accurate, except for this planetary system here. It's a standard, Type II planetary system featuring one green world in the fourth position."

"So, what about it?"

"It's not there. We have detected no sign of it, not via scanning or visual sighting."

His stomach was full-on aching. "Perhaps it was destroyed; its star gone to nova."

<*Oh, Bel, please . . .*> "A nova'ed system is quite a mess. We'd easily see the remnants of the system, if that were the case. It's simply not there."

"There's actually sort of a hole there where it should be," Taara added.

He stood and went to the window. He wanted to return to his quarters and rest. He was amazed Gwen hadn't detected it; she was in-tune with all his inner workings. "Perhaps the Black Abbess made a mistake."

"She hasn't made any yet. She even gave the planet a name: Punt."

The word stuck in Stenstrom's head.

Punt?

The moment he heard the world the room began to spin around him. He'd never been sick a moment in his life; now the room spun around him in a hopeless wobble. "Punt? As in the Nillists of Punt? The sect hoping to destroy the universe?"

"It's probably a coincidence," Gwen stated.

"What?" Taara cried. "Come on, how could it be? I'll tell you what it is, Punt's a Planar World. There one moment, gone the next."

"*Planar World . . .*" a voice echoed out of nowhere.

"Not possible. Planar Worlds are a physical impossibility."

"Oh, yeah? Then where is it? And, one more thing that Gwen forgot to mention, we're detecting trace amounts of Shadow tech, precisely in the area where the Punt system should be." Odd memories forced their way into his head. Punt, he'd been there, he remembered it. The sky there was a whitish negative image. Taara, was with him, a different Taara, tall, goddess-like. The Shadow tech billowing into the sky.

Which way was up? Which way was down? He didn't know. The table they were sitting at seemed to be riding a violent storm. Gwen and Taara swirled about.

A third person was sitting at the table, staring at him from the other side. An unfamiliar face smiled at him. "*Hello, Lord Belmont,*" came a sultry voice.

Colors clashed in front of him.

"Bel, what do you think?" somebody asked.

"*Yes, Lord Belmont, what do you think?*" came an unknown voice.

He fell to the floor.

"Bel! He's down! He's down! Summon the Hospitalers!"

The storm of chaos subsided. Dull obscurity sharpened into ebon clarity. Stenstrom sat in a vast room. Smooth marble, lofty columns and fine accessories, it reminded him of a great Vith hall with the lighting turned down. The gothic décor appeared to be all black, but it might have been dark blue or possibly brown; it was difficult to tell.

He was seated at the end of a long table. How long did it go, a hundred feet, two hundred, possibly longer? A legion of high-backed black chairs were tucked neatly in at either side of the table. Each chair, and there were too many to count, was occupied by a silent figure, all sitting straight with practiced posture; he could see their elegant silhouettes.

All the people at the table appeared to be female; it reminded him of his mother's table back in Tyrol, full of his twenty-nine sisters. His sisters, except for a few, also sat with perfect posture, chin up, shoulders back, slender and stately in their chairs.

The figures were all lock-still in their seats, like wax statues rendered in sitting positions.

He got out of his chair with a loud drag across the floor and approached a nearby figure. "My lady?" he asked. The woman, her gaze fixed on the table's surface, did not move. He stooped down to look at the side of her face. It was a somber black-haired woman.

"Recognize her?" a soft voice asked, filling up the room. It startled him.

"Who's there?" he asked, reaching for his NTHs, which were not present.

A figure sitting at the distant end of the table moved slightly and responded. "Me. I'm here."

He squinted. The figure was too far away to make out clearly. "Show yourself!"

"As you wish." The figure stood and walked around the table. It approached with slow, measured patience, its footfalls noisy and hollow. Like all the others in the hall, it was female. She wore an odd, tight-fitting costume, like the Astro Traders in their body-fitting elastic suits he often saw scrubbing down the hulls of shipping at port. In the dim lighting, her costume seemed made out of black liquid. It flowed seamlessly into her shoes which sported impressively long heels making a din of noise with each step:

POCK! POCK! POCK!

The sound of each step bounced across the room.

"Do you recognize her?" the figure asked again. She wore a light cape which took flight in fluttering rolls as she walked.

"Where am I?" he asked as he watched her approach.

"Where? Where have you been for the last month or so?"

He thought a moment. "The Hall of Mirrors?"

"Yes. Well done."

The woman arrived at his side at last. In addition to her odd costume, she wore a bizarre helmet that was perfectly round, like a ball. The only part of the woman's face he could see was her pale chin, her mouth, and her nose. The rest was covered up by her helmet. A sharp visor drew a glowing purple line across the helmet where her eyes would be. "You're sick, right now. Gift-Valve, I think they call it."

"I don't have Gift-Valve."

"Yes, you do."

He looked around the hall. "If this is the Hall of Mirrors, then where is the Anatameter?"

"Over there." She pointed down the hall. Stenstrom looked but didn't see anything. "Don't bother," she said, "it's not yours."

She gestured to the lady seated at the table. "Not to change the subject, but I'll ask again: do you know this woman? I'm quite curious."

"I can't really see her face, just her profile."

"Oh? Look again." Stenstrom turned his attention back to the woman. She now looked directly at him over her left shoulder. She was pretty and proud; her expression was small-mouthed and somewhat sad.

"I don't know this woman," he said.

"Are you certain?"

"Yes, I'm certain."

"I didn't think you might. You couldn't know them all, could you? You aren't the All-in-One, are you?" She stood there, her liquid-like costume flowing around her.

"What? Who are you?" he asked.

"Me? I am the person who has been worshipped for ages. There are many who follow me. There are many who seek me out." She bowed with a flourish. "I am often called the Shadow tech Goddess."

He was taken aback. "You are the Shadow tech Goddess?"

"That is correct."

Stenstrom looked her over. She radiated an innocuous other-worldly power. She was alluring and charming, certainly not what he had expected. He had expected something more grand, something incalculable, inconceivable, incomprehensible, and irresistible. Standing before him was a shapely and oddly dressed woman, but nothing more. She seemed to be something that could be faced, could be dealt with if need be, not a force of nature radiating fear, not a singular individual, an elusive beast always just out of reach. He touched her hand; she did not react or pull it back. She allowed him to examine it. Her hand was small and delicate, and perfectly tangible. Her costume felt like warm latex. She took his hand and laced her fingers with his. "I am flesh and blood, sir, I assure you."

"And you are the destroyer of all things?" he asked.

"I destroy things from time to time, yes. Why must you be so glum?"

"I was expecting something different."

"Like what?"

"Something more impressive, I suppose." She made a slight surprised expression with her mouth. He quickly responded. "I'm sorry, I didn't mean to offend you. You are certainly attractive and stately; that's not how I envisioned the Shadow tech Goddess. Why am I not quaking in fear right now?"

She threw her head back and laughed. "Would you like to be? What is it about men and being afraid? Men love to be afraid, I've observed. Perhaps it's that little rush of excitement you receive afterwards, like you'd just withstood something or accomplished something important. Fear has an addictive quality to it."

"I don't enjoy being afraid."

"Ah well, then. I apologize for not being what you expected."

He called her attention to the seated figures. "Who are all these people?"

Still holding his hand, she led him down the length of the long table, passing one silent female after another. "These are your loves, Lord Belmont, across the various realms, realities, and pocket-plains of the Universe. There are so many of them, aren't there?"

"These are my loves?"

"Indeed. As you touched on earlier, you are in the Hall of Mirrors, and what comes out of the Hall of Mirrors, I'm certain you've been told; your loves, and here they are."

They passed woman after woman and he didn't recognize a single one. The woman who called herself the Shadow tech Goddess lifted her hand. "Here at this table, sit the *Covus*, the also-rans, the one-timers, the ones who are more infrequent in your life. If you took an accounting of each one, you would, no doubt, begin to see a few here and there you know."

"How can I not know them?"

She shrugged. "There are many of you. Their exploits took them on vastly different paths. Here are the results, a lot of ladies at a very long table. Might be a man or two mixed in here somewhere."

He ran his gaze up and down the table, so many. An army of souls sitting there motionless.

"I'm told you killed one of these ladies sitting here, horribly I might add, and that you stole my Anatameter at Clovis."

She placed a demure finger to her chin and tapped it. "Did I? I have no memory of that. I don't steal things."

They reached the end of the table at last. There was an open doorway leading to a colorful outside area, a harsh contrast from the dim, dark hall.

"Are you saying it didn't happen?"

"No, I'm saying I didn't do it." She looked around, touching her helmet with her left hand. "You did lose the Anatameter, that's certain enough, and you've been stuck here in the Hall ever since, barely managing to avoid my wraith." She smiled. "So far you haven't annoyed me. Unfortunately, there's more to worry about in the Hall besides simply me. There are quite a number of horrors residing here, all focused in on you at the moment. Would you care to see?"

"What are they?" he asked.

"Come with me outside. I'll show you."

She held her gloved hand out for him to take, then led him outside into the glare leaving the infinitely long table and the ladies sitting there behind.

11—The Garden of Horrors

They exited the hall to a bright, harshly colorful garden. The Shadow tech Goddess' ebon costume glistened in the light. She led him down a cobbled path. To his left, he saw a steep cliff trail down to a distant beach. Hints of white stone structures huddled against the shoreline. Black water lapped against the sand. The sky was a harsh, oversaturated grayish-white.

Shadow tech. He could smell it in the air.

"What do you want?" he asked as they walked.

"I don't know what you mean." she replied happily.

"What do you want? You've brought me here; you've shown me all this. You must want something—and, for the record, I don't believe you are the Shadow tech Goddess as you claim."

"Why not?"

"Somehow, I don't think the real one would be so conversational."

"I've been worshipped here for ages."

"Then I believe your worshipers are deluded."

She laughed a little. "Because I like you, I'll allow that remark to pass."

"So, my question stands, what do you want?"

She didn't address his question. She led him farther down the path. At last, they reached a curved stone fence and a black iron gate. "Here we are. This is what I've wanted to show you." She opened the gate and swung the door out. "Go ahead, please enter."

Through the gate was a vast walled-in courtyard. It appeared to once have been a lavish garden landscaped in potted, semi-circular boulevards with trees, hedges, and flowering plants. All the flora in the courtyard was withered and dormant, rattling dead leaves racing in the breeze. In the center of the courtyard was a dry fountain. Two giant-sized figures stood in its center. The Shadow tech Goddess breathed deep and took in the desolate scene. "This is what I call my Garden of Horrors."

Garden of Horrors? Stenstrom took a step in and the garden came to life around him, seemingly drawing energy from his presence. Leaves sprouted and flowers bloomed, plump fruits appeared on the trees, and hedges turned dark green. Spots of rich color reached up from the ground, a gaggle of scents from fresh flowers, pine needles, citrus, and new growth, plowed into his nose. The fountain, too, came to life, gurgling black water. "See how my garden blooms in your presence?" the Shadow tech Goddess said, admiring the scene. "Have you ever stopped to wonder why things happen to you, Lord Belmont, like my garden celebrating your arrival in leaf and flower? Why do things happen in your presence? Why are people so drawn to you? Do you know?"

"I don't know what you mean?"

She smiled and pinched his cheek. "Ah, so modest. Is it false modesty, I wonder? You know exactly what I'm talking about. All the ladies you've attracted in your young life, and not simply attracted as a passing fancy, but who have become devoted to you one way or the other. Look at the Sisters, look at your loyal friends. Look at your various enemies; they are drawn to you too. Why?"

"It must be because I have money," he replied.

She laughed. "Money, really? There is indeed something very special about you. You appear in every universe, node, and alternate reality to be found. That is unheard of. Most everyone, myself included, do not appear in all the realms. Most everyone else has to content themselves with a few appearances, say twenty to thirty percent at a time. There is a formula that determines how many Universes a given person appears in, and that applies to the gods as well. But you—you defy the formula. In every reality one cares to examine, there you are. There is a name for your special condition: *Kaidar Gemain*—the "One who is Everywhere". To the *Kaidar Gemain* comes the favor of the Universe and the reward of power. Look at the power you possess; you have yet to properly appreciate it. People are drawn to you because of it; even though they might not be aware of why they feel the way they do. Their feelings might not always be positive, but they are there just the same and they are always passionate. Congratulations, sir, you are an Extra-Planar entity. Surprise!"

Stenstrom thought to protest, but something told him she was right, that she was telling him the truth. She might by lying about her identity, but her information rang true. He gripped her hand tighter, taking comfort in it.

They strolled through the elaborate twists and turns of the garden. Stenstrom found himself enjoying the colors and textures of the place, and he found the company surprisingly pleasing as well. This woman pretending to be the Shadow tech Goddess was quite charming. They approached the fountain in the center of the garden and inspected it. Standing there at an elongated height was a man and a woman. They were slender and elegant, of fine features. He didn't recognize the man, but he recognized the woman instantly.

"Queen Wendilnight!" he cried. "I know her!"

"Indeed, and this is her husband, a man with many names whom I refer to as 'Fiddler Crowe'. They are folk of Cammara."

"The Gods of Cammara?"

"If you like. Fiddler Crowe is an accomplished craftsman in the rare art of creating Anatameters, and Queen Wendilnight has a mastery over time. As a side note, her lore states that she is in dire need of rescue."

"Rescue?"

"Yes, from a terrible enemy. Perhaps you are the one to rescue her."

Queen Wendilnight's words came to him: *". . . when you came to rescue me . . ."*

He tried to stay focused. "You call this place the Garden of Horrors; it seems misnamed. I find it rather lovely. Why do you call it that?"

"Because you are surrounded by horrors, even now. Check the garden, peer into the foliage and you will see why."

They wandered about. He approached a thick, dark green hedge speckled with red berries and moved the foliage aside. Deep within the growing mass of the hedge was a carved figure.

He pushed branches aside and uncovered it, smelling the woodsy scents of sap and hedge needles. Standing there carved in perfect rock was Gwendolyn, wearing her Fleet uniform, her hat in her hands. "What is an image of Gwendolyn doing here?"

"Because she is a 'horror,' of sorts. This woman is an Extra-Planar entity known as a *Merthig*. She appears at your side most often, more than all the rest."

"Gwendolyn is no monster."

"No, I didn't say she was. The *Merthig* draws a great deal of power from you that manifests in various ways. Hence her status as a *Merthig*."

"Rubbish."

"Does your Gwendolyn exhibit any unusual abilities? Can she do things other people can't do?"

"She is a powerful telepath."

"Really? Actually, she's not. Were she not a *Merthig*, she would be simply another person about the League with ordinary skills. That amazing telepathy she has is because of her association with you. She possibly has latent skills; however, her dealings with you across the realms fuel her telepathy to much greater levels."

"Her whole family has it. She had it long before she met me."

"Time, as we see with Queen Wendilnight, is not entirely linear, sir. She is at your side in many places, and not all at once. There could have been a version of her with you when she herself was merely a little girl, or, for that matter, before she was born. Given that, even if she hasn't met you yet or is far away, her frequent place at your side in the various universal realms gives both her and her family power; they benefit by proximity. That is the hallmark of the *Merthig*. It's a completely symbiotic relationship; you benefit from her presence as much as she benefits from yours. Hers is a standing of privilege, a place of power. Many beings contend heatedly to be a *Merthig*."

"What beings?"

"More Extra-Planars. Keep looking. See for yourself."

Stenstrom stepped away and Gwendolyn's statue disappeared behind the hedge. Moving to another area of the garden, he spied a figure seated amid a growth of well-tended roses. It was the statue of a woman with long hair. She seemed quite large, much larger than Gwen, especially in the legs, hands and feet, but she sat in a less proud, less confident manner with her eyes slightly downcast. "Who is this?" he asked.

"This woman is a *Merten*. A *Merten* is almost a *Merthig*, but not quite and their fate is usually not pleasant. The Universe speaks through a *Merten*, encoding messages in their flesh that can be read, usually by killing them."

A message in her flesh? "Melazarr?" he whispered in wonder. "Is this Melazarr of Caroline?"

"Probably. You may pursue a *Merten* if you wish, but be prepared for a great deal of hard work keeping her alive. Come, there is more to see."

In a far corner of the garden, hidden behind a stand of trees on a shallow hill, was yet another statue. It was a tall female who gazed out over the whole of the garden beyond. She wore a suit of some kind, like a pilot's suit complete with straps and hoses to connect to a life-support system. There was a holster with a gun carved near her shoulder. She seemed so familiar. It was maddening. "Who is this?" he asked, eager for the answer.

The Shadow tech Goddess put her hands on her hips. She seemed slightly perturbed. "One who has no place."

"What does that mean?"

"It means she has no place in the Universe and is not worthy of further thought. There isn't even a name for a creature like this. Your time is not unlimited here. Move on."

Stenstrom was adamant. "But . . ."

The Shadow tech Goddess pulled him away. "Come, there is more to see." Down the hill next to an orange tree was a statue carved in a sitting position on the ground and another in the tree branches, crouched on all fours. He recognized the statues from a distance. "Taara here too? And Kat as well?"

"These are *Covus*," the Shadow tech Goddess said. "*Covus* are random events the Universe throws you way, oftentimes during tranverses in universal flow or when there is no *Merthig*. *Covus* can help reinvigorate patterns of force. I consider them a good thing to have happen every once in a while, a nice change of pace. The table in the Hall is full of *Covus*."

Near the wall was a patch of bizarre plants stuck in the ground in all manner of confusion. The plants resembled distorted people. They had husk-like arms and legs, shoulders, and bloated heads. "What are these?" he asked.

"Punts. These are Punts. These people have lived in the fallout of a Shadow tech vent for centuries, and look what it has done to them. They have become not quite human. See for yourself."

Stenstrom inspected one of the Punts. Its skin was dry and crinkly, like a corn husk. With minimal effort, the covering of skin came away revealing a dark and utterly alien skeleton underneath, brimming with odd, wheel-like organs, extra parts, and a predatory, alien head. They seemed to be composed entirely of Shadow tech. "You and your lady friends will be encountering them at some point, I'm certain, as they are avid followers of mine, always wanting this and that. When you do, be on your guard."

She led him away from the Punts and down a boulevard of flowering ivy. "Be careful, there is a very dangerous entity in this area just ahead." They passed under a cluster of hemlock trees where another statue lay half-hidden. He couldn't make out what it was. It didn't seem to have a human shape.

"Please excuse me," she said and made her way deep into the trees to the statue. A fog blew up around her, obscuring the statue. Two points of white light appeared in the fog, floating like a pair of eyes, followed by an ominous clacking sound, like a pair of scissors opening and closing.

CLACK . . . CLACK . . . CLACK . . .

He thought back. Melazarr had mentioned something similar aboard his ship, a fog, and white lights; and that something within the fog had attacked her.

The Shadow tech Goddess emerged from the fog a moment later and took his hand. "I'm sorry, please this way. Please."

She led him away. With her free hand she adjusted her helmet and toyed with her face as if she'd been weeping.

"What was that, ma'am?"

"A demon," she abruptly replied, wiping away tears. "Please, this way."

They reached a section of curved ivy. "Here we are," she said. Stenstrom stepped up and reached into the ivy, pushing it aside, uncovering a menacing set of iron bars covering a dark, hollow space.

"Are you certain you wish to see? There is a reason why the creature residing within is behind a locked gate."

He leaned in.

"In this cell is something very dangerous, something you should deal with very carefully. As you are the *Kaidar Gemain*, the 'One who is Everywhere', there is also one called the *Tempus Findal*, or, the 'One and Only'. The *Tempus Findal* appears in only one Realm, and they, on a subconscious level, fret for their existence, feeling their aloneness in the multi-verse. The *Tempus Findal* usually doesn't start out that way. They oftentimes face a mass extinction across the realms and they all die out in a common, seminal event, except for one; and that one remaining soul becomes a planar creature of extraordinary power. They can only die in the spot and manner in which all the others died, thus they are, essentially, immortal.

"This person, craving the power you command, will be drawn to you, cannot resist not being near you. Wherever you go, it will follow, hoping to sink its hooks into your soul. No prison can hold it for long. The Hall of Mirrors and the Anatameter meant to prevent planar passage are ineffective against it; the *Tempus Findal* may go wherever it wishes. It feeds off your energy. It will replace those around you whom you love and trust. It fills you full of doubt, fills you full of fear and turns you to chaos. Unlike the *Merthig*, which is a beneficial relationship to you, the *Tempus Findal* is nothing more than a relentless parasite that will lead to your doom."

"And that person is behind this gate?"

"Of course not. This is simply a facsimile, a representation, but it should be real enough to help make my point. Go ahead, see what is there."

He came in to have a look. The iron bars and the darkness behind it awaited. As he neared, a chalky white arm shot out to the elbow, its hand reaching and grasping in a crazed manner, trying to get at him. The greenish nails on its fingers were cracked and uneven. It rattled the bars as it struggled.

The Shadow tech Goddess pulled him away a step or two. The chalky hand lost some of its ferocity. It pulled back a bit and held the bars tentatively, then slowly reached out to him, palm up, fingers extended. "See how its bearing changes? When it has fed off of your power long enough, it becomes sated for a short while. During that time it can be charming, reasonable, sympathetic even. Sometimes, it even forgets what it is and believes itself to be mortal. But, always, it will fall back into that ravenous, mindless state you saw before. The *Tempus Findal* has the strength of twenty men and can make you feel fear such as you have never known. Most troubling, it can make you feel sorry for it, make you serve its own ends. It tells lies, Lord Belmont, and you will believe them. You will believe every word it says and then it will have you."

"Lies, like the lies you're telling me right now."

"What lies?"

"That you are the Shadow tech Goddess. I don't believe you."

She shrugged. "Believe what you will. But, believe this, the *Tempus Findal* will be the ruin of you if you let it."

"How so?"

The Shadow tech Goddess pointed to area patch of dead growth near the bars. "Look there."

Stenstrom cleared the withered growth. Toppled over and covered in old runs of poison ivy was the statue of a man wearing what looked like a Fleet uniform. The statue's head had come away from its body, looking up, shedding tears of bird droppings. He took a long look at the face. "Captain Duval?" he said, astonished.

"Indeed. Here he is, Captain Duval, Lord of Willshire, wasted and cast aside, a recent victim of the *Tempus Findal*. Captain Duval was a *Kaidar Gemain* as well. He was favored. He had power granted to him by the Universe. His *Merthig* granted him extraordinary power over the Hall of Mirrors. He could call it to him when he wished and walk its halls in relative safety. And then, all that came to an end. The *Tempus Findal* got him. It killed his *Merthig*. It pursued him across the realms, then wormed its way into his confidence, gained his trust and his reliance, all the while gorging on him. It gorged itself so much that he faded from one realm of existence entirely."

"It killed him?"

"It did worse than merely kill him. He simply no longer exists in one plane. No longer a *Kaidar Gemain*, he became a *Kaidar Gogol*, the 'One Who is Almost Everywhere', and there is nothing worse than that. He became a powerless after-thought, an also-ran. The Universe abandoned him. The Hall of Mirrors abandoned him and he didn't even have the *Tempus Findal* anymore, for it abandoned him, too. All he has to look forward to now is oblivion."

"He is looking for the Shadow tech Goddess. He says he loves her."

"Does he really? My, that is flattering. Unfortunately, I will not see a *Kaidar Gogol*. He may search for me all he wishes, but he'll find nothing but an empty chair."

"The man is insane," Stenstrom said.

"Is he? He was a great man once. Now look at him, an oddity in the Shadow tech Goddess' garden."

"And now you say this planar entity, this *Tempus Findal,* is after me?"

"Oh, yes, and you will never be rid of it. It will kill and lie and do what needs to be done until you belong to it. And when it has you, it will drink deep until you are a *Kaidar Gogol* too."

He felt a fist of raw fear come blasting out of the bars, twisting him into a knot, ready to bring him to him knees.

"You feel that? That is the fear it can create. Overwhelming, isn't it?"

He struggled to speak. "I've . . . I've felt . . . this before . . ."

"I imagine you have. See, it wasn't me. Your time here is nearly done," the Shadow tech Goddess said. "You are being pulled back into your body. Soon you'll be back aboard your ship, all shined up and ship-shape. I have something I wish to give you first."

She pulled a wooden box from a nearby pool, then held it out. "I would like to give you what is in this box. I want to help you protect yourself from this relentless creature. That is why I've presented myself to you."

"To help me?"

"Indeed. Whether you believe I am the Shadow tech Goddess or not is irrelevant." She opened the box. Inside was a bolabung made of black, shiny material. He picked it up: Shadow tech.

"This bolabung will shield you from the fear the *Tempus Findal* creates. Wear it and be protected."

The second item in the box was a stone dagger made from blackened sandstone and sharpened to a razor point. The handle was made from hammered silver and gold. "What's this?"

"This stone knife is made of material taken from the site of the *Tempus Findal's* mortality. This dagger is lethal to it."

"So, you want me to kill it?"

"Do what you will. I'm simply offering you the tools to protect yourself." She glanced at Duval's toppled statue. "I truly don't wish to see you join Captain Duval in my garden."

He took the bolabungs and the knife and made them vanish. "Why are you offering me these things? You must want something?"

He felt himself being pulled back away from the Shadow tech Goddess and her Garden of Horrors.

"I want you in my debt . . . That's what I want."

* * * * *

"Taara, he's back!"

Gwen was sitting over him, holding his hand. Taara's little face barged in, her sideburns dangling. "Hey, welcome back, Bel. You had us worried."

He tried to sit up, but Gwen and Taara held him down. "Not so fast. Just relax."

"Where am I?" he asked.

"Dispensary," Gwen answered. "You came down with a sudden and rather severe case of Gift-Valve."

"I don't have Gifts of the Mind; my mother's Tyrol heritage suppressed it. How could I get Gift-Valve?"

Gwen reached over and picked up a report. "The Hospitalers detected a fair amount of Cadispar in your system. Cadispar can easily make your system susceptible to the rigors of Stellar Mach."

He puzzled over that. "How did Cadispar get into my system?"

"I'm thinking it happened on Planet Fall when that annoying little man tried to get himself on the ship. I did some checking in our ship-board archives, which is up-to-date from the time we shipped out of Planet Fall. Ottoman John, associate of Professor E. Com-Pressor, University of Arden, is actually, through various subtle connections, affiliated with none other than Hannah-Ben Shurlamp."

"In other words, you were poisoned, Bel," Taara added. "I guess Professor Shurlamp is playing for keeps."

"We'll deal with her when we return to Kana. How long was I out?"

"Two days," Taara said. "We postponed our SM to give you and some of the others suffering from Gift-Valve time to recover. We've already got the next one calculated in twenty-six hours."

"What about the ship? If Professor Shurlamp could get to us in Planet Fall, she could have sabotaged the ship, or rigged it."

"We've been all over the ship while you were sleeping it off. No rigs, no sabotage," Taara said. "If there's one thing the MOLLY is good at, it's sniffing out rigs."

"I had a vivid dream. I dreamt I was walking with the Shadow tech Goddess."

Gwendolyn adjusted his sheets in a loving manner. "You did? Tell me?"

"She was wearing a costume and a helmet. I don't think it was her, though. I think she was lying."

Gwen gently probed in with her mind. <*Sounds like a fascinating dream. You'll have to allow me to see later.*> "Taara, when can Bel be released?"

"Any time."

"I need to get back to the bridge," he protested.

"No, no," Gwen said. "You still need rest. We're on fast approach to Eng. You come back to our quarters and continue your recovery. I'll take good care of you."

Part of his dream came back to him: *Gwendolyn, a Merthig: symbiotic relationship.*

Gwendolyn took him back to his quarters and tucked him in. She had a few duties in engineering to perform, but promised to be back as soon as she completed them, and bring dinner from the mess.

While she was gone he rose, troubled. He fetched his HRN. He wondered if what he had seen was simply a delusion or if he had actually walked in the presence of a person claiming to be the Shadow tech Goddess. He wondered if the horrors she had warned him of were real, too. *The Tempus Findal. Is that what I saw at Sarfortnim College in the amphitheatre?*

He searched the vast interior of his HRN, typically full of arcane brick-a-brack. There, he found two unfamiliar lumps in the pockets: a bolabung of black Shadow tech on a leather cord and an ominous knife with a blackened stone blade.

PART 3

ENG

1—Eng

Stenstrom was still recovering from his bout of Gift-Valve. He recounted to Gwen his experiences, all that he'd seen: the hall, the legions of women, the Garden of Horrors, and the other-worldly woman who called herself the Shadow tech Goddess. Gwen had sorted through his thoughts, to assist him in analyzing his dreams. All she saw was a blank void. Being a very logical person, Gwen deduced that all he experienced was a Gift-Valve fueled hallucination tinged with bits of partially-remembered detail from his experiences in Clovis. But it had certainly seemed real to Stenstrom so he asked her to research some of the terms the Shadow tech Goddess had used:

Kaidar Gemain.

Tempus Findal.

Merthig

Merten

Covus

Kaidar Gogol.

She checked the ship's archives and library. Nothing. The terms had no meaning.

It was just a hallucination, she said.

But, what about the bolabung and the stone knife? He showed them to her. "Are you certain you didn't make these yourself?" she asked, holding them up. "You've got a whole arsenal of arcane kit on you at all times. I think you made these items and just don't remember doing so."

She discounted the trinkets as the products of an absent mind and his dreams as hallucinations. But, the dreams didn't stop. Every evening, with Gwen curled up next to him, he dreamed of someone sitting in the room with them watching them sleep. He saw its form sitting near the wall. He felt its eyes upon him.

Gwen saw nothing, wrapping him in a techo-plast haze and the haunting dulcimer-filled wind stream of her more grounded mind night after night.

One night he awoke in a terror that had come upon him from nowhere. He struggled out of bed, feeling his heart ready to fail, feeling unwanted eyes upon him. He took the bolabung the Shadow tech Goddess had given him and put it on. Wearing the bolabung, the fear, though not quashed entirely, faded to manageable level. He took the knife and inspected his quarters, ready to defend himself if need be.

He found nothing except a pulled out chair near his bed.

The chair was warm, as if recently occupied.

Stenstrom went back to bed wearing the bolabung, determined never to remove it, and he kept the stone knife within easy reach

Three days from Eng.

He had the same old dream, somebody sitting there in the dark watching them sleep, only this time, the figure spoke. *"Better wake up . . ."*

Then, noise, confusion. Something was attacking the ship through the night of space.

Ambushed! The *Seeker* being an old *Straylight* had a minute blind sensory spot on the aft dorsal quarter of the ship—a flaw that never had been suitably corrected due to the stiff framework of the vessel. It was an issue easily compensated for by flying in a slight zig-zag pattern. However, here in the middle of nowhere, the helm was flying the ship straight and true.

The enemy ship came blasting through the blind spot, the attack precise and well-placed, hammering the underside of the *Seeker,* taking out SM coils 1, 4, 6, and 8 in the first few moments.

He started to yell a command to the Com, but nothing came out of his mouth. Through his windows, he got a good look at the attacker as it soared past: a Sprint-class League vessel.

It was the *George Parr*—it had to be.

In his dream, he whirled in mute frustration. How? How were they found??

Sar Beams, crashing into the hull. Gases venting, debris flailing out and sparkling.

He tried to bark out the order to return fire: Run out the damn guns and open up! Loose the canisters! Again, nothing came out of his mouth.

The door to his quarters opened and two figures darted in. The figures fetched both he and Gwen from bed. He was dressed quickly in the dark.

Then, he was helped out into the corridor, along with the limping, sleepy Gwen.

No, no—I need to be on the bridge! The bridge!

He was being led down to Deck 10.

The solid structure of the ship rocked again.

Beat this goddamn tub to quarters and return fire!

And then he dreamed of fog, and hands raised in prayer, a yellow star in the distance.

Fog all around.

He became aware of fast cold air moving over him. He awoke and sat up.

He was not in his quarters; nor did he appear to be on the ship. He was on a desolate shelf of dusty ground in the middle of a wilderness. The sky overhead appeared very low to the ground and was mottled with fast-moving brackish clouds. A chill wind blew past him.

Gwen lay on the ground next to him wearing her partially unbuttoned uniform. She immediately reacted to the bite in the wind and put her arms around her chest, trying to stay warm. "Where are we, Bel?" she yelled. "What happened?"

He took off his HRN and put it over Gwen's shoulder. She gratefully accepted it and ran her arms through the sleeves.

"Your guess is as good as mine!" he shouted back. "I had a dream the ship was under attack by the *George Parr*. I was trying to shout orders and get to the bridge, but I had no voice, and was led into the holds by a pair of shadowy figures!"

Gwen turned a little white. "I also dreamed of that."

He tried the tregador. *<Taara, you there?>* He expected the worst. *<Taara!>*

Thankfully, she answered. *<Bel? Creation, where are you?>* she replied. *<We thought you'd been sucked out or something.>*

<I'm not sure where I am. I'm on a planet surface, I don't know where or how.

Gwen's here with me. Never mind us; what's your status?>

<We're nominal. Still getting damage reports from all over the ship. We've lost a fair amount of our starboard SM coils and are venting on decks nine and ten, aft section. Should have that fixed here soon.>

<Casualties?>

<Six so far, mostly from the areas that were vented. But the sounding continues and several crew are still missing.>

<What about the attacking vessel?>

<We were able to rally and lay into it with canister and Battleshot. Though it felt really rotten firing on a League ship.>

<Was it the George Parr?>

<Aye. We tagged it a good one. We blew off its port wing and it retired. Our sensing capabilities aren't the greatest right now, so her current whereabouts are unknown, though I've got lookouts posted. A-Ram was standing at the helm for the engagement. He flew us through.>

<A-Ram?>

<Yeah, but he's gone again. Our Lacerta friend on the George Parr *mashed up our sensing units pretty bad with TK.>*

<All right, Taara. I want you to come about and return to the League, making as weather a time as you can. Make sure you waggle so they can't sneak into our blind spot again.>

<What about you and Gwen?>

<We're fine. I think, given A-Ram's presence, that Alesta put us to the Road. I think, there's a good chance that we're on Eng.>

<Really?>

<So, don't worry about us. Get back to the Fleet, inform them what has happened and then have them send out a combat box to get us. We should be fine until then. Perhaps, in the meantime, Alesta and A-Ram will collect us. One can only hope.>

<I'd rather have you on the ship, Bel.>

<That makes two of us, but the situation doesn't favor that, does it? Go on. We're fine and since we've got our tregs we can stay in contact as we will for a fair time. Get my ship to safety and if you see the George Parr, *lay into it with canister. You'll have the advantage of range. And Taara . . .>*

<Yeah?>

<I'm glad you're all right. Thanks for getting my ship out of that mess. Keep me updated.>

He tregged off and the two of them took a good look at their surroundings. They were atop some sort of plateau; a scrubby valley stretched off into the distance below them. The lighting was very poor. Gwen was rather put off. "Can this truly be Eng?"

"I believe it is."

"It's so dark and foreboding. Perhaps it's merely twilight, or dawn."

She looked around, not liking her surroundings one bit. "If this is Eng, this is not what I expected. I've been doing a fair amount of research on the subject. Many of the texts indicated it was a place rather like Kana. I thought it would be like Kana. This can't be Eng, Bel."

A fierce gale of wind kicked up the tails of his HRN.

"Perhaps the texts are wrong. The phantom of the Black Abbess at Magravine indicated Eng was a fairly inhospitable place and she didn't seem to miss it much. This must be Eng."

They both looked around, trying to take it in. It was an enormous moment, though a radically different one than Gwen had envisioned. "I had hoped it to be a cheerier place, full of the memory of our ancestors."

"As you said, the footsteps of our ancestors are long since covered up. Anything that was built would have been claimed by nature long ago. This is just another aimless world now, populated by who-knows-what."

<Bel,> Taara tregged in. <We're good. All venting is controlled for now, but we'll need a Dry-Docking to get fully repaired. The engineers are hard at the coils, and, good news! One of the crew thought to be dead has popped up, safe and sound. Are you sure you want us to make sail back to the League? We can be there at 2/3 sail in about five days. I don't want to leave you two behind.>

<I know, Taara, but you have your orders, and I expect them carried out. I want my ship and crew made safe. And, like I said, if Alesta brought us here, perhaps she'll bring us back straight away.>

Gwen recovered from her initial disappointment and began taking analytical stock of their situation. "Looks like there's a moon off in the distance. A big one. I don't recall seeing a large moon through the telescope." She pointed with her FEDULA.

A huge round object rose into the sky, obscured in haze and cloud. "What else could it be? It's too big to be anything on the ground," Stenstrom said.

"Let's get off this shelf and find some shelter for the rest of the day.

We can figure out our course of action later."

"A moment," he said looking at the ground. He produced a MARZABLE and plunged it down.

"What are you doing, Bel," she asked, impatient to find shelter.

"By leaving a MARZABLE here, I'll be able to relocate it with certain Holystones, should we need to return to this spot for any reason. I'll leave additional ones every day or so, as it appears we have far to journey." He checked himself over. The Shadow tech bolabung was around his neck, safely hidden under his clothes and the stone knife was in its usual spot.

They found a safe trail into the valley below and soon discovered a dry cave with a spring of potable water nearby. Being rather hungry, they decided to separate. Stenstrom, using his extensive herbal lore went looking for plant forage in the woods, while Gwen with her FEDULA and MiMs pistol went hunting for meat. She took a few MARZABLE with her in case she got lucky and managed to bag something big.

Wandering through the woods, Stenstrom found an assortment of rough but edible plant life: seeds, tuberous roots, and leafy greens. His years of study with his sisters and his mother were paying off. As this was an alien world, he rightly expected the plant life to be just that—alien. However, he spotted a number of trees and plants that seemed rather familiar. In fact, the leathery black trees with the weeping branches looked an awful lot like the Nadine trees common to the north of Kana. He cut into the trunk of one and tasted the dark brown sap that came out. Sweet, husky flavor. Tasted a lot like the Nadine syrup they made every morning in Blanchefort Castle.

His conversation with Alesta and A-Ram returned to him. He recalled the Elder's practice of collecting the animal and plant life of their previous home worlds and seeding Kana with it. If that tale was true, then it was possible the hearty Nadine trees of north Kana were in fact native to this world, not Kana—and therefore this planet could only be Earth, Cammara, Emmira, Lemmuria, or Eng.

He had a strong hunch though that this was, in fact, Eng.

He didn't have to worry about losing Gwen. She stayed in his head, giving him frequent updates. She was becoming more at-ease sharing her thoughts with him, and was liberated by it, sharing not only thoughts, but feelings, impressions, and other empathetic tidbits. She was always in his head now, nesting there. It was like holding her hand. He felt how hungry she was, as well as her growing frustration. Gwen was proving to be a poor hunter, making a lot of noise, wasting time in the same spots over and over again and not hiding her presence well. He didn't place much stock on her bagging anything substantial today.

It began to get very dark and they returned to the cave, Gwen having had no luck. They cleared the cave as best they could and Stenstrom built a roaring fire near the cave's mouth using a red Holystone. They ate nuts and roasted stringy leaves, and downed them with brackish water from the spring, his usual supply of small beakers coming in quite handy. The meal was rough, but it filled their bellies.

"Tomorrow, we're eating meat, I promise you," she said, struggling with her leafy meal.

"You'll need to improve your hunting skills a bit; we both will."

As the evening progressed they sat by the fire and looked at the occasional stars through the breaks in the clouds. Gwen had a bellyache from their coarse dinner and he held her.

Their shared thoughts drifted around each other.

So, here they were, just the two of them; the first to set foot down on Eng in a hundred millennia, sitting on the dirt by a fire.

26 Bells, Kana Standard was the time, according to her ever-present watch.

She put down her various mental blocks design to keep out the thoughts of others. It felt good to stretch out. No noise, no stray thoughts. They were alone.

Their thoughts chattered back and forth.

<If this was a quiet evening at our manor, I'd sit you down and play you a tune on the dulcimer. I'm quite accomplished at it.> In fact that's what she wanted for her dowry gift—a grand, gilded dulcimer. Brand new, never been played. There it was, splashed out in her thoughts.

<And what color would you like?>

She didn't care, whatever color he wished to get her. Visions of a midnight blue dulcimer, or a red one, or possibly provincial pearly white flashed across her thoughts. And then, they'd play a game or two of cards. She dreamed of such evenings with him.

<Though I'm a far-flung engineer in the Fleet, I'm really just a homebody at

heart. I love being home.> She wished they had some cards now.

He laughed and waved his hands. A fine deck appeared and Gwen gasped.

"How did you do that?" she exclaimed, taking the deck and sorting out the cards.

"Magic, remember?"

Hold up—his voice. They had shared the evening and not spoken a word. It had all been in his head. Amazing how fast he'd become accustomed to Gwen's telepathic ways. The words of the Shadow tech goddess came back to him:

Merthig, symbiotic relationship. "She draws a great deal of power from you."

She shuffled the deck. For the card-game she decided to use her voice to teach him how to play. "Very well, Lord Belmont. I'm going to introduce you to a game called Crazy-Eights."

Cheered by the cards, warmed by the fire, Gwen crossed her legs and dealt the cards and they played in the flickering firelight.

<*Two stars there in the north, and a smaller greenish one to the south. And, I think I see a nebula on the western horizon. Damn clouds. What time is it? Goodness, it's 2 Bells.*>

He awoke some time later. The hard ground of the cave bothered him a bit. Actually, it bothered him a lot. He'd have to find bedding, or create a hammock of some kind. Sleeping on the ground was too much.

Gwen was gone. She had been tucked into his side when they had finally nodded off after an hour or two of cards. He could feel the wedge of her thoughts buried in his brain. It didn't trouble him as much anymore. He'd become used to it.

He sat up.

Gwen sat at the mouth of the cave. She was wearing his HRN, and apparently nothing else other than her watch; he could see her bare feet and legs stretched out in front of her. Her clothes were all neatly folded nearby in typical Gwen fashion. He got up, a little stiff, and joined her. She had efficiently cleaned out his coat pockets; an impressive volume of Holystones—all organized into colored piles, arcane bits of Tyrol kit, pens, papers, string, cinnabar strikers, lockpicks of various kinds, silver candlesticks, and the Shadow tech Goddess' stone knife were all laid out in orderly fashion. The only thing she had missed was his MARZABLE, which she could never find—only he could find it.

She was sitting out in the cold by the dying fire holding a pile of his papers, busily scribbling notes and checking her watch. She was looking upward, holding his Megaeye to her face. She'd come to terms with the disappointing reality of Eng and the scientific part of her nature had returned in full.

He seated himself next her and she scooted into him a little. The sight of her sitting nude under the HRN was still quite a thing to see. His coat kept her perfectly warm and comfortable from top to bottom. She didn't need anything else.

"What are you doing?" he asked.

She reached out and put her warm fingers to his lips. "Shhh . . ." She wanted him to share his thoughts with her. Talking was unnecessary, pedestrian, the way other people did things.

Here, on Eng, let them be truly together. He relaxed and let the waters of his thoughts flow and mingle with hers.

<*What are we doing?*>

She was trying to map the constellations and accumulate data as they went. She was very empirical, and thorough, keeping a running log of sun up and sun down, Moon cycles, charting the stars, that sort of thing. She planned on doing this every night.

<*The sun went down at precisely 22 Bells, fifteen beats. All this information shall be invaluable when we return home. I'm anticipating the sun's rise to record its exact time. We have no idea when that will be at this early stage.*>

She resumed her work. These damn clouds were making things difficult.

<*Is there an infra-red prism on this Megaeye?*>

He took it from her and gave the lens a twist.

<*Ah! Thank you!!*> She kissed him and took it back.

A few random thoughts of taking up the hem on his coat crossed her mind. It dragged to ground when she wore it.

"As it fits me just fine, we'll leave the hem where it is," he said aloud. At least he thought he'd said it with his mouth. It was hard to tell anymore.

She giggled. She entertained a few passing thoughts of breakfast, something warm and comforting and she indulged in an erotic flash of what sex would be like on the hard ground.

<After the sun comes up and I record the time, let's have sex.>

A large break in the clouds passed overhead and she made more notes.

<Until we secure a steady source of food, we probably want to conserve our energy.>

She silently agreed. She reached over and handed him her scabbarded FEDULA. She wanted him to be a dear and etch their names into the wall of the cave somewhere. They needed to create tangible proof that they had been there.

That was crucial. Screw that bitch, Shurlamp.

<Oh! Look at that constellation!> She plotted its shape in her notes and recorded the time of its rising.

He pulled the blade from its scabbard. The FEDULA was a tiny, rapier-like sword that felt flimsy and tin-like in his hand.

She objected to him holding it in such a limp manner. This wasn't a gilded museum piece or a show pony, this was her FEDULA. She fought the Lacerta tooth and nail at Caroline with this tiny weapon.

She took it from his hand. *<Tin-like show-pony, eh?>*

She promptly plunged the delicate blade into the solid rock of the cave floor, burying it near to the hilt in a shower of colorful sparks.

Her thoughts came in a bundle. *<It's made of a blend of metals found in a unique quarry near our home in Zenon.>* Images of a rubble-strewn rock quarry entered his mind. A tiny Gwendolyn standing there with her father and her sisters, digging, finding bits of shiny metal gummed up in the rocks. Gwen sunburned, with a basket full of rocks. A large hat tied to her head to help protect her skin as she dug. The smelting and casting.

Gwen watching the craftsmen hammer the metal she'd picked from the quarry with her own two hands.

<I'll show you someday soon. I'll take you there; it's a place of riches. I'll show you it all.>

She then pulled it back out of the ground and showed him the blade: perfect, just as stainless, delicate and un-notched as before. Gwen put it into his hand, then got behind him and demonstrated how to properly hold it, guiding his arms with her arms. Not being a swordsman, he was clumsy with it.

<No, no . . .
Here . . .
Adjust your grip.
Like this . . .>

He felt the contour of her naked ribs and stomach behind him as she silently instructed him. Effortless, he carved their names into the wall of the cave:

Here was Lord Stenstrom and Countess Gwendolyn of Belmont-South Tyrol,
Re-Discoverers of the Planet Eng
March 17, 004772ax
As before, we walk here again.

A crimson diamond appeared in the east. Dawn. Gwen grabbed her notes and pen.

<March 17: Sun up: 5 bells, twenty-six beats, or 05:22 HST.>

Later Gwendolyn, after her long night, was sound asleep next to him, still nude within the posh safety of his coat, one of her arms draped over his shoulder. His Megaeye weighed down the stack of notes she'd made and his pen was neatly arraigned near her head.

He groaned; his innards felt rough from dinner last night. Sashing his NTHs, he let Gwen continue to sleep and set out to find more forage, preferably something a bit more protein-heavy and easier on the digestion. He felt a bit naked without his HRN as he set out into the scrubby woods in his linen shirt, but Gwen needed it more than he did right now. It was cold this morning, probably somewhere just above freezing, though he felt the temperature rapidly rising with the sun. He wandered through the old forest, finding more of the same from yesterday: seeds, coarse leaves, and roots. He gathered the various bits, though he didn't relish the thought of having to eat them again.

Ah, look there! Through the trees he spied a vast meadow. On a distant hillock in the center of the meadow he thought he saw a robust ground covering of white flowers. Flowers meant the possibility of fruits and berries; the petals themselves might be rather succulent. Flowers also might attract some type of insect life, which might in turn attract larger, flesh-bearing predators such as birds, which might bring even larger game.

Stenstrom had never considered himself much of a hunter and was rather a pacifist when it came to animal life. He was, however, somewhat amazed by how quickly the veneer of civility and pacifism fell away when faced with the Mother of Realities: an empty stomach in a barren land. Adoring animals were best left for another, more satiated time.

He readied his NTH's and made his way to the hillock. Being larger and farther away than he first thought, it took quite a while to walk there. When he reached it, he was pleased. He found dark blue berries growing in abundance. They seemed edible and had a rather sweet taste. A wondrous find, Gwen would love these, and he eagerly gathered as many as he could. His HRN would be ideal right now for carrying such a haul. Higher up the hill, the plants that were in flower should bear fruit later on. He marked the hillock with a MARZABLE.

Off in the clear morning distance, he saw the same gigantic moon Gwen had pointed out yesterday hulking low on the horizon and appearing rather mottled and brown in the morning light. It seemed to be in the same position as it was yesterday. He continued his work, picking sweet berries with abandon. He cursed the loss of his HRN stuffing berries into his pockets. He'd probably need to return and get more. He'd head back to the cave and bring Gwen and his HRN along with him.

That moon?

The huge moon on the horizon hadn't moved one little bit in all this time. In fact, as he watched the morning sky slowly fill with clouds, he was certain he saw a cloud disappear *behind* the moon; therefore, it could not be a moon. It had to be something colossally huge on the ground, something so large the very thought of it sickened him to some extent.

He hurried back to the cave and woke Gwen up.

✳   ✳   ✳   ✳   ✳

"You're sure?" Gwen said as she chewed her breakfast of berries, popping one in after the next.

"I'm certain."

"Let me see," she said, her nest of mentality opening up. She gently sorted through his thoughts and saw the image of the giant sphere in the distance with clouds moving behind it.

"So, what does that mean? What could it be?"

"I really don't know. I've a feeling that our destination is that thing—whatever it is. A-Ram's instructions weren't clear and Professor Shurlamp certainly gave us no insight. Perhaps that monolith yonder is a structure of some sort. Perhaps that is the Shrine of Boraster."

"Bel, that thing breaks the clouds."

"I'm just saying. I think we should make our way in that direction. It's an obvious point of interest in any case."

Gwen finished the berries. "All right. What are we waiting for?" She stood, still nude other than his HRN.

"Your clothes, Gwen."

She laughed. "You know, being here all alone with you is rather liberating. Why bother with clothes, other than stout shoes to protect my feet? Seems pointless, really." She took his HRN off and handed to him. She instantly recoiled, feeling the cold hit her full. Teeth chattering, she quickly dressed, as Stenstrom gathered the objects she'd removed and returned them to their proper place in his coat pockets. Her Fleet uniform was poorly suited to the cold conditions and he didn't need telepathy with her to understand how desperately she wanted his coat back. He handed it over.

"You're going to have to carry everything if you're going to wear my coat." He reached in and pulled out his MARZABLE, startling her.

<Where did that come from?> she thought. *<I emptied your pockets.>*

He let her see it, holding it and testing its well-balanced weight.

She wondered if she was holding it correctly. Gwen being a master swordsman with a full-sized blade, was not a dagger-user.

"Like this," he said, taking it from her. Quickly moving his hands, the MARZABLE vanished. He shook his hands and three appeared between his fingers. "I know what you're thinking, that these are all extensions of the original one I just showed you. As long as I have the original MARZABLE on my person, I can produce as many of these extensions as I choose. I'm never without another MARZABLE to throw. I'll wager one of these will fetch us dinner this evening."

Dinner—food!! She smiled. She was hungry; he felt the blossoming emptiness of her stomach even after her breakfast of berries.

They set out from the cave, Stenstrom retracing his route through the woods to the hillock. They climbed up the side and gathered more berries, Gwen doing more eating than collecting.

There was the huge round shape in the far distance to the west, low on the horizon as before. He pointed it out to her and she stopped eating in mid-chew, amazed at the sheer size of it.

Her logical, scientific mind had trouble accepting that such a thing could be artificial.

He thought it might be a statue, possibly of Boraster himself.

<Impossible!>

<Why not? What does an Elder look like?>

<They don't look like anything. They are ethereal.>

<They are not.>

Regardless of their silent disagreement, it was clear that the massive shape in the distance should be their destination. They finished up on the hillock and set out, moving west through the forest.

Eventually, the forest gave way to a long, open step-land dotted with hillocks; a very unique sort of landscape Stenstrom had never seen before.

This was Eng, an alien world after all, regardless of the fact that many of the tree and animal species he'd spied looked familiar. They looked about, seeking to discover some trace that their ancestors had stood upon this cold, forlorn ground. But, as Gwen had mentioned, too much time had passed. Other than the gigantic shape in the distance, they saw nothing but wilderness.

Gwen's open mind ticked out nuggets of logical information. *<Nothing of our people will be left upon the surface. Nature will have re-claimed it all. One hundred thousand years is a long time. Anything left of our ancestors would be underground where the forces of time move at a slower pace.>*

<What about the giant-sized eminence ahead? It seems to have survived nicely.>

<I dispute that is an Elder-Made construction.>

And on and on it went. silent, friendly banter conducted between two people who would one day be married; walking alone yet completely at ease in each other's company.

The climate was relentlessly windy and cold; good thing for his HRN as Gwen would be suffering without it. They followed a shallow stream of clear, cold water twisting through the hillocks. Stopping for lunch,

Gwen gathered materials to sustain a fire while Stenstrom fished in the stream. He had a bit of success, managing to snag a few odd creatures resembling eels with his thrown MARZABLE. They cooked them and ate, both savoring the taste of meat on their tongues. They stared at the huge round object dominating the horizon.

2—The Welcoming Colossus

Continuing on, they covered a good fifteen miles before retiring for the day. There was no cave for them to shelter in this time, so they made do against the leeward side of a steep hillock for protection against the wind. The coat was just large enough to admit him as well, and they snuggled together on the ground in the flickering light of the small fire Stenstrom had made, eating eel and the last of the berries they'd collected.

Gwen pulled her arms out of the HRN's sleeves and got her notes out again, taking more readings and compiling more data. Her bare arm with its gleaming watch poked out of the HRN with the Megaeye, hoisting it skyward.

<This is actually kind of nice; peaceful and new things to discover. A few more days of data and we'll have a nice baseline detailing if the days are getting longer or shorter. I have no idea what season this might be. I hope we're not at the outset of winter.>

<If that be the case, I'll never get my coat back.>

A few more notes, then she got back inside the cozy nook of the HRN and began dreaming of dulcimers and quiet evenings at home. She dreamed of Belmont Manor, though her ideal version of it wasn't what actually existed on the shores of Tyrol. He was certain she'd have changes she'd like to go over with him. Her thoughts always had just the two of them at the manor rolling about the vast hallways and sitting rooms alone, but he had to interject. Belmont Manor was never empty, with the staff and his army of twenty-nine sisters always coming and going, and his father's occasional presence. His sister Lyra, still unmarried and in no particular hurry to change her status, lived there full-time. One never knew who or how many of his sisters were going to be in attendance for dinner at his departed mother's grand table, and that's how he liked it. All of his sisters and their families were welcome at any time.

Roughing it, under the fast-moving cloudy skies, they eventually drifted into sleep.

$$\bigstar \quad \bigstar \quad \bigstar \quad \bigstar \quad \bigstar$$

<*Wake up . . . .*> came a crawling voice.

During the night, Gwen was startled awake. Their minds hooked together, Stenstrom awoke as well. In the cloudy dark of the steppe, they both saw a light on the horizon, low at first but steadily rising and forming a strong, mist-clogged beam lancing through the clouds.

A loud chattering sound filled his ears—no, not his ears, his mind. The sound was deafening, growling with chaos. Gwen quickly closed up the walls of her mind, shutting herself and Stenstrom back in and forcing all else out.

He stood. The voices came from the light in the distance. He produced his Megaeye and trained it upwards.

A ship prowled through the cloudy night sky. It had the fine lines and white paint of a League ship: long, thin, straight as a pencil, lit up in standard Fleet running lights. It was a Sprint-class vessel, no doubt about it.

It was the *George Parr!!*

Curiosity, mixed with dread and cold terror, filled them. Frustration too, at this high-flying and inconvenient interloper wrecking the open-minded solitude they had enjoyed. <*How in Creation did they get here?*>

Stenstrom trained the ship in his Megaeye. As the ship rose into the southern sky, he saw a number of reddish scanning lights drift down like nets of irresistible energy and pan about the steppe in long, sweeping arcs, hauling in troves of data.

Gwen pulled him down to her side and covered him with the long tails of the HRN.

<*It's scanning for us, Bel!*> she sent to him in blaring surface chatter. <*This whole continent should be under their eye! They'll have us zero'ed in seconds.*>

Her years of experience came into his thoughts, the courses on the topic of scanning energy she'd taken at Fleet. Memories of tracking a tiny field mouse across a heather from orbit and the sheepish delight as she, just for fun, locked the ship's guns onto it as it scurried through the brush. She didn't fire, of course.

Now, the two of them were the mice in the field, and the hand controlling the guns from above might not be so kind. Stenstrom got out his Megaeye again and hoisted it to his face.

<*The port anterior wing, along with its various packages of scanning*

instrumentality, is missing. Taara said they'd shot it off in their previous engagement and she was correct, so their scanning capabilities aren't at full. Look how low they're flying; and I think I see it trailing smoke.>

<Even still, if they catch us in those lesser scanning cones, they'll zero us by our heat.> She looked at the few flickering embers of their fire with horror. *<This fire will have us made, Bel! The optics on a Sprint ship are without peer!>* She kicked at it, trying to douse the flames. Curls of smoke went up.

The ship settled in a slow port turn, lazily orbiting. *<It's about eighty miles west. It just seems to be sitting there.>*

As Stenstrom watched, several tiny craft emerged from its bays. *<They've launched several Sub-Orbitals. They're coming down to the surface.>*

He stood, seized Gwen about the waist, and tore off across the hilly landscape as fast as he could manage with his TK.

The TK quickly tired him, but he couldn't stop. He had to get distance from their campsite—a lot of it, otherwise the *George Parr* would zero them, open up and roast the both of them alive in a Sar Beam.

Flying low, the darkened ground whizzed by, the coattails of his HRN slapping against the grass. Part of him was glad the *George Parr* was here on Eng instead of harassing the *Seeker;* that meant Taara had time to get away to safety. His other half wondered if they were moments away from getting fried.

They'd traveled several miles to the south and stopped on a bluff to get a better look at the ground party in the Sub-Orbitals. Gwen took control of the Megaeye and zoomed in. *<I see a crew of six. They're hard at assembling some sort of emitter, possibly a Com station. I see the components for a portable Com shed, an antenna, and a Type 6 thermoplant for power. They already have it on-line, and they've set up a sentry post to guard it.>*

As they crouched on the ground and watched, they saw what the *George Parr's* crew was up to. Powered by the portable thermoplant, a colossal hologram punched its way into the night sky, at least a mile high. As the hologram took shape and formed, Gwen's mouth dropped open.

<That utter bitch . . .>

A grand hologram of Professor Hannah-Ben Shurlamp sprawled across the landscape, powdered arms held out in welcome, her wigged head splitting the clouds.

She spoke in a vast, thundering cone. "WELCOME, FRIENDS, TO

THE WORLD OF ENG, HOME OF OUR ANCIENT ANCESTORS. I, HANNAH-BEN SHURLAMP, EVOR, AND MY TEAM OF HARDWORKING EXPERTS, HAVE LABORED LONG TO REDISCOVER THIS PLACE OF RICHES EMBEDDED DEEP IN OUR COLLECTIVE HISTORY, AND OUR WORK NOW BELONGS TO THE AGES. I GIVE YOU . . . ENG!!"

She even had a gigantic holographic representation of her dragonball desk. Her hologram seated herself behind it and sat with practiced polish.

<*We ought to destroy that wretched thing,*> Gwen smoldered.

<*We can't, it's guarded. Best leave it be.*>

The hologram spoke once again. "OH, AND TO LORD BELMONT AND LADY PRENTISS, I REITERATE THAT YOU OUGHT TO HAVE ACCEPTED ME AS YOUR MENTOR AND BENEFACTOR. NOW, IF YOU ARE INDEED HERE ON ENG, THERE SHALL BE NAUGHT REMAINING OF THE PAIR OF YOU BUT A FEW FREE MOLECULES AND TRACE GASES. YOU HAVE BROUGHT THIS FATE UPON YOURSELVES." The hologram looked back in the direction of their camp. Scanning beams issued forth and panned about.

<*Creation, Bel, they've zeroed our camp!*> Gwen's thoughts surged through his skull. The *George Parr* banked and proceeded to the area, its cones focused on a single spot, joining the hologram's cones in a dance-hall craze of spotted light.

<*Those are Fleet crew on that ship. They wouldn't knowingly fire on two Fleet personnel,*> Gwen thought. <*Even if Captain Duval revealed himself to be a capering madman and ordered them to do so anyway, the crew would surely mutiny.*>

A moment later, there was a flash of night-searing garnet light and a great trembling shook the land. The *George Parr* was firing. The weight of deadly Sar Beams came down from her forward ventral bays like the fist of God and devastated the area where they'd camped. They extended the shot in a long, hot blast, banked around and then staggered fired, carpeting the entire area in a TAT-TAT-TAT of devastation, Professor Shurlamp's hologram looking on impassively. They then began firing in different directions, trying to triangulate in on Gwen and Strenstrom's position, but the variables and the time since departure were too great and their shots were bad misses.

<So, you were thinking, Gwen? Answers your question, doesn't it.>

The Sar Beams quieted and scanning cones filtered down again, panning about, assessing the damage done. Professor Shurlamp still sat at her holographic desk. The ship maneuvered over the destroyed area of their camp in an ever-widening series of concentric circles. Unlike the deafening gas-compression engines of his *Seeker,* the *George Parr* made almost no noise; it was wraith-like in the clouds. A lazy plume of blasted earth rose into the night air like an organic surrender flag. The hologram cleared her throat.

<Come on. We need to create some distance between us and them!> Onward he TK'ed, gaining more and more speed, more and more distance, low, bouncing off the ground, Gwen huddled up inside the HRN. From far away, they heard a rolling contented laughing, tinged with a bit of wickedness floating by them on the wind.

A small, chiding mental voice worked its way through Gwen's mental barriers. *<Jo-boy...>* he heard. *<Jo-boy... I'm back. I know you're down there somewhere, you fucking little bastard! We saw your campfire and thought we'd knock, but it seems you weren't home, were you? We can't find your blasted, stinking remains anywhere.>*

It was the Lacerta, yet again. She stopped and waited, perhaps hoping for a response of some kind. Then, she continued. *<So much the better. I'd rather it be you and me, alone on this wretched planet, where we can settle this up in person and nobody's going to interfere. I really hope that . . . fucking bitch is down there with you, too. You know the one I mean, the one who gave me the little brain scramble the last time. Oh, what I'm going to do to her. Had me in the tank, she did, and I still can't hear out of my left ear. I'm going to show her what her guts look like. Hehehechecheheeeee . . . .>*

There was another pause. *<I'll bet you're wondering how we found you? Suffice to say, it wasn't all that hard. Professor Shurlamp pointed us in the right general direction, Duval's associates helped out after they took apart that miserable slut from Caroline; and your Hospitaler had all sorts of information, too. Oh, I'm sorry. You thought she'd off-shipped, didn't you?>*

He was alarmed and crashed into the ground in a tumble. Gwen fell out of his grasp and rolled in the grass.

Morgan! Morgan didn't get off the *George Parr*? But how? Taara told him she was off on the *Caroline* and safe. Worry and dread filled him.

<So, for starters, I'm going to take your bitch and I'm going to rip her ear off and make her eat it! An ear for an ear, it's only fair. Then, you and me can finish up what we started on Caroline. It's going to be a great fight; people would pay good money to watch a fight like that. And I'm looking forward to putting my hands all over you. Be seeing you around, Jo-Boy. Oh, by the way, take your garbage back . . . .>

As Stenstrom watched, something small was jettisoned out of a ventral port of the ship and fell to ground in a slow crumple.

<Have a nice night, hahahahahahaha!> came the Lacerta's thoughts, then the *George Parr* bore away and disappeared in the direction of the giant shape far to the west. Professor Shurlamp's hologram sat at her desk, waiting to either greet newcomers from the League or rat out their position, whichever came first.

Stenstrom went on for another few miles, finding a good place to set down and hide in the rotted-out base of a fallen tree near a river. Though it was a little wet, the tree would mask their more obvious scanable signatures well enough for the time being.

Gwen was exhausted. He settled her in for sleep deep within the trunk. The process of its decomposition made its interior slightly warm, so she should be just fine. He took his HRN back and left, fading into the shadows and moving swiftly near the ground with TK.

Though it probably was a trap, he headed back in the direction of their campsite, giving the Professor's hologram a wide berth. He had to know what had been cast out of the ship.

He hoped he was wrong.

When he arrived later, the area was raked and furrowed from the Sar Beam attack, like a shelled battlefield of churned earth. The hillock where they had camped was no more—flattened and scorched, wreathed in smoke. Mixed in with the furrows were numerous sensing cubes known as "Warblebugs" deposited by the *George Parr*, hoping to lock onto him should he be dumb enough to return and take the bait the Lacerta had dangled in front of him.

The cubes lay there, throwing out various beams of light and radiation reading movement, temperature, chemical composition, and so forth. An alien fly buzzing across the field could trigger any number of scans and the *George Parr* would have it zeroed in an instant.

However, none of the cubes laying there could detect Stenstrom. His Tyrol fade into the shadows being just that, a melded shift into a pocket dimension. He was there, moving through the destroyed landscape, but he wasn't at the same time.

From the west, the Professor's hologram stirred and stood up. It turned its gaze in his direction, scanning cones saturating the area. After a minute or so, Shurlamp seemed satisfied that nobody was present, and returned to her desk. The framed holographic picture of her portly teetotaler husband floated in mid-air behind her, just a little touch of home.

In the middle of all this tumult was a huddled form laying in the dirt. He knew what it was without having to look.

He knelt down beside Morgan-Jeterix's corpse, gazing at her: the beautiful Hala face, that braided hair. Her twisted, broken body encased in her Hospitaler bodysuit.

How he once dreamed of cutting her out of that bodysuit to get to the steaming flesh within.

Lying in the dirt here and there were her Hospitaler tools, glinting in the mute light.

What happened Morgan? Why did you leave? he pleaded into her dead face and got no response. Covertly, he gathered up her tools, then bore Morgan away, escaping all notice.

Morgan-Jeterix, his friend, his midnight fantasy and woman he could have made his lover, was dead.

When he thought it safe to do so, he stopped in a glen and made his final peace with her, cradling her small, firm body in his arms and whispering into her dead ears.

How I could have loved you, Morgan. How I wanted to. I simply chose a different path.

Then the recriminations came. What if he'd picked her over Gwen? Would she be alive even now? What would have happened to Gwen? Was this his fault? Was his status as some sort of Planar Entity the cause of this? The regrets, what it might have been like to have made love to her, if just for one night.

He had felt Gwen's death in the Ruins of Caroline, and he now felt Morgan's. So much life. Such a free spirit, and all that she would have given to him. Why would such a person offer a dull man from Tyrol her love?

"*People are drawn to you . . .*" the Shadow tech Goddess had said.

Gwen loved him, and Morgan loved him, too—and he loved her in return, only in a different, less nurturing, more carnal way than he loved Gwen. He thought about A-Ram's disk and the conference room. He wished Morgan's name had been on it.

He held her for a long while. He found a good green spot that he thought reminded him a bit of the Hala-lands on Kana where Morgan had come from. He thought, perhaps, this spot might please her, might remind her of home, and he buried her in a grave dug with his own two hands; the Sisters' strength not failing him. Giving her a final kiss on the cheek, he covered her up with heavy stones and carved her a headstone with his MARZABLE:

Here lies Morgan-Jeterix,
Lady of Thompson and Samaritan of the Grand Order of Hospitalers.
. . . a path not taken

He looked back one last time and said his final goodbyes. The pile of rocks he made sank down and settled a little. He didn't want to leave her there, but what choice did he have? Perhaps, when the Fleet came to rescue him and Gwen, they could exhume Morgan and take her back to Kana. He flew away at last on his TK, hearing her ghost calling out to him as he departed:

I loved you too, Bel . . .

His thoughts darkened as he covered ground. Captain Duval or the Lacerta had killed Morgan in cold blood, and now were seeking their blood as well with the help of Professor Shurlamp and her gigantic hologram.

Darkness entered his mind and the desire for revenge took control of his soul. This place, this Eng of old, was going to be a tomb, either for him or for them. He was going to find the *George Parr* and attack, and then he'd pit his strength against theirs: a foulmouthed, wretched, debauched, strung-out, balled out, Kooked-up murderous ex-Sister and an ex-*Kaidar Gemain*. Both of them were going to die; whatever happened after that was irrelevant.

He moved on in the direction of the massive monolith in the far distance. He figured that's where the *George Parr* was making berth. He passed a stream. From the air he saw large fish swimming lazily through the water.

Gwen would love those.

Small matter. Before the dawn, this would be settled one way or the other.

Something knocked on his thoughts. *<Bel? Bel . . . where are you?>*

Gwen. She was awake, searching for him. He thought of her, alone and bewildered in the tree. He wondered what would happen to her, should he fall. The Lacerta would surely get her too.

He put his fury aside and calmed himself down. *<I'm here, Gwen. Finally waking up?>*

<Where am I? It smells in here.>

<You're in a rotten tree stump. A fine place for a Countess, isn't it? Stay in there; it's warm and safe. Are you feeling hungry?>

<I'm starved!>

<I'll be back soon and I'll have fish.>

<Ohhhh, sounds delicious. Please hurry. I love you, Bel.>

<I love you too, Gwen.>

He TK'ed faster and made to get some of those fish he'd seen. He was hungry, too.

3—THE TEMPUS FINDAL

When he returned to the tree, Gwen already had a small, smoldering fire going inside the tree stump. She had created a number of relief holes for venting the smoke with her FEDULA, but the air inside the stump was still heavy and hard to breathe. She coughed under her breath and stayed low.

"We have to be careful, Bel. Even with a diminished sensing capacity, the *George Parr* and Shurlamp's bloody hologram can detect minute variations in heat, smell our smoke if we let the fire burn too hot, and hear our conversations if we talk too loud."

Her throat was ragged from the smoke. She hacked and shut her mouth. She entered his mind.

<I suggest we forget our mouths for the time being and keep to the covert realms of our mental connection.>

<Fair enough.> He filleted the fish and put them over the fire. His mind parted as Gwen settled in. Her throat hurt from the smoke, her ankle hurt in the damp morning air, and she had an odd slow burn deep within her, like a bundle of ache stretching outward filling every part of her and hurting just enough to be noticeable and annoying.

<I've started my monthly cycle, Bel. It's going to get worse and worse for a week or so. I've never disabled my womb. We don't do that in Zenon.>

Taara was always a little bundle of bad energy when she was on her cycle. *<That reminds me. Taara, are you out there?>* he thought over the tregador.

<Taara?>

No reply. Odd. She should be responding right away, unless she was asleep or in the shower and didn't have it on her wrist. He was certain the *Seeker* was safe. The Lacerta would have mentioned something should they have further damaged her; still, the silence was worrisome.

He'd try her again later.

Soon the fish was ready and Gwen eagerly pulled the pieces off the fire, transferring them from hand to hand as they were hot.

<Oh, this is good,> she thought, savoring the hot fish. *<I've always been a dainty eater, but seems since we've been here I've not thought about much other than my stomach. I wish we had some seasoning, a little salt and pepper would do well. Some lemons, too.>*

<I'll keep an eye out for such things, if they're available. I'm sure we'll find something out here we can use to add flavor to our dinner, as it looks like we might be out here for at least a few months.>

<I estimate we'll be here at least four months, given the possible disabled state of the Seeker, *the informing of the Fleet, the callout and assembling of an armada, and the return trip at speed. The sailing speed of the vessels sent for our rescue is also a concern. And, that is assuming we can stay low of the* George Parr.*>*

<I'm thinking we shouldn't delay. We find this shrine, then we get at the Anatameter and turn the knob. Then we're done with it. As for this situation here, we'll just find some nice quiet part of the world where the George Parr *and Shurlamp's hologram can't find us to hole up in until the Fleet arrives.>*

Gwen grabbed another piece off the coals. *<I think our best bet is to go underground. I'm certain there's underground habitations left by our ancestors we can repatriate. All we need do is find and make use of them.>*She swallowed a bite of fish. *<The thing they threw out last night, what was it?>*

He darkened and didn't answer. Gwen nudged into his thoughts.

She was devastated for a moment as images of Morgan's broken body and her grave of stones filtered into her mind. *<I . . . never meant for that to happen. I thought she was safely off the* George Parr.*>*

<I did too, but apparently not, and it cost Morgan her life.>

<It might sound odd, given our often contentious working relationship, but I considered her a friend and I admired her skills. Of course, I didn't approve of some of her vices. I most certainly never intended to go to bed with her. But she was a good Hospitaler and a fine lady. I know you liked her Bel, and I'm sorry.>

He nodded.

They finished their meal and crept out. The giant tree stump they'd sheltered in was the largest feature of a narrow wetland that went on for about a mile until the ground dried. Beyond, the landscape fell away in a large escarpment that dropped down into a tumbled valley that stretched to the horizon.

There, at the edge of the escarpment, they got their first really good look at the vast shape in the distance, the gigantic monolith.

It was a spheroid, roughly egg-shaped and apparently lying on its side. At some point in the past, it might have been standing upright, doubling its already staggering height. It was made of a brownish stone that was irregularly cut, like a relief atlas. It had a facial disk of some sort, though there were no discernible features. It also had a pair of great, curved protrusions, like a set of rough-hewn horns that met over the top. One "horn" curved directly over the top of the monolith, the other was beneath it, mostly buried in the ground. To the east, about fifty miles away, Hannah-Ben Shurlamp's hologram sat quietly at its holographic desk, busy doing nothing.

Stenstrom got out his trusty Megaeye and looked the monolith over. Magnified, he could see layers of hanging clouds condensing around its girth. It was so huge, that seeing it blown up through the lens of his Megaeye made it lose its identity as a shape, and appear as nothing more than the continuation of the land tipped on its side.

Gwendolyn settled into his mind and looked through the Megaeye with him.

<It's got to be at least fifty miles away still.>

<More like a hundred. Look at it.>

Stenstrom noticed something tiny and slow-moving circling the heights of the monolith. It looked like a white gnat buzzing about and harassing the horned head of a water buffalo.

<The George Parr—*there she is. Look at the contrails.>*

<They're just loitering around, casting their net, waiting to zero us. And recall, Duval is also after the Anatameter for his own purposes.>

<Then we're moving out together. We'll use TK. Stay low to the ground and avoid bodies of water. Duval will focus his scanning beams there, expecting us to use them for cover . When we near, we'll have to suspend the TK and walk. The Lacerta will be able to detect it if we get too close.>

Gazing at the monolith in the distance with grim determination, Stenstrom stood and put his Megaeye away Gwen smiled and adjusted her FEDULA, locking it in place. She put her arms deep into the depths of his HRN, encircling him.

<Well, I'm ready to go. Mmmmm, I can't think of a finer way to travel. Hold me and let's fly, Bel.>

He put his arms around her and TK'ed into the air. As usual, the TK didn't feel like he was really flying. It felt like the dream of flying; like he wasn't really in the air, just imagining it and he would soon awake, going nowhere and not moving at all. He skimmed the ground, slow at first, then picking up speed. Though the Sisters' strength filled him, he had the memory of having the normal strength of a man, and carrying the rather dense and heavy Gwendolyn gave him the phantom feeling of muscle fatigue. He even thought for a moment that he might drop her or crash into the ground, but he relaxed and allowed the Sisters power to move through him. Eventually, carrying Gwen felt like nothing and he settled in, picking up more speed, becoming a creature of the air. The tails of his HRN beat the ground and kicked up the leaves. He plunged into the valley, hugging the contours of the land. Gwen, now familiar with the interior of his HRN, found his Megaeye and got it out, holding it to her face.

<*We're covering the ground well; must have gone several miles already. I think if we bear to the south and come up on the monolith heading north, the natural shape of the thing will blank the Geoge Parr's scanning cones and shield us to some extent from Shurlamp. I see a storm coming in as well from the west. That should further confound their scopes.*> She moved the Megaeye around and centered on the George Parr. <*There she is, still orbiting aimlessly, and still trailing smoke. They must be heavily damaged and might require Dry Docking. I estimate she's about ten thousand feet up. Never thought I'd loathe the sight of a Fleet Sprint ship.*>

The speeding valley opened up into a broad flatland dotted by mirror-like pools of standing water and isolated pockets of tall fern-like growths. Herds of gazelle-like animals peppered the landscape, moving amongst the ferns, using them as cover. Stenstrom did his best to avoid them to prevent an attention-attracting stampede.

As they neared, the monolith came into clear focus, framed by the line of stormy clouds behind it. The "Face" of the monolith appeared to be composed of a number of eyes lumped together, creating a very alien display. Gwen's thoughts spiraled. She had always thought the Elders were more spirit than flesh, more conception than reality, and certainly not a horned, eye-covered creature of distinctly alien note. She sketched as best she could with her arms confined by Stenstrom's embrace.

They darted into the structure's massive shadow as a tempest boiled in from the west, pelting them with frigid rain.

Gwen huddled within the folds of his HRN, protecting herself from the rain. This rain would chill her down to the marrow otherwise. She noticed something to the west.

<*Bel! What's that? That ground-covering of large fern-like plants, just there, several miles west.*>

<*I see it.*>

Gwen scanned it with the Megaeye. <*Look how the ferns are situated. They seem to be laid-out in a systematic, grid-like pattern; see there . . . and there as well. I'll wager there's something beneath the surface creating a steady pressure of warmer air the ferns are taking advantage of. Bear west, Bel, bear west! We might be on the verge of a grand discovery!*>

Stenstrom veered to the west. As Gwen said, the ground was dotted with patches of dense fern cover. He saw a flat spot and dropped to the ground. The ferns were huge, nine feet tall and provided good cover. Gwen hopped out and together they searched the area. The ground felt a bit warmer, possibly from the humidity created by the ferns. As Gwen searched about, he moved on foot to the fern's edge and surveyed what was before them.

<*Still about thirty miles away. I don't like the looks of this. The* George Parr *and* Shurlamp *have got the area covered. We go much farther and they're going to have us zeroed regardless of what we do.*>

<*We might not have to worry about that. Bel, come here!*> Gwen sent, excited. At the base of a thick stand of ferns, she had discovered a vent leading down into the ground spewing humid warm air. It seemed man-made. <*This seems to be a relief duct of some sort. I'll wager there's a massive complex beneath. We might be able to go to ground and access the monolith from underneath, safe and out of the eye of the* George Parr.> She cleared away the ferns. <*Can you help m—*>

Suddenly, Gwen went silent. The air grew heavy and Stenstrom felt a tangible wave from the vent hit him full.

He knew what it was. Fear given form. Gwen was locked in place at the opening of the vent, unable to move or think; she couldn't even draw her FEDULA and defend herself. Then something emerged from the vent and begin pulling her down into the hole.

The Shadow tech Goddess' bolabung under his shirt seemed to be working. He felt the ferocity of the fear, but the bolabung took just enough off that he could still function, still act. He seized Gwendolyn by the shoulders and pulled her back. Whatever had hold of her wasn't letting go and he engaged in a brief tug-o-war with Gwen as the prize. With a final jerk he pulled her free. He readied to take Gwen and TK away, but there was the *George Parr*, there was the hologram. If he came out of the ferns they would be zeroed in seconds.

"... *bel* ..." came a hideous voice from the hole. "... *i'm going to kill her, bel, and then ... hhhhhehehehhe ... and then ..."*

His guts roiling in fear, he watched a pale clawed hand creep out of the hole and rake the ground, making deep ruts.

Protecting Gwen as best he could, he produced the stone knife and held it out. "I have a weapon. I'll put you to the grave."

The clawed hand pulled back a bit. It spoke again. "... *but why? you won't kill me, I loooove you. It's the Merthig, isn't it? I'll stop her heart and then we can be together!"*

A fresh wave of terror crawled out of the hole and slammed into both of them. He grit his teeth and felt his guts constrict. Gwen, eyes dilated, convulsed.

Gwen had no protection.

Gwen was dying of fear.

He had no choice. He took her and TK'ed fast out of the ferns heading toward the monolith as fast as he could.

"... *there is no place you can go that I can't follow ... hhhhehehehehee ...>*

As he feared, Hannah-Ben Shurlamp instantly detected them as they broke into the clear, snapping her head around and painting them in the red blare of her scanning cones. "THERE YOU ARE, YOU GUTLESS COWARDS!!"

The *George Parr* high overhead wobbled fitfully and came about. She seemed to be having issues maneuvering, and she also seemed to be having difficulty maintaining altitude. Thrusters fired. The smoke she was trailing had gotten worse.

The hologram pounded on her holographic desk. "WHAT ARE YOU WAITING FOR? FIRE! FIRE!"

Gwen stirred in his arms. <*Gods, what in Creation was that? I've never felt such fear.>*

<Tempus Findal.>

As the effects of the fear subsided, Gwen lifted the Megaeye. *<The George Parr is listing hard. See that, their thermoplant is out. The damage the Seeker did to her must have been significant. They're running on nothing but gas compression and thrusters. I think they've got an internal fire, too. See that?>*

Stenstrom glanced up. The *George Parr* was in certain trouble, even the hologram looked up at it, wondering what was going on. He spied a number of tiny objects blossom away from the ship like bees exiting a hive.

<They're deploying Ripcars, Sub-Orbitals, every ancillary vessel they've got. I count twelve craft in all. They've abandoned ship!>

Gwendolyn followed the *George Parr* as it came down in a long, smoking curve. It rolled over in a terminal dive, flaming and shedding parts as it disappeared beneath the horizon. She turned her attention to the smaller craft that had emerged from it. *<She's end-of-mission, but we've got Ripcars coming our way, Bel. Six of them.>*

Stenstrom strained and TK'ed faster, the great bulk of the monolith blotting out the sky. *<Then we have no choice but to fight.>*

At last they reached the perimeter of the monolith, the area doused in shadows. The monolith was craggy in the extreme, offering them innumerable places to take cover. They dove for the crags and drew their weapons. Just as they situated themselves, the swarm of Ripcars came in.

<Oh, Good Creation. Look at them, Bel,> Gwendolyn said, giving them the once-over. *<They're bloody K-Listers, right off the damn boats. Duval's replaced his reputable Fleet crew with K-Lister trash. Small wonder they couldn't keep their ship flying.>*

<K-Listers? You mean washouts?>

<Riff-raff who couldn't pass muster. I can see their 4-D tattoos, a giant 'K' printed right on their disreputable faces along with their list of offences.>

The Ripcars, six of them, roamed about, searching for them. Gwendolyn didn't like what she was seeing. *<Gods, they're mounting `99's, three guns per ship. Fast-firing guns like those will punch through this rock like nothing. And I'll wager they're kitted out with incendiary loads as well.>*

Standing tall in the lead ship was Lt. Remm Deckard, the first officer they'd met in Blanchefort village, her large hat and blue hair streaming in the breeze.

The Ripcars came in fast. "There! There they are!" one of the K-Lister lookouts called, pointing in their direction. There were five crewmen aboard each Ripcar: one flying the ship, one operating the scanning devices, and the last three manning mounted `99 guns. In Gwen's mind, Stenstrom could see dark blue "K's" stamped on their faces. K-Listers, dishonored washouts who'd found safe haven on Captain Duval's renegade ship. They wore segmented ansel-plas armor to protect them from shrapnel and return fire. Stenstrom aimed and fired his NTH's at an approaching Ripcar. He hit the lookout and the man went limp, sliding into the bowels of the ship. The armada formed a battle front and brought their guns to bear. The K-Lister crew seemed eager to begin.

"Get down!!" Stenstrom cried.

A storm of unrelenting gunfire erupted and they choked on clouds of pulverized stone as their cover was quickly scoured through.

<Follow me!> Gwendolyn sent, pulling him through a tight passage to another section of rock.

<We're going to have to fight, Bel. I could Pop them, but the Lacerta will be sure to hear it, then we'll have to deal with her as well.> She drew her tiny MiMs and cocked it.

"What are you going to do what that?" he asked, noting the MiMs wasn't a very practical weapon in an actual battle situation. He waved up a green Holystone and threw it to their right. It cracked open and spewed a tangle of sticky webs. Instantly, the armada maxed fire on it.

Stenstrom rose up and took aim at a nearby Ripcar hovering about twelve feet above the ground. He fired in rapid succession, hitting two K-Listers manning guns and a scanner, his shots passing right through their protective plating. The pilot reacted with shock seeing his fellows fall and tried to swerve away. Stenstrom lined him up and fired, killing the pilot. The Ripcar heeled over and went down hard, the composite structure of the vessel splintering against the ground.

"There!" Remm Deckard cried. The armada reset their formation.

They resumed cover and continued crawling to their left until they reached a dead end. A cloud of destruction followed them. Literally up against a wall, they had nowhere else left to go. "Gwen, stay down!" Stenstrom yelled as he faded in the Shadows and leapt out into the open.

<Where are you going!> Gwen sent in a panic. Invisible, he ran out

under the armada, picked out a ship and fired up through the hull, pumping shots, aiming in the general area of where the pilot would be situated. The ship shuddered, a limp arm appeared over the rim, and then it careened down, hitting the ground nose first, dead and wounded people squirmed together in their harnesses. The remaining four Ripcars jostled about in confusion for a moment.

"He's there!" Remm Deckard yelled as the Ripcars re-orientated themselves to fire on his position. He sprinted to his right, moving away from where Gwen was hidden.

He popped off two more shots and then got zeroed by a gunner, the force of the gunfire knocking him down. He should be dead, torn to pieces, but, as usual, the Sisters were with him and he lived, absorbing the damage, the bullets bouncing off his HRN.

He was still hooked into Gwen's mind. He saw the white of the K-Lister's eyes standing out against the dark blue of their 4-D tattoos as they hammered away with their guns. The pilot suddenly stood up in his seat, looking about dumbly. He grabbed his head, blood squirted out through his fingers.

Gwen, she'd Popped him hard and the man was dead. The Ripcar lurched and flipped over in midair, dumping all but two out into open space where they fell to the ground, badly wounded from the fall.

<WHAT THE FUCK IS GOING ON!!!> came a hideous mental wail. <OHH, BELMONT!! JUST A MOMENT!!>

The Lacerta! She had heard Gwen's Pop and had them zeroed.

<I'LL BE RIGHT THERE!! DON"T GO ANYWHERE!!>

A cloud of smoke formed in front of them. The Lacerta Wafted in with considerable aplomb. She stood on the rock face, not bothering to get out of the way of the hail of bullets from the Ripcars. The bullets went around her, or, in some cases, stopped altogether and fell to the ground, her field of TK protecting her. Eyes wide, she stood before Stenstrom.

"Knock, fuckin' knock, Jo-Boy!" she yelled over the din of gunfire as he tried to stand. He waved up a red Holystone, ready to throw it at her and set her ablaze. She reached out and cupped her hand around his preventing him from throwing. She squeezed with impossible force, cracking the Holystone in his palm. A fireball erupted, enveloping both their hands.

<*Bel!*> Gwen sent.

"Ah, look what you did," the Lacerta said, putting the fire out with TK. "Now you're going to have to buy me a drink or something."

She locked his gaze and he couldn't look away.

She Buzzed him, scrambling the interior of his mind into chaos. It was an oddly lilting sensation as the floor to his reality dropped away, and he heard a rousing brass band playing somewhere as he forgot who he was.

4—THE SHRINE OF BORASTER

Stenstrom inhabited the shadow lands for an undetermined length of time, witless, in a whirlwind of chaotic thoughts and disjointed psychedelia. He dreamed meaningless dreams and things he should have known became unknown.

Sounds and voices punched through the dark.

Did you kill him?

Nah, I didn't kill him. I touched him up nice. Wake up, Jo-Boy!

Hey?

HEY!

All at once, the various moving parts of his mind that had been shot off into the far corners of oblivion piecemealed themselves into place, crawled back into order, turned in the correct sequence. There was daylight and encroaching humid twilight.

"Well, well, well, welcome back," came a voice.

Looking up at a distant rock ceiling, Stenstrom lay on an earthen floor. Reddish sunlight came in from his right. He thought he must be well above the clouds. His lungs ached in a slight but persistent demand for thicker air.

His hands were tightly bound in a thick, cocoon-like length of wound-up wire studded with an assortment of ant-like moving charms. The charms slid back and forth along the length of the wire. He strained to get a better look at the wrappings; pewter eyeballs blinked back up at him. He was trussed up in an ANGRY MISER wire, studded and activated. If he managed to get out of his bonds, the charms would react and blow him to Creation's Gate. He wondered how large a bomb blast could he survive. He wondered.

Standing in front of him, lank and tall in her lacy black gown, was the Lacerta, along with Captain Duval and his first officer, Remm Deckard with her beady eyes hidden behind her big hat and blue hair. A trail of ashes like little sailboats riding the waves of fate drifted down lazy from the Lacerta's usual cigarette. K-Lister crew regarded him with a disinterested, somewhat sour note. They were all armed with Inseroth "Hot" rifles. He wondered where his NTHs were; they were missing from his sash.

And where was Gwen?

"Is he finally cogent?" Duval asked.

"Ya'," the Lacerta said in her wheezy, accented voice, spewing ashes. She put her foot on his chest and pressed down with crushing strength. The sole and heel of her shoe dug into his chest; he even felt the subtle shiftings of her foot moving around within her shoe. "How you doing down there, huh? I made sure to wrap you up nice and tight. Didn't want ya' to get lonely or nothing."

He took note of his surroundings. He was near the opening to a vast ledge. There was an abundance of reddish daylight drifting in tinged with a hint of gold indicating the onset of dusk. No clouds at all, he must be very high up the face of the monolith. If he concentrated, he could hear the faint ghost of Hannah-Ben Shurlamp's hologram speaking far below. Nearby a large Sub-Orbital was parked, all its hatches and doors open. It was loaded with mixed bag of crates and tankards of supplies they had managed to throw in before the *George Parr* sank.

"And there is no possibility he can escape?" Duval asked.

The Lacerta pushed him down again. "Nah!" she said.

"Well, then, shall we escort him to the Shrine? He has a duty to perform. It will be the last of his life."

They all turned to the Lacerta. She winced and toyed with the dressings covering her right ear. The wound Gwen had inflicted upon her on Planet Fall, the devastating "Pop", still seemed to be an issue.

"We're waiting," Duval said. He placed his hands at his hips, opening his Fleet coat. Stenstrom caught a glimpse of his NTHs jutting out of the Captain's waistcoat. So, Duval had claimed them as a prize. That was inconvenient.

"Yeah, yeah, give me a sec, `kay? You guys ever try walking?" The Lacerta moved her hand away and Stenstrom saw a few blots of blood seeping through the wrappings. After a moment she composed herself and stood tall, adjusted her bodice, and quickly he and all else present were TK'ed into the air where they drifted into the interior like a swarm of floating rocks. The Lacerta did not TK herself. Instead, she walked on her three telescoping metal legs from the VUNKULA hidden under her gown, expanding them upwards to full stretch, lifting her high into the air, their pincers clacking on the stone far below. She moved at Stenstrom's side. He felt the invisible cloud of her TK moving around him, tickling in a coy fashion. She even winked once as they moved deeper into the interior.

The journey inward was like a trip down a giant gullet. The rosy sunlight quickly faded to a jewel-like purple glow rising up from the floor in gentle veils. The walls and looming ceiling shifted from a craggy ochre stone to a smooth, gemstone polish surging with inner light. On and on they went. They passed over a yawning gulf and Stenstrom felt the depths and the cool emptiness of it beneath him. The "clacks" from the Lacerta's VUNKULA ceased as she TK'ed herself across the void. Soon, they reached the other side, her clacking resuming.

She intruded her thoughts into his. <*Damn, you smell good,*> her mental voice thundered. <*Anybody ever tell you that? Huh? Any Sisters ever tell you that? No?*> He felt the indistinct fingers of TK press about his face as if she were kissing him.

Carried by the cushioned airiness of the Lacerta's TK they entered a great purplish, greenish chamber surging with energy. This must be the Shrine of Boraster, Stenstrom thought. The ceiling went up and up into a great dome so lofty it had to be least two miles high. Stenstrom mused Professor Shurlamp's giant hologram would fit nicely under it.

They arrived at the center and the Lacerta set them all down. The K-Listers scattered. They got their "Hot" rifles out, the charged battery packs buzzing slightly and ready to fire.

"Bring him here," Duval said.

In the center of the Shrine was a fluted column rising up about four feet. A great pulsing gem sat on top of the column charging the Shrine in its light.

"There it is, at long last. The Anatameter," Duval said.

The Anatameter, stolen from Clovis and relocated to this remote place, sat as a king atop its pedestal, no longer a "ruddy little nothing" as Gwen had called it. Here, it shown like an emerald heart surging with power.

"Now, sir, here we are at last," Duval said, his voice lost in the enormity of the shrine. "Seems such a terrible long way to go for such an innocuous thing . . ." He looked around the shrine and let his hands fall. "I mean this place is certainly grand and epic in scale, but we've seen many grand places here and there in the League and in Xaphan space, haven't we, Lt.?"

Remm Deckard nodded, her hat brim flopping about. The Lacerta snorted. "I kinda' like it!" she said, her voice bouncing around the interior. She slapped Stenstrom on the back. "Whadda' ya' think?"

A beeping came from Remm Deckard's coat. She pulled out a Fleet J-Raster transponder and spoke into it. She said a few words to Duval.

"What's that, you say?" Duval said, consulting with her. "Well, then, go on and return when you can." She returned the J-Raster to her coat, then left.

Duval turned his attention back to Stenstrom. "Here we are, the Shrine of Boraster at last, and the Anatameter. In my younger days, when I was still buttoned up and tied down in Remnath, these devices in St. Mary's Axe came to me readily, and I had but to touch them and new worlds were opened up to me. But now, with my wife gone, these devices no longer come. All that was once available to me is now shut. I sometimes feel that I have lost favor with some unknown greater power."

Stenstrom's dream came back to him, the toppled statue of Captain Duval in the Garden of Horrors. The *Kaidar Gogol*—he who had it all, but no longer; a victim of the *Tempus Findal.*

Duval hovered over the Anatameter. "And now, as I recall, if I touch it, it will bring St. Mary's Axe to us, and the way to the Shadow tech Goddess will be open at long last." He pushed up his sleeves and placed his hands on its surface. The vibrant face of the Anatameter went dark and cloudy and seemed to recoil at his touch.

Duval pulled his hands away and it came back to life. He sucked in his breath in frustration. "I've lost my old magic. Where has it gone?"

Duval pointed at Stenstrom. "You, touch it. Burgon promised it would work for you. Touch the device."

Stenstrom stood there defiant He didn't move.

"I said, touch it!" Duval repeated. Some of the K-Listers, filthy-minded, snickered.

Stenstrom refused.

A K-Lister crewman came up and raised the butt-end of his weapon, ready to club Stenstrom over the head with it.

"Easy, easy, I got hold of this, I got hold of this," the Lacerta said, interjecting. In dramatic style she clapped her skinny hands on Stenstrom's shoulders, her fingers spread out in spidery fashion, and squeezed. His joints popped under the crushing pressure. Like a mother guiding a willful child she led him step by step to the Anatameter. She clamped her hand onto his bound wrists and moved his arms for him. Her strength was hydraulic-like and unstoppable. Perhaps he could have resisted, but he bided his time. She pushed herself into the contours of his back and mid-section, grinding him into the column. Her right hand wandered between his legs to his crotch. He felt her bloom of heat pressed up into his back and heard her quivering, rapid breaths. She was aroused. "Yeah," she whispered. "You like that? You like that?"

"Lacerta!" Duval cried. "What are you doing? Put his hands on the Anatameter and be quick about it."

She forced his knuckles against it, skinning them.

"Is something supposed to happen?" the Lacerta asked as she pushed against him. The Anatameter seemed to be inert.

"According to Burgon, yes. Lacerta, let him go; perhaps your presence is fouling the workings of the device."

The Lacerta pushed Stenstrom to the floor and stepped back. "No problem, sweet guy."

Duval drew an NTH from his sash and pointed it at him. "Now, stand up and lay hands on the device." He shook the NTH. "I'm told this weapon is not to be trifled with."

Stenstrom did nothing. Duval cocked the hammer. "I will gun you down."

The Lacerta rolled her eyes. "We're getting nowhere. I'll be right back." She marched off into the crowd of K-Listers. "Outta' the way!" she barked.

There was a commotion and crazed whimpering. The Lacerta came up through the ranks. She was dragging a female crewman with her, her hand embedded in the girl's black hair. "Go on, do it!" she barked as she roughly pushed the girl into Stenstrom. The girl stumbled and fell on top of him.

Sobbing, smelling of sweat and fear, her clothes dirty, she righted herself and helped Stenstrom to his feet. He recognized her. She was the same crewman he had stolen the Vith helmets from in Blanchefort Village, the same one Duval had previously been terrorizing. She was crazed with fear and exhaustion, near delirium. She held him by the shoulder with her trembling fingers and led him to the Anatameter.

"Here," she whispered. "Please, sir, please . . . they'll kill me." Tears cut through the grime on her tortured face. "I don't know you, but they'll kill me. If you've any mercy in you . . ."

She was lost in her own fear-clouded world.

He glanced at Duval. "I touch this and then what?" he demanded, trying to stall.

"And then there is St. Mary's Axe. There is the Shadow tech Goddess."

"She does not exist on this plane."

"She lives in St. Mary's Axe. I shall offer her this universe as a gift. What wonders we shall create together, and all awaiting you, sir." He stepped forward. "So get to it! Do it, now!" He pointed the NTH at the girl and cocked the hammer. "Do it, or this worthless girl dies, right here, right now. Think I won't kill her?"

"She's doomed regardless if you have your way? Isn't that right?"

The Lacerta seized the girl and threw her into the ranks of K-Listers. "Come an' get it, boys, she's all yours!" The K-Listers pushed and shoved her, bouncing her about. Cloth tore, her breasts came spilling out. They hooted and groped.

"All right! Don't hurt her!" Stenstrom said. Duval glanced at the K-Listers and they stepped away. The girl stood there, exposed, weeping. She covered herself with her hands.

The Anatameter awaited. It was faceted and elaborate, conceived of alien design, awaiting his touch. Stenstrom placed his hands on the surface of the Anatameter. As his fingers touched it, he felt a slow rumble from within and a noticeable bloom of heat. A secret door opened, and a moment later the straight stone passage of the Hall of Possibilities appeared at the rear of the Shrine. It looked like a mundane hallway running left and right in what appeared to be a perfectly straight line. It stirred Stenstrom's memory. He'd encountered this before in Clovis.

"Behold!" Duval cried in triumph. "Burgon was right! By Creation, he was right! It is St. Mary's Axe returned to me at last, and, down the right hand corridor is the Shadow tech Goddess, the end of our journey!"

Duval turned to the K-Listers. "My friends, I'm looking for a small detail to kindly scout ahead and secure the central corridor there. There's extra pay in it for any who participate."

K-Listers, each armed with rifles, went ahead and carefully entered the corridor, taking up hi/low defensive positions.

"Do you see anything?" Duval asked.

"No, sir!" one of them replied.

With all eyes on the corridor, Stenstrom pulled his hands away from the Anatameter and the Hall of Possibilities vanished along with the K-Listers inside.

"What happened?" Duval cried.

Stenstrom lunged at Duval, hoping to seize his throat with his tied-up hands. The K-Listers raised their weapons. "Lacerta!" he cried. "Lacerta help me!"

The Lacerta pulled Stenstrom off and punched him hard in the jaw, sending him to the ground. Her fist was like a shaped bar of iron. A bristling forest of Heat guns came down, pointed at him.

"No, no!" Duval cried. "We need him alive to maintain the connection to St. Mary's Axe. All of you, he must be alive to operate the Anatameter."

He pointed at the girl. "Crewmen! I want ten men abusing this girl, and make every moment of it hurt!"

A K-Lister tossed his Hot rifle aside and pushed the girl to the floor. He mounted her.

"All right, I'll do it!" Stenstrom said. Nobody seemed to be listening. All were intent on the spectacle and the girl's helpless screams. "Did you not hear me, Duval, I said I'd do it! Leave that poor girl out of this!"

"I'm sorry, Paymaster. Ten men is the price she shall pay for your arrogance. Crewman, continue and take your pleasure." The K-Lister began his work.

Stenstrom couldn't bear it. He had to help her. He strained, feeling the wire stretch a bit. The Lacerta put her arms around him and squeezed. She whispered into his ear. "I'd hate to Buzz you again, love. 'Cause, you know what, I'm keeping you for myself."

The girl begged for mercy.

Full of rage, Stenstrom let fly with TK. He picked the offending K-Lister off the girl and sent him, trousers dropped, flying across the face of the Shrine into a far wall where he hit with life-ending force.

Stenstrom strained and broke the Lacerta's grip and snapped the ANGRY MISER wire confining his wrists. He stuffed the broken wire into the Lacerta's face and pushed her away. "Oh shit!" she cried as the charms went off in a red explosion, knocking her back and shredding several K-Listers. He lunged for Duval when the Hall of Possibilities appeared by itself at the far end of the Shrine.

All eyes turned to it. Like a vent spewing poison gas, raw, palpable fear saturated the Shrine. In a gibbering mass, the K-Listers stumbled out in a panic. One was nude, having torn himself out of his own clothing, another had chewed her own fingers off. They all seemed insane with fright.

Stenstrom felt a blaring wall of fear slam into him, filling the Shrine in a dense, uncomfortable humidity. Everybody reacted, even the scorched Lacerta who held her stomach and bent over. Stenstrom was prepared, the Shadow tech Goddess' Bolabung around his neck deflected much of it, though the effect was like trying to breathe through a straw.

"Do you feel it?" Duval cried in triumph. "Do you feel the love of the Shadow tech Goddess?"

The K-Listers scattered in heavy-limbed confusion into the Shrine, some crawling, others stumbling like jellyfish with bones. A few lay still. They seemed to be dead, dead from fright.

The Shrine hushed to a vacant silence, marred only by the occasional ripcord of ragged breath from an insensate mob.

Stenstrom took the girl and pulled her away from the cowering K-Listers. He covered her up and held her to him, trying to protect her from the onslaught of fear.

In the corridor, a figure appeared from the right and turned to them, standing like a pagan idol in the center of a tempest-fueled fear cloud. It stood motionless in the shadows, and then it glided a step forward. It was a tall female wearing a black, somewhat dirty suit that clung tightly to its lithe form. The suit stopped at her forearms, revealing chalky white skin. Her hands were splayed out and claw-like, sporting green nails that were pitted and broken. On her head was a great conical helmet made from smooth, semi-shiny metal. The helmet bore no human features. It was completely smooth, like a bullet. At either side of the helmet, approximately where her ears might be, were a number of twisting spokes that went out about ten feet. The spokes moved as she walked with airy, gauzelike grace.

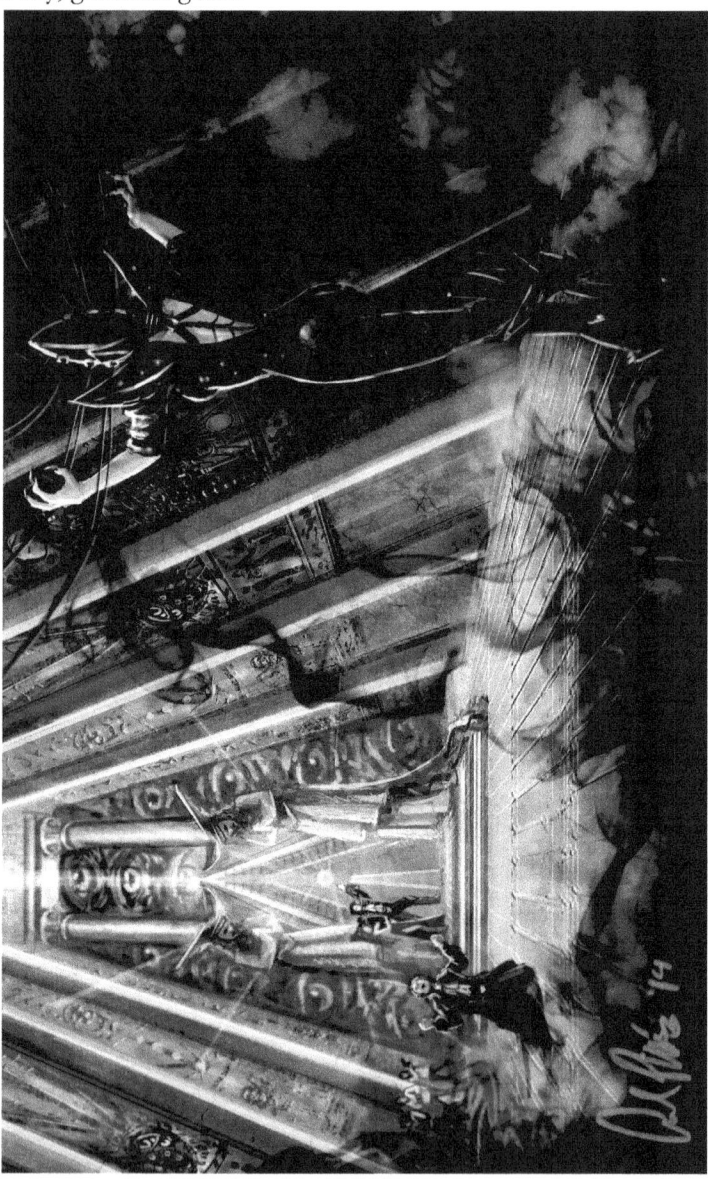

She stepped carefully into the Shrine, one foot in front of the other, heading for Duval. She appeared to be focused on him. She quickened her pace and raised her arms in a semi-threatening posture.

One of the K-Listers somehow managed to level his rifle and fire, hitting the woman in the chest with a flaming plasma burst, pushing her back a step or two.

"YOU FOOL!!" Duval cried, slobbering. He aimed Stenstrom's NTH and fired, killing the K-Lister. The woman balled her fists and the drifting cloud of fear ramped up to a crushing wall. People moaned and withered, weapons clattered to the floor. K-Listers gnashed their teeth in fear. Some died on the spot. Duval dropped his NTHs and fell down to his knees, beseeching her forgiveness.

Then she reached Duval. He managed to grovel-out a few words. "Muh, muh, my Goddess, my q-q-queen. I have come from f-f-f-fields far away to bask in your p—presence once again, to beg thee to perform thy work, to lay this unclean puh, puh, place waste and allow a new world built in its ashes. I-it is a guh-guh gift I h-have brought y-you."

The woman approached noiselessly and loomed over him, opening and closing her claw-like hands. Duval held up his hands. "I am here f-f-for you . . ."

She seemed to approve. With slow dramatic gestures, she motioned for him to take her clawed hand and follow her, which he did in a star struck haze, stumbling after her. They made their slow way back to the Hall of Possibilities, passing slobbering ranks of terrified K-Listers the entire way. They entered, turned to the right, and the Hall disappeared.

5—The Lacerta's Pit

When the Hall of Possibilities vanished, all within the Shrine regained their senses. The K-Listers muttered in an angry mob, raising fists and hoisting weapons. Stenstrom TK'ed his NTH pistols back to him.

"Let's get that guy!"

"Give us that bitch!" one of them called. "And when we're done with her we'll take our pleasure with him, too!"

Stenstrom raised his NTH's and cocked them. "Then who dies first?" he shouted.

He was picked up in a merciless TK and thrown to the ground. The Lacerta again. He struggled to break it. She drove her heel into his chest. He felt the dangling tails of her VUNKULA clacking together under her skirt. Several feet away, the crewman lay in a crumpled half-fetal position absently covering her breasts. He had to get her to safety and he had to turn the bloody knob and be away.

"I'm gonna' make you suffer for the explosion," she said.

Furious, Stenstrom lay under her heel and struggled, his thrashing knocking her shoe loose. She kicked it aside and rammed her hot, sweaty foot into his face.

"What? You trying to get me out of my shoes, out of my clothes? Don't worry, hon'. That's going to happen soon enough. Don't you fuss."

The K-Listers congregated in an angry mob. "Let's kill the Privateer and have our fun with the girl!" one clamored. "His job is gone and done. We get triple the pay once he's dead, Captain said so!"

The Lacerta scrunched up her foot and shoved her stockinged toes into his mouth. "No, no, boys, he's mine. He's gonna' be my personal punching bag and sex toy, see? Doesn't that sound cool? You guys can have the chick." She clapped her skinny hands together and gazed greedily at Stenstrom. *<So, what game are we going to play first?>* she sent.

A K-Lister snuck up behind her while she was preoccupied and clamped some sort of crab-legged device onto the back of her neck, right in the center. It penetrated all her layers of protection as the legs of the device bit into her flesh with a wretched crunch.

"What the fuck?" the Lacerta gurgled in utter shock.

"And, we get quintuple if you're dead too!" the K-Lister cried.

The device came to horrid life. Lights flashed. Minute turbines turned and exhausts howled. Flakes of crystallized blood pulsed out of tiny exhaust ports in a garish cloud, creating a miniature crimson snowstorm in her vicinity. Stenstrom had seen one of these devices before, in Xaphan space. It was a Midas Hemolizer, a cruel device that could drain a full grown man of blood in mere minutes. It was made of rare metals that could penetrate mental defenses, like a Black Hat's Sten field, or a Sister's TK. It was made to assassinate an unwary Black Hat, or even a Sister.

The Lacerta screamed and stumbled about as if blindfolded. The K-Listers sprang into action. "Kill her! Kill him, too and let's feast on the little bitch!" they cried.

The K-Listers came up, ripe with the euphoria that came with the passing of fear, and leveled their Hot rifles. They pulled the trigger and flaming red balls of plasma spewed out. The Lacerta, losing blood fast, in agony, rebounded and deflected the shots, one went into a group of K-Listers standing nearby, killing several. She jumped in front of one of the K-Lister and pulled the rifle from his hands before he could pull the trigger again. She grit her teeth and Buzzed the man with full force. He clutched at his head and screamed, but didn't fall. A second K-Lister came in knife drawn and attacked. She caught the knife and broke the man's arm in a gory display. Blood flowed from her neck in a dusty, chugging cloud. She stood there stupidly, wondering why the first man she'd Buzzed wasn't dead. How could he not be dead? He also drew a knife from his belt and stabbed her in the shoulder as she killed the second man with his own knife.

They went down in a heap, the Lacerta still only wearing one shoe. She Buzzed him again, and this time something short-circuited on the man's temple in a flash and a puff of smoke. The man's features flickered and a mask-like appliance covered with circuitry appeared over his face sporting small holes for his eyes and nose.

"Ah! You're wearing a fucking facekatron, are you, you fucking fuck!" She gripped his temples and pulled. "Think that's going to save you from me, do you? Huh? Come on, give it to me! Give it to me, you piece of crap!"

The facekatron he was wearing came away bit by bit in a bloody peel, pulling off his skin and a layer of muscle with it. She tossed it aside, hoisted him up and Buzzed him again, and this time, with nothing to protect him from her power, a geyser of blood and greenish brain matter erupted from both of his ears. Enraged, she threw his dead body somewhere into the group of massing K-Listers.

Others came in, and she fought them all at once, swinging a Hot rifle around like a club, caving in skulls, punching and snapping with her three VUNKULA tails forming a perimeter of dead bodies around her.

"Keep at her, boys, the Hemolizer will have her down in no time," someone said.

"Like hell!" she spat. The Lacerta spun about, trying to get at the Hemolizer. She reached up with her VUNKULA tails and grabbed onto it, pulling, smashing, desperate to get it off. The K-Listers pressed in, hoping to overwhelm her. The Hemolizer malfunctioned, sending tiny drills out the front of her neck and mouth in a twisting whine.

Elsewhere, Stenstrom was desperate to get to the girl and take her to safety. She was deep in the masses of K-Listers. He fired continuously with his NTHs, dropping K-Listers left and right. They returned fire, but Stenstrom moved fast, side to side, TK'ing over it or, in some cases, he just let the shots hit him, doing no damage. He lobbed red Holystones into their midst, setting fire to four and five at a time.

One of his NTHs malfunctioned, the cinnabar striker cracked. He sashed it and waved up a MARZABLE dagger to spilt skulls and slit throats. There was bountiful chaos in the Shrine: oaths shouted, dying screams, profanity uttered, and enraged mumbling mixed in with the crackling of multiple fires, the breaking of bones, and the mechanical drilling sound of the Hemolizer slow killing the Lacerta. Soon, the pile of death he left rivaled hers.

The K-Listers were on their J-Rasters, calling in backup. A Ripcar slewed into the Shrine, the occupants whooping and hollering. Stenstrom had learned to fight like a Sister. He grabbed onto the Ripcar with TK and took control of it. The people aboard screamed in helpless terror as the ship picked up speed and height at his command. Stenstrom rode the craft into a far wall hard, and that was the end of that.

Nearby, the Lacerta, still trying to deal with the Hemolizer attached to her neck, fought back against the onslaught. She darted with her tails. Sabers emerged from the wrappings at her wrists. Heads and body parts flew. She set fire to the K-Listers with her TK and worked her VUNKULA tails with lightning-quick strokes. Though she was a debauched, foul-mouthed pig, Stenstrom had to take a moment to admire her, fighting this lot all by herself, compromised as she was. And she was still wearing only one shoe.

Stenstrom hacked and burned his way to the girl. Several remaining K-Listers came running at him. Stenstrom methodically dispatched them, beating them to death with his fists.

"Hey, hey, hey! Get over here and help me!" the Lacerta yelled from behind, surrounded by attacking crew. "Help me with these fuckers! You and me, come on!!" Flashes of gunfire danced across the Shrine.

He scooped up the crewman and TK'ed fast into the air, the tails of his HRN spreading out around him like wings. Several plasma shots came up from below. He answered with his remaining NTH. Down below, the floor looked like a confused dance, the few remaining K-Listers running about and the lone Lacerta fighting them with a gusher of blood spraying out amid pockets of fire and smoke.

He TK'ed out of the Shrine and down the long corridor. There was the Sub-Orbital and the ledge to the outside, clear stars twinkled in the sky. It all seemed rather peaceful. The Sub-Orbital was packed with hastily assembled goods from the ship. He made space, placed the girl in the Sub-Orbital and checked her over. She was scratched and partially catatonic, but she was alive. Drawing his second NTH, he replaced the cracked striker. "Stay here, miss, I'll be back shortly. You should be safe here." She blinked and turned her cloudy gaze to him. She weakly held her hand out for him to take. "I'll be right back, then we're leaving. Stay here."

He launched himself back down the long corridor into the Shrine. It was eerily quiet, like the uneasy hush of a drunken lull after a particularly wild party. There were bodies everywhere and in every sort of position, most supine on the floor. Some were on fire, some were crushed, some were collapsed down in a tiny, boxlike shape. The Ripcar he'd ridden into the wall was still stuck there like a squashed fly. In the center of all this carnage was the Lacerta, face down, her lacy clothes shredded and burned, her VUNKULA destroyed, bloody sabers sprouting from her wrists and crystallized blood still coming out of the battered Hemolizer in fitful crimson puffs. She was still wearing just one shoe.

She seemed to be still alive, though just barely. She groped at the Hemolizer on her neck, her sabers scraping on the floor. She couldn't reach it. She offered him a hint of a toothy smile. "Sorry, darlin'... think I'm too tired to fuck tonight, `kay? We'll do it tomorrow. I'll... put on something nice for ya'."

Stenstrom sashed his NTHs. She was on the verge of death. Despite himself, he couldn't leave her like that. She had fought a hoard of K-Listers while being drained of blood. She'd fought well and she deserved a bit of consideration.

She looked up weakly, her makeup smeared into a harlequin nightmare, her hair a mess. Her lenses were smashed. The stumps of her VUNKULA tails wavered. He knelt down and examined the Hemolizer on her neck. It was dug in, deformed, smashed, but still operating at a greatly diminished level, doggedly chugging out fitful puffs of powdered blood. It whined in unsteady fashion like a dental drill.

"You... son of a... bitch..." she gurgled.

He saw the rugged and simple construction of the device. It would be difficult to destroy it by crushing or smashing, as the Lacerta had tried. It wasn't really designed to come off. The best way to get it off was by manipulating its locking mechanism. He produced his lock picks and set to work.

The Lacerta chattered in a slow mumble. "I'm... going... to... make you... my... bitch," she said as he worked. "It's... going to be good. You know... it's going to be... real good."

"Keep quiet and stop squirming," he said.

With bloody hands, she tried to grab him. He pushed her hands away. Delirious, she babbled. "I got this fortress out there. I... took it from a Xaphan Warlord. He was a real... pussy, you know, he and his crew. So, I took... his fortress and hung him out on a stake. It's got this nice pit up in the courtyard, chains and mildew and everything. Now that's a dungeon . . . you can be proud of. I'm . . . I'm gonna' put you in that pit. When I want to fuck, I'm going to get you out and we'll fuck. When I . . . want to fight you, I'll get you out and we'll fight, like fuckin' . . . fuckin' gladiators or somethin'. Might even invite my friends over to let them see . . . what I got in my pit." She spoke in a dreamy fashion, as if this horrid slave pit she was describing was some lovely vacation spot she looked forward to visiting.

"I said be quiet. You fought well and deserve to be treated like a warrior, so save your strength, sit back, and keep your foul mouth shut. Perhaps you'll walk away from this and return to you stolen holdings someday. However, don't expect a visit from me." He got through the locking mechanism and pulled the Hemolizer away from her skin, exposing an indentation and several gory holes. It had inserted a number of wires and drills into her neck. He worked them out one by one.

The Lacerta refused to stay quiet. "My bitch . . . you're . . . you're going to be my bitch. If you want to save me . . . go ahead, that's on you. You're going to be in my pit. You're . . . going to dance for me and my fuckin' friends. Maybe we'll fall in love or some crazy . . . shit . . . like that? What do you think?"

The Hemolizer was off. He tossed it aside. She continued. "I'm going to . . . kill your woman and I'm going to put you . . . in my pit," she said. She blinked, her eyes glassy. Her death seemed near. "Hey, mister . . ." she whispered. "Mister . . .?" He couldn't hear what she was saying. Hearing a person's last words was an important duty in Belmont, even for an enemy. He leaned in to listen.

WHOOSH!!!

One of her VUNKULA tails, undamaged, shot up, its beak covered in slimy salve—possibly some hideous tranquilizer or poison. It went for his neck like a scorpion's tail applying a killing blow to an intended victim. He caught it cold; its beak inches from his neck, and, with the Sisters' strength, he pulled the metal tail apart and tossed it aside.

"Ah, shit . . ." she groaned.

Enraged, he pulled her up by the scruff of her neck and raised his fist to hit her. She was flaccid in his hands, neck lolled, mouth open, arms limp at her side, her face slathered in sweat. The Lacerta was defenseless.

There was no fight left in her.

"Whatcha' do that for?" she whispered. "I just wanted to knock you out and take you to the pit. Hit me, go ahead . . . hit me; make it hurt . . . I want you to hurt me."

He let her go and she slumped back down, nudging against other dead bodies around her. He'd wasted enough time. He'd done his duty for a fellow warrior.

There was the Anatameter on its pedestal. He'd come all this way. Now, it was time to turn the knob. He placed his hands on it and the Hall of Possibilities returned. He tried to turn the knob but it was gone. Where was it?

Blast!! Where in Creation was the bloody knob?

What had Alesta said?

"The Shadow tech Goddess stole it . . ."

The Shadow tech Goddess was in her lair now with Duval and the Anatameter's knob, and he would have to walk the Hall of Possibilities and fetch it.

NTHs drawn he walked across the Shrine and went in, the cold of the stone closing in around him, like he was in a dank cave. He turned to his right and went down the corridor. Duval and the Shadow tech Goddess and his knob were down there somewhere in the darkness waiting for him.

6—THE SHADOW TECH GODDESS

Stenstrom plunged into musty darkness. The floor was littered with debris and the air heavy from wet stone. He couldn't see; just like in the old culvert back home burgeoning with gothic darkness and the floating round eye of his mother's flaming cigarette. An ebon tunnel that could be home to any number of imagined horrors, stretched before him. Though in this case, a real horror awaited him at the end.

The Shadow tech Goddess.

His Megaeye was gone, probably lost in the bloody fight with the K-Listers. No, wait—Gwen had it. She was always grabbing, always taking it. A very annoying habit.

Where was Gwen?? He had to comfort himself with the fact that she could take care of herself and was probably safe somewhere at the bottom of the monolith.

He held his NTHs at the ready, but they shook a little in his hands. He hated the dark; and he was tired of inhabiting dark places and wondering what lurked out of sight. He craved the sunshine and occasional stormy skies of his home in Tyrol by the sea. Sashing one of his weapons, he shook up a yellow Holystone, but it didn't do much to cut through the dark. He cocked hammer and fired a glowing green NTH shot down the corridor. The globe lit up the walls of the corridor with an emerald green ring that drifted for a long distance before sputtering out. He didn't see Duval and he didn't see the Shadow tech Goddess in the green light. He appeared to be alone.

He continued on, feeling his way along the left hand wall, feeling the accumulated grit and sediment pass under his fingers. Every so often he encountered a drafty empty spot. In the dim light of the Holystone he saw small rooms with no doors situated along the corridor, about one every fifty feet. They were about the size of a broom closet. These were the Nodes of Reality, he recalled A-Ram saying. Both good and bad things were supposed to come out of them. This one seemed empty.

The next one down sputtered faint orange light. NTHs ready, he entered. Something in the room took up most of the space. There was a table, slightly slanted, made of sterile metal. A female lay atop the table, and she seemed to be in distress. Her arms and feet were shackled, her neck slightly arched in anguish.

Leaning in, he gasped.

It was Queen Wendilnight! He remembered her beautiful face from her visit in his office where she presented him with the Anatameter.

Her words came back to him. *"Exactly how I remembered it when you came to rescue me . . ."*

And what had Hannah-Ben Shurlamp said?

"A demon is said to live there, and there is also the persistent story of a trapped woman, a goddess, requiring rescue . . ."

He tried to free her, but she was rigid, like a statue. Time seemed to stand still around her. She might have been here chained to this table for untold ages. And, another thing, she was missing the left side of her body. It had been replaced with robotic parts of extreme complexity.

He marveled at it in horror. Shaking up a MAZARBLE, he slid it into her hand so that he could re-locate her later. "My queen, I will return for you."

Stenstrom turned to leave to resolve the matter with Duval and the Shadow tech Goddess, then rescue Queen Wendilnight. He bumped into a tall statue that hadn't been there before, blocking his exit from the node. It was a statue of Queen Wendilnight, and . . .

Wait.

The statue looked like Queen Wendilnight, but it carried a completely different feel. Wendilnight was angelic; this statue seemed quite the opposite. He sensed evil and chaos leaking out of it. Her expression was diabolic, her eyes wide; and here her flesh-side was located on the left, the robotic parts on the right. The robotic parts were sadistic, studded with wire and knives. He tried the push the statue aside, or topple it over, but it wouldn't budge. It was locked in time.

There is a woman requiring rescue and there is a demon haunting the Shrine. Both two opposite halves of Queen Wendilnight.

He squeezed past it and re-entered the corridor.

Far down the corridor, Stenstrom made out a distant smudge of indistinct light hovering before him. It was so dim he couldn't really see it when looking straight on. When he looked to the side, the smudge popped out of the dark like a blue halo, reminding him of the old Witchlights glowing on moonless nights on Merian Hill he and his sisters could see from their bedrooms. They never had discovered the source of those lights.

Step by step he continued on. Gwen needed him; the terrified crewman whose name he didn't know needed him, and, apparently, Queen Wendilnight needed him, too.

He passed another Node; this time he thought he saw someone sitting within. Shining his Holystone he peeked in, NTH ready. There was a pile of clothes jumbled together in a rough sitting shape. He found a Fleet coat over a white shirt and a pair of black pants, a gun belt with MiMs pistol—loaded, a large hat, and a blue wig. Were these Lt. Remm Deckard's clothes and her officer's gun? If so, where was she? It was as if she had simply vanished, leaving her clothes behind in the rough arrangement of how she'd worn them. Deckard herself was nowhere to be found.

He exited the Node and continued, still seeing the blue Witchlight in the distance. A face appeared on the wall in the dim glow of his Holystone, causing Stenstrom to jump back a bit. It was a somber woman's face drawn in chalk within an elaborate cartouche looming high into the upper reaches toward the ceiling. Kat the Black Hat had told him once that the face of the Shadow tech Goddess was hidden somewhere in the Hall of Possibilities. Was this the face of the Shadow tech Goddess? It was a woman with blue eyes and a slightly squared-off chin. She had strong cheekbones, wide, thin lips, a small nose, and a massive Shadowmark that nearly covered the entire right side of her face. She had whitish blonde hair that seemed to be cut rather short, in a fashion his mother once favored. Her face in chalk was stern and expressionless.

Stenstrom tried to compare the image in chalk with the woman of his dreams who claimed to be the Shadow tech Goddess. Their complexion seemed to be a similar shade. The one from his dreams had worn a helmet covering all except her nose, mouth and chin, so that was all he had to go on. He gazed at the portrait. They were similar, though the one depicted here seemed to be slightly more squared-off in the face. It was difficult to tell. She had a rather unassuming, unremarkable face. She lacked the wry smile and energetic feel of the one from his dream whom he imagined would be stunningly beautiful under her helmet. She had a rather large Shadowmark; but many ladies, jealous of the growing popularity of Black Hats in the League, were painting Shadowmarks on their faces these days, some being quite large, like hers.

This woman could literally be anybody. Pass her in the street and one wouldn't think twice.

Yet here she was, the face of the destroyer mirthlessly staring down at him; and possibly waiting for him at the end of this corridor. With her chalk eyes seeming to follow him, he backed away and continued.

The dim blue smudge got ever closer. Now, he could see it clearly, whitish blue, like a patch of drifting moonlight. He dropped his Holystone; it wasn't helping.

At last the corridor ended in an archway. Beyond the archway lay an ornate gothic room bathed in soft blue light that seemed to come from everywhere. There was a clean checkered black and white tile floor and lacy iron furnishings and accents laid out in a tasteful manner. Great windows looked out on swirling pitch black. It looked like the parlor of some grand manor, with the exception that everything was made of iron. Iron picture frames holding nothing hung on the walls and iron vases sported arrangements of iron flowers riveted together. A grand iron staircase was situated in the center of the room, twisting upward beyond his field of view.

He heard the subtle notes of crying within.

Stenstrom, pistols drawn, entered.

Sitting at the top of the stairs in a vast chair was the Shadow tech Goddess. She wore tattered black clothing through which glimpses of chalky white skin peeked through. Her face was obscured by her featureless conical helmet. Resting in her arms like a sleeping baby was Duval, head facing upwards, mouth open. The Shadow tech Goddess held him, rocking back and forth slightly. She wept.

Other than the fitful sounds of her crying, the room was unearthly quiet.

He moved to the steps and looked up. She seemed to take no notice. Duval was limp in her arms.

"You stole my Anatameter. You forced me here, far across the deep sea, far from the fields I know. Here I am. What do you want with me?"

Nothing. No response.

"You killed my countess."

She stopped weeping and her helmet moved slightly. She was staring at him. "Can you come to me?" she asked in a muffled voice.

"I require the knob to the Anatameter."

"Then come."

Stenstrom was certainly not at ease in the room with the Shadow tech Goddess, but he also felt none of the crushing fear he'd felt in the Shrine. He eased up the stairs, NTHs raised, the two figures waiting at the top. Soon he stood over them.

The helmet tilted up as she glanced at him. "He's dead," came her muffled voice.

"Give me the knob."

"I can't let him go."

Stenstrom sashed one of his NTH's and removed the helmet from her head, then let it fall to the iron platform with a noisy clatter. He was shocked by what he saw. He nearly fell off the platform.

"M-Morgan?"

Sitting there was Morgan-Jeterix, the woman he'd watched fall from the *George Parr*, the woman he'd grieved over and built a cairn of stone. A woman he loved.

She was dirty and her braided hair was a mess. She bore a somewhat crazed expression, but she seemed otherwise uninjured. Her complexion, unlike her usual tanned self, was deathly pale, like a Monama, her eyes round and lamp-like. She wore her Hospitaler bodysuit, though it was filthy and torn, her flesh showing through in various spots. Her hair was ragged, the braids coming out to a hopeless tangle. Her blonde hair was a tepid green shade and her hands were tipped with ragged greenish claws.

"Morgan! Morgan, what happened? I saw you fall from the ship. I held your dead body. I wept over it. I buried it."

Her lamp-like eyes gazed up at him, full of sorrow. "I know you did. I listened to you."

"You were dead, Morgan."

She shook her head and spoke in a heavy voice. "I can't die, Bel."

I can't die, Bel . . .

The room closed in on him. The words the Shadow tech Goddess had spoken in the Garden of Horrors returned: *"Beware the Tempus Findal, a creature that is virtually immortal and will lead you to ruin."*

The Tempus Findal. Morgan????

"Are you a *Tempus Findal*, Morgan?"

She closed her eyes. "I really don't know what I am, Bel. I have heard of that name. I've read it in arcane books pulled from the shelves of forgotten libraries. I looked at old drawings and pictures, seeing a monster there on the page, a parasite. Can that be me?? As a Hospitaler, if I were to diagnose myself, what else could I be? I have all the symptoms, the evidence seems clear."

Things fell into place. Things finally made sense. "Morgan, was that you I encountered in Clovis? Did you steal the Anatameter? Did you kill my Countess?"

Morgan seemed desperate for a moment. "I . . . yes, no. I . . ."

"Did you steal the Anatameter?"

"Yes, yes I did. I can go wherever I want, sometimes."

"And did you kill my countess?"

"No! No, I didn't kill anybody there. You do believe me, don't you?"

"The Tempus Findal tells lies, and you will believe every word . . ."

"Why did you come at me like that? Why the fear? Why do you look like this?"

"I don't know."

He took her by the scruff of the neck and dragged her out of the chair. Duval's body tumbled to the ground. Keeping his grip, he pulled her down the stairs.

As in the Garden of Horrors, things in the Shadow tech Goddess' sanctum came to life around him. The iron was replaced with wood, soft fabric, and fresh flowers. The picture frames filled in with vibrant color. Morgan groveled at his feet.

"Lies, Morgan!"

"I love you! You know I couldn't hurt you."

"You mean like at Sarfortnim College? Was that you coming at me off the slab like a corpse?"

"I don't know, Bel. Sometimes I'm not myself, sometimes something comes over me and I can't help it! I'm sorry!"

"And what about at the vent when you tried to stop Gwen's heart?"

"I . . . I . . . didn't mean for that to happen. I was just trying to scare her away."

He shook his hand and produced the stone knife. "And what about Duval? Did you tell him the same things? Did you proffer innocence and now here he is, dead. You killed him, right?"

Morgan wept and spoke in sobs. "I didn't kill him, I swear it! I wanted to give him what he wanted most: the Shadow tech Goddess. I wanted to bring him to her. That's what this is all about! That's why I stole the Anatameter, to come here so I could take him to her. I saw her here once, long ago."

He put the stone knife to her throat. "Then, you better start talking and it better be the truth!"

Morgan looked at the knife. Her eyes darted. She put her hand in her mouth and chewed her nails. Her nails were green and ruined. She tried to compose herself.

"This knife, the stone it's made of, do you know where it comes from? It's masonry from my manor home in the green Hala-lands. I've told you of the fire that happened there, how my father saved me. I never told you *when* that fire happened, Bel. It happened a long time ago. If you were to visit my home in Hala today, you'd find just a pile of blackened stones in a forgotten, overgrown field. Just like what you'd find at Caroline, only no one goes there to find love. No one has lived there in centuries; the locals think it's cursed."

"I was told you are an extra-planar creature of a particularly dangerous note and that I should kill you with this knife, right now."

Morgan was desperate. She wanted to embrace him, but he kept her away with the knife. "I didn't ask for this! I didn't ask to survive! Soon after the fire, I fell into depression, madness. I was committed to a convent to live out my days. I felt so utterly alone. None of my *Wvulgrom* selves survived the fire. They all perished, only I lived, and I felt the weight of that. It's a feeling I wouldn't wish on anybody, Bel.

"In the convent, I became aware for the first time of a presence that I was drawn to. I didn't understand, I couldn't explain it. It was like a bouquet of flowers that I longed to hold and breathe in deep. It was all I wanted; my every moment was set to it. Imprisoned in the convent, I became a raging beast and I saw myself as a monster for the first time reflected in the window. I made that convent tremble with fear and, with my own hands, I broke out and began chasing that bouquet of flowers I so longed to touch. I went on a long journey, not simply across Kana, but across the planes as well. I could go to whatever universe I wished; though I didn't understand it fully for a long time."

"And did you find your bouquet of flowers?"

"I did. In Hannover, by the icy bay; not the Hannover we know, a different one, universes away. It was a young man, a student. I longed for him and I worked my way into his graces." Morgan's eyes grew distant. "I think . . . I might have murdered somebody, perhaps his lover or other hangers-on in my way. I don't remember."

"And then?"

"We married. I was so happy, to hold him close; it filled me with power. I could smile and laugh again." Morgan blinked in sadness. "But, it didn't last. Like a bouquet of flowers, he wilted and became nothing; it was as if the universe had turned its back on him. And I too . . . I felt the calling of a new bouquet elsewhere that I longed to hold; and I left him behind. I walked the planes, searching once again. I've made that search many times. I've had many husbands; I've had many wives, all just fleeting moments in the sun. All the lies I've told, all the people I've pretended to be, the names I've called myself . . ."

"And then Captain Duval. You got to him and became his first officer?"

Morgan nodded.

"And then you killed him."

She fell apart and erupted in emotion. "No! No! I didn't! Yes, I pursued him, decades ago and yes . . . I killed his wife, and then I latched myself to him. I loved him. I let him do to me whatever he wanted, all while I was seeking out my next target. I'm old enough that I know how to stalk, how to put myself in the correct position to encounter my next love; so I placed myself aboard Gwen's scouting ship and I waited. I forgot what I am during that time, I thought I was just a mortal woman again. That happens a lot, until I wake up."

She looked up at Duval's body at the top of the stairs. "And then I saw you, Bel, in the Kestral's pit, and I fell in love all over again. For the first time in ages, I actually felt like I was in love, and not simply satisfying a need. I wanted it to be different this time, I swear it. I wanted you to love me, too. I realized what I had done to Duval. I watched him go mad, watched him become a merciless tyrant."

Morgan's voice cracked with sadness and she wept uncontrollably. "I wanted to give him back some of what I stole! He was a great man once . . . and . . . and a kind man. He could walk the planes just like I could, his St. Mary's Axe. He had a wife and children . . . and I took that from him! He went mad because of me. Me! They all did! And, for once I didn't want to turn my back and move on. I wanted to show you that I still have feelings, and I wanted to make things as right as I could. I listened to him plot and rave about the Shadow tech Goddess. I wanted to give him what he wanted. I wanted to bring him here and lead him to her! I wanted him to be happy again! And, do you know what we found here in this room? Nothing . . . no Shadow tech Goddess, just this empty helmet sitting atop the stairs. I revealed myself to him and Duval was devastated that she wasn't here. He couldn't bear it and what was left of his mind gave way. I . . . I gave him peace. I didn't want him to suffer!"

She turned to Stenstrom at the end of the knife, her eyes puffy and desperate. "You do believe me, don't you, Bel?"

"I'm told you tell lies."

"Yes, yes, I tell lies, and sometimes I tell the truth as well. I don't want to be a monster, Bel. I don't want to hurt anybody." Her face cringed in anguish. "I'm just a woman who survived a fire, and look what happened to me! I don't want to be a deceiver. Morgan-Jeterix of the House of Thompson will not be the deceiver of the man she loves."

"Is Morgan-Jeterix actually your name?"

"Yes, it is. The name I was born with long ago. I wanted you to know my name."

She held up her clawed hands. "Look at me, the only way I can be young and beautiful again is to take from you, or Duval. I'm not safe. I tell lies. I go mad, and then I'm ok for a while. Perhaps it's best if you just kill me. Take the knife made from the stones of my old manor and do it, I've lived too long and caused too much sorrow." She smiled. "I'm glad yours is the hand, Bel."

He stood there with the knife for what seemed like a long time. Eventually, he lowered the blade and sat next to her. His hand found its way into hers, her head eventually came to rest on his shoulder.

The Shadow tech Goddess had told him he would believe the *Tempus Findal's* lies. Whether or not he believed everything she said was irrelevant.

He couldn't harm Morgan. He took the stone knife and shattered it.

"So, what are we going to do, Morgan? I can't kill you."

"I don't know, Bel. What can we do? I can't kill you either."

He noticed the Shadow tech Goddess' helmet lying forgotten on the floor. The previously empty pictures on the wall now moved with livid color. He watched the scenes unfold for a minute and was struck with clarity and inspiration. He picked up the Shadow tech Goddess' helmet. "This helmet, Morgan. It's a cause for celebration. Look . . ."

In one of the portraits on the Shadow tech Goddess' wall, a charming scene unfolded. A tall blonde-headed woman in a gown with a large Shadowmark on her face walked in a leafy grove carrying a basket. Children walked with her, and a handsome man as well. They sat down in a lovely spot and enjoyed a simple lunch together.

"See, there she is. The Shadow tech Goddess. Look at her. Family and children, an afternoon in the sun, those simple things are all the weapons that were ever necessary to prevent the coming of the Shadow tech Goddess. She is not here in this forlorn room because she is out there, living her life. Even she, a destroyer of universes and the stuff of nightmares, isn't locked into a fate, isn't consigned to a particular damnation. In this universe and perhaps many more, even the Shadow tech Goddess has a place she calls her own, contenting herself with being a simple wife and mother."

Morgan took the helmet and gripped it hard, her knuckles standing out. "I see. I see! And if she can have that, then why can't I? Why can't I, Bel?"

He recalled more words the woman in his dream had spoken to him: *The Anatameter will turn you into a new man.*

"Come, let us create a place just for you, Morgan, and there, together, we'll figure out a way to help you make that place all your own." Morgan stood and brushed herself off, bouncing with life and hope. She went up to the top of the stairs and placed Duval in the chair. She said a few words of goodbye to him and returned to Stenstrom's side, then took his hand.

No Shadow tech Goddess. She's not there. She doesn't exist on this plane, at least not in that particular form, unaware of the fate that could have befallen her. The love he felt for Morgan-Jeterix had never been greater. He'd witnessed what he thought was Gwen's death in Caroline, and his love for her was confirmed, and he saw Morgan's apparent death, and the same was true.

The Tempus Findal will tell you lies, and you will believe them. It will make you feel sorry for it.

What did it matter? If this adventure had taught him anything, it was that he had the capacity to love many times over, even the *Tempus Findal and the lies she might be telling*. Perhaps that was best gift the Universe had given him.

She approached and put her arms around him. She parted her lips and kissed him. He felt the passion, the burning of it and the transfer of energy from his soul to hers. He controlled it, giving Morgan just what she needed, and, when they parted, she looked like herself again: tanned, tattooed, with no trace of green tangles and green claws.

Morgan took a last look at Captain Duval and they went back out into the corridor, hand-in-hand, past the Shadow tech Goddess' portrait.

They passed the node where Queen Wendilnight was imprisoned. "Don't worry about her," Morgan said. "A different version of you saves her."

Stenstrom peered into the node. It appeared to be empty.

Morgan pulled him along. Her eyes grew wide with excitement as the Shrine approached.

7—Escorting the Gentlemen

When they walked back out into the Shrine, Stenstrom was surprised to find A-Ram and Alesta waiting in the shimmering glow. The dead K-Listers were gone. The Lacerta was gone. "It's so good to see you both!" he said, overjoyed. "Where have you been?"

A-Ram shook his hand. "Off helping you, Bel. This Shrine is a confluence of realms. Most planar sockets, like the one in Clovis, can only access the next plane adjacent to it, but this one can access any plane, anywhere. For ages, this Shrine has been deactivated. We're told the Sisters did it way back when, and it took a lot of work to get it functioning; and that is what several of your *Wvulgroms* were off doing. Their contributions have all led up to this, a functional Shrine of Boraster, clear of all the demons that once haunted it. And now, all we need to do is turn the Anatameter and finish."

"Hello, A-Ram!" Morgan said, popping out. "Have you two missed me?"

"Morgan . . . again . . ." A-Ram said. "You do tend to get around, don't you? Bel, Morgan is . . ."

"Yes, yes, he knows," Morgan said, anticipating their reaction. "I told him everything. We are onto a marvelous discovery."

A-Ram flushed slightly. "Morgan, you know we love you, but we've seen you act in a strange manner lately."

"And I'm sorry for that," she said.

"It's all right, A-Ram," Stenstrom said. "We will find a place for Morgan and right what ails her."

"It could be dangerous, I'm just saying."

"Then so be it. I love Morgan as much as I love Gwen, and I'll not abandon her. There is a way to fix anything."

A-Ram thought about it and smiled. "All right, this is the place to do it. I shouldn't expect anything less of you, and we will try to help as best we can. For now, we're here to perform a very important duty with you, and once that's done we can assist with Morgan and Gwen."

"Speaking of Gwen, have you seen her, A-Ram? We were separated."

"Look there," A-Ram said, pointing.

At the mouth of the Shrine, two figures entered. It was Gwendolyn assisting the crewman from the *George Parr*, her arm around her. Gwendolyn saw Stenstrom and her face lit up. "Bel!" She handed the crewman off to Alesta and ran across the Shrine, plowing into him before embracing him tightly. Morgan stood back and watched. A-Ram kept a close eye on her.

"Gods and Creation, Bel, I was worried sick! I was down there all by myself. I killed a few more K-Listers, and then A-Ram and Alesta came for me."

"Hello, Gwendolyn," Morgan said.

Gwendolyn blinked in surprise. "M-Morgan? I thought you were dead."

"Sorry about that. I heard you had a little fright recently, Gwen. Are you alright?"

"I'm fine. I'm glad you're not dead."

Stenstrom didn't think to wise to allow Morgan and Gwen to interface much; it might not be safe. He got in between them. "How's the girl?"

Alesta fussed with the crewman. "We found her wandering by the ledge when we arrived. She's shaken and will need time to recover, but I think she'll be fine," she said. "Her name is Crewman Jessa. She's from the House of Walpole. She's a Barrow, like me."

"What happened to all the bodies?" Stenstrom asked.

A-Ram was confused. "There was nobody here when we arrived."

"There were dozens of dead K-Listers from the *George Parr* here. And what about the Lacerta?"

"What?" A-Ram asked. "We didn't see her, and thank Creation for that. We've had our fill of her lately, that's for certain. We did see a ladies shoe over there near the Anatameter, but there was no lady in it."

With Gwendolyn taking care of Crewman Jessa and Morgan hovering in the wings like a buzzard, Alesta escorted Stenstrom to the Anatameter. "So, Bel, It's time. We are going to make a few adjustments on the Anatameter, and then alternate versions of you will appear here in the

Shrine. We will escort them back to where they need to go and this will be over. Seven turns, alright, since you've already turned it once already in Clovis."

"Who taught you all this?" Stenstrom asked.

"Queen Wendilnight and her husband Fiddler Crowe. They were in your debt."

"My debt?"

"You rescued her, Bel." A-Ram shuddered a bit. "We'll tell you about it later."

A-Ram got the familiar ochre disk out of his pocket, the one with the names etched on the face. One of the names was discolored. "You ready?"

"I suppose so."

"Oh!" Morgan cried, "Here's the knob. You'll need that." She came up and placed it back atop the Anatameter. "I took it. Sorry. Here it is."

Alesta eyed her with a bit of scrutiny. "Thank you, Morgan. Now, it's not that we don't trust you, but we don't trust you. You've proved yourself to be a bit of an unpredictable menace and general nuisance of late."

"Me??"

"Yes, you. Please, step back. A little farther, thank you."

"Awww, you're no fun," she said, stepping back several paces. "Are we still friends?"

"Of course we're still friends, but we don't trust you either."

Alesta and A-Ram laid their hands on the Anatameter, their fingers sinking into hidden recesses. Working in unison, they turned two secret dials. As they did so, the vast empty space of the Shrine filled up with a gallery of haunting images locked in time. Stenstrom saw himself repeated over and over, some wearing his familiar HRN, others wearing different garb. Some were hopeful and bright-eyed, others haggard and weighed down. "What is all this?" Stenstrom asked.

"These are *Wvulgroms* of you, and we must send the correct ones back to where they are supposed to go; the Anatameter has its hooks in them as well. The others who have no stake in this will fade back on their own after we're done," Alesta said. "Bel, touch the Anatameter's surface."

Stenstrom laid his hands on the Anatameter. In the Hall of

Possibilities, eight Nodes lit up in vibrant life, each a small window into a different universe.

"Before we continue, let's go ahead and get Gwen and Crewman Jessa back to where they belong," Alesta said. "Since you've already turned the knob once, that realm is already open."

"We're going?" Gwendolyn asked, getting her things together.

"Just you and Crewman Jessa, Gwen," Alesta said. "Your presence here could cloud things up. We'll be along in just a few minutes."

Gwen put her arm around Crewman Jessa, leading her to the Hall. "Morgan, are you coming?"

She shook her head and crossed her arms. "Nope, *Merthig*. I'm going someplace else."

Gwendolyn was puzzled. "What did you call me?"

"Nothing, Gwen." A-Ram and Alesta led Gwendolyn to an open Node. Inside was the bridge of the *Seeker,* the lights, the bustle. Taara was running around in her Marine coat yelling at people as usual.

"Please hurry, Bel," Gwen said as she walked in with the crewman at her side. Taara and the bridge crew reacted seeing Gwen arrive, then the Node went dark.

"I thought she'd never leave," Morgan said.

"Morgan, you promised to behave," Alesta said as they returned to the Anatameter.

"What did I do? Let's continue please, I'm anxious to see where I'm going."

"Go ahead, Bel," A-Ram said.

Stenstrom turned the knob once clockwise.

CLACK!

A-Ram released the Anatameter. Holding the disk out in front of him, he wandered out into the ranks of Stenstroms populating the Shrine.

"Do you need help?" Morgan asked.

"No, thank you," he replied. Soon he returned leading a Stenstrom wearing an HRN by the hand.

"Ooooh, I like this one!" Morgan chirped. A-Ram escorted the *Wvulgrom* to the Hall of Possibilities. They headed to a Node of Reality depicting what looked like a fine restaurant with a view of the sea. Seated at a cozy table was a beautiful, fawn-haired woman of the highest quality.

She looked back through the Node and smiled. Stenstrom didn't recognize her. The *Wvulgrom* of himself entered the Node and the woman stood to greet him; she was very tall on her long legs. The pleasant scene vanished and the Node went dark. "That was Melazarr of Caroline," A-Ram said as they returned. "She cleans up quite well."

"Why does a bloody *Merten* like Melazarr get that one?" Morgan asked. "I wanted that one."

"Because that's where he belongs," A-Ram said, checking his disk. Two spots were now darkened in. "Morgan, are we going to have an issue again?"

She stepped back and stewed. "No," she said, somewhat put off. "No, no, no, I said no, didn't I?"

Six more to go. Stenstrom turned the knob.

CLACK!

A-Ram waded off into the crowd once again. To Stenstrom's surprise he returned with a small woman, leading her by the hand. Stenstrom thought for a moment it was his sister, Lyra, for she had rich black hair similar to Lyra's, but the woman was far too small in stature to be her. His only conclusion: he was face to face with a female version of himself.

"Oh, Stenibelle, you little cutie!" Morgan cried, jumping up and giving her a hug. "I want this one!"

"Morgan, you promised to behave. Step back, please." A-Ram and Alesta greeted her warmly. "Stenibelle" was wearing a variation of his clothing, all at a smaller scale including a tiny HRN coat. He thought she was very pretty. They escorted her to the Hall of Possibilities and went to a Node lit up with a rich country home setting. Someone tall wearing a Fleet uniform sat by a pool. The female version of himself entered the Node and the figure, who appeared to be Gwendolyn, stood to greet her. The Node went dark. Five left. "You would be very proud of her, Bel," Alesta said, returning. "In another universe, you are a woman. She showed such bravery."

"I'm certain of it." Stenstrom turned again.

CLACK!

Following his disk, A-Ram selected another from the group, a somber version of himself. Morgan looked hopeful. "How about this one? Can I have this one?"

"No, Morgan." A-Ram and Alesta greeted him and took him to the Hall. In the lit-up Node was an odd beach scene splashed with tropical sun and a distant wall of black hanging over the water. Through the line of trees, he saw the rusting remains of a large starfaring ship leaning slightly off its keel. It looked Xaphan in design. A goddess-like woman with short black hair came wading out of the water carrying a handsome catch of meaty fish on a line. Stenstrom was shocked, not by the scene, but by who came out of the water. "T-Taara?" he gasped. She was everything Taara was not: tall, busty, curvy, utterly alluring. The only reason he recognized her was because she had Taara's bearing, her spirit. The *Wvulgrom* of himself entered the Node and the goddess-like Taara welcomed him with her typical enthusiasm. The Node went dark.

Stenstrom had to shake his head. Wow . . .

"Why does Taara get that one?" Morgan asked.

"Because that's how it has to be, Morgan. We're not making this up, you know."

She huffed.

A-Ram and Alesta returned and he continued.

Four more turns.

CLACK! CLACK!

The next two were more *Wvulgroms* for alternate versions of Gwen. A-Ram fished two more Stenstroms from the group and took them by the hand to the Hall of Possibilities. Each time, there was Gwendolyn sitting at a dulcimer playing a lilting tune. They bade A-Ram and Alesta goodbye and entered the Node which went dark.

Morgan was getting unruly. "Gwen again! Over and over it's the *Merthig!*" she said, an edge in her voice. "When do I get my turn?"

"Just be patient, Morgan," Alesta said.

"I don't want to be patient!"

Two more to go. A-Ram gave Stenstrom a look encouraging him to hurry. Stenstrom turned the knob again.

CLACK!

A-Ram checked his disk and selected a particularly rugged and somewhat sad-looking version from the group.

Morgan reacted violently. "No! No!" She pushed A-Ram away and put her arms around him. She was back to her monstrous appearance:

claws and tangled green hair.

"Morgan, stop," Alesta said.

"Mine!" she spat. Stenstrom felt a wave of fear radiate from her.

A-Ram and Alesta seemed nonplussed. "Morgan, you promised."

"I don't care what I promised. I want him!"

Alesta drew a jade jug from her robes and pulled the stopper. Instantly, Morgan was captivated. She released the *Wvulgrom* of Stenstrom and seized the jug from Alesta's hand. She sniffed it. She drank from it. Whatever was in the jug seemed to calm her. She resumed her normal appearance and sat down. "I'm sorry, I'm sorry. Thank you, Alesta. I'm better now." She glanced at Stenstrom, ashamed. "See, Bel . . . I'm a mess."

"What did you give her?" he asked Alesta.

"A tonic that helps soothe her soul. Morgan herself gave it to us, just for these select occasions when she loses control. Please, don't ask me what the tonic is made of; you don't want to know, trust me."

"How did you ward off her wave of fear?"

"Bolabungs. She gave them to us while she was in a more lucid state. They work quite well, in fact." Morgan gave her the jug back and Alesta returned it to her robe.

They set back to work and escorted the *Wvulgrom* to the Nodes. In it, Stenstrom saw his grand dining table back home in Tyrol; he would know it anywhere. A small woman in black stuck her head around a corner. She bounded up with great agility. She was wearing a mask. She pulled it off revealing a beautiful face and thick blonde hair. Her face lit up in excitement. The woman in black climbed up on him in joy. Then, hand in hand, they walked away and the Node faded to dark.

"Was that Kat?" Stenstrom asked, feeling a tinge of longing after seeing her die in Caroline.

"Yes. She is an amazing woman. We're glad to have made her acquaintance."

One more turn, one Node left. "Now we can see about Morgan," A-Ram said.

"About time!" she replied, perking up after her brush with insanity.

A-Ram and Alesta placed their hands back into the Anatameter and turned the hidden dials. The vast ranks of Stenstroms faded away, leaving the Shrine mostly empty again. Alesta spoke up. "Bel, we've learned that the final slot is sort of a wildcard—any name can appear there. We're just trying to find a good spot for Morgan so that her name will appear."

A-Ram showed him the disk. All seven names were now colored in. The final spot was still blank, occupied with a twisting sort of nebulousness.

Morgan came up. "Here, let me help. I've been working this thing a lot longer than you two have. Make room!"

"Morgan, don't!" Alesta said.

She turned the hidden dial and a series of barbed spikes erupted from the surface of the Anatameter like a quill of needles. Alesta and A-Ram pulled their hands back, while Morgan kept hers in place.

Alesta was injured, her hands bleeding. Morgan's hands were run-through, but she doggedly kept them where they were.

"Morgan, what are you doing?" Stenstrom demanded. "Alesta's hurt."

"I'm doing what I have to do, Bel. Alesta, let me see your hands."

A-Ram held Alesta close. "I knew we couldn't trust you, Morgan!"

"You have a place to go after this is over. I don't. Let me see her hands."

Reluctantly, A-Ram lifted Alesta's hands; they were both bloody. Keeping her impaled hands on the Anatameter, Morgan leaned over and looked them over. "Alesta has several deep punctures of the phalanges on both hands. Easily treatable, and I suggest a mild Type 2 analgesic taken by mouth for the pain. I'm sorry you were hurt, Alesta, and I dearly hope this hasn't ruined our friendship. You must understand, I want to be better too." Bleeding, Morgan turned the dial a bit further.

An eerie red light came from the Hall of Possibilities and stained the interior of the Shrine in a bloody pall.

A-Ram was alarmed. "Morgan, we were warned about this. The Red Nodes, the dying plains of reality claimed by demons. They're too dangerous."

"Check your disk, A-Ram," she said.

"It's too dangerous."

"Check your disk!" she screamed. A-Ram looked at the disk, no change.

Morgan turned the dial further, her hands shredding. More red light from the Hall. Stenstrom heard a distant, forlorn wail that chilled his blood.

"Morgan!" A-Ram yelled. "Stop! Look at the disk!"

Morgan glanced at it. In the eighth spot that had been occupied by a hazy cloud, was the name: MORGAN-JETERIX.

Morgan pulled her hands free of the barbs; they were both terribly mangled and run through.

Out of the ruddy dark, a figure appeared. It was a single *Wvulgrom* of Stenstrom, only this time he was stark naked and seemed to be a clear slate, as if newly born.

Morgan put her hands on him, leaving a trail of blood. "Oh, yes, he will do. He will do fine. I love him already."

"You can't take him to a dying land, Morgan. Look at him," Alesta said.

"I will protect him, and I will be his queen, and whatever horrors are there, we will face them together. This is what I was promised and this is what I accept. Please, Bel, turn the knob and keep your promise to me."

Alesta protested. "And what of him? He's like a new born babe. What does he want?"

Morgan went to Stenstrom and showed him her mangled hands. "I swear, Bel, I will clothe him, shoe him, and give him all the love I have to give. Look what I am willing to sacrifice for a place of my own, be it as it may. Turn the knob for me, Bel."

All eyes were on him.

He waved up a single MARZABLE dagger and put it in his *Wvulgrom's* hand. "I will trust you, Morgan, that you will do right by yourself and by this innocent version of me. Take a dying place and make it better. If you need my help, then come to me and I'll give it." He carefully turned the knob.

CLACK!

Morgan put her arms around the naked *Wvulgrom* of Stenstrom and walked with him to the bloody red Hall of Possibilities. One of the Nodes seethed in a cyclone of red. She looked back once more. "I love you, Bel. A-Ram, Alesta, I love you all. I swear, he will be the final love of my life."

She then walked with her Stenstrom through the node and it went out, turning to quiet black once again.

The turning was done. The Hall of Possibilities faded and was gone. The dials on the Anatameter turned by themselves and the nest of barbs pulled back. The light it emitted went out and they were plunged into darkness. Stenstrom shook up a yellow Holystone and the three of them huddled around its yellow glow. "How are your hands, Alesta?"

"They hurt, but I'll be all right." She was worried. "Did we do the right thing, Bel?"

""He is part of me. He can handle himself."

"I don't know if Morgan can be trusted."

"Only time will tell. If she can't, then I will go and assist him. I think she was sincere. I might be wrong, but I have faith she's in a place all her own now."

In the light of Stenstrom's Holystone, A-Ram gathered their things together. Stenstrom checked Alesta's hands, they were bloody but, as Morgan had said, nothing that couldn't be treated. "How are we getting back to the ship?"

"We're taking the Road. I'm ready immediately. I want to go home," Alesta said.

Several minutes later, they were back on the *Seeker* in the Merian's hold on Deck 10. A-Ram took Alesta to the dispensary to have her hands looked at. Stenstrom returned to the bridge. Gwendolyn and Taara were there.

In the cone, he saw the ship was in orbit over a turbid green world he assumed was Eng, and, he noticed the guns were locked. "Who are we shooting at?" he asked as he stepped out onto the bridge.

"Bel!" Gwendolyn cried.

"I'm back. How's Crewman Jessa?"

"She's down in the dispensary getting checked out. I think she's going to be fine. I'm so glad you're back!"

"Me, too."

"And Morgan?"

"We found her a place to call her own."

Taara was all smiles. Stenstrom embraced her. "It's good to see you, Taara; though I believe I ordered you to make sail back to Kana, didn't I?"

"Yeah, but I couldn't leave you here, Bel. We're just about back to 100 percent. We can out-fight that Sprint ship any day."

"It sank earlier."

"Gwen told me. We've got details out rounding up the survivors. Might as well give them a ride back to Kana where we can drop them off at the stockade."

"I see the guns are locked onto a target in the southern hemisphere. What are we shooting at?"

Gwendolyn blushed.

"Professor Shurlamp's hologram, Gwen wants to take it out. We were just about to obliterate it when you arrived."

"I was thinking of the planet's best interest, Bel. It could be creating hard radiation or emitting byproducts harmful to the environment," Gwen said.

"Seems a waste of a good canister missile."

"Can we please destroy the hologram?" Gwendolyn begged. "As a pre-wedding gift to me."

Stenstrom laughed. "Go head. I suppose I'll not hear the end of it if we don't."

Gwen beamed. "Fire!" she cried.

A single canister missile clanked out of the bays and made its lazy way down through the clouds, its tail fire creating a jumpy pinprick of light. It bloomed in momentary light on the edge of dusk and glowed like a dying ember.

"Direct hit. So much for H-B S's hologram," Taara said.

Stenstrom turned. "Fine then, with Professor Shurlamp's apparatus in flames and our interest in the Shrine done, let us make sail back to the League. Perhaps we'll return someday. The way is now open."

As the *Seeker* hurtled way from lonely Eng, Stenstrom and Gwendolyn went down to the dispensary to check on Alesta. They had two weddings to plan, and the rest of their lives to consider.

Epilogue—The Woman with the Gun

The Woman with the Gun

In the silent Shrine soaked in darkness, the Anatameter sprang back to life on its own, shifting and twitching, belching sprays of color across a giant empty room eager for light.

Something shimmered and a man appeared near the device. He wore a hat and a long HRN coat. He knew who he was, yet he didn't know. He knew of many things, all the lives he'd lived, all the places, all the adventures, all the dreams hovering in front of him like a grove of ripe fruit.

All the loves . . .

He struggled to bring it all under control, to make order out of an infinity of clashing thoughts and contrary dreams. He took in his surroundings and he knew exactly where he was; he'd been there many times. Still, he took a deep breath and spoke. "Where am I?"

A soft voice in the dark replied "Here, with me."

A figure emerged from the darkness. It was a tall, light-haired woman wearing a flight suit and a pair of heavy treaded boots. Life support hoses clanked. The butt of a gun stuck out of a holster near her left shoulder.

He searched back through all the lives he lived, the infinite cloud of loving faces before him scented in a white noise of perfume, trying to place her. "I know you," he said. "You came to me in . . . Clovis. You claimed to be my countess, my wife, and I believed you, though I had no memory of that. It's all so clear now. You are not my countess in any realm. We are not married."

The woman laughed a little. She transformed before his eyes, changing shape into a beautiful blonde woman in a gown, all in a storm of whirling sand.

Now he knew who she was. "Lilly?"

Lillian of Gamboa, his once and former love, an arcane creation of the Sisterhood of Light, stood there in a familiar form.

He reviewed all his other lives. In no place was Lilly standing at his side. She was an outcast and an oddity.

"The lengths I had to go to get to this place. The parlay, the dreary days in the presence of the Gods of Cammara. I even used the *Tempus Findal*. She's not the only one who can tell lies."

"To what end?"

"To create a new you. All my previous attempts failed; the Universe would not have it. Everywhere I went, someone else was at your side, predestined by Universal design and no matter what I tried, they all ended in failure. The Sisters hoped I would be alone and miserable forever, until I had no choice but to return to them or go mad and fade into dust. They never gave me any credit for being intelligent, crafty, determined . . . and in love. Of all things, they should at least know that. They put it in me, and that love was the only thing of theirs I didn't reject.

"So I sat and pondered, trying to figure this puzzle out. I performed research. I read all I could. I became an authority on Extra-Planar entities. I ventured far and walked in dark places. I wept. I raged. I learned about the infinity of the universes and *Kaidar Gemains*, the Gods of Cammara and their Anatameters, and I even learned of the Shadow tech Goddess. And I learned that while there was an infinite number of you, there was always room for one more. That's what the custom made Anatameter does, creates a new, superior version of you whom the Universe has not pre-selected a mate for. So I went to the Gods of Cammara and begged them to make me an Anatameter just for you . . . and they did. Though the labor of Fiddler Crowe and Queen Wendilnight was not free or easily affordable. The things I had to do in payment; the ages of servitude, the treasures I had to guard and the demons I had to face . . ." Lilly closed her eyes.

"I faced them too," Stenstrom said.

His hands prying the Frog's mouth apart, revealing Queen Wendilnight within . . .

The Punts reaching for his throat.

The Demon in the fog. . .

Lilly nodded. "Yes, you did."

"You have labored for nothing, Lilly. I have a great willingness to love, that is a constant; yet for you I feel nothing. The Sisters took my love for you from me. You know that."

Lilly twitched in anger hearing the Sisters' name uttered. She composed herself and removed a golden locket from around her neck. She held it out. "Take it, Bel. Look at it."

He took the locket and opened it. Inside was a skillfully painted portrait of his face. On the left side were three irregular bits of shiny metal. "You'll recognize your old hermelins; the ones that used to reside in your mask and were replaced the day the Sisters humiliated and discarded me. They lay forgotten on the ground when the Sisters cast them aside. I took them, and placed them within my locket for safe keeping. I have kept this locket with me. For a long time, it was my sole possession. I carried it through limbo. I painted your portrait years ago when I was a prisoner at Westron. Of all the treasures I've protected, this was the most precious. When the Sisters wouldn't let me see you, I looked at it, for hours sometimes, to keep myself sane. I am a full-fledged person. I once was a construct of sand, a Nargal. I am now a person. I suppose I have Lady Vendra to thank for that. She tried to poison me, and instead she set me free."

"You killed Lady Vendra."

"Did I? Again, we are in the Place of Many Places. In some realities I killed her; in others I did not. In any case, she certainly deserves it, wouldn't you say?"

Stenstrom stood there, not knowing what to think. "She deserves justice, not summary execution."

Lilly shrugged. "Perhaps in some places she received that. May I have my locket back?" He handed it to her. She opened it, turned it over and tapped the three hermelins out onto her palm. They glinted in the Anatameter's light. So fragile. "Here are the Hermelins that once rested in your mask. They contain all the love you once had for me; the Sisters put it there. I have guarded these tiny bits of metal with all the fury I possess. Take them and all your love will come back. No tricks, no magic—these are your feelings, simply siphoned out of you by force. These are the feelings I earned."

Her eyes began to tear. She held the metal shards out. "Wherever you go, I can follow. Embrace me as hard as you wish, and I'll not break. I've no lies to tell. All you need do is accept back the love you once felt for me."

Stenstrom looked at the hermelins. The many aspects of him all spoke up.

"*But, Gwendolyn, what about her?*"

"*But, Morgan, what about her?*"

"*But, Melazarr, what about her?*"

"*But, Kat?*"

"*But, Christiana, what about her?*"

"But, Lady Miranda . . . ?"

"But, Taara . . . ?"

And on and on.

"There are many realities, Bel. There are some out there just for Gwendolyn, and Melazarr and Taara, and even one for the *Tempus Findal.* And now there's one for me, too. We have an infinity of choices. Here, this Shrine can be our palace, our safe harbor from whence we can go anywhere. King and queen, or if you prefer, simple husband and wife. Have I not demonstrated my devotion?"

He thought about it for a moment longer. "The woman with the gun, the one from Clovis, the one who guided my friends A-Ram and Alesta, who was she?"

"Just a face I made up. Why?"

"I admired her courage and mourned her passing."

"She is me; just with my hair up and shed of this gown. All this hair the Sisters gave me, I look a lot different with it up. I used the same face to befriend and guide Lord A-Ram and Lady Alesta. I've always loved A-Ram and, I must admit, I enjoyed making his acquaintance throughout this process. He's like a brother to me. It's his feelings that set me free, his heart is my heart. How I would love to stand with you at his wedding to Alesta. I can be that woman again for you, if you wish it."

The woman with the gun stood there before him, holding the little bits of metal in her hand.

"Why the gun?"

She glanced at the pistol holstered at her shoulder. "I, I don't know. I thought it made me look less threatening, nothing hidden. I thought it made me look like a normal woman, one who needed a gun to protect herself, who needed life support to sustain her and heavy boots to protect her feet."

Stenstrom, who was all Stenstroms, thought about it and then held out his hand. Lilly beamed, and carefully put the hermelins into his hand, closing his fingers around them. They sat there, cold and metallic in his palm.

And it all came back—all his feelings for Lilly, long since gone and absent. The longing, the carnal wonders, the careful angst as he pined for her from afar. The joy of the day she picked out his HRN. The sadness he felt seeing her cry on the dock in Minz. The thrill at seeing her afresh. All of it came home.

"Lilly!" he cried, picking her up and spinning her around, his voice echoing around the Shrine. "Lilly!!" She laughed and threw her head back, savoring the moment, all her planning and preparation and no small measure of sacrifice a success.

And together they left the Shrine and walked the empty passes of forgotten Eng, savoring the familiar wildness, a place of old memories and unfinished dreams lost in time, holding its breath, waiting to create new ones afresh. Together they explored the deep places built by the Elders of old and watched the skies at their leisure, waiting for the League to return once again.

The King and Queen of Eng, hand in hand, would be there to greet them.

AUTHOR INFORMATION

Ren Garcia is a Science Fiction/Fantasy author and Texas native who grew up in western Ohio. He has been writing since before he could write, often scribbling alien lingo on any available wall or floor with assorted crayons. He attended The Ohio State University and majored in English Literature. Ren has been an avid lover of anything surreal since childhood. He also has a passion for caving, urban archaeology and architecture. He currently lives in Columbus, Ohio with his wife, and their four dogs.

PUBLISHER INFORMATION

VISIT THE LOCONEAL BLOG AT

www.loconeal.com

Breaking News
Forthcoming Releases
Links to Author Sites
Loconeal Events